Also by Jorge Amado

Showdown
Dona Flor and Her Two Husbands
Gabriela, Clove and Cinnamon

The War
of the Saints

Jorge Amado

Translated from the Portuguese
by Gregory Rabassa

BANTAM BOOKS
New York   Toronto   London
Sydney   Auckland

The War of the Saints
A Bantam Book / December 1993

Book design by Maria Carella

Library of Congress Cataloging-in-Publication Data
Amado, Jorge, 1912–
    [Sumiço da santa. English]
    The War of the saints / Jorge Amado ; translated from the
Portuguese by Gregory Rabassa.
        p.   cm.
    ISBN 0-553-09537-4
    I. Title.
PQ9697.A647S7913   1994
869.3—dc20   93-5310
                                                              CIP

Published simultaneously in the United States and Canada

Bantam Books are published by Bantam Books, a division of Bantam
Doubleday Dell Publishing Group, Inc. Its trademark, consisting of
the words "Bantam Books" and the portrayal of a rooster, is
Registered in U.S. Patent and Trademark Office and in other
countries. Marca Registrada. Bantam Books, 1540 Broadway, New
York, New York 10036.

PRINTED IN THE UNITED STATES OF AMERICA

RRH   0 9 8 7 6 5 4 3 2 1

This is the small tale of Adalgisa and Manela and a few other descendants of the love between the Spaniard Francisco Romero Pérez y Pérez and Andreza da Anunciação, the beautiful Andreza de Yansan, a dark mulatto girl. Herein, to serve as example and warning, are narrated events unexpected and curious without a doubt, which took place in the City of Bahia—events that couldn't have happened anywhere else. The importance of the date is relative, but it must be understood that everything described here took place in the short span of forty-eight hours, toward the end of the sixties or the beginning of the seventies, more or less. No explanation has been sought; a tale is to be told, not explained.

The idea for this novel took shape some twenty years ago, as did the title, *The War of the Saints*. Only now, in the summer and autumn of 1987, the spring and summer of 1988, in Paris, have I put the story down on paper. It's been fun to write; if someone else has fun reading it, I'll consider myself satisfied.

—Jorge Amado

The War of the Saints

The Crossing

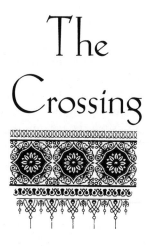

Casting Off

That day, though the hour was surprisingly late, the *Sailor Without a Port* was only just entering the far side of the Bay of All Saints, from upriver, under full sail—the sea, a blue mantle, the lover told his beloved. And strangely enough, in the wake of the wind, Maria Clara's voice was not to be heard trailing off in the throes of a love song.

If it happened that way it was simply because, in addition to the customary cargo of aromatic pineapples, cashews, and mangos, at Santo Amaro da Purificação the sloop had undertaken the responsibility—the mission, we should say—of transporting to the state capital a statue of Saint Barbara of the Thunder, famed for her eternal beauty and miraculous powers. Despite the evident displeasure of the vicar, the parish had agreed to loan the statue, to be displayed at a highly touted religious art exhibit that was being celebrated in prose and verse in the press and among intellectuals: "The cultural event of the year," as the newspapers proclaimed. In order to carry out this sacred commission, the sloop's captain, Master Manuel, had had to put off his habitual morning departure, delaying almost twelve hours, but he did it willingly: It would be worth the trouble, and besides, Dona Canô never requested favors, she gave orders.

The vicar felt less upset when he learned that a priest and a nun were also going along; he was young and modern, hair in disarray, wearing civilian clothes, while she was on in years, thin, pale, in a black habit. Divine providence, which never fails, had sent them to accompany the saint.

"Look after her during the crossing. Pay particular attention at the mouth of the river—the currents are tricky there, and the wind blows hard. God go with you."

Aided by the vicar, the sexton, and Dona Canô, amidst the prayers and applause of a fidgety gathering of church biddies, the priest and the nun proceeded with the embarkation ceremony. During the slippery descent, however, they preferred to entrust the litter that bore the figure on its pilgrimage into the seafaring hands of Master Manuel and his wife Maria Clara, who deposited it with reverential care in the stern of the sloop. There, standing erect, the majestic effigy of the Catholic saint looked like a ship's figurehead, a votive carving for the bow, a pagan and protective entity.

The Nun and the Priest

As the late afternoon breeze filled its proud sails, the sloop sped along with the saint. At the helm, Master Manuel smiled at the reverend father and the good sister: Don't be afraid, Saint Barbara's in no danger.

Sitting alongside the litter, Maria Clara saw to the stability of the saint, prevented the lurching of the sloop from upsetting its balance. "Don't you worry," she had added to reassure them, while she examined and praised the extravagance of the lining of the litter, made with all the refinements of brocade and ribbon, trimming and lace fashioned for the occasion by the devout ladies of the sisterhood of Our Lady of the Good Death in the neighboring town of Cachoeira, pious old women, first-rate artists. Oh, if it had been up to them, the saint would have traveled all covered with gold and silver, old gold, sterling silver, but the director of the museum had peremptorily turned them down. He'd even refused the sisterhood's reliquary—nasty man!

They had been trustworthy vows, those of the captain and his wife, yet the old nun, huddled in her worn and severe habit, trembled for the safety of the figure throughout the long voyage, because of the river currents or the rough seas of the gulf. But she didn't say a word, didn't let her concern show; only prayed, reciting over and over the beads of her rosary, until the breeze that fluttered about the carving came to comfort her bony hands. For her the trip was long and worrisome; she breathed easily only when the sloop headed in toward the market ramp. All had gone well, God be praised! she thought. The saint and her sack of thunder and lightning would soon be in the Museum of Sacred Art, where the director, a German monk with several advanced degrees, a scholar three times over, a renowned author, in his impeccable white cassock, awaited her impatiently. He'd developed a breathtakingly daring thesis concerning the origin and the artist of this famed piece of religious sculpture. Only then, delivered from her prison of fear, would Sister Maria Eunice close her eyes, let out a sigh of relief, and succumb at last to the soft enveloping breeze.

The priest, for his part, didn't look like a priest—how could anyone recognize him as a father when he was wearing blue jeans and a flowered shirt open to the wind, with no tonsure shaved into the center of his flowing hair? He was a good-looking fellow who drew women's stares. The habit doesn't make the monk, teaches a wise proverb that dates back quite a bit, to a time before such changes in costume and custom were common. In spite of the apparent disorder in his clothes and hair, his lack of cassock and tonsure, this was no hippie on his way to the peace and love colony in Arembepe, but an ordained priest, sincere in his vocation and his apostolate, devoted to his mission. In the distant parish that was his charge, the faithful were God's unfortunates, slaves of the rich, humbled by the age-old law of violence.

For him the trip had seemed longer, endless even, because he'd been living amid impunity and injustice and had every reason to believe he was being summoned to the capital for something besides praise or encouragement. He'd heard of provocations and threats, he'd read items in the papers denouncing and condemning the subversive activity of certain priests. His name, Father Abelardo Galvão, had appeared in the press, in twisted stories that turned facts upside down, invented things, slung mud, vilified him. That was all infamy and villainy, the priest pondered to himself. In truth, all he knew about Patrícia was the crystal tone of her voice, the enigma of her smile, the coquetry of her look. With these venomous insinuations, the bastards were trying to hide the corpses that lay rotting in the mangrove swamps among the guaiamu crabs. The priest was traveling with three dead men on his mind. He knew who had ordered them killed, everybody knew. It did no good to know, however; the ones who give orders to gunmen sail on, unsullied and inaccessible, beyond good and evil. The land has its owners, only a few, and they can be counted on the fingers of both hands—only a few, but they are implacable.

Some Modest Information Concerning Bahia

In spite of the fact that Maria Clara's soft voice, recalling oaths of love, joys, and sorrows, couldn't be heard, as she sat beside the figure of the saint she was actually humming little popular tunes, a special offering owed to saints and the enchanted. Her melodies didn't carry to the nun or the priest but summoned green swarms of water hyacinths that encircled the stout hull of the sloop. On their fleshy stems the newly opened blue flowers bowed, greeting Saint Barbara of the Thunder. The Paraguaçu River has the smell of tobacco and tastes like sugar; the vessel sailed between cane brakes and tobacco fields.

In the seas of the gulf, schools of fish greeted the sloop. A cortège of octopuses, rays, and skates accompanied its wake. The sun spread gold over the sky of the Bay of All Saints.

It is well known that the Bay of All Saints is the doorway to the world. Immeasurable, all other inlets in Brazil can fit into it, with space left over for the estuaries of Galicia and all the fleets in the universe. As for its beauty, there's no possible comparison, nor does the writer exist who is capable of describing it.

A flock of islands, each more delightful and dazzling than the one before, grazes on this sea of dreams, shepherded by the largest island, Itaparica, settled by Portuguese and Dutch soldiers, Indian tribes, and African nations. In the depths of the waters, in the realm of Aioká, lie the hulks of caravels armed for war, Portuguese noblemen, Batavian admirals, colonists and invaders expelled by dauntless Brazilian patriots. Itaparica is the mother of the new nation, the soil of freedom during the battles for independence commemorated every January.

Prudence ordains us not to speak of the glories of the Bay of All Saints—it's best to remain silent so as to avoid resentment and jealousy; its fame is already in the mouths of seafaring men, in the songs of troubadours, in the letters and reports of navigators. We won't give in here to voicing the glories of the bay, nor will we sing praises in its name. Modesty is the perquisite of true greatness.

In the bosom of the gulf, in the breezes of the peninsula, set on the hill, rises the City of Bahia, its full name, Cidade do Salvador da Bahia de

Todosos Santos, exalted by Greeks and Trojans, celebrated in prose and verse, capital of all Africa, situated in the east of the world, on the sea lane to the Indies and China, on the meridian of the Caribbean, fat with gold and silver, perfumed with pepper and rosemary, copper-colored, flower of mulattery, port of mystery, beacon of enlightenment.

Much more could be said concerning this City of Bahia were it not for our modesty and prudence. Now, toward its docks, bearing their tales and humming their songs, heads the *Sailor Without a Port,* Master Manuel at the helm, his wife Maria Clara watching over the litter. As passengers it carries a priest and a nun and the image of Saint Barbara of the Thunder, who is leaving her simple altar in the main church of Santo Amaro da Purificação to take part in the religious art exhibit in the capital. Muted, Maria Clara's voice is in the diving of the fish, the flight of the sea swallows.

The Musician on the Drum

That afternoon, up on the market ramp, sitting on an empty kerosene barrel, a well-dressed black man wearing a white suit, bowtie, and two-tone shoes that shone with the glow of their polish was playing solos on the *berimbau* for a small audience of fruit vendors, idle urchins, and a pair of lovers. There was no group of *capoeira* foot-fighters to accompany him; the black man was playing for the simple pleasure of playing, the sound coming out of the remote past, from the depths of slave quarters, telling of the horrors of captivity.

Looking out in the direction of the sea fort, surprised, the musician recognized the outline of the *Sailor Without a Port* sailing along with the first shadows of dusk, instead of at the fringes of dawn, as it usually did, when it would carry the morning star atop its mast and Maria Clara's voice would awaken the sun:

> The handsome sailor
> Carried off by the mermaid . . .
> How sweet to die in the sea,
> In the dark green waves of the sea . . .

Dusk and dawn are equally good times to come and to go. Life is made up of the unexpected—isn't that what gives it its charm? The black man stopped playing, sharpened his ear, and heard the horn announcing the end of the crossing. Where had Maria Clara's voice been lost? Why couldn't the sailors' favorite melody be heard?

I'll give you a comb for your hair
The sky and sea I give you are fair . . .

With the majestic sound of the conch-horn, a triumphant cry echoed across the bay. What good news was the captain announcing to the city and its people? An intoxicating aroma of fruit enveloped the dock, the perfume of ripe jackfruit.

In the softness of late afternoon, in the opulence of the sunset, the sea and its fish delivered the sloop with the precious litter and the beauteous statue to its port of call, the vessel touching the cement of the market ramp. Maria Clara stood up, went to furl the sails while Master Manuel dropped the rope with the stone that served as an anchor. The *Sailor Without a Port* came to a halt as the sun was exploding in the sky, in the evening sky of Bahia, in all the nuances of red, from rose to scarlet.

The Landing

Father Abelardo helped the nun to her feet. The two took deep breaths of relief, each disembarking in his and her particular haste. They had watched over the saint during the crossing and were no longer needed since, close to the ramp, the museum van could be seen parked and waiting to pick it up.

To receive the precious image the director had chosen Edimilson Vaz, a young and talented ethnologist and his trusted assistant. The director himself had been unable to go; at that precise moment he was hosting a well-attended press conference for both the print and broadcast media, to give them the details of the great exhibit, whose grand opening was scheduled for two days hence, on Friday evening. Attending the press conference were journalists from Bahia, correspondents from important newspapers from the south of the country, and crowning all, a representative from a chain of Portuguese newspapers, a certain Fernando Assis Pacheco. Even as the sloop was anchoring at the market ramp, the director had already begun to discourse on the antique carving of Saint Barbara of the Thunder. Why thunder, why did she have a knapsack full of lightning bolts where a castle and a palm tree should have been? he asked rhetorically. She was a capital work of the imagination that in just a few minutes would be lighting up this room, dazzling all you journalists! Speaking of thunder and lightning, dates and places, saint-makers and sculptors, there is some disagreement among musicologists, historians, and art critics, some pro, some con, yet all are extremely competent and the director even more so, his impeccable white cassock, his seraphic look making him seem roguish, even devilish, at times.

Before Master Manuel and Maria Clara had finished mooring the sloop and managed to lift out the saint, the saint herself got down from her litter, took a step forward, smoothed the folds of her cape, and walked off.

With a sway of her hips, Saint Barbara of the Thunder slipped between Master Manuel and Maria Clara and gave them a smile of complicity and affection. The *êbômin* then held her hands open before her breasts in a ritual gesture and said: *"Eparrei, Oyá!"* When she passed by the priest and the nun, she waved politely to the nun and winked at the priest.

Off went Saint Barbara of the Thunder, along the market ramp, heading toward the Lacerda Elevator. She was in a hurry because night was coming on and the time for the *padê* had already passed. The well-dressed black man bowed at the sight of her, touched the ground with his fingers, then lifted them to his forehead and repeated: *"Eparrei!"* The black man was Camafeu de Oxóssi, an *obá* of Xangô, a vendor in the market, a soloist on the *berimbau*, former president of the Children of Gandhi Afoxé, and not even he himself knew whether he had just happened to be present, or whether he had been allowed to witness this event through the work and grace of the enchanted ones. Before the lights came on in their lampposts, Saint Barbara Yansan had disappeared into the midst of her people.

The Press Conference

The Wait

As he continued speaking in his almost unaccented Portuguese, relieving the dryness of his material with unexpected colloquialisms—he was discussing his extensive research in foreign archives, commenting on various specialized studies, exhibiting his archaeologist's passion—Dom Maximiliano von Gruden, director of the Museum of Sacred Art, kept an eye on the window of the main entrance door, waiting. The van's delay was beginning to worry him.

The television crews had taken some quick shots at the start of the press conference, showing the monk, prominent and elegant, surrounded by journalists, bowing effusively to the "special envoy" from the Portuguese press. Now they were already getting ready to leave. TV time is as precious as gold and is measured in fractions of a second. To stall them, Dom Maximiliano had to make use of lots of smooth talk—and smooth talk was what he had a lot of. No one was more adept than he, offering another round of whiskey to keep the technicians and cameras in the room. "Just a few more minutes, friends, so you can film the arrival of the statue—it's on its way; we've received word that it just left the waterfront."

It was a lie; he'd had no word yet at all from Edimilson Vaz about the precious cargo—but what was wrong with an innocent lie when it served a just cause? Just—and imperative, in this case. He wanted to ensure that millions of television viewers all over Brazil glued to the eight o'clock news would see Dom Maximiliano von Gruden welcoming the image of Saint Barbara of the Thunder, a unique treasure of Brazilian art: a precious masterpiece, scarcely known and even less studied. Dom Maximiliano had just established its genealogy—its lineage, descent, nearly the precise date of its origin—in a book he had originally written in German, then translated into Portuguese; its publication in Portuguese was to coincide with the opening of the religious art exhibit set for Friday. A copy of the German edition, published in Munich in a masterful job of printing, was now lying as if forgotten on the long, antique, authentically Dutch table. Even the reporters, who were unaccustomed to dealing with museums and antiques, were aware of the perfect harmony of this room, the authenticity and value of each of the works on display there—be it a statue, painting, or piece of furniture.

On the cover of the book, reproduced in color, was a picture of the carving. It was easy enough to pick up the book with a casual gesture and thumb through it in front of the cameras: the crowning glory, the apotheosis of a triumphant career of an illustrious saintly man. Well, *saintly man*, we beg your pardon, isn't quite the proper expression: the *illustrious* museum director, shall we say, the talented researcher, the erudite and reputable art historian, the doctor *honoris causa* from four universities. Dom Maximiliano von Gruden was all this and more—but he was no saint.

The Special Envoy

As Dom Maximiliano listened to a question that the bearded Portuguese journalist was asking, he half-closed his blue eyes and smiled. In addition to the TV crews with cameras, radio reporters were clutching their tape recorders, while the newspaper reporters were content with pad and pencil. With an aura of modesty and meekness, his thinning hair, pale face, and spotless cassock, Dom Maximiliano looked like a wax museum figure himself. It was a tricky question that the Portuguese asked him, smacking of malice, hinting that the director had been auda-

cious—hasty, perhaps—in the conclusions of his book. But extending his
arms as if he were going to bless the provoker, the monk opened his eyes
and replied, his voice pear-shaped, oozing:

"In just a few minutes, my dear colleague will be able to judge for
himself, with the eyes that God has given him to see and learn. The best
proof is the statue itself; anything said without a proper look at the work
in question is little more than speculation and hearsay. If I were given to
boasting, I would state that the conclusions of my thesis were dictated in
person by Saint Barbara of the Thunder, from up there in heaven where
she resides." He permitted himself a small, mocking chuckle. How's that,
you fop?

The cruel truth, however, was that only when he heard Assis's full
insidious, aggressive question, did the monk become aware that an un-
derlying plot was being hatched by his two confreres to discredit him in
the eyes of the press. He hadn't suspected anything two days ago, when
the Lisbon correspondent had appeared in his office touting letters of
recommendation: He was a journalist of renown on the peninsula, almost as famous in Madrid as in Lisbon, and the author of important
articles on art and literature that had made their mark across the entire
European continent, quoted in the cultural pages of *Le Monde*. Fernando
Assis Pacheco was likewise a poet idolized by the critics. And the man
who had introduced this Pacheco to him with such descriptive flourish
had the authority to do so, as fellow Bahian and connoisseur. He was
none other than the art critic Antônio Celestino, whose weekly column
ran on Saturdays in *A Tarde*.

At that meeting Dom Maximiliano had been delighted that the
Portuguese journalist had come all the way from Lisbon to attend the
upcoming press conference on Wednesday, and he hadn't worried about
the seeming trifles—obvious as they were in retrospect—that he now
knew bespoke conspiracy. One single question, however, put forth craft-
ily by this interloper while all were awaiting the arrival of the litter with
the saint, had been all that was necessary. All that was necessary to reveal
the threads of the intrigue and have them unravel, to illuminate, machi-
nating behind two no-accounts, the hated figure of the unregenerate
J. Coimbra Gouveia, the director's stubborn, insolent rival, whose only
pleasure in life seemed to be challenging and denigrating the studies of
his Bavarian-born Bahian counterpart.

No, this Fernando Assis Pacheco—a great journalist and poet, at
least in the eyes of his black ladies—hadn't turned up in the office of the
director of the Museum of Sacred Art, sipping imported whiskey, because of the mere happenstance of a vacation trip to Brazil, as had
happened on his previous visit, or so he had said. Nor was he there only
out of intellectual curiosity, or an ostensible interest in the origins and
authorship of the statue. Dom Maximiliano, on introducing Assis

Pacheco to his local colleagues, had given him the title of "special envoy," in order to enhance the press conference's prestige. A special envoy —no doubt about it, he was, but not of any journalistic enterprise; rather, Assis was the special envoy of the rascal J. Coimbra Gouveia, who at that moment was probably scratching his balls, stretched out in a greasy armchair in the director's office of the Pena Museum, a stunning view of the Sintra Mountains framed in the window.

The Telephone Call

Yes, it was hidden intentions, unconfessed designs that had brought the vile Assis Pacheco to Bahia at the exact moment of Dom Maximiliano von Gruden's greatest triumph, just when the intellectuals of the nation were bowing reverently before the eminent doctor who had just put an end to an age-old controversy, clarifying once and for all the multiple questions concerning the carving of Saint Barbara of the Thunder. The perverse Assis, consumed with the slaver of envy, was trying to besmirch his reputation. Dom Maximiliano lifted the hem of his cassock slightly to protect it from the slaver of envy.

Now he could see why the conniving Celestino had been so eager to get an advance copy of his opus, on the pretext of writing an article and running it before the book was available to the public—he'd said he wanted to be the first to salute such a significant event in Luso-Brazilian cultural life. And Dom Maximiliano had believed him—but then what mortal, tell me, is immune to an avalanche of praise? If such a man exists, his name isn't Dom Maximiliano von Gruden. He had enjoyed scribbling in the copy—one of the first five sent him by the publisher—a warm inscription, unsparing in adjectives of praise for Celestino. He was still awaiting the article.

The idea of a plot was so far removed from his mind that he'd forgotten the ties of friendship that existed between Celestino and Coimbra Gouveia; that the former proclaimed himself the "modest disciple" of the latter, and that the latter stayed at the former's opulent residence on his trips to Bahia to prowl around churches, convents, and sacristies. In the midst of his monumental sprees—some of which Dom Maximiliano took part in and, to be fair, praised the quality of the edibles and the wine—those Portuguese know how to take care of themselves—the foreigner announced discoveries capable of revolutionizing the study of tiles and sculpture. Nothing of this had occurred to Dom Maximiliano as he autographed, with that excess of praise, his advanced copy for the "astute Antônio Celestino, model of art criticism." Now he realized that this "model" had sent the copy to Portugal that same day, by air mail most certainly, which allowed the infamous Gouveia to submit it to the microscopic scrutiny of his refutation.

A week later, when Celestino had appeared in his office with the Portuguese journalist in tow, Dom Maximiliano still hadn't suspected anything. He had opened his arms to the recent arrival, effusive, picturing himself in the pages of newspapers in Lisbon and Oporto, proclaimed as the ultimate, uncontestable authority. The monk had an innocence that contrasted with his fame as a wise man—wiser than a churchmouse, Professor Udo Knoff, a specialist in mosaics, would have said of him; they were intimate enemies. No, it took the poisonous question at Wednesday's press conference to set before him the filthy reality of the plot. He felt like a boxer who, at the moment he's been proclaimed champion, receives a stealthy punch in the stomach. He recovered immediately, however, with an urge to liquidate his adversary once and for all; his mocking smile underlined his immediate and peremptory reply.

Dom Maximiliano didn't have time to savor the journalist's embarrassment, his bewilderment: The telephone rang, and without concealing his excitement, the director went to the desk, eager to hear the news that the van bearing the work had departed. At that precise moment the misfortunes of the director of the Museum of Sacred Art, on the eve of the grand opening of the religious art exhibit, began. They lasted two days: a century at least.

The Oratory Cabinet

While Dom Maximiliano, still euphoric, answered the phone—"It's me, Edimilson, hello . . ."—the newspapermen took advantage of the break, some to leave without waiting to see the statue, others—the majority—to refill their glasses. A thirsty horde, they rushed over, crowding around the oratory cabinet that had been converted into a bar—a trick of Dom Maximiliano's, who hid bottles of imported whiskey there, along with a port wine that had been aged in its keg on the Douro.

"Is this a neat trick, or isn't it?" asked the austere and discreet Professor Renato Ferraz, director of the Museum of Modern Art, as he sipped a double shot of sacred Scotch—neat, with only two ice cubes.

As for the oratory cabinet, it was "sumptuous, large in size, and artistically rendered," as the aforementioned Antônio Celestino had noted in an article on "The Treasures of the Museum of Sacred Art of Bahia." It had come from "the winding streets inhabited by seventeenth-century woodcarvers, from the Rua do Piolho or the Beco das Caganitas, the Rua da Indiaria or the Viela dos Gatos, the Cangosta dos Marchantes, in the city of Braga in the Minho region, a piece of genuine polished Portuguese baroque." Sitting in the director's office, the precious article of furniture continued to be useful, except that instead of images of saints, it now sheltered expensive liquors; but they too were objects of widespread and heated devotion.

As the refined Celestino was savoring a glass of port, drop by drop, sigh by sigh, he listened to the acid commentary of Professor Ferraz; but the taste of the ambrosia—smooth!—would not allow him to agree or disagree. According to Ferraz, Maximiliano was overbearing, sophisticated, wily, tricky, presumptuous, et cetera and so forth; but no one would deny his competence, initiative, or authority.

A beam of light fell onto the glass of true and tawny wine in Master Celestino's lordly hand. The blaze of sunset enveloped the church and the convent, came in through the windows, spread its gold out on the stone walls; the sun plunged into the garden among the acacias.

The Busybody

"What?" Almost a shout, the question caught the attention of Guido Guerra, a young scribe just starting out in his career in journalism and literature in search of some sensational item capable of propelling his name out beyond the provincial borders. Eyes wide, mouth open, Dom Maximiliano von Gruden was listening, flabbergasted, but he recovered when he noticed the interest of the reporter from *Diário de Notícias:* He closed his mouth, half-closed his eyes, regained control. The journalists toasted the imminent arrival of the vaunted statue.

"I don't understand—repeat what you said. . . . Calm down—repeat it!" His voice barely audible, out of the corner of his eye, the director examined the gathering. The alert Guerra, however, remained attentive: "It's best that you wait for me there. I'll be right over." He paused again, controlling his impatience, and finished, demanding imperiously, "Wait for me there, I told you that already!"

He hung up, faced the group, which drew closer, and although each word cost him an effort, when he spoke, his voice sounded calm. Resuming his cordiality, Dom Maximiliano even managed a smile.

"I must beg your indulgence," he said. "I brought you here so that together we could receive the incomparable statue of Saint Barbara of the Thunder, who for the first time has been removed from her altar in the main church of Santo Amaro in order to be part of our exhibit. I've just learned that something unforeseen has caused a small delay in the schedule we set up and that we'll only be able to greet our celestial guest tomorrow." He broadened his smile.

"What time tomorrow?" Leocádio Simas's anxiety was well founded. He was familiar with the customs that Dom Maximiliano had established for press conferences at the museum, and he knew that in the afternoon whiskey was served, while in the morning only fruit juices, albeit a wide selection: Spanish plum and hog plum, maracock and custard apple, mangabá and cashew. Even Surinam cherry, a delight.

"I still can't say exactly what time," the director replied, "but I'll let the newsrooms know as soon as I have precise information." With a discreet gesture Dom Maximiliano ordered the beadle to lock the door of the oratory cabinet before Leocádio, a notorious lush, could sop up another drink.

"What exactly happened that's causing the delay?" the indiscreet Guerra inquired, his face avid, his nose like a parrot's beak with the sensory ability of a hound. He didn't touch whiskey, preferring the nectar of tropical fruit. He should have had a drink instead, the director thought.

What *had* happened? That was just what Dom Maximiliano wanted to find out, and the sooner the better. He went over to the busybody Guerra, swallowing his impatience and irritation, his brain working at full speed in search of some way of holding back the whispering, the mistrust of the dangerous meddler. Guerra was most dangerous, thought Dom Maximiliano—he lived by sticking his nose where it had no business. Wasn't he the reporter who uncovered the embezzlement in the corn cooperative accounts with a piece of investigative work that was nothing short of notorious, unleashing a monumental scandal? Dom Maximiliano took him by the arm and drew him away from the others. He still didn't know what to say. In order to stall, he whispered in his ear, "If I told you, it would be in the paper tomorrow, and it might—"

"I promise not to publish anything without your consent."

Dom Maximiliano wracked his brain but couldn't find an explanation worthy of belief. Then the reporter himself, playing detective, came to his aid by hinting, "Could it be that the vicar has made yet another demand?"

It was Guerra who had revealed in his paper the difficulties created by the parish priest of Santo Amaro. His position had been sympathetic, criticizing what he called the vicar's "mean-spirited and retrograde attitude" in opposing the loan of the image. Now Dom Maximiliano took advantage of the opening and went straight through it—an imprudent act that he would later regret:

"Keep the information to yourself. I'm telling you in confidence, and you've got to promise me that you won't let it out."

"I promise! As God is my witness!"

"All right, then. The vicar isn't satisfied with the assurances and guarantees give by the museum, and he has demanded one more document. Since the image is so valuable, I can't say that he's wrong. You people in the press go about spreading so many lies about the museum, and this poor man of God who runs it, that now you have the result."

"Lies, Dom Maximiliano? What lies?"

"Wasn't it one of you who suggested that when we gave the statue of Saint Peter the Penitent back to the Chapel of Monte Serrat, what we were returning was a copy, keeping the original in the museum?"

"And is that a lie, Dom Maximiliano?"

Dom Maximiliano smiled, shaking his head to ignore the provocation, but Guido Guerra was insatiable: He wanted to know what new document the vicar had demanded.

"A guarantee of fiscalization, from the Historical Commission." He invented that on the spot, not knowing how. Then he rested his hand on the reporter's shoulder in a friendly gesture: "Please, Guido, not a single word about this matter—the vicar might be offended. I'm sharing a confidence with a friend, I'm not giving a story to a journalist. I must be able to count on you."

Offended? The director knew that the vicar, a suspicious man, instilled with the greatest ill will, would raise holy hell if the innocent invention had the misfortune to reach his ears—and he would become one more enemy to add to the long list of those who couldn't wait to attend Dom Maximiliano's funeral.

"Rest easy, sir. I'll be as silent as the grave." The journalist's expression was prudent, respectful: It would have been the face of a saint, except that he was ugly as sin.

Dom Maximiliano had never been in so much of a hurry. Even so, he took his time now, going from reporter to reporter, shaking hands, lamenting the time wasted for the television people who had brought all that equipment here for nothing. And it really was a great pity—Dom Maximiliano von Gruden was born to appear on television, a man of bearing and elegance. He embraced Assis Pacheco as if he still hadn't noticed any of his hidden intentions, leading the Portuguese poet along:

"We'll have another chat, my dear Antônio Alçada Baptista." Even when he was at his wit's end he still managed to offend the bare-faced fellow by "mistaking" his identity. Poets are sensitive—their vanity is on the surface of their skin. "We'll clear up all doubts."

He waited to see them through the doors, to witness the end of their huffing and puffing with the television equipment, then dashed down the steps. God in heaven, what had happened? Over the telephone, little Edimilson had seemed lost, he hadn't been able to put two words together, had kept repeating nonsense.

The Festival

Saint Barbara, also called Oyá, also called Yansan, entered the *barracão* dressed in the colors of dusk, the evening star on her forehead, the green perfume of the sea on her ebony breasts. They hadn't been expecting her, but there was no surprise or turmoil; the drumming merely grew stronger, and the circle of holy *êbômins, ekedes,* and *iaôs* bowed reverently. Along the way Oyá had gathered up injustices and evil deeds, carrying them in a bundle under her left arm, while in her right hand were her thunder and lightning.

Getting out of a taxi, Maria Clara, Master Manuel, and the *obá* of Xangô, Camafeu de Oxóssi, drew back to let her pass: *"Eparrei Oyá!"* The taxi driver, too, bowed in greeting. His name was Miro and he was always laughing. He declared himself to be a son of Ogum, but evil tongues whispered that the "owner of his head" was Exu. It was gossip that rolled along on the wheels of idleness and sloth, and anyone who wanted to was welcome to believe it.

Resting on her knees and forearms, Oyá lay at the feet of Mãe

Menininha do Gantois, mother of goodness and wisdom, queen of calm waters, immense and majestic. An *iyalorixá*, a *mãe de santo*, a priestess, she was large enough to gather in her lap of hills and valleys all the complaints, torments, and entreaties of her sons and daughters, the people of Bahia. Sitting on a shabby throne, an armchair with a high back, she was gripping the *adjá:* Her blood daughters, Carmem and Cleusa, were on either side, her other sons and daughters—those of the saint— out in front. Mãe Menininha do Gantois, the most beautiful Oxum, incomparable; Oyá lying at her feet.

The *iyalorixá* touched Barbara Oyá on the forehead and, taking her by her bare shoulders, lifted her up and hugged her to her breast. Then Oyá stood up straight, turned her body around, and all could see her breasts and behind. It was a delight to see her and desire her, but her war cry imposed silence, making even the boldest people tremble. It could be heard from one end of the city to the other—she'd come to do battle, let all know that! Hands on hips, she greeted the circle and the musicians, then the aged and the notable, stopping in front of each to embrace, chest against chest, heart against heart.

Miguel Santana Obá Aré sang a chant in her praise that few still remembered, something forgotten from the past:

Ialoiá é du aná tá
ai mi arê arêê
ialoiá é du aná tá
ai mi arê arêê
ô lindé bochiré
é ialoiá
é ialoiá ô ô

Having danced in front of Obá Aré, Oyá was puzzled why the old babalaô wasn't sitting in the place that was his by right, alongside the *mãe de santo* priestess. Instead, one of those modern Africanologists had climbed up there, half-baked, mediocre in learning, overloaded with pride, holding forth with pompous nonsense to a pair of simpleton tourists who were barraging him with questions about mysticism, parapsychology, and negritude.

Why did Obá Aré sit on the edge of an ordinary bench set out for visitors and not in one of the wicker chairs reserved for guests of honor? Wherever he sat, that was where the throne was, the *ogan-da-sala* said, trying to explain. Oyá agreed with that notion, but she didn't accept it as an excuse for such inexcusable presumption. Sketching a gesture in the air, she dumped the insolent pretender out of the chair he'd dared to occupy. The Africanologist found himself violently shaken by Oyá, with a gale force that uproots trees and flings them far away. Lifted up and thrown onto the ground, he felt a punch in the chest and another in the pit of his stomach, along with a couple of slaps on the face. He got up, groggy, gasping for breath, and rounded up his troop of nitwits—he was a tour guide—and beat a hasty retreat.

Oyá, a soft breeze that comforts the faces of children and old people, with a courteous step and a salaam of respect, led Miguel Santana Obá Aré, the venerable *obá*, so proclaimed by Mãe Aninha, the unforgettable, and had him sit down where he was supposed to. Smiling, gladdened, Mãe Menininha handed him the *adjá*. He shook the bell, calling on the enchanted ones. The festivities took on more rhythm and the joyfulness of restrained laughter and mute applause. What had happened had not passed unnoticed by those capable of discerning—the kind of people who said "Bless you" and not just "Good evening."

Before Oyá went into the circle, a white whore approached her, forty or so years old, with bleached hair, prettyish. She spoke breathlessly, so eager was she:

"I've been looking for you for a week. I came up from São Paulo. Sister Grazia from Halfbreed Pajeú's shop in Bás said I should ask you where my ring is. Sister Grazia is a medium, she consulted with the Halfbreed, and he said that when I get the ring, everything will turn out right: Marino will come running back and never leave me again. Go to Bahia, that's what he said. At the *candomblé* look for the girl with the evening star, she'll tell you where the ring is. I just happened to come by here, I've already been to ten temples, I was ready to quit, catch the bus home tomorrow. But I heard about this ceremony—the ring is copper, with the head of a lion."

"Your ring's with that man in the white hat," Oyá answered, indicating Camafeu de Oxóssi, who came over to take his appointed place beside Miguel Santana.

The woman from São Paulo ran toward him.

"My ring, tell me—" and she described it.

"I've got it, yes, ma'am. I received a shipment of necklaces, bracelets, and rings from Lagos. I sold the rings—there was only one left over, that very one you described. Come by the market tomorrow, and I'll give it to you. Ask for Camafeu de Oxóssi, everybody there knows me."

"How much will it cost?"

"It won't cost you anything, it's a present from Yansan. If you want, you can bring an offering to her, a white dove. Turn it loose by the docks."

If Oyá had wanted to ride one of her horses, there were four at her disposal in the circle; sitting among the visitors could be seen Margarida do Bogum, the wife of the *ogan* Aurélio Sodré; Yansan Oiaci, and others. But Oyá contented herself with dancing in the midst of the *filhas de santo,* making obeisance to Oxalá—here, the Oxalá of Mãe Menininha's daughter Carmem, a splendor; and to all of Oxalá's children: to Omolu and Euá, to Xangô and Oxum, to Oxóssi and Yemanjá. A more bewitching Yemanjá than Maria Clara's had yet to be seen in any *candomblé*, whether in Bahia, Angola, Cuba, or Benin.

Oyá left before the festivities were over—she had lots to do. She'd come to the City of Bahia to finish a task begun this past January on Bomfim Thursday. She had come to free a young woman named Manela from captivity and to teach her aunt Adalgisa what it means to have to wear a packsaddle. Oyá usually rode her horses bareback, but she was going to put a packsaddle on Adalgisa; that was how she'd ride her—to teach her tolerance and joy and the goodness of life.

The Stray Dog

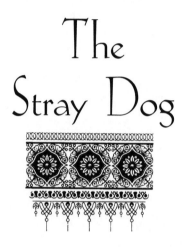

Edimilson's Visions

Edimilson kept repeating the same absurdities to a perplexed and perturbed Dom Maximiliano von Gruden, almost hysterically. In order to avoid drawing attention, the director had driven over in his own private VW Beetle, avoiding use of the museum car. He'd parked alongside the empty van. "The statue, tell me—what's happened to the statue!"

Edimilson's skinny silhouette with its curved shoulders was forlorn on the deserted waterfront. Both of them were forlorn—Dom Maximiliano insisting, demanding concrete facts ("Stop all this nonsense!") and the assistant helpless, waving his hands. They were like two puppets beneath the lampposts, the dim light of which was unable to drive away the dense shadows of the damp and secret night. The distant sounds of conversation and laughter were coming from the Ladeira da Montanha, where the hubbub of life was starting up in bars and brothels. A star had come out over the sea fort.

Edimilson, on the verge of fainting, was swearing by God and all the saints that he had seen the carving standing on the litter at the stern of the sloop when the *Sailor Without a Port* was putting in to the market ramp. Even though he had seen it only in the glimmer of sunset, when strange shapes and figures run across the sky and fall to pieces in the sea, he'd instantly recognized Saint Barbara of the Thunder: He knew the statue because he'd gone to Santo Amaro several times with Dom Maximiliano, combining the functions of assistant and chauffeur. He'd even held it in his arms, then, fascinated.

"It was her—yes! I'd put my hand in fire and swear to it!"

The fire of hell, in fact—if it were only that simple. Because Edimilson knew what had happened, even though it made no sense: All of a sudden the figure had begun to grow, to change, and before he knew what was happening, right there she'd turned into a beautiful dark woman, a flesh-and-blood creature, dressed in traditional Bahian dress. She had left the sloop and gone off—he swore by Christ's wounds and Holy Mary's virginity.

But when it came to explaining this to the director, Edimilson was unable, no matter how hard he tried, to satisfy the fierce and threatening Dom Maximiliano—you can't explain what has no explanation. His hands were shaking, he was sweating, he felt chilled and frightened, he was ready to burst out crying. It was a miracle of God or a trick of the devil, but he'd seen it—he certainly had seen it: "May Saint Lucy strike me blind if I didn't see it!" He swore and swore again, on the soul of his departed mother, an oath of death. The most inexplicable thing was that while he was watching it happen, he hadn't even been that surprised. How could that be? It was the devil's business, certainly, Dom Maximiliano, there's no other explanation.

Dom Maximiliano von Gruden didn't believe that the devil had anything to do with it. In confidence one day, Edimilson had confessed to the director that ever since he was a child, he had been given to visions: At nightfall trees would seem to be transformed into old hags, and with black shawls over their shoulders, they would run through the garden foretelling dire events. His studies at the university hadn't cured him, nor had his knowledge of dialectical materialism, which he had studied secretly under the influence of Dr. José Luiz Pena, a substitute professor and a Marxist.

⊷⊶

The Vicar
and the Populace

Aside from the delirious Edimilson with his cock-and-bull story,
the alarmed museum director could find no one in the area of the ramp
who was of any help to him—no living soul capable of furnishing a valid
explanation. They provided good will, perhaps, and pleasant conversation, but no help. Master Manuel and Maria Clara had left in a taxi, in
the company of Camafeu de Oxóssi—Your Worship knows who that is,
don't you? Everybody knows Camafeu, even the governor. In the taxi
driven by Miro, that good-for-nothing. The other people who'd been
present when the *Sailor Without a Port* arrived—fruit vendors, the
urchins called captains-of-the-sands, a lover with his beloved—all had
left, each in a different direction. That was all the director managed to
find out; in the market the last stalls were closing up. Of the nun and the
priest, there was not a word.

When the vicar had reported the departure of the sloop from
Santo Amaro on the telephone, he had told Dom Maximiliano about
a priest and a nun, passengers into whose care he'd entrusted the exalted statue—so much the better to have divine providence watching
over the saint. So it was necessary now for Dom Maximiliano to find
the priest and the nun—that was his first order of business. Most
probably the statue had been left with one of the two religious people
for safekeeping. And if it hadn't, Dom Maximiliano would get a serious recounting of what had actually happened when the sloop arrived,
from the mouths of those responsible. But how could he find them if
he didn't know their names or addresses, or the nun's convent, or
where the priest was staying?

Telephoning the vicar of Santo Amaro to ask for clarification and
tell him what had happened at the same time—my dear friend, so sorry,
our priceless carving has disappeared, simply taken off!—was the last
thing Dom Maximiliano wanted to think of doing. That wild man would
go berserk, raising a scandal and telling the whole world. The vicar had
agreed to make the loan only with great reservations, and not even all
their guarantees and assurances had entirely overcome his mistrust or
eliminated his apprehensions. He'd resisted as much as he could, but his
grumbling had finally given way under pressure from the cardinal, an
imperative request. He hadn't hidden his antagonism, however, bringing
the matter up in his Sunday sermon. His own opposition to loaning out
the saint reflected the unanimous feelings of the people of the town.
Now, was he supposed to telephone the vicar? Never—Dom Maximiliano wasn't that crazy. The matter had to be cleared up, the figure recov-

ered, without a word of its disappearance getting back to Santo Amaro, either to the priest or to the populace.

Should he go from convent to convent in search of a nun, go to the Curia to find out who the priest was? Should he go to the police to report the matter? Should he talk to Manolo at the Casa Moreira and ask him to warn antique dealers? Should he tell Mirabeau Sampaio to keep his eyes open and inform principal collectors that whoever bought the statue would be out his money? He would follow clues every which way. The world had collapsed upon Dom Maximiliano von Gruden, and it was crushing him; the sunny day of his fame and triumph had changed into a night of opprobrium and bitterness.

Desperate, the illustrious monk roamed the empty waterfront, crying out to heaven. A stray dog accompanied him for a few minutes, then stretched out on the pavement and howled into the darkness of the sea—the only sign of solidarity that Dom Maximiliano was destined to receive.

The Demons

What crimes had the monk committed, what terrible sins had been his, for him to suffer such an awful punishment, for his life to be subject to such a fearsome test? Have pity, Lord! The strangled invocation of the monk mingled with the howling of the dog through the shadows of the docks in the silence of the night.

Delirious, the monk imagined Edimilson, an angel in panic, catching sight of a gang of demons bearing on their shoulders Dom Maximiliano's sins. The torchlight procession headed toward Monte Serrat, where, at the entrance to the chapel, beside the holy-water font, Saint Peter Penitent was waiting to receive the visitors—but was it the genuine Saint Peter, sculpted by Frei Agostinho da Piedade, or was it a copy manufactured at the museum on the orders of Dom Maximiliano von Gruden—who knew? Not even Edimilson himself, a completely trustworthy employee, knew for sure. The demons led the way in the dance of sins, Dom Maximiliano followed, shoulders hunched over, his burden heavy.

He now confessed himself a sinner—venial sins, mortal sins—but what could temptation, weakness, and carelessness mean to a monk who had done so much—a monk who had done so much and was still doing so much—for the glory of God and his kingdom on earth?

The land of Bahia, where fate had led him to live and work, a land where everything is intermixed and commingled, where no one can separate virtue from sin, or distinguish the certain from the absurd, or draw the line between truth and trickery, between reality and dream. In this land of Bahia, saints and enchanted ones make miracles and sorcery, and not even Marxist ethnologists are surprised to see a carving from a Catholic altar turn into a bewitching mulatto woman at the hour of dusk.

The Leather Strap

Adalgisa at the Street Door with the Five Wounds of Christ

Adalgisa's yell shook the foundations of the Avenida da Ave-Maria: "Inside, right now, filthy brat! Slut!"

Manela scurried off, fleeing her aunt so that when Adalgisa lifted her arm for the slap, the girl was nowhere to be seen. She must have gone through the always wide-open door of Damiana's house. To Adalgisa it even looked like a brothel, with all that coming and going of people, in and out.

Damiana was a candy-maker, and in the morning she prepared pots of dough for the cakes of cassava, corn, and sweet manioc that an insolent troop of black urchins peddled from door to door in the afternoons to regular customers. A masterful sweets-maker, Sweet-Rice Damiana was famous—oh! Damiana's sweet rice, just thinking about it makes your mouth water—not just in the Barbalho district; her clientele was spread throughout the four corners of the city. During June, the month of the festivals of Saint John and Saint Peter, she couldn't fill all the orders for corn and coconut mush, tamales, and honey-corn cakes. It was a happy, hard-working house. Comparing it to a brothel showed an excess of ill will, but Adalgisa wasn't one for halfway measures. Besides, Adalgisa knew nothing about brothels, outside or in. If she chanced to pass a woman of pleasure on the street, she would spit to the side to show her disgust and disapproval. She considered herself a lady, not just an ordinary woman: Ladies have principles, and they demonstrate them.

An expert in amplified speech, she didn't lower her voice but yelled so the neighbor woman would hear her:

"I swear by the Five Wounds of Christ that I'm going to put an end to that love affair if it's the last thing I do in my life! God will give me the strength to stand up to such lowlifes trying to take a young girl down the wrong road, the road to perdition! The Lord is with me—I'm not afraid, nothing can touch me, that nigger business won't get anywhere with me. I'm cut from better cloth, don't need to mix with any common people. I'll get the sin out of that girl if it costs me what health I've got left."

Adalgisa was always complaining about her fragile health, because in spite of her healthy appearance, she was subject to recurring migraines, continuing headaches that often persisted day and night, turning her mood bitter, driving her out of her mind. She blamed her acquaintances and relatives, not to mention the whole neighborhood, but especially her niece and her husband, for all the migraine attacks that persecuted and plagued her. Dona Adalgisa Pérez Correia, of touted Spanish blood on her father's side and whispered African blood on her mother's, was the nightmare, the terror of her street.

Adalgisa's Hips, and the Rest of Her Body

It wasn't even a street: The Avenida da Ave-Maria was nothing but a blind alley, a cul-de-sac, to use Professor João Batista de Lima e Silva's pedantic phrase. Still a bachelor in his forties, the professor lived in the last little house on the alley, also the smallest. Whenever he heard Adalgisa's ill-tempered echoes, he went to the window, lowered his reading glasses, and rested his eyes on his irritable neighbor's hips.

Adalgisa was certainly irritating—but she was a knockout in looks. Everything has its compensation. In the mediocre setting of the alley, bereft of lawns and gardens, of trees and flowers, the real compensation was Adalgisa's derriere, which reaffirmed the beauty of the universe. The fanny of a Venus, Aphrodite's bottom, worthy of a painting by Goya—so meditated the professor. He, too, exaggerated somewhat, as can be seen.

The rest of Adalgisa's body was nothing to be sneezed at either—quite to the contrary, the professor allowed, feasting his eyes: full, firm breasts, long legs, black braids encircling an oblong Spanish face with eyes of fury, burning dramatically. A pity she had such an aggressive demeanor. On the day Adalgisa lost her arrogant, mocking, and disdainful ways, her air of superiority, on the day Adalgisa left the Five Wounds of Christ in peace and smiled without rancor, without affectation—oh! on that day her beauty would transfix the heart, inspire the poets' verses.

From her father's side, the Pérez y Pérezes, Adalgisa got her pious and penitent behavior, displayed in Holy Week processions in Seville, carrying the cross of Christ. She acknowledged only that side of her family, not wishing to know anything about her mother's. She took no pride in her Goya hips, and if she knew about Venus, beautiful but missing both arms, she'd never heard tell of Aphrodite.

The Junior Partner

The angry cavalcade of threats reached its peak of rage when Adalgisa recognized, sitting behind the wheel of the taxi parked by the entrance to the alley, Miro. The mangy dog was waving at her, that cynical, cheeky, insolent pauper! But then, noticing that she was also being observed by the professor, a solid citizen, teacher, journalist, she nodded courteously, feeling obliged to explain her fury and bad manners:

"I'm bearing my cross, paying for my sins," she said. "That's what comes of raising other people's children: blame and mortification. That wretched girl is leaving me all skin and bones, ruining my health, driving me to my grave. Never seen anything like it, a girl barely seventeen."

"That's youth." The professor tried to make excuses without knowing exactly what Manela's crime was. He suspected that she'd been fooling around with her boyfriend—could she have actually done it already? A girl of seventeen? The aunt was blind; she hadn't noticed that Manela was all woman, headstrong and wiggly, an appetizing body, ready for bed. Wasn't she a candidate for Miss Something-or-Other? "You've got to be patient with young people."

"More patient than I've been?" Adalgisa was horrified. "You don't know the half of it, professor! If I were to tell you—"

If Manela still hadn't, the professor thought, she was wasting her time. Drugstores sold the Pill without requiring any prescription. Freed from the fears of pregnancy, the girls of today live it up, in a wild hurry, their tails on fire. They don't follow Adalgisa's ideal of chastity and honor.

As everyone was tired of hearing, Adalgisa had had no gentlemen friends until she met Danilo, her first and the only one, the man who had led her to the altar a virgin and pure. Well, a virgin, maybe—pure is more doubtful. There's no morality capable of passing through a year-long engagement unscathed; a few daring things, minimal as they might be, always end up happening: a hand on the breast, a tool between the thighs. Danilo Correia was a modest but enterprising clerk in the notary office of the Wilson Guimarães Vieira, and a former soccer star; he was the worthy opponent of the professor at checkers and backgammon, fortunate husband, exclusive master of those sumptuous hips and the rest of Adalgisa's body, that chaste, virtuous woman—what a pity! the professor thought.

Actually, Professor João Batista de Lima e Silva was mistaken. He knew Adalgisa was chaste, but he hadn't guessed she was prudish. Danilo at the very most was a junior partner. The one who actually mastered Adalgisa's body, who determined the rules in her bed, was Christ our Lord.

Historical Note

This is a solemn promise. In a little while we'll return to the burning and controversial subject of Adalgisa's prudishness, her Catholic bed, governed by her father confessor each Sunday in the confessional of the Church of Sant'Ana, before ten o'clock mass and holy communion. We will also get to the Spartan personality of her confessor, the Reverend Father José Antonio Hernández, a Falangist, incorruptible, master of the fires of hell, missionary to Brazil—*me cago en Dios,* what a painful, rotten mission!—custodian of Adalgisa's purity. When we do, we will recount, with all the necessary details, the bitter vicissitudes of the clerk Danilo Correia, her noncompliant victim.

First, however, the figure of Manela must come to the fore, now only barely glimpsed as she disappeared from her aunt's sight into the wide-open door of fat Damiana's house. From Damiana's house emerged the appetizing smell of spices mixed with coconut milk and grated lemon cooking in the oven: vanilla and clove, cinnamon, ginger, almonds, and cashew nuts.

In Professor João Batista's ponderings, doubts about Manela have been raised. Why did her aunt Adalgisa want to punish her? Was she still a virgin, or did she already know the taste of what's good? Was she or wasn't she running for Miss Something-or-Other? It's important to clear up such uncertainties because a few pages back it was announced that it was to free Manela from captivity that Oyá Yansan, the *iaba* who has no fear of the dead and whose very cry lights up the craters of volcanos on the summits of mountains, was visiting the City of Bahia, her sack of thunder and lightning strapped over her shoulder. So in the end, what was the question of Manela?

Her name was Manela, just as it's written—not Manuela, as was asked whenever her name was seen or heard, as if to correct a spelling mistake or mispronunciation. It was a name she inherited from her Italian ancestor, whose memory was kept within the family because the beauty of that first Manela, a scandalous and fatal beauty, had become legendary. Two dashing and foolish lieutenant colonels, in disrespect of orders, had fought a duel over this earlier Manela; one governor of a province had conceived a passion and killed himself for her; one priest on his way to the honors of a bishopric had committed a sacrilege, reneged on his eminence, tossed his cassock aside, and run off to live with her.

In order to familiarize oneself with the extensive and lively chronicle of Manela Belini, with the precise details of names and dates, titles and offices, a reading of the chapter in *Supplement to the History of the Province of Bahia,* by Professor Luís Henrique Dias Tavares, is recommended. It records the triumphs of this diva in the theater, who sang operatic arias for ecstatic audiences; the deadly duel with swords in which the honor of La Belini was bathed in blood—only a few drops, but sufficient; the rumors about the governor's suicide; and the concubinage with the priest, which resulted in the Bahian family and the tradition of the name Manela. It's pleasant reading, in spite of the title.

Luís Henrique Dias Tavares, historian, is the alter ego of the fiction writer Luís Henrique, or Luís Henrique *tout court,* as his colleague and intimate friend João Batista de Lima e Silva would say. The fiction writer used the episode of the priest to create a charming picaresque novel. It's difficult to say who deserves greater praise, the historian or the novelist —it would be best to read both.

Eufrásio Belini do Espírito Santo, the descendant of the sacrilege, liked retelling stories about his great-grandmother during rounds of beer and conversation—a gorgeous Italian woman she was, whose hair blew in the wind. The day he had a daughter he gave her the name Manela. He was a romantic and a reveler.

Manela's Procession

Our Manela did not come from Seville; nor did she participate in any Procession of the Dead Lord on Good Fridays. No, her procession was that of Bomfim Thursday or if you will, the washing festival, the waters of Oxalá, the most important festival in Bahia, unique in all the world. Nor did our Manela wrap herself in atonement and penitence, cover herself with a black mantilla, or recite the litany to the sinister sound of rattles: "*Mea culpa! Mea culpa!*" Her aunt Adalgisa so repented, pounding her chest. But Manela came wrapped in joy and merriment, dressed in the dazzling traditional white dress of a Baiana, a Bahian woman. On her head, balanced over her torso, she carried the jug of scented water for washing the Church of Bomfim, and she went along dancing and singing Carnival songs to the irresistible sounds of the music truck.

That year, for the first time, Manela took her place among the Baianas on Bomfim Thursday. In order to walk in the procession—unbeknownst to her aunt, needless to say—she had played hookey from her English class in the intersession program at the Americans' institute. She played hookey in a proper fashion, however, because the day before the procession the class had unanimously informed Bob Burnet, the teacher, of their decision not to attend that day in order to take part in the washing festival. Curious about Bahian customs, young Bob not only went along with the idea but proposed that he keep them company, and he did so with his well-known thoroughness: he *samba*-ed ceaselessly under the burning January sun, bloating himself with beer. He was what you'd call a nice guy.

Manela changed her clothes at the house of her other aunt, Gildete, who lived nearby in Tororó. Manela's parents, Dolores and Eufrásio, had died in an automobile accident several years ago, while returning in the early morning hours from a wedding party in Feira de Sant'Ana. Eufrásio, who was behind the wheel, hadn't had time to get out of the way of a truck loaded with cases of beer. After the funeral, Adalgisa had taken charge of thirteen-year-old Manela, while Gildete took charge of Marieta, Manela's sister, who was a year younger. Although Gildete was a widow and mother of three children, she had wanted to keep both girls, but Adalgisa wouldn't allow it: The sister of Dolores, she was just as much an aunt to the girls as Eufrásio's sister was. She took on her responsibilities, fulfilled her duty. God had not given her children, so she dedicated herself to making a lady out of Manela—a lady of principle.

Adalgisa kept to herself her opinion of the fate that had been awarded Marieta, relegated as she had been to an environment whose customs she considered censurable—and Adalgisa never passed up an occasion to censure them. Gildete was the widow of a shopkeeper at the market and a public schoolteacher. She was not a lady, although she was a very good person. So that we keep everything out in the open, it's worth quickly mentioning the general opinion of all their friends and acquaintances, who agreed that in the lottery of orphanhood, it was Marieta who had won the grand prize.

On Bomfim Thursday, Manela had arrived at the steps of the Church of the Conceição da Praia, the dwelling of Yemanjá, to begin the revelry. She'd come early in the morning in the company of Aunt Gildete, Marieta, and Cousin Violeta, and they mingled with dozens of Baianas as they waited for the procession to form. What do we mean, dozens? Actually, there were hundreds of Baianas gathered on the steps of the church, all in the elegance of their ritualistic white costume: the wide skirt, the starched petticoat, the smock of lace and embroidery, the low-heeled sandals. On their arms and necks they displayed silver *balangandã* bracelets and necklaces, jewelry and armbands in the colors of their saints. The pot, jug, or jar on the turban atop their heads carried scented water for their obligation. *Mães de santo* and *filhas de santo* of all Afro-Bahian nations were there—Nagô, Jeje, Ijexá, Angola, Congo—and copper-colored beauties of the mulatto nations, full of coquetry and merriment. Manela, perhaps the prettiest of all, was blooming with excitement. Up on the trucks the *atabaque* drums were throbbing, calling the people together. Suddenly music exploded from a Carnival truck, and the dancing began.

The procession wound all the way from the Church of the Conceição da Praia, along the Lacerda Elevator, up to the Church of Bomfim on Sacred Hill, for a distance of six miles, more or less, depending on the quantity of devotion and cane liquor consumed by the participants. Thousands of people—the procession was a sea of people—it stretched out of sight. Cars, trucks, carriages, and donkeys festooned with flowers and sprigs, carrying full barrels on their backs; all ensured there would be no lack of scented water for the ceremony. In the trucks were lively groups, whole families, *samba* clubs, and *afoxés*. Musicians clutched their instruments: guitars, accordions, ukeleles, tambourines, *capoeira berimbaus*. Popular singers and composers were there, like Tião the Chauffeur, River Man, Chocolate, and Paulinho Camafeu. The voices of Jerônimo, of Moraes Moreira were heard. In riding breeches, white jacket, dandified, kinky cotton hair, Batatinha, "Small Potatoes," smiled while crossing the street. People shook his hand, shouted his name, "Batatinha!" embraced him. A blond—American, Italian, from São Paulo?—ran over and kissed him on his black and beautiful face.

Rich and poor mingled, rubbing elbows. In the mixed-blood city of Bahia, all shades of color exist in the flesh of its inhabitants, ranging from a black so dark it's blue, to milky white, the color of snow, and in between the infinite gamut of mulattos. Who isn't a devotee of Our Lord of Bomfim, with his countless miracles; who doesn't cling to Oxalá, bearing the unfailing *ebós?*

Also present were the commanding general of the region, the admiral of the naval base, the brigadier of the air force, the president of the Assembly, the presiding judge of the Superior Court, the president of the Honorable Chamber of Aldermen, bankers, cacao barons, entrepreneurs, executives, senators, and deputies. Some paraded in black limousines. Others, however—the governor, the mayor, and the head of the tobacco industry, Mário Portugal—followed on foot along with the people. There followed a mob of demagogues—that is, candidates in the upcoming elections—canvassing every mile, butting in, distributing fliers and embraces, kisses, smiles, and pats on the back to potential voters.

The procession swayed to the music from the trucks: religious hymns, folk songs, Carnival *sambas,* and *frevos.* The accompaniment swelled along the way, the multitude expanded; people clambered down the hillsides, the São Joaquim market emptied out, latecomers disembarked from ferryboats and launches or arrived in sloops. When the front of the procession reached the foot of Sacred Hill, a voice well known and loved rose from the music truck of Dodô and Osmar—a hush descended over everyone, the procession halted, and Caetano Veloso intoned the hymn to Our Lord of Bomfim.

Then the march up the hillside resumed to the beating of the drums, to the singing of the *afoxés* about the waters of Oxalá. The mass of people headed for the Church of Bomfim, which had been closed by a decision of the Curia. In years past, the procession would wash the whole church and honor Oxalá on the altar of Jesus. Someday it will go back to being that way. Today the Baianas occupied the steps and the entrance to the church; the washing began, and the obligation of the *candomblé* is fulfilled: *"Exê-ê-babá!"*

Our Lord of Bomfim arrived in Bahia from Portugal during colonial times riding on the mournful Catholic vow of a shipwrecked Portuguese sailor; Oxalá arrived from the coast of Africa, during the time of the traffic in blacks, riding on the bloody back of a slave. Today they hovered over the procession, Our Lord and Oxalá, fused in the breasts of the Baianas, plunged into the scented water, and mingled. Together they are a single uniquely Brazilian divinity.

The Two Aunts

That Bomfim Thursday was decisive in Manela's life. The procession, a happy time of singing and dancing, the ceremonious Baianas, the square on Sacred Hill festooned with paper streamers and decorated with fronds of coconut palms, the washing of the steps of the basilica, the possessed women receiving the enchanted ones, the sacred ritual, and having lunch with her cousins at a table of love, eating and drinking, dendê oil running from her mouth down her chin, her hands licked, cold beer, *batidas* and the warmth of cane liquor, cinnamon and clove, prancing around the square with her sister, her cousin, and the boys, parties in family homes and the public dance in the street, the music trucks, the lighting of the footlights, the colored bulbs on the facade of the church, she wandering amid the crowd with Miro beside her, leading her by the hand. With a sense of lightness, Manela felt capable of taking flight, a free swallow in the euphoria of the festival.

That morning, when she had first arrived at the Church of the Conceição da Praia, she had been a poor, unhappy girl—oppressed, lacking a will of her own, always on the defensive: timid, deceiving, disheartened, submissive. Yes, Auntie. I heard, Auntie. I'm coming, Auntie. Well behaved. She'd attended the procession because Gildete had demanded it with an ultimatum of fearsome threats:

"If you're not here bright and early," her aunt had said, "I'm coming to get you, and I'm a woman capable of slapping that so-and-so right in the face if she so much as dares say you can't come with me. Where did anyone ever hear tell of such a thing? She thinks she's carrying the king in her belly, but she's nothing but a stuck-up bitch. I don't know how Danilo puts up with all that crap—it takes balls."

Hands on hips, on a war footing, Gildete finished:

"I've got some accounts to settle with that busybody, going around talking about me, treating me like a street walker or some hoodooer. She'll pay me for that someday."

Yet, big-hearted, cordial, loving, a piece of coconut sweet, Aunt Gildete held no rancor; the threatened revenge, the promised vengeance, never went beyond words. On the rare occasion when she lost her temper, she would become transformed, capable of uttering the worst absurdities.

Wasn't Gildete the one who had stormed wildly into the office of the secretary of education like a crazy woman, when the government attempted to cancel student lunches in order to save money? "Calm down, my dear teacher!"—that was all the secretary had said to her. He lost his composure in fear of physical assault as he faced Gildete's robust figure, itching for a fight, her harsh accusations defending the poor children, her imperious figure—and he hastily left the room. Panicky stenographers tried to restrain her, but Gildete had pushed them away; all determination, ignoring protests and warnings, she crossed through anterooms until she got to the sanctum sanctorum where the secretary issued his orders. Her photograph later appeared in the newspapers with an exposé about the plan to do away with elementary school lunches—it had been a carefully guarded secret until then—resulting in such a wave of protests, including the threat of a strike and a demonstration, that the measure was canceled, and Gildete even escaped a negative report in her service file. Instead of a reprimand, she was praised; for the governor took advantage of what had happened to get rid of the secretary, whose political loyalty he had doubted anyway. The governor attributed the authorship of the disastrous idea to the secretary, then threw him to the wolves.

Along with the praise came a certain notoriety: Newton Macedo Campos, a combative opposition deputy, referred to the incident in a speech in the State Assembly, praising Gildete to the skies, calling her an "ardent patriot and distinguished citizen, paladin of children, paragon of teachers." In addition the union tried to coopt her for its leadership, but she refused: She enjoyed the praise but had no ambitions to be a paladin or a paragon.

On Bomfim Thursday, Manela turned her weakness into strength and did as Gildete had instructed her. Early in the morning, she set out for Gildete's, taking advantage of the fact that Adalgisa was gone for the morning—she and Danilo had left to attend the seventh-day mass for the wife of one of his co-workers. Manela carried her English books and notebooks so that when she came home for lunch, they would think she had been off at her class. To be back for lunch, Manela planned to check her watch, leave the procession in time to pick up her dress and her books, and catch the bus—the whole thing was well orchestrated in her mind. Trembling inside, astounded by her own audacity, she had changed her clothes had put on the petticoat and wide skirt, her breasts naked under the Baiana smock—oh, if Aunt Adalgisa ever saw such a thing!

To say that Manela wasn't sorry she had come, that she was in love, would be to say very little. By the time she finally did take the road back home that day, poorly timed rather than according to her schedule, she was a different Manela. The real Manela, the one who'd hidden herself away ever since the death of her parents, had almost extinguished herself in fear of punishment—the punishment of God who, omnipresent, sees everything and makes note of all for a settling of final accounts on the Day of Judgment. And she had lived in fear of the punishment of Aunt Adalgisa, who reared and educated her. Auntie, ever watchful and nosy, had collected her dues for whatever she saw or found out with a good tongue-lashing and the leather strap, too!

As the twig is bent, so grows the tree. Manela had been thirteen and a half when she came to live with her aunt and uncle, so she wasn't that young. But according to Adalgisa, her parents had brought her up very poorly: She was a teenager full of wiles and will, accustomed to bad company, consorting with trash, loose with her schoolmates at movie matinees, only pretending to take part in programs for children, running off to festivals on the square. Why, her parents had even taken her to *candomblé* temples, that was how irresponsible . . .

Adalgisa had taken her in hand, put a leash on her. She'd laid down strict hours: She couldn't let her set foot on the street, and as for festivals and movies, she could go only if accompanied by her aunt and uncle. *Candomblés?* Not even to be mentioned: Adalgisa had a horror of *candomblé*—a *sacred* horror, the adjective imposes itself. A short rein and a strong wrist would bring Manela under control. Adalgisa would punish her with no misgivings or pity. She was fulfilling her duty as an adoptive mother—and one day, established in life, Manela would thank her for it.

The Hour of Noon

"Exê-ê-babá!" The palms of her open hands at chest level, Manela greeted Oxolufã, Oxalá the elder, as he arrived at the entrance to the Church of Bomfim. Bending over in front of Aunt Gildete, she watched Gildete quiver, close her eyes, and bend her body over her knees, possessed. Leaning on her broom as an improvised *paxorô*, Gildete came out doing the dance of the enchanted one: Oxalá, old, debilitated, but free from captivity at last, from the jail where he'd been punished without any trial or sentence, was celebrating his freedom. When he showed himself on the square, the bells were ringing, announcing the hour of noon.

Noon was the hour when Manela was expected back at the Avenida da Ave-Maria for lunch, dressed again as a student, skirt and blouse, her breasts held in by a brassiere, carrying the schoolbag with her English text and her notebooks, as if she were coming from her class at the institute. Good afternoon, Auntie, how was the mass?

But she must have forgotten, or decided not to, and when she heard the bells, it was no longer any use if she remembered, because at half-past noon on the dot, Uncle Danilo was sitting at the table and Aunt Adalgisa was serving him his repast. Whenever Manela happened to be late, her prepared plate would grow cold waiting in the kitchen. That day Adalgisa didn't even fix up the cold plate, and she herself barely tasted the beef stew with dwarf beans—she stopped with the first forkful, choking with surprise and indignation. Her mouth was as bitter as bile, her head was bursting, mute. She did not want to believe what her eyes had seen—she'd rather go blind.

The Waters of Oxalá

Anyone who moves backward is a crab, Aunt Gildete had stated the night before, using proverbial phrases, popular tales, and folk wisdom to sum up her diatribe against Adalgisa. Returning to her normal self, sitting with her nieces, stroking the head of her daughter Violeta who was crouching at her feet, she'd mentioned the legend of the waters of Oxalá and recounted it—if you'd like to hear it, I'll tell it to you. She cleared her throat and spoke what follows, perhaps a word more, a word less:

"The ancients tell, I heard from my granny, a Grunci black woman, that Oxalá went out one day through the lands of his kingdom and the kingdoms of his three sons, Xangô, Oxóssi, and Ogum, to find out how the people were getting along, with the intention of correcting injustices and punishing evildoers. In order not to be recognized, he covered his body with the rags of a beggar and set out, asking questions. He didn't get very far; accused of vagrancy, he was taken to jail and beaten. Just on suspicion they tossed him into the clink where, forgotten, he spent years on end in solitude and filth.

"One day, happening to pass by the miserable jail, Oxóssi recognized his missing father, who had been given up for dead. Quickly freed, he was loaded down with honors, and before he returned to the royal palace, Oxalá was bathed and perfumed. Singing and dancing, the women brought water and balm and bathed him. The most beautiful among them warmed his bed, his heart, and his parts for him.

" 'I have learned with my own flesh the conditions under which the people of my kingdom live, and of the kingdoms of my sons. Here, there, everywhere, whim and violence reign, rules of obedience and silence: I carry the marks on my body. The waters that put out the fire and washed the wounds are going to extinguish despotism and fear. The lives of the people are going to change.' Oxalá was true to his word, he put his power as king into play. That's the story of the waters of Oxalá. It passed from mouth to mouth, crossed the ocean, and so it reached our Bahian capital city. A lot of people who walk along in the procession, carrying jugs and jars of scented water to wash the floor of the church, don't know why they're doing it. Now you know, and you can pass it on to your children and grandchildren when you have them; it's a pretty good story, and it bears a lesson."

Oxalá didn't manage to change the lives of the people—that was easy to see. Even so, we have to recognize that no word spoken against violence and tyranny is entirely vain and useless: Somebody who hears it just might overcome fear and start to rebel. Just look at Manela following the path of Oxalá in front of the Church of Bomfim, just at that moment when she should have been hightailing it home.

The *Ekede*

When the noon bells rang, in her affliction at the lost hour, Manela clung to Our Lord of Bomfim, for whom nothing is impossible. On the upper floor of the sacristy was a whole tier filled with thanks and ex-votos, the awesome museum of miracles, attesting to and proving the power of the patron saint.

At the same time that she was invoking a divine protection—Have mercy, my Lord of Bomfim!—with an instinctive hereditary gesture, Manela joined in the ritual of the *ekedes,* the acolytes of possessed women who are under the care of the *orixás* who have revealed themselves. She took off her immaculate sash to wipe the sweat from Gildete's face; hands on hips, fists clenched, Oxalá was muttering commands.

Manela began to sense the enormity of her transgression, the size of her sin—it couldn't have been greater, alas, it couldn't! She'd have to invent a plausible explanation, figure out an acceptable excuse that would restrain Aunt Adalgisa's pitiless arm and shut her cursing mouth —some insults wound deeper than a couple of slaps. It was normally difficult for Manela to get around her aunt, who was mistrustful and speculative, but sometimes Manela managed to convince her and escape a sermon, a bawling out, and the leather strap. Not that she was deceitful by nature, but in times of panic and humiliation, there was nothing she could do but lie. Worse still was when nothing came to mind, and all that was left for her to do was confess her error and ask forgiveness: I'm sorry, Auntie, I won't do it again, ever again. I swear by God, by the soul of my mother. Today, Manela knew, such an entreaty for forgiveness couldn't forestall punishment; the best it could do was soften it—and would that even be worthwhile?

Manela wiped Aunt Gildete's face, and without thinking, as if obeying orders—orders muttered by Oxalá, perhaps—she followed Gildete through the entire triumphal dance of the enchanted one, commemorat-

ing his regained freedom—the end of his solitude and filth. She was
getting dizzy, she felt a tingling in her arms and legs, she tried to keep
her balance, was unable to, bent her body over, let herself go. As if in a
dream, she saw herself as someone else, soaring in the air, and she
realized that she didn't have to invent excuses or make up lies to tell her
aunt because she wasn't committing any crime, misdemeanor, or error,
any sin. There was nothing to confess, no reason to beg forgiveness and
deserve punishment. With a leap of freedom, Manela danced in front of
Oxalá, *Baba Okê*, father of the Sacred Hill of Bomfim—she and Aunt
Gildete went on in front of the church in the midst of the cadenced
clapping of the Baianas. How did she know those steps, where had she
learned that dance, acquired those fundamentals? Sprightly and light-
footed, standing up against captivity, guilt and fear no longer weighed on
her shoulders.

Oxolufã, or Oxalá the elder, the greatest of all, the father, came for
her and embraced her and held her, hugging her against his chest, trembling and making her tremble. As he went off, he shouted quite loud so
they would know: *"Eparrei!"* and the Baianas repeated, bowing before
Manela: *"Eparrei!"*

Once this change had come over Manela, Yansan, who had been
present, left as suddenly as she had come. She carried away all the accumulated filth, all that dirt, to bury in the jungle: hesitation and submission, ignominy and pretense, the fear of threats and shouts, of slaps in
the face, of the leather strap hanging on the wall, and worst of all, the
pleas for forgiveness. Oyá had cleansed Manela's body and straightened
out her head.

So it was that the fright and mortification that had overcome
Manela when the bells marked the hour of noon were followed by complete release: Filled with joy, in the rejection of yoke and harness, Manela
was reborn. That was how the waters of Oxalá flowed on that Bomfim
Thursday. They had put out the fires of hell, *axé*.

The *Coup de Foudre*

On that Bomfim Thursday, under the scalding and luminous January sun, at the end of the washing ceremony, Manela met Miro.

It was a *coup de foudre*, as Adalgisa's dear and esteemed neighbor,
Professor João Batista de Lima e Silva, familiar with the French language
and its literature, would have said upon learning about the case. But it
was love at first sight only as far as Manela was concerned, because if one

could believe Miro, he'd had his eye on her for some time and was only waiting for a chance to state his intentions.

Manela was busy on the steps of the church, scattering scented water over the delirious crowd—*filhas de santo* in trance were receiving *orixás;* seventeen Oxalás were hanging about the entrance, ten Oxolufãs, and seven Oxaguinhãs—when she heard someone say her name, calling her insistently:

"Manela! Manela! Look, here I am!"

She looked and she saw him, squeezed in along the steps, his pleading eyes fastened on her. His open mouth displayed white teeth against his black face, and unbelievable as it might seem in that horrible crush, his feet were dancing a *samba*. Manela leaned over and emptied the last drops from her clay jar over the big-mouth's kinky hair. His hair was combed out in an Afro, a symbol of the world struggle against racism made popular by American Black Panthers. Manela couldn't remember seeing him before, but what difference did that make?

Miro reached out his hand and said:

"Come."

The Flight of the Swallow

Overwhelmed by a feeling of relief, of well-being, the all-consuming urgent desire to live, an insidious euphoria, a sweet sadness, the liberated swallow flapped her wings, ready to take flight and discover the world. Manela laughed wildly.

On the square around the basilica and on the streets at the foot of the Sacred Hill, the people had started Carnival: A month and a half of frolicking and merrymaking would follow, of endless celebration because no one should have to tolerate the harshness of life uninterrupted for a whole year. The gift of celebrating festivities even under calamitous conditions belongs exclusively to our people as a favor from Our Lord of Bomfim and Oxalá: The two together add up to one, the God of Brazilians, Bahia born.

Samba groups and *afoxés* paraded by, the Children of Gandhi gave their first performance of the year, and the melodies from music trucks echoed across the horizon of houses on stilts barely raised above the water and mud in the swamp of Alagados. The urchins called captains-of-the-sands went through the crowd peddling Bomfim ribbons, medals and scapulars, colored figures of saints, clenched-fist *figas* and leather-bag *patuás*. Crowds of tourists came and went, all bubbly and excited.

Arranged on aromatic trays were *acarajés, abarás,* fried fish, crabs, *moqueca* of aratu crabs wrapped in banana leaves, and corn cakes. At the jammed, noisy lunch stands, meals of coconut and dendê oil were served: minced herb *caruru, vatapá, efó,* diverse fried dishes, and different *moquecas*—so many of them!—spiced chicken stew with shrimp and pumpkin, *hauça* rice. Ice-cold beer, *batidas,* and jackhammer soup, an incomparable aphrodisiac. Sumptuous baskets of fruit: *manga-espada, carlota,* custard apple, and *itiuba, manga-rosa,* sapotes, sapodillas, hog plums, Malay apples, cashew fruit, Surinam cherries, jambos, Chinese gooseberries, eleven types of banana, and slices of pineapple and watermelon. Everything was sky-high in price, but even so, the stands couldn't hold the vast and voracious clientele—it was a gut-stuffing spree.

In several of the houses set aside for pilgrims or rented to summer visitors who were there for the festivities, small orchestras—guitar, accordion, flute, tambourine, ukelele—livened up family groups. Among the embracing couples there was no lack of those getting on in years, old-timers joining in with the young, remembering the good old days. The great majority of people, however, danced in the open air, on the street, to the electronic sound of the music trucks: *frevos* and *sambas,* Carnival *marchas:* "The only ones who don't follow the music trucks are those already dead," the minstrel says. A dance without limits, with no quitting time, perennial and boundless, it can only be seen to be believed.

They didn't stop their frolicking when a happy band of merrymakers gave off the inaugural Carnival shout on Bomfim Thursday to sisters, cousins, lovers, hangers-on, friends and strangers. Manela was the heart of the group, and no one outdid her in liveliness. Having been mortally ill, with the miracle of her recuperated health she wanted to enjoy everything she had a right to enjoy. On the pavement she danced the Brazilian dance of the people, of the *masses,* as the most dispossessed segment of the population was beginning to be called. To the lulling sound and soft melody of the Periperi Live-Wire Jazz Group, wrapped in the arms of her swain, she fluttered in the blue heaven of her life. She danced the *samba,* foxtrot, rock, bolero, rhumba, and twist, she even did some steps of an Argentine tango—Miro was unpredictable; one step after another, one dance after another, a beer here, a *batida* there, a shot of liquor afterward, the euphoria growing. Such, indeed, was living.

The Blessed Candle

Gildete broke her fast of that day at the Queen of the Sea food stand. She presided over the full table and the inconsequential gab, laughed with her children and her nieces, needled the lovers. In the middle of the afternoon she withdrew: A widow in her fifties could no longer compete with the music truck.

She'd left her daughter and nieces in the care of the boys. Her son Álvaro was in his third year of medical school and was courting a fellow student with engagement and marital intentions; and Dionísio was a good-looking cutup who took care of the stand in the Model Market, a Romeo, always surrounded by women. At the table, a pair of twin sisters —one with dyed hair, the other a brunette—were vying for his attentions. Dionísio was making out with both of them: So? they were twins, weren't they? But not only were Gildete's sons looking after Manela, so was the suitor himself: Miro was never more than a step away.

Sitting at the head of their table, savoring her cleaned-out siri crab, Gildete was trying to discern from her niece's face what was going on in her heart: Manela had said nothing about having to return home, Gildete noticed. She showed no sign of haste or hurry. She had seemed worried that morning, looking at her watch all the time, anxious on occasion, but it appeared that starting with the washing ceremony, the distant thought had ceased to consume her.

The signs of worry on Manela's face had given way to a certain exaltation: talkative, uninhibited, laughing either with or without reason, she let her hand rest on Miro's hand. Miro was outdoing himself with his gab, his humor, his buffoonery, his charm. Had her niece given the cry of independence, of Liberty or Death? her aunt wondered. An elementary schoolteacher, Gildete loved giving children examples from the history of Brazil. Getting up from the table to go catch her bus, when she took leave of Manela she whispered in her ear:

"Don't you want to come with me? If you want, I can go with you to Adalgisa's house. Leave everything to me."

"Thank you, Auntie, but you don't have to. I'm not ready to leave yet. I'll stay with the girls and come with them. Don't worry, Auntie, everything's okay."

Gildete's eyes lingered on Manela's face, and behind the immoderate liveliness, the fever of the festival, and the courting, she could make out the girl's spirit, her definite decision—there was no doubt about it, she'd proclaimed her independence. In any case, she, Gildete, would keep a sharp eye for whatever might come about—and she would intervene, should it become necessary. Enjoy yourselves, she told her children, picking up her empty pot and broom that she had used in the washing ceremony.

When the washing ceremony was over, the doors of the basilica had been opened to the public. The faithful entered, went over to cross themselves before the miraculous statue of Our Lord of Bomfim, and asked for his blessing and protection. Baianas who earlier had been in trance at the entrance now knelt in the nave of the church reciting the Lord's Prayer. Crowding into the sacristy, tourists were buying tickets to the Museum of Miracles. They asked if they were allowed to take pictures. They took pictures. Church biddies were selling candles, and the brotherhood was adding up donations and gifts. A mulatto priest, no longer young, was contemplating the festivities in the square. He remembered the days when the whole church could be washed; he'd never noticed any lack of faith or devotion or any signs of disrespect in the ceremony. He never understood why his superiors in the Church hierarchy had prohibited this pious and moving celebration: the people washing the house of the Lord. Was it really "black people's stuff," as he'd been told? But didn't all Bahians have some black blood? Nearly all certainly, with a few, rare exceptions.

As Gildete passed before the basilica, she changed course and went in, bought a holy candle, and lighted it. She made the sign of the cross as she stood in the line of the faithful, placing the candle in one of the many holders fronting the main altar. She knelt before the image of Our Lord of Bomfim, murmured a Hail Mary, crossed herself, and picking up her jar and broom, went on her way.

The Lovers

When Manela came down the steps, Miro led her by the hand to the Queen of the Sea food stand, edging their way through the crush of people. At the table Dionísio's good humor was already helping the cousins have a good time: Álvaro with his girlfriend, the Don Juan with the twins, taking care of both of them with diligence, skill, and competence. When Dionísio saw the couple arrive, he asked Miro, shouting in order to be heard above the uproar:

"Hey fellow! What's all this? Is Manela your girlfriend?"

"Do you know of any other?" Miro challenged him.

Seeing the curiosity stamped on Manela's face, Dionísio explained to his cousin:

"This wiseguy tells me he's going to go get his girlfriend, then he comes back with you. I didn't know you two even knew each other."

They sat down and squeezed in at the head of the table, which was small for the number of occupants. Manela's eyes alighted on Miro's, looking for an explanation of his impertinence. But before the rascal could explain the charade, he was ordering *moquecas* and *batidas*—a *moqueca* of soft-shelled crab and a maracock *batida* for her, for him a *moqueca* of ray fish and a lime *batida*. Only then did he say something, staring at her with such a look of tenderness and enchantment that she lowered her eyes and blushed—and in the dazzling light of the summer sun no one noticed that Manela's face was flushed. But that was no reason to ignore this significant detail.

"You don't remember," Miro said, "but I met you four or five years ago at the Gantois Candomblé during the festival of Oxóssi's jugs. You were there with the late Eufrásio and the late lady your mother, Dona Dolores. I remember it as if it were only yesterday. You were a very young girl. I lost track of you after that, but I never forgot you. Just the other day I found out that you were the cousin of my buddies here and Marieta's sister. Right then I said to myself: 'I've got her now—she's not going to get away from me again.' "

"Sweet talk and holy water never hurt anyone," Manela jested. She joked for the sake of joking and asked questions for the sake of asking questions. Harmless jests and questions weren't going to stop what was destined to happen.

"And what if I don't want to go with you?" she asked flirtatiously.

"Why shouldn't you want to? I've got no shortage of girlfriends, God bless me! This nigger here is the Jesus, Mary, and Joseph of girls—you'd better believe it! What I need is you. I already told you that I never forgot you, and that I've been looking for you all this damned time. You cast a spell on me!"

He laughed with pleasure, a convincing and confident laugh. Manela laughed too, and they laughed together. Dionísio laughed without knowing why, his twin girlfriends accompanying him. They were possessed by an uncontrollable *foú-rire*, as Professor João Batista would have put it had he been there. Dionísio, roaring with laughter, pointed out his cousin and his friend to the twin sisters and everyone else gathered there. He still hadn't decided which of the two he would finish off the festivities with. Maybe with both of them, in order to stay on the crest of his wave of sexual promiscuity. Finally managing to control his laughter, he commented, "A pair of boobies. Halfbreed love. Not for me, no siree."

From that moment on Manela and Miro were inseparable. They walked about the square holding hands, tied Bomfim ribbons on each other's wrists: three knots in each ribbon, each knot a secret request. Miro offered her a straw hat to protect herself from the sun and a paper fan to cool herself with. Mostly they walked behind the music truck, not even realizing that evening was coming on. Night caught them in the mournful cadence of a blues, dancing cheek to cheek at an impromptu dancing party given by the journalist Giovanni Guimarães and his wife, Dona Jacy.

Dona Jacy served fine liqueurs, delicious drinks made by Carmelite nuns; Giovanni was discussing politics with friends. The generals, he said, are too dim-witted, incompetent—the dictatorship is on its last legs. Dr. Zitelman Oliva replied, "I'm sorry, my dear Giovanni, but I don't think so. Unfortunately, that gang of muddlers is set to stay around for a long time. Unfortunately," he repeated, sadly and realistically.

Each year, in order to give recompense for a prayer that had been answered, the Guimarãeses rented this house on the Sacred Hill and eagerly celebrated the saint and benefactor. "If I get pregnant," Dona Jacy had offered, "I promise my Lord of Bomfim . . ." Dona Jacy did get pregnant and gave birth to a beautiful girl who had been baptized with the sonorous Slavic name Ludmila.

But wasn't Giovanni a Communist, and one of the most fervent of them at that? Ah, why should one thing impede the other? What is the ideology patrol doing here? Out! Quickly! Back to the bottom of hell, to the whore that bore them! There's no room for thought police in these ecumenical pages.

—❦—❦

The Kiss

Before the blues, foot-dragging and languid, Manela and Miro had spun around to rock and swing, flirted in the *samba* and the rhumba, and they'd showed off to applause with a demonstration of the Argentine tango. Miro danced like a prince or a caliph, and Manela wasn't far behind, a pair of virtuosos, impassioned to boot—it was a moving scene to watch. "It's a pleasure to know that feeling still exists in a world dominated more and more by crude materialism and selfish interests," commented Dona Auta Rosa, wife of the painter Calasans Neto, visibly moved. She was addressing her remarks to the Belgian philosopher Michel Schooyans, a Catholic priest, professor at the University of Louvain, a distinguished guest, a foreign celebrity. Politely the distinguished guest agreed, although not without a touch of impatience: If he'd had his way he'd be out in the streets watching that extraordinary spectacle of the festival of the people of Bahia. He loved the people, he adored Bahia, and being a modern and enlightened priest, although an adversary (philosophically speaking), he was no enemy of materialism.

Dancing was not included in the list of prohibitions laid down by

Manela's aunt—a surprising bit of liberalism. Perhaps it was because Adalgisa liked to dance herself and did it with elegance and pleasure whenever she attended the Spanish Club cotillions or soirées at the home of families of her acquaintance. Needless to say, she danced exclusively with her husband.

In her single days, before she had met Danilo, Adalgisa had won first prize in a hotly contested *paso doble* contest in the salon of the Galician Center, her partner the dextrous Dmeval Chaves, who in his younger days had been a clerk in a bookstore. Adalgisa still owned and wore the gold brooch with amethysts—the prize donated by the Galicians of the Casa Moreira, a reputable establishment that dealt in antiques. When Manolo Moreira had presented her with the piece, using improvised but inspired words, he had compared her to Terpsichore, labeling her the "Bahian muse of dance." For these and other reasons, at birthday parties, baptisms, and weddings, Manela had permission to dance—within the bounds of decency, of course.

Bounds of decency, alas! Who was there to define them in the absence of Adalgisa on a Bomfim Thursday, night having fallen, after so much beer had been drunk at the food stands, the *batidas* and *caipirinhas,* not to mention convent liqueurs and an even sweeter and more intoxicating malmsey, the uninterrupted declaration of love? When the lights went out in the room—had a fuse blown, or had some shameless person turned them off? How was one to know?—Miro kissed Manela on the mouth and ran his hand over her breasts.

The Impudent Hussy

It wasn't until nine o'clock that night that Manela finally appeared at the end of the Avenida da Ave-Maria: Aunt Adalgisa was waiting for her in the doorway. That lazybones of a husband had gone out so as not to witness the scene, leaving his poor, sick wife the worry and obligation. As foster mother, Adalgisa had assumed all responsibility and she was rising to it even in the state she was in, at the limits of her scant strength: her heart palpitating, a bitter taste in her mouth, her head ready to burst.

She didn't permit Manela to utter a single word. "Don't you come to me with any lies, you shameless hussy! I know everything," said Adalgisa. Her aunt's open and heavy hand landed a slap on each of Manela's cheeks, right there at the street door, in full view of the neighbors.

Manela entered the house under a rain of blows. Sharp slaps and Adalgisa's angry voice insulted her with the worst names possible, accusing her of having evil instincts, calling her a hoodooer and a hussy; not content with that, she dragged out of the peace and tranquility of the cemetery the memory of Manela's father Eufrásio. "You take after that boozing nigger," Adalgisa cried, "the drunkard who killed my sister, poor thing." She passed over her poor thing of a sister's own origins, her own manners and ways, attributing to the blood and influence of her brother-in-law the deplorable propensities that drew her niece stubbornly away from the good path and led her into sin and perdition.

Adalgisa was forgetting that in her sister Dolores, the other side had prevailed, the African side. The Spanish blood that flowed in both their veins hadn't imposed its rules and customs on Dolores, hadn't made her white. But Adalgisa, loyal to the Catholicism of their father, Don Francisco Romero Pérez y Pérez, nicknamed Paco Negreiro in homage to his preference when it came to females—Adalgisa had followed the path of the Spanish colony and Holy Mother Church with no deviation. Dolores, on the other hand, had been true to the plebeian side of the family, their mother's. Andreza da Anunciação had been nicknamed Andreza de Yansan because of the matchless grace she showed when receiving the thunder spirit in the circle of the possessed women. *Dolores,* although she still mingled pleasantly with the Galicians and attended mass piously, had never missed a festival on the square, the call of Carnival, or the obligation of the *candomblé.* At the centuries-old *axé Casa Branca* she had shaved her head, a favorite daughter of Euá.

Dolores's African roots were accentuated in her daughters—dark girls, copper-colored—because Eufrásio, in spite of his grandmother and the surname Belini, was himself also quite dark, a Brazilian of many mingled bloods: Belini Alves do Espírito Santo, Italian, Portuguese, and black. With so many white boys from good families, why in the devil, Iberian Adalgisa wondered, had Dolores chosen that Cape Verdean? What had she seen in him besides his guitar and his singing?

It was only when Manela heard her aunt carrying on unreasonably against Eufrásio tonight, calling him a cane-liquor-swilling murderer, that Manela opened her mouth and raised her voice, interrupting the harangue and stemming the flow of bile:

"Don't you talk about my father! Talk about me, say whatever you want to, I don't care—you're my aunt, I live in your house, you've got every right to. But keep my father's name out of it. He isn't here to defend himself!"

The outburst was so unexpected, so unusual and absurd, that Adalgisa fell silent, stunned. While she was ranting, she hadn't noticed the strange look on her niece's face, silent till then, taking the blows without a word, without weeping or begging forgiveness, as she usually did. What had happened to her submissive and fearful Manela, the one who would burst into tears and, still sobbing, fall to her knees asking for clemency? "Enough, Auntie," she would say, "I swear I won't do it again, I swear by my own salvation, on the soul of my mother!" Well, she'd finally loosened her tongue, gotten her voice back—and only to tell Adalgisa to be quiet! What had happened to induce the child to do something so daring, so outrageous? What was going on?

"I'll teach you, you ingrate!" Adalgisa, recovering herself, shrieked. "I'll tear your tongue out, you slut!"

She went to the back of the room and took the leather strap down from the wall.

The One O'Clock News on TV

Adalgisa normally listened to the radio all day long; she knew the schedule of the main programs by heart, and she never missed the amateur hours and country music programs, her favorite shows. She was inseparable from her transistor radio, carrying it from room to room: in the bathroom early in the morning, on her dressing table in the bedroom, in the kitchen while she prepared lunch, on top of her sewing machine in the parlor. She would turn it off only in the evening, to follow her TV soap operas. She watched two, the first at seven and the second at eight; the first she almost always watched with her husband, who was also a fan. When she finished her homework, Manela would join her aunt and uncle.

The television set, a fine expensive one, hadn't undergone the same wear and tear as the transistor radio. It was reserved for the nighttime: for soap operas, miniseries, movies, and live broadcasts of important events. Danilo preferred sports; his passion was soccer. He'd once played for Ipiranga, the soccer club closest to his heart, his one and only. He'd started out there while he was still a boy, and he had become famous—a renowned forward. He'd turned down offers in the millions from the other Bahia and Vitória clubs. He never switched his jersey until he took it off for good when a serious injury removed him from the playing field permanently.

Another of Danilo's preferences was the news—he never missed a broadcast, even at one o'clock, sitting at the table in the middle of lunch, keeping up with what was happening in Brazil and in the world, starting with the latest news of Bahia. Adalgisa wouldn't pay much attention to the news. The twists and turns of politics and the direction of the universe didn't interest her much, except for fashion shows and news from the courts of Europe—Spain, Monaco, England. She would drool over the English royal family. "How charming!" she'd exclaim whenever she caught a glimpse of the Queen Mother on television.

Well, it so happened that on that Bomfim Thursday, having turned on the TV set as usual so Danilo could follow his news, Adalgisa nearly had apoplexy when she spotted her niece Manela on television, right in the midst of the washing ceremony of Bomfim. The depraved girl was actually sprinkling perfumed water on the kinky head of some hustler: Days later, the hustler would turn out to be the driver of the taxi, of the vehicle with the unbearable horn, parked at the entrance to their street. It was good that Adalgisa had time to sit down. Danilo exclaimed, "Why, it's Manela—look, Dadá!" Danilo found it very funny, the wretch! His Dadá murmured, "Oh, my God!" and put her hand over her heart to stop it from bursting.

Transmitted live from atop the Sacred Hill, the report on the washing ceremony began by showing a lively image of Manela beside the railing, a pitcher in her hand—no one who saw her would ever forget her. Then, after showing the governor and the mayor in turn waving to the crowd, the cameras zoomed in with successive shots, some really quite striking, of the Baianas dancing on the steps of the basilica in honor of Oxalá. Adalgisa recognized Gildete leading Violeta, Manela, and Marieta. Gildete and Violeta, impenitent followers of *candomblé*, mother and daughter, not satisfied to force those impious and savage practices on the niece Marieta, a defenseless orphan, were now secretly corrupting Manela behind the back of her foster mother—stabbing Adalgisa in the back!

One of the cameras singled out Manela several times, showing her swinging her hips shamelessly, her face glowing with sweat and abomination, her feet possessed by the devil, Adalgisa thought. The announcer didn't see her in that light as he effused with praise for the washing ceremony, for the Baianas, and for Manela in particular. He called his viewers' attention to the purity of the ritualistic white garments, the necklaces and bracelets. According to him, these were the authentic expression of the culture. In Adalgisa's opinion, they were the barbarous and provocative adornments of *candomblé*. A cynical pedant, a closet satyr hiding behind a Che Guevara beard, currently the vogue among these sassy young men, the news announcer declared himself incapable of "describing the café au lait beauty" of Manela as it deserved to be praised, incapable of "lifting it to the proper heights, of finding the inspiration of a poet, the talent of a Godofredo Filho, the fantasy of a Carlos Capinam" necessary to do justice to it. Poet or not, the announcer outdid himself over the adolescent grace, the proud demeanor, the Bahian beauty of that flower of the Brazilian race, fulfilling her duties as a *filha de santo* in the procession of the waters of Oxalá. With what pleasure Adalgisa would have bashed the braggart if he had been there before her in person and not on the screen. On the screen, Manela's face, licentious, laughed like that of a fallen woman, Manela's feet did *macumba* steps, her half-naked breasts swung in the loose robe—her face, feet, and breasts on the one o'clock news! On a program seen and heard in the state capital and throughout the region by thousands of people! Such shame! Such a scandal!

"Manela's riding high!" Danilo said, proud of the praise for his niece's beauty, which he considered well deserved. But he never got to say "well deserved." He swallowed the end of the sentence, because Adalgisa looked at him in such a way, with eyes so full of deadly fury and pain, that the good Danilo, horrified at once, realized his mistake and began to perceive the actual criminality of what had happened. Manela had joined the procession of her own free will, without asking their permission, without Dadá's approval, and even worse, she had gone at Gildete's invitation. And he, lummox of an uncle, had applauded her!

Flower of the race! Adolescent beauty! Proud face! On the television set Adalgisa saw only the sweaty, vulgar lasciviousness—that's the proper word—of a shameless wench: hypocritical, perfidious, false, disloyal, the worst kind of trash, turning herself over to the nefarious practices of witchcraft! Stabbed by this betrayal, the dagger piercing her breast, Adalgisa got down from her cross with a death-rattle and turned off the television. Danilo laid his napkin aside and, without waiting for coffee, sneaked out of the house.

Succumbing to an unbearable headache, a knot in her stomach, a feeling of nausea, and a growing, generalized hysteria, Adalgisa raised her dying eyes to the print of the Sacred Heart of Jesus enthroned in the room: Stand by me in this crisis, oh Lord! she prayed. Give me the strength to correct this sinner, to bring this stray lamb back unto your fold!

The Code of Punishment

To say that Manela had never been struck while she was living in her parents' home would be to lie, would falsify the facts of the narrative, an unfortunate habit quite common today among the illustrious gentlemen who write History—the grandiose kind, with a capital H. They do it whenever they have a mind to, depending on the interests of those in power, accommodating facts to the pleasure of dictators. "It's not a question of distorting History," they explain, "but rather of cleansing it of events and personages who compromise its essential ideological purity."

Every so often Eufrásio and Dolores did warm Manela's bottom in payment for some overdaring bit of mischief—a few whacks, to make things clear more than to hurt her. But it was a beating all the same, worthy of that ugly name. Manela had only had one real one, and she'd deserved it. She had been twelve years old and was in the first year of a high school at the Manuel Devoto school, where she was a member of a gang of smart-alecks.

Summoned to the school one day, Eufrásio had found himself sitting among other fathers and mothers in the principal's office. He was informed that the threat of expulsion was hanging over Manela and her cohorts because of a serious breach of discipline they had committed the previous afternoon. The parents knew how hard it was to find an opening for a child in a free public institution. Eufrásio owed the one here for Manela to a certain big-shot by the name of Dr. Wilson Lins, who besides being a writer was a well-known politician.

Indignant that the teacher of moral and civic education had given a grade of zero to everyone in the class out of pure meanness, forty students—twenty-two boys, eighteen girls—had poured a generous amount of dendê oil over his gradebook and, since there was still some left in the bottle, on the seat of the chair where the despot would place his skinny behind. Mean-spirited, intolerant, unpleasant, and a major in the army, the teacher now had the principal up against the wall. The threat of mass expulsion was an empty one—the principal could hardly expel an entire class, and luckily the major was retired. But that was no reason for Eufrásio to let the matter drift off like a cloud, and he had given Manela a good hiding.

Manela's otherwise pleasant life, imbued with the love and trust of her parents, without fear or lies, had ended when she moved to the house of her uncle and aunt after the tragic automobile accident. The scolding and punishment had begun immediately. It was severe and continuous, especially during the first year, when Manela still had ideas of resisting Adalgisa's orders. That was before she changed tactics to pretending and lying, hiding things from Adalgisa.

It began, and it continued. Scoldings and slaps on the face became customary, humiliating and painful, unavoidable at first. Adalgisa had learned from Father José Antonio, her moral adviser, not to use the word *punishment:* "a mother doesn't *punish*," he told her, "she sets an example, she corrects." Adalgisa would say, "Manela deserves corrective measures, I apply them, I fulfill my duty because I'm bringing her up with respect for God's law, making a lady out of her."

Manela had no complaints about Danilo. Her uncle had never raised a hand to punish her or opened his mouth to call her names, to curse her as a street urchin, ungrateful wretch, common wench, heathen. True, he'd stopped defending her against his wife's rigors—he'd made an attempt but then desisted, not daring to go up against the hot-tempered Dadá, a bundle of nerves with her everlasting migraines. Still, to himself, he disapproved of the educational methods his solid, pious, and wrathful wife used. Besides, there was a great deal about Adalgisa's way of acting and behaving that he found fault with or deplored.

Jovial and mild, Danilo had introduced his niece to the subtleties of checkers and backgammon, had taught her to play patience and to do card tricks. Patience and tricks were what Manela needed to bear up and turn away, to obey and disobey, to follow and break the rules that proper conduct dictated and life demanded. It was a severe and a strict code: for each lapse a proper punishment.

In devising a variety of punishments for Manela, her torturer had few equals. Being forbidden to go to the movies with her uncle and aunt, being locked in her room when her favorite series was on television, forbidden to visit her classmates, deprived of her weekly visit to Aunt Gildete, getting no dessert, saying her rosary aloud and on her knees: these were some of the more frequent punishments. Scoldings, raps on the head, tugs on the ear, and slaps on the face were also abundant. And when the fault or mistake or sin went beyond the merely venial, hanging on the wall was the leather strap, ancient, shapeless, fearsome—and efficient. Aunt Adalgisa's list of mortal sins, quite a bit longer than the one in the catechism, assured that the leather strap was put to use—it had been a present from Father José Antonio when he learned that his beloved parishioner would rear her orphaned niece: "It will be useful for you," he had said. "Don't have any scruples about using it—correcting someone who does wrong is no sin, it doesn't offend God, it pleases him. It's in the Bible, *mi hija:* Punishing with firmness is one way of showing mercy."

There was no time to lose, to put off till tomorrow what could be done today. The day after Dolores and Eufrásio's funeral, when Manela came home from school, her eyes still swollen from weeping, Adalgisa took her to confession and had her recite the credo. "Let's take advantage of the moment," Adalgisa had said, "and make things clear once and for all, get everything out in the open, so that later on you won't say you didn't know. If you're obedient and well behaved, if you get good grades at school, if you behave with decorum and dignity, show fear of God and devotion, and don't displease your uncle and aunt, you'll have everything you want and the right to rewards."

What these rewards were, Manela never knew, but she was immediately aware of what was forbidden her: keeping bad company; going to matinees, watching television, going to dances or festivals on the square or anywhere else unless accompanied by her aunt and uncle; hanging out in the street, talking to boys, flirting. And above all, she had to maintain the greatest distance possible from *candomblé, umbanda,* and all such witchcraft. It goes without saying that these are centers of perdition, where the devil ensnares the souls of Christians.

Adalgisa didn't prevent Manela from visiting her aunt, Gildete, her father's sister, but those visits had to be limited; no more than once a week, and that was already a lot. And if Manela's sister Marieta wanted to see her, let her come to Adalgisa and Danilo's house—weren't they her aunt and uncle, too? It was a long, repetitive monologue, Adalgisa's voice soft and loving at times, aggressive and threatening at others. She angered easily.

The end justifies the means, as has already been taught by Hitler and other fathers of their country, the "genial guides" of their people: "I will make a lady out of you, no matter what the cost." To conclude her discussion on an elevated note, Adalgisa had pointed out the leather strap on the wall, hanging between a print of the Most Holy Virgin and a yellowing picture of Adalgisa and Danilo, happy on their wedding day. If necessary, she, Adalgisa, an aunt with the duties of a foster mother, would not think twice about using the strap, unhesitatingly and unsparingly. "It will be for your own good. Someday you'll thank me."

The Almost Miss

Manela did not learn the weight of the strap, feel the sting of the lash, as cutting as a knife blade, until about a year after that initial, definitive oration. In the meantime she had come to consider it as more or less a symbolic object, with no other purpose than to warn and intimidate.

She'd become rather adept at the art of hoodwinking her aunt, putting things over on her, lulling her watchfulness, deceiving her with complicated webs of lies and inventions. The better to convince her aunt, Manela had even engaged in a kind of friendly conspiracy with school-mates and neighbors, who were themselves distressed at the restrictions and corrective measures imposed on Manela. Not even murderers in jail underwent such despotic punishment, said Damiana, the next-door neighbor who was obliged to listen to the moans and slaps, the pleas for forgiveness. "That woman's a viper, she has no heart," Damiana would announce loudly to anyone who wanted to hear.

Adalgisa had grown accustomed to hearing Manela's confessions and realized that the girl admitted her errors even when she knew she wouldn't escape punishment; so that for months Adalgisa was prepared to believe Manela's explanations, her excuses for being late, her reasons for going out visiting: "You know, Auntie, I'm late because I was with Telma, we went to the Portuguese hospital where her father's a patient: a cancer operation, poor man—there's no hope." Adalgisa was interested: "Cancer? You don't say. Has metastasis set in already?" Operations and hospitals, sickness and suffering, were subjects she enjoyed. In all of the excuses Manela put together there was always a germ of truth, and if it became necessary, an accomplice would come along with the trickster to the door of her house, ready to confirm the deception—especially when it might be particularly suspect.

But the pitcher can go to the well only so many times before it breaks and the water is spilled; the fibs grew in number until they became so frequent that Adalgisa finally grew suspicious. Acting as if she suspected nothing, playing dumb, she began to scrutinize Manela's excuses, justifications, and movements vigorously. It wasn't long before she uncovered her niece's duplicity, and she proceeded to inflict twice as much punishment as seemed advisable and equitable since the misstep had been accompanied by a lie, one of the seven mortal sins in the catechism.

It was only by accident that Adalgisa found out that Manela had entered the Miss Springtime contest. She found out just in time, however, God be praised, to prevent the worst from happening. Adalgisa was taken by surprise, paralyzed, horrified just for a brief instant, but mind you, she didn't let on. Quickly she recovered, and proceeded to go to war.

Adalgisa was a milliner and it was a customer at her hat shop who had called her attention to it, Dona Norma Martins, a rich lady, a member of the upper crust and a competent gynecologist, but in spite of that a simple soul. She'd ordered a fancy hat, to wear to the wedding of the daughter of Dr. Jorge Calmon, editor of *A Tarde*. The event had Adalgisa working night and day, six hats in all of top quality, to be delivered by the end of the week.

One day Dona Norma was making idle conversation as she tried on the creation, decked with artificial flowers and a discreet tulle veil. She never missed a chance to talk about her son, who was a high school student but already had a penchant for the piano—more than a penchant, a vocation—and she mentioned Manela:

"Renatinho is leading the campaign for your daughter."

"My daughter?" Adalgisa was surprised but immediately understood to whom the physician was referring. "Oh, yes! You mean my niece, my foster child. I've been rearing her since her mother, my sister, died. Does your son know Manela?"

"Know her? Well, I can only tell you that Renatinho is all excited about campaigning for her. He told me that the decision is between

Manela and that girl who worked in the D'Aversa film, I can't remember her name. . . ."

It was a garbled story, and Adalgisa thought it a mistake, a mixup in people: "Campaigning for Manela?" she asked. "Are you sure, Dona Norma? Campaigning for what?"

"For the Miss Springtime contest, of course. Isn't your girl the candidate of Ariovaldo's newspaper? You know, the one that comes out on Sundays; it has some good articles. It's entertaining, but it probably won't last very long: it goes after the government too much." She laughed, thinking about Ariovaldo's paper.

Adalgisa rested her arms on the back of the chair that had been set near the mirror for trying on hats: her legs were weak, and her head throbbed. She forced a smile, then managed to articulate:

"The contest. I know . . ."

Luckily Dona Norma had gone to find her purse to pay for the hat, which was tasteful but expensive.

"It's beautiful, Dona Adalgisa," she exclaimed. "You're an artist. I hope your girl's the one they pick. Renatinho says she's the prettiest of them all. Congratulations."

Adalgisa thanked the woman for the congratulations and her praise of Manela: "That's very kind of your son, Dona Norma." But as soon as Dona Norma left the shop, Adalgisa went off fuming to the house of Dona Aydil Coqueijo, another customer, who was always good for gossip and information. Nobody would be more up on this shameless business of Miss Springtime contests and popular music festivals than Dona Aydil and her husband, a man of many accomplishments: He was an austere magistrate, esteemed jurist, law professor, writer of pleasant newspaper columns, prize-winning composer, gifted pianist and guitarist, polished speaker, and an inspirer and promoter of deals and successes, not to mention president of this, that, and the next thing.

It was a pushover. Adalgisa didn't even have to confess the reason for her interest; as soon as she mentioned the contest, the woman, obliging and enthusiastic, told her everything she wanted to know, adding a few choice asides. The Miss Springtime contest took place every year in the month of September; the candidates represented various newspapers in the city, the promoters of the contest, and a few commercial establishments that took care of the expenses by donating funds. A jury made up of well-known people made the final decision after the contestants paraded in folk costume, evening gowns, and then bikinis.

"Bikinis? You mean two-piece?" Amusing herself, Dona Aydil teased the milliner: "Adalgisa, don't make such a face—bathing suits are old hat." The judging would be on Sunday, two days hence, in the Vila Velha Theater. Dona Aydil planned to go see the young buds parade. "Nobody can beat these young girls today," she said. "Are you interested? If you want to go, I can arrange tickets for you and your husband."

About the scandal sheet that Manela was representing and the location of Sunday's orgy, Adalgisa needed no clues—she knew about them from Father José Antonio. She'd remembered his harsh words of condemnation. The weekly rag disseminated Russian poison, red propaganda, he'd told her. The upright clergyman could think of no explanation for the absurd apathy of the authorities—why hadn't they prohibited its circulation? It was edited by a mud-slinger whom they called a good writer but was good for nothing but pornography and subversion. Hadn't he been arrested for just as much? He signed his name Ariovaldo Matos.

And at the Vila Velha Theater the worst kind of shows were staged, the most degrading; plays that challenged proper customs, morality, and religion, shows with songs of protest, disrespectful and obscene comics, lewd dancing actresses. There debaucheries and bacchanals were held in honor of Odum. It was a place where the intellectual rabble gathered, from Glauber Rocha to João Ubaldo Ribeiro, down-and-out drifters, enemies of the established order and the sacred precepts of divine law.

Adalgisa returned home from Dona Aydil's house with a mouth of bile and a stone in her heart: Manela was clearly marching quick-step toward slime and putrefaction, toward the abyss—they were waiting for her in the red-light district and in hell. Sitting in the parlor, Manela looked up from her studies when her aunt arrived, and she welcomed her with an innocent smile:

"On Sunday, Auntie, I have to tell you—"

"On Sunday. I know. Yes," Adalgisa said, and she went to the wall where the leather strap hung. Who knew, was there still time to halt the fall and the curse?

Manela was then fifteen years old—one and a half of those years spent in this captivity after her parents' burial—when the leather strap finally made its presence felt. Manela's aunt showed no compunction or pity: She worked methodically over her whole body. All she spared was the girl's face. When she ran out of strength and stopped lashing, she locked the former favorite for the contest in her room, and put her on bread and water, starting that Friday in September until the following Sunday night—so that she could meditate and repent.

When Manela got to school on Monday, her head down, her body so battered that she was scarcely able to sit down, her eyes puffy from weeping, dejected and demoralized, she learned that Marilda Alves, the girl from the film, the candidate of the evening paper O Estado da Bahia and the columnist Renot, had been unanimously proclaimed Miss Springtime.

The Leather Strap

When Manela returned home after the procession of the waters of Oxalá, Adalgisa lifted the leather strap again. The first blow caught her at kidney level, cut into her flesh. But more cutting and intolerable was the insult that her aunt spat out:

"Whore!"

During the two years that had passed since the Miss Springtime contest, Adalgisa had flicked her arm with the leather strap frequently. But before she brought it down again on this day, Manela took a step forward, and without shouting, her voice only a little louder than usual, serious and categorical, she commanded:

"Stop, Auntie. Get rid of that strap if you want me to have any respect for you."

"Whore! Heathen!"

Adalgisa swung again, and the whip whistled in the air, but this blow failed to catch the heathen whore. A pilgrim from the festival of Bomfim, her body clean, her head clear, Manela grabbed her aunt's wrist with her right hand, and with her left she pried open her fingers. She took the leather strap and cast it aside. Eyes bulging, incredulous, stunned, bereft of action or words, Adalgisa stared at her niece and saw Satan before her. The end of the world was at hand.

"Never whip me with that strap again. It's all over, Auntie, if you want me to continue living in your house and obeying you."

Adalgisa quivered from head to toe, ran both hands over her flushed face, drooled out of the corner of her mouth, closed her eyes, whimpered deeply as if her soul were coming out of her chest, and dropped to the floor.

Her body in contortions, her arms and legs trembling, froth coming from her mouth, her heart pounding against the floorboards, Aunt Adalgisa looked as if she were possessed.

The
Via Crucis

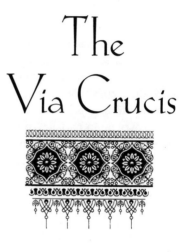

The Chief of
the State Police

Some months later, leaning back in his swivel chair, lifting his hand in an elegant and affirmative gesture, Dr. Calixto Passos, chief of police for the State of Bahia, was speaking to the alarmed director of the Museum of Sacred Art:

"Another one!" he exclaimed. "If it goes on like this, there won't be a single statue of any value left in all the churches of Bahia. Do you know, my dear director, how many have been stolen in the past three months? Sixteen, no less! Not fourteen, not fifteen—sixteen!"

He smiled for emphasis, enjoying the sound of his own voice. A magistrate who had been applauded ever since his days in law school, when he had been the orator of his class, he had become a lawyer in civil practice with powerful financial organizations as clients, and an extremely successful politician as well. "Calixto Passos: talent in the service of justice," a hack journalist had written in a fit of adulation when Passos had been chosen to head the State Police. Inspector Parreirinha could only agree with this ass-kisser's estimation of his boss. Standing beside the desk, he nodded energetically, seconding the chief's statements and savoring every pearl: He considered the police chief to be most astute, most astute indeed. Dom Maximiliano von Gruden, by contrast, considered Dr. Calixto to be the mother of incompetence.

Dr. Calixto leaned toward the monk and lowered his voice in a tone of confidence and complicity:

"The guilty party or parties? We all know who it is: Somebody with a skullcap who has itchy fingers. But nobody dares accuse someone with a skullcap of being a thief. Who'd dare do that to a tonsured head?"

This man was an absolute ass, a complete fool, Dom Maximiliano said to himself as his disgust overwhelmed any glimmer of sympathy. There he went, the conceited boob, repeating the asinine litany of "the under-the-table sale of statues that have somehow disappeared from churches and chapels, the illicit and scandalous traffic that priests themselves carry on in parishes in the interior." And these were poor parishes, some very poor, with no money for the barest of necessities, and a few pieces of wood, old and blessed, lying in sacristy attics are so tempting—who wouldn't sell them? the police chief asked rhetorically. Dom Maximiliano swallowed his indignation, saliva, and bile.

―❦―❦

Digression on the Profane Cogitations
of Dom Maximiliano von Gruden
Concerning the Sale—No, the Exchange of
Statues and Other Religious Objects
While the Chief of the State Police,
All Excited, Speechifies

Acting either independently or as agents for important antique dealers, the police chief told the director, roving swindlers go hunting through the interior in search of merchandise. Tirelessly they go from village to village, from town to town, from plantation to plantation, from house to house. They return with their trunks filled to the brim with valuables and junk.

From up above, the gods themselves follow the laborious and extended journeys of these faithful proselytizers of race and belief with benevolent sympathy. Yahweh, the Jehovah revealed on Sinai, the Syrio-Lebanese good lord of the Marionites, and the merciful Jesus of the

Vatican guide the steps of these intrepid workhorses—all under their protection—to the nooks of an ark or an oratory in a village where an incomparable piece awaits the dealer: David, Salim, or João da Silva.

To the shepherds of the souls living in penury in the village, the dealers seem to have been sent by divine providence in response to their prayers. The village priest is paid in current coinage, in gold pieces for the piece; in reality, the dealers pay a miserable amount. They lie, cheat, and bamboozle, and if an opportunity presents itself, they steal and appropriate. Be that as it may, the priests consider themselves twice-blessed because even the few pennies they have obtained for those useless curios will shore up the shaky finances of the parishes, cover the alms deficit, and supplement the paltry donations.

With the support of the faithful and the applause of the devout, a priest will proceed to acquire a gaudy plaster statue, the blue paint on its mouth still fresh, its miter and tiara painted red, to take the place of the worm-eaten old trash that was exchanged opportunely—saints are not sold, they are exchanged—for hard cash. The altar improves with the replacement: the modern statue cuts a striking figure; the church biddies rejoice. Overdue debts are cleared up, charitable work is kept alive, beggars and poor people in the village are cared for, as are widows and orphans, and the meager rations of the devoted pastor improve, as do those of his housekeeper and his godchildren, poor things. The housekeeper, who in her youth was the most provocative temptation in the parish, still preserves traces of beauty, pristine and appetizing, on her aged face and mistreated body.

In these times of inflation and crisis, even in the unblemished exercise of religion one must know how to defend oneself, and how to give things that small Brazilian touch, without which there would be no soup kitchen for the poor and the fare of the miserable village families would be scant and scarce. In the state capital when the ecclesiastical authorities, severe and threatening, hear of the traffic in blessed statues, the patrimony of the Church, they belch out their indignation, rail against impiety and sacrilege, and label it as crime and scandal. But what do those pampered monsignors, who enjoy the stewardship of the archdiocese, know about the poverty, the dog's life, of priests exiled to the interior, poor devils living by God's grace? Satan preaching Lent: It's easy to criticize with a full belly.

If it weren't for his good manners, which obliged him to be discreet, Dom Maximiliano would have surprised that swine of a police chief by declaring that such traffic, if examined in the light of the interests of culture, actually performed an undeniable service. Stolen or bought for a song by the wandering dealers, pieces of noteworthy value escaped the destruction to which they might have been condemned in the scrapheaps of convents and rectories. Instead, they are rescued, passed from hand to hand, profit to profit, and end up safe and sound, well cared for, in private collections or museums.

The church authorities would have regarded this opinion of the museum director as heretical. They had already labeled him agnostic and impious. To Father José Antonio Hernández, in fact, Dom Maximiliano von Gruden was the perfect example of a person who shouldn't be a monk at all. He was an atheist and an anarchist—particularly dangerous precisely because he attired himself in the white cassock of the Benedictines. In these days of disorder and disrespect, of liberation theology and other diabolical blasphemies, the enemies of the Faith and of Christian doctrine hide in cassocks and habits. The wolves cover themselves with the skin of sheep.

The Guffaw

Dom Maximiliano girded himself patiently—although patience was not his cardinal virtue—as he waited for an opportune moment to interrupt the chief of State Police's trivial, tedious babble and return the discussion to the matter at hand. Given the seriousness of the case and the urgency of clearing up the mystery, identifying and apprehending the criminals, and recovering the statue, Dom Maximiliano had addressed the matter with energy and in detail at the start of the meeting. He'd insisted on the need for secrecy in conducting the investigation; he had been thinking about the vicar of Santo Amaro and his probable reaction when he found out about the disappearance of the statue—that is, he would tear the world apart.

Dom Maximiliano described the intrinsic and extrinsic value of the sculpture, a priceless jewel, the patrimony of Bahia and Brazil. It dated from the 1800s, contemporary with the creative genius of Aleijadinho; in the opinion of experts only pieces proven to be of Aleijadinho's authorship could surpass it and—in short, who knew?—it might even carry the same value. Indeed, it's the only image of Saint Barbara of the Thunder that depicts her clutching a bundle of lightning bolts instead of the usual palm branch. Museums in Europe and the United States would pay, there's no arguing, any amount of dollars to have the priceless statue in their collections.

Dom Maximiliano called attention to the opening of the exhibit, scheduled for two days thence: at that point the value of the statue would become even greater. And his book would be published during the solemnities—he briefly outlined his rather audacious theory that the press had made so much of. Courteous and hypocritical, the police chief stated that he'd heard some reference to it.

Whether or not he'd heard of it was of little importance to Dom Maximiliano. What mattered was that despite his briefing the blowhard police chief had never come to realize the magnitude of the affair; for him, it was just another instance of the countless thefts of sacred objects that took place in the interior of the state. Dom Maximiliano realized he had been wasting his breath and his words. His precise and learned briefing had come to naught in making the police chief understand that no, it wasn't just another theft of a rundown statue of unknown value, that likely had little significance except to the worms.

Fixing his dead-fish eyes on Dom Maximiliano's blue ones, insinuating in his whispering little laugh, Dr. Calixto Passos finished his thought: "In certain cases it isn't exactly a question of robbery, at least not one committed by an outsider. I mean—"

He placed his two hands on the desk, glanced up at Inspector Parreirinha, who was drooling with admiration—the police chief had killed the snake, now he was parading the stick—and went on:

"I mean—transfer . . . the pieces change owners. For example: Not a week ago two statues that had been stolen in Laranjeiras were discovered in the warehouse of a firm on the Rua da Independência. They'd been brought from Sergipe and sold here"—silence for a fraction of a second, to let the suspense grow—"by someone in the priest's family."

"But as I've already said, doctor—"

The police chief raised his hand and interrupted the director of the Museum of Sacred Art to ask him:

"Tell me, my dear director: How well do you know the vicar of Santo Amaro? You may tell me in complete confidence, just between the two of us." Inspector Parreirinha turned to look out the window, as if he were paying no attention. "Do you, my dear director, deem him a person worthy of trust, or—"

Even before he heard this confidential question, Dom Maximiliano von Gruden had reached the limits of his endurance. It took a superhuman effort for him not to run out into the street screaming like a lunatic. But when he heard the chief of police for the state of Bahia ask him about the honesty of the vicar of Santo Amaro, he gave vent to the loudest guffaw ever heard in the whole parish.

-&- -&

The Chief of the
Federal Police

In marked contrast, Dom Maximiliano's meeting with Colonel Raul Antônio Parreiras at least had one practical result: The director recovered the litter that had borne the statue and that had been left behind on the sloop and was permitted to bring it to the museum.

At the request of this chief of the federal police in Bahia, the *Sailor Without a Port* had been towed from the market ramp to the navy wharf. The colonel had made arrangements by telephone with the naval authorities at the base for the immediate disposition of the sloop that had carried the statue. He assigned an agent to keep a lookout around the market ramp.

"With the navy holding the sloop, the couple that owns it will have to show their faces. We'll listen to them, roast them a little; they certainly must know who's responsible. There's no doubt but that they're accomplices. We'll find out soon enough."

He was referring to Master Manuel and Maria Clara. Without losing any time, the colonel had sent a policeman to pick up the sloop captain and his wife—Federal Police headquarters were actually located on the waterfront, in a former cargo warehouse between the market ramp and the Bahian Navigation Company docks, a few steps from where the robbery took place. But the policeman came back empty-handed; after landing, the suspects had left in a taxi for an unknown destination. This information was obtained from a two-bit huckster downing a beer after hours at the Xispeteo, a hookers' dive at the foot of the hill.

At the Federal Police, Dom Maximiliano rose up out of the depression into which the chief of the State Police's incompetence and bombast had plunged him. The colonel listened to the museum director with attention and interest: He seemed appropriately convinced of the capital importance of the problem. Dressed in civilian clothes, he had been tending his fingernails at the start of the conversation, alternating between scissors, pick, and emery board for the delicate task. He had hardly looked like the bully he was reputed to be.

He appeared pleased by the visit of the director, a well-known and celebrated intellectual. He understood the reasons for his request for secrecy: "Not a word, you can rest assured; we're used to working quietly and off the record here. Otherwise it would be impossible to deal effectively with criminality and terrorism." He went on unhurriedly, the whole evening at his disposal. The opinions he gave concerning the robbery impressed Dom Maximiliano: He didn't waste his time on oratorical flourishes, and he expressed himself convincingly in the language of a technocrat, an expert.

"Here at the Federal Police we've been giving this series of church robberies the kind of attention that it deserves, and we've gathered a thick dossier covering the matter in some detail over the past twenty years, maybe longer. In my opinion there's an organized mafia behind these crimes, a well-organized one. It's no longer a question of sporadic thefts, the way it used to be."

The chief of the State Police had liked the sound of his own voice; but the chief of the Federal Police preferred to display his knowledge.

"The age of amateurs is over, the days of raids by would-be artists into the interior of the state, as far as Sergipe and Alagoas, to steal saints from convents and chapels. These artists were all broke and got more money from such robberies than they did from their own paintings and statues. Today they're filthy rich, all of them, earning as much as they want, they don't have to steal statues or rob convents anymore—they're regular nabobs. The only regret I have is that I don't know how to paint myself. . . . Their criminal activity eventually became public knowledge, you've only got to peruse an article about Carybé or Jenner Augusto. Mário Cravo's jeep became part of folklore, the statues they stole are almost all in the hands of collectors, here or in the south, in the homes of fat cats: Clemente Mariani, Odorico Tavares, Orlando Castro Lima."

Methodically, before he put the pick back in the drawer along with the scissors and emery board, the colonel used it to open a hole in the tip of a Suerdieck cigar, then took his time lighting it. He took a drag, blew out the smoke, and leaning back, pressed the button behind his chair. He asked Dom Maximiliano if he wouldn't like to wet his whistle with a little cold beer; bottles and glasses were brought, and only after serving the director and himself did he continue.

"At the present time, Dom Maximiliano, the situation is much more serious than it was back then. We're up against a ruthless gang that cares nothing about the consequences when they carry out their criminal acts. I call your attention to the following fact, *proven:* Pieces of real value disappear, and they're never seen again. Why? Because they've been shipped out of the country. We've followed the trail of some of them and found that they ended up in Portugal and Spain, Switzerland and France. There's an international traffic in antiques—you must be aware of that, it's well known. Behind the disappearance of your notorious Saint Barbara we're going to discover, I have no doubt, the hand of the same gang, this mafia. We've got to act quickly to prevent something that valuable from being shipped abroad."

Dom Maximiliano had heard a great deal of tiresome chit-chat and prattle about the mysterious traffic in sacred objects. In a recent conversation Mercedes Rosa, director of the Costa Pinta Museum, and Carlos Eduardo da Rocha, director of the State Museum—two distinguished people, albeit chatterboxes—had told him things that made his hair stand on end, about individuals of the highest respectability. But now a responsible authority was telling him of the existence of an organized and dangerous international gang. Even the Museum of Sacred Art possessed pieces of obscure, if not suspicious origins, but Dom Maximiliano preferred to ignore how they'd reached his exhibition halls of the convent of Saint Theresa. Or could it be that he really didn't know?

The prospect of Saint Barbara of the Thunder being shipped abroad —a possibility raised by the chief of the Federal Police, no less—completely threw him: "Do you think, Colonel, that there's a real danger that the statue will be sent abroad?"

"Most certainly, yes. I'm not a man to joke about serious matters. I think, all in all, that there hasn't been enough time yet for them to have sent it off, that it's still hidden somewhere in the city. We've got to find it, within twenty-four hours if possible. I'm going to put my men to work on it right away, get things going immediately. We'll check cars and buses leaving by the highway and all flights at the airport. We've got the statue's dimensions—we'll inspect anything that looks suspicious, open every suitcase or crate capable of holding it. You can relax, leave it all to me; I'll keep you up to date on how the investigation is going."

He got up to escort Dom Maximiliano to the door and gave him a last, frightening, even terrifying revelation:

"Do you know where the money goes that's obtained from these church robberies, especially from items sent abroad? You don't know? I'll tell you: It goes into subversive activity, terrorism, urban guerrilla warfare, to Communists and those watermelon priests, the ones who are green on the outside and red on the inside. Does that startle you? I could show you evidence, concrete proof. But I won't, so as not to prejudice the investigations we're involved in."

He laid his heavy hand on the monk's thin shoulder:

"A lot of priests are in cahoots with Communists. I'm not telling you anything new, it's a notorious fact. For me, for those responsible, for our national security, those priests are criminals far worse than the Communists themselves. Besides being enemies, they're traitors." Indignantly, categorically, he repeated the word: "Traitors! But we're going to put an end to them—to them and to the Communists, that whole mess of perverts. All of them."

Now it wasn't just upset, anxiety, and exasperation that consumed Dom Maximiliano; he felt chilled to his balls. The cordiality that had hung over the meeting vanished, giving way to a heavy atmosphere of warning and menace, as the colonel suddenly acted like the firebrand everyone said he was. With his iron fingers slightly pressing on the fragile shoulderblade of the museum director, Colonel Raul Antônio Parreiras continued, staring into his eyes:

"I know everything about you, Reverend Father"—he drew out the syllables—"absolutely everything! I know that you don't openly support our patriotic government, but you don't fight it either. You stay on the sidelines of politics. You don't plot against the Revolution, our worthy Revolution of 1964 that saved Brazil from Communism. Just keep it that way, and no one will bother you, I can guarantee. Stay far away from subversion—that's the advice I'm giving you."

He softened his voice, relaxed his pincer-fingers, and smiled with his lips and his eyes, all amiable again.

"Thank you for your visit, I've been most pleased to meet you personally and to chat with you." He extended his hand to Dom Maximiliano. "Keep well—you'll have news from me in just a little while, good news, you can count on it."

He ordered a policeman to accompany the renowned intellectual to his car, which carried the litter. Intellectuals, what a rotten breed . . . the colonel spat on the pavement, then rubbed his foot over it.

—⊱⋅⊰—

His Excellency
the Auxiliary Bishop

Dom Maximiliano's *via crucis* on that night of trials had begun not with Dr. Calixto Passos but when he met with the combative and influential Monsignor Rudolph Kluck, auxiliary bishop of the archdiocese of Bahia. Their long conversation was conducted in German, the mother tongue of warriors.

After sending Edimilson back to the museum, the perplexed director had left the docks and gone to the cardinal's residence in Campo Grande. Before anything else, he had to inform the cardinal of the situation, decide with him on the measures to be taken, and ask for his advice and support. His Eminence had shown great interest in the success of the religious art exhibit, and his mediation had been decisive in making possible the loan of the statue.

But in Campo Grande Dom Maximiliano discovered that the cardinal had departed to accompany the university rector to Brasília to try to obtain from the responsible authorities, if not a commutation, at least a softening of the drastic measures that had been imposed on some students in retaliation for their recent general strike and demonstrations. They sought to help them avoid losing an academic year.

In the cardinal's absence Dom Maximiliano telephoned the auxiliary bishop, the second person in the archdiocese, and asked for an immediate audience. "If it's really that urgent, you can come: I'll wait for you," His Excellency consented.

Dom Rudolph was a German like Dom Maximiliano, but besides their nationality, their origins, they had nothing in common. Opposite they were, poles rather like fire and water, salt and sugar, the egg and the frying pan. The museum director was thin and tall, prim, pale, and elegant, while the incorruptible theologian was robust, thick-set, ruddy, unkempt, and uncouth.

On the rare occasions when they had previously met, they had treated each other formally and ceremoniously; otherwise, they barely tolerated each other. There were those who attributed the auxiliary bishop's nickname, "Lefebvre of the Poor," to Dom Maximiliano's malice. The director had indeed applied it to Dom Rudolph on the occasion of the publication of yet another volume of his already-considerable theological opus—four fat tomes—analyzing and condemning race-mixing and religious syncretism, defending the rigorous purity of the faith and the exactness of dogma. The jest went unappreciated, however, because no one in those parts had the slightest idea who Monseigneur Marcel Lefebvre was and what role this leader of French integralists had played in the internecine battles of the Church, apart from a few rare prelates and Professor José Calazans, who had chaired a seminar on Vatican Council II and couldn't bear hearing mass conducted in Portuguese.

It was rumored that Dom Rudolph had been named auxiliary bishop in order to compensate for the fact that the new cardinal of Bahia, the primate of Brazil, was considered sympathetic to the progressive positions of a part of the clergy called the Church of the Poor on social and political matters; on doctrinal questions, the cardinal leaned toward the conservatives and supported the traditionalists. This was a current contradiction throughout ecclesiastical spheres, where religious men found themselves squeezed between the misery of the population and the dogmas and mysteries of doctrine, between demands for agrarian reform and the Latin mass. But let's go on, since there's no room for such metaphysical matters in these skeptical pages.

Dom Maximiliano and Dom Rudolph said a lot of things that Wednesday evening, not all of them pleasant. Dom Rudolph, playing deaf to the director's concerns, continued the stormy catechism he always gave in articles and reviews, homilies and sermons, radio preaching —he used the radio assiduously as the most popular means of communication. From the window of the cell on the upper floor of the Ursuline convent where he lived, he was accustomed to contemplating the vista of the city of Bahia—Bahia? no, to him it was named Salvador. It was beautiful without a doubt, he couldn't deny it, but it was inhabited by idolatrous heathens and halfbreeds, the majority of them black, ignorant of the hegemonies of race and culture—that is, the Aryan race and Western culture—who broke the law, disobeyed the gospels, conjoined all the colors of the rainbow, and in illicit beds of love, mingled their blood and their gods.

It was most urgent, Dom Rudolph believed, to separate the wheat from the chaff, good from evil, and white from black, to impose limits, to draw boundaries. Certainly, it was difficult for him to hold his belief in this incomparable paradigm locked in his breast, but he had to. He didn't dare preach it—it wouldn't have suited the reigning disorder that had begun with the end of the war, with the defeat. The perfection of the world, as he saw it, had taken refuge since then in South Africa.

The Episcopal Ring

The fact that their conversation was in German made it all the more harsh and labored. After listening without interruption to the detailed report of the director of the Museum of Sacred Art, Dom Rudolph's first comment was on Edimilson's testimony:

"So you see, Dom Maximiliano, where miscegenation leads—to a weakness of the spirit, to idiocy. That assistant of yours, if you'll pardon me for saying so, is a cretin."

Dom Maximiliano swallowed silently. He didn't plan to challenge his hierarchical superior, argue theses, exacerbate his usual ill will. The auxiliary bishop would not forgive a touch of independence or an acid tongue such as his. The situation called for sanity and respect, so the monk lowered his head.

Taking advantage of that rare moment, Dom Rudolph rubbed his hands, closed his eyes, and spoke slowly to savor his syllables and pauses, distilling the venom drop by drop:

"I've been told about your—what was the phrase? Oh, yes! Your 'cohort of angels' at the museum. That was what they said. . . ."

Dom Maximiliano swallowed dryly, forced himself to be patient, and leaned back. Dom Rudolph continued implacably:

"I thought they were referring to statues in the collection, the stone or wooden angels. But I was mistaken. The angels meant were the employees." He raised his voice: "If they were capable, at least, and not mental defectives . . ."

Without changing his posture—the day of reckoning would come,
the Lord Bishop would be answered eventually—Dom Maximiliano
mused:

"We can talk about the employees of the museum anytime Your
Excellency wishes. I'll be happy to explain the criteria used in hiring,
which were set, incidentally, by the rector, not by me. But right now I'd
like to limit our conversation to the disappearance of the statue."

It was said and done: The auxiliary bishop was malignant and malicious, but no one was more vigilant and responsible than he when it
came to matters of doctrine or church goods. With the finger upon
which gleamed the Episcopal ring, he touched the monk's curved shoulder. "You're right. It's a serious matter. Let's get to it."

By mutual accord, they established a plan of action. Dom Rudolph
dictated the tactics and strategy, analyzed each step to be taken. He was
all the more efficient since the responsibility for the lost statue was the
province not of the archdiocese but of the Federal University, to which
the Museum of Sacred Art belonged.

The auxiliary bishop would take care of tracking down the priest
and the nun, and he recommended that Dom Maximiliano act as if he
were unaware of their existence. Let the police discover the fact on their
own or through third parties. That would give the ecclesiastical authorities time to hear their story.

"I know the priest in question," Dom Rudolph said. "He was called
in—he has an appointment with me tomorrow morning at the archbishop's palace. Maybe you've heard of him—Father Abelardo Galvão,
vicar of Piaçava, out in the backlands, just this side of Conquista. You
don't know who he is? He's the one who attacked Colonel Joãozinho
Costa's property at the head of an armed band; he created a problem
that's still giving us headaches. The best course is probably to keep him
out of police hands for as long as possible. I don't know who the nun is,
but it won't be hard to locate her. Leave the two of them to me."

The auxiliary bishop advised Dom Maximiliano not to lose a moment in seeking out the chief of the State Police and the chief of the
Federal Police. Coming from Dom Rudolph, the advice seemed more like
an order. The auxiliary bishop spoke to both officials on the telephone,
asking for their help and setting up the appointments. He stressed the
need for the greatest secrecy in the investigation; if the news got out it
could cause a devil of a mess. Had Dom Maximiliano thought about the
reaction of the people at the Historical Trust? he asked. Dom Maximiliano indeed had considered it and feared it, but he was more afraid of the
reaction of the vicar of Santo Amaro, he replied.

The vicar of Santo Amaro? Having already learned about him the
hard way, Dom Rudolph was wary of the harshness and bad manners of
that insolent, rude, but popular rustic. Once when he'd tried to get him

to rid the festival of Our Lady of Purification of impurities, of the fetishist filth that desecrated it so thoroughly, he got a resounding and disrespectful no for an answer: The people are the ones who celebrate the saint, the vicar had said. "Your Excellency is going to get nowhere with all this nonsensical intransigence, sternness, and rigidity." Neither instruction nor intimidation had moved the vicar: "Name another vicar, if you really intend to go through with the foolishness of turning a celebration into penance," the vicar had said. "With such a jackass idea it's easy to tell that Your Excellency is a foreigner with little understanding of what makes this country tick."

The two men knew they'd have to inform the vicar eventually of what had happened, but they could delay it and maybe avoid his wrath.

"It would be best to leave it for tomorrow. It's possible that by noon we'll have a solution to this affair."

For once in their lives Dom Rudolph and Dom Maximiliano found themselves singing the same tune, lyrics and all.

The auxiliary bishop hastened to put an end to the conversation, since the time for the museum director's meeting with the chief of the State Police was drawing near:

"Recommend haste and secrecy to him; explain to him about our worries."

A diplomat by calling, Dom Maximiliano confided:

"Tomorrow I will have sent Your Excellency a copy of a book I've written. It has been published to coincide with the exhibit. The fruit of much investigation and study—I think it will put an end to the debates about the origin of the statue of Saint Barbara of the Thunder." He grew modest: "It's not my triumph, of course. All glory belongs to the Church."

Dom Rudolph replied that he already knew of the book and its importance, and he thanked him for the copy—"Don't forget to inscribe it"—then, not wanting to be surpassed in erudition, he speculated as he said good-bye:

"If we were dealing with the appearance of God, we could speak of a theophany. But since it's a matter of a *dis*appearance, what can we call it? The word *enchantment* occurs to me. The enchantment of Saint Barbara of the Thunder. What do you think, Dom Maximiliano?"

He'd used the right word without knowing it, but then, Dom Maximiliano did not know it either. Instead, he felt that the bishop was exulting over his ruination. He lowered his head, and Dom Rudolph raised his hand and blessed him. The episcopal ring, symbol of the hierarch's rank and power, glinted on his index finger.

The Litter

The first floor of the former Convent of Saint Theresa, now transformed into the Museum of Sacred Art of the Federal University of Bahia, was still lighted up when, almost at midnight, Dom Maximiliano von Gruden stopped his Volkswagen Beetle in the courtyard and, with the help of the doorman, pulled the litter out of the back seat.

Two museum helpers—two mulatto boys, or two of the angels from Dom Maximiliano's "cohort," as Dom Rudolph had malignantly put it . . . Dom Rudolph, that no-good . . . that crude Prussian peasant with an evil spirit and the tongue of a viper—two boys were arranging the pieces for the religious art exhibit in rooms normally occupied by the permanent collection, under the direction of the architect Gilberbert Chaves, who had offered to help set it all up. Dom Maximiliano greeted Gilberbert, inquired about Dona Sônia's health, and began his inspection, accompanied by everyone present. He stopped before the spot reserved for the statue of Saint Barbara of the Thunder. Under the attentive gazes of the architect and the workers, Dom Maximiliano lingered, looking at it.

"Are we going to set up the statue now, director?" they asked. "Where is it?"

"Not just yet. We'll set it up the day after tomorrow, a few hours before the opening, to avoid people coming here and wanting to see it and interrupting our work." He concluded, to head off any objections, "There are some people to whom we can't deny entrance. The best thing is to avoid any unanticipated visits." He tried to smile and actually managed it. "Saint Barbara is well guarded."

"Where did you put her, director? In the church?"

"No. Far away from here, in a safe place."

Gilberbert Chaves was studying the litter that the doorman had set down on the floor, examining its details:

"The litter is a work of art all by itself—a delight. It deserves to be shown too."

"In an exhibit of arts and crafts, without a doubt. It really is a gem. But it doesn't fit in with ours." Dom Maximiliano turned to the doorman and ordered: "Put it in the storeroom, Almério, so we can return it with the statue."

Followed by his three helpers, the director went through the rooms. The arrangement of the pieces was going along nicely. He praised their work, but while he was walking he made small changes, moving a crucifix from here to there, adjusting the position of a pair of small pedestals, having a shrine carried into the main hall. Then one of the boys came up to him:

"I almost forgot to tell you that the vicar of Santo Amaro telephoned three times. The first time he asked if the sloop had arrived yet, and I told him yes and that you, director, had gone to the waterfront to pick up the saint. He telephoned again, twice, wanting to know if you'd come back yet. He left a message for you to call him as soon as you got in."

"It's late now—it's already after midnight."

"He said no matter what time it was."

It would be opportune here to let our readers know that the vicar of Santo Amaro answered to the name of Father Teófilo Lopes de Santana, but everybody called him Father Téo, and Missy Marina, his housekeeper, when they were all alone, called him Teteo.

Gilberbert Chaves said good-night, and the two boys accepted his offer of a lift and went with him. Dom Maximiliano, all alone amid the images, returned through the exhibition rooms with slow steps, lingering to look at each piece. It was really an exceptional display—rarely had such wealth been exhibited in Brazil. There were so many pieces, all of them outstanding. In the places of honor stood sculptures by Frei Agostinho da Piedade and Frei Agostinho de Jesus, and the Christ on the Column, tragic and dazzling, by Chagas the Halfbreed, a loan from the Carmo Museum. Only down south in Minas Gerais, thanks to the heritage of Aleijadinho there, could something comparable have been achieved. Dom Maximiliano felt his eyes grow moist. This was his work, the fruit of his labors, of his knowledge, of his love. But when his dimmed eyes alighted on the empty pedestal destined to receive the statue of Saint Barbara of the Thunder, his monk's heart grew somber.

For him the stupendous, the incomparable exhibit of Bahian religious art was proving a failure, a disaster, a nonevent. It seemed that it would mark the end of his career, not the climax—indeed, the end of his life. No, suicide didn't occur to him, but he did consider resigning and returning to his cell at the Abbey of Saint Benedict.

The Quarters

Dom Maximiliano was famished—he hadn't touched food since his frugal lunch at noontime, a glass of milk, a small cheese omelette, a slice of papaya. Exhausted by the onerous day and the bitterness of the evening, he faced the steep stairs that led up to the attic containing the museum storerooms and his own recently constructed director's quarters: a small parlor, a large bedroom, a complete bathroom. My anchorite's cell, he would mutter, suppressing a laugh.

In the parlor, stacks of books in five languages, not counting Latin, overflowed their cases onto the floor. On the English desk with secret drawers sat the small portable typewriter, blank paper, pens, pencils, and erasers—he used pencil to correct his manuscripts—and a jade letter opener, a souvenir from a visit to China. In the bedroom were two black leather easy chairs, modern and comfortable, and a beautiful small jaca-wood table, a gift of the craftsman João dos Prazeres; atop it in a seven-teenth-century bowl of blue and white Macao china flourished a rare green rose plant, sent from Goiás by the esteemed Sister Amália Hermano Teixeira: historian, museum worker, and botanist. There was also a basin and a pitcher of Portuguese ceramic from the convent in Mafra, baked by the artist José Franco, and painted with blue flowers and birds by his wife Helena. And a luxurious bedcover of embroidered vel-vet covered a double bed of ivorywood.

Not a single print, not a single image hung on the walls. There was only an old photograph clamped between two panes of glass that showed in a landscape of pines under the snow, a German village; and in a restored antique frame was a modern colored woodcut by Emanuel Araújo of a muscular and lithe cat on the prowl in the Brazilian night. In the angle between the walls, over a colonial prie-dieu, hung a fair-size Italian print of the David by the divine Michelangelo.

Dom Maximiliano von Gruden went into his quarters, *garçonnifère de bon vivant,* cell of an anchorite, knelt beside the bed, lowered his head until it almost touched the velvet cover, and prayed. He struck his fist against his chest and asked for God's forgiveness.

Giroflê

Much of what happened during Yansan's visitation to the city of Bahia will never be known: where she slept, or with whom she played the sweet game, or on whose loving chest she lay her head at a late hour in repose, enjoying the sleep of the just. But it's not because of the darkness that this is unknown—quite to the contrary, there was too much light, preventing anything from being seen by eyes that earth will someday devour.

Gossip was guaranteed, and a buzz of rumors was indeed rife in *candomblé* temples and universities, in bedrooms, cultural centers, fairs, and marketplaces. It was all confused, inconsequential babble—nobody really knew what was going on. Talk for the sake of talking requires neither effort nor economy.

Such was the bewilderment experienced—or imagined—by the photographer Bruno Furer, which was widely commented upon in prose and verse and ended up as a pamphlet story written by the street singer Coelho Cavalcanti. The high artistic quality of Furer's professional work is common knowledge. We must make note, however, of one detail that wasn't all that widely divulged: Furer nowadays works exclusively for the painter Carybé (alias Hector Júlio Páride de Bernabó, the name of a Venetian marchese or a Buenos Aires honky-tonker), whose work he has been documenting for decades. Because of this he's traveled hither and yon, covering the five continents, from Patagonia's barrens to Leningrad's winters, his trips financed entirely by the paintbrush magnate.

On that first night of the visitation, Bruno Furer was carrying an enormous case stuffed with slides and photographs under his arm, and the two cameras he was never without hung from his shoulder. He arrived at Master Carybé's house around midnight and delivered material that was to be handed over to a dealer from London—a set of forty-five reproductions of Carybé's most recent paintings and the Iguatemi panel. Bruno had just finished shooting the final canvas, and he was extremely weary—he'd worked right up till the last moment to finish the job and deliver it on time. The English dealer was leaving on a morning flight the following day.

Upon his arrival, Bruno found the house empty. Carybé and Miss Nancy had gone out to dine at the house of the banker Victor Gradin: Their daughter Grace had just modeled a series of ceramic pieces, and she wanted the opinion of the bellwether of the arts before putting them into the kiln. In spite of being a millionaire, she was an accomplished professional. Unable to wait, and familiar with the couple's crazy habits —they never locked doors, didn't believe in thieves—Bruno went into the living room to await their return.

Carybé's mansion in Boa Vista de Brotas looked more like a vast museum, such is the nature and quality of what was on display there. A seventeenth-century Spanish altar takes up a whole wall of the living room. It holds, in almost perfect condition, twelve original paintings by Mejías el Zurdo—the Lefthander—only one of which is slightly damaged. The altar is an extraordinary piece whose presence in Brazil was made possible only by a conspiracy of friends with the participation of various antique dealers, writers, entrepreneurs, and customs officials.

This isn't the place to dwell on all the works of art that make up Carybé's holdings, but in order to convey some faint idea of the importance of the collection, it's worthwhile to point out a few objects, even if we only know of their existence by hearsay.

There's a Greek caryatid that Carybé obtained from the São Paulo collector João Agripino Doria in exchange for an oil painting and three watercolors by the master of the house; and there's a Croatian Saint George, a monumental sculpture in granite found in the atelier. In the dining room are three ex-votos painted by Toilete de Flora in the middle of the last century, as well as three icons: Russian, Macedonian, and Bulgarian. The last is an original by the icon painter Krastu Zakhariev from Triava, dated 1824: it features Saint George and Saint Dimitri together, in red, white, and gold. How did those ancient Orthodox saints from such distant homelands, seemingly unexportable national treasures, end up in the Brotas district of Bahia? The question remains unanswered. It would not be circumspect, in this tangle of churchmen and artists, to talk about pilfering, to reveal plots, accomplices, falsifications, bribery, and smuggling. Besides, Carybé was not lacking in astuteness and experience, according to what the chief of the Federal Police told us a while back.

Also imported illegally was a superb oratory that Carybé had unearthed in Portugal, in the attic of the ancestral home of local politician Manuel Castro's great-grandmother. Carybé had put sugar in her mouth, spoken honeyed words, and brought back the oratory in his luggage to give to her distinguished Brazilian great-grandson, a modest remembrance from his Portuguese relatives. "Wouldn't Manuel be offended by that Portuguese junk?" the great-grandmother had worried. The victim of recurrent attacks of amnesia, Carybé had forgotten to deliver the "modest remembrance," and even today Manuel Castro is unaware of the oratory's existence. Carybé made up for his forgetfulness, however, by giving Castro fresh and detailed news of relatives whom he didn't know across the sea, gracious and pleasant noblemen and women.

No one was offended by the Portuguese booty. Scenes from the life of Saint Mary of Egypt covered the inside of the oratory's niche, painted by a medieval primitive artist—actually, *naïf,* Professor João Batista had said during a pleasant lunch in honor of young Miss Nancy's birthday. They were strange scenes, lascivious—even libertine to be perfectly frank —showing the blessed girl Mary, merry and young, plying her trade in a brothel, stark naked, with no veil of allegory; they showed her later, an unfortunate old woman covered with sackcloth, scourging herself in penance amidst weeping and blood.

So that the inner paintings could be seen and appreciated properly, Carybé kept the oratory empty and the doors always open. In doing so, he endowed Saint Mary of Egypt with the role of patron saint of whores —so lovely in the seraglio, but so gloomy in the convent.

Bruno turned on the crystal chandelier to lay the folder containing the prints and slides on the birdfoot-based table. Startled, he found himself face to face with a statue of a saint inside the niche—more precisely, a strange Saint Barbara: a marvelous image! Carybé had placed it inside the oratory even though it blocked the picaresque episodes from the life of the Egyptian saint. Where could Carybé have gotten it? It wasn't a piece you came across for sale in any antique shop, and it hadn't been there the night before.

Bruno moved closer to admire it better—though not a specialist, he knew something about antiques, having lived in close contact with collectors, and rare was the day he hadn't photographed reliquaries, images, furniture, or paperweights. Now he knew he was standing before something truly sensational. Spellbinding! he would have defined his feelings if he'd known the term, but since he didn't, he thought and exclaimed: Damn!

He had a feeling he'd seen it before. Where, God in heaven? He couldn't place it. Later, while he was driving back to Boca do Rio where he lived, it came to him in a flash: It was Saint Barbara of the Thunder, the ever-so-famous statue in the main church of Santo Amaro. How the hell had it ended up in the oratory in Carybé's living room?

When he got home he woke up Gardênia, told her what he'd seen, asked her what she thought. "You never know with Carybé," she said. "Don't you remember the painting by Jenner that he swiped from Mirabeau's office when things were at their busiest, right under the noses of the servants, and nobody was ever the wiser? Anything's possible when it comes to Carybé. But to steal Saint Barbara of the Thunder from the church of Santo Amaro—I think that's going too far even for him. You must have been dreaming. I can't believe it."

Later on that night, just before dawn, Pergentino Three-Time-Loser entered the garden of Carybé's house and jimmied open the door of the studio. His plan was to get hold of the treasure of the Orient. While he was incarcerated in the House of Detention, he had attended a series of lectures intended to raise the intellectual consciousness of the detainees. There he'd heard the essayist Cláudio Veiga state that in a Goan chest in Carybé's studio was hidden the treasure of the Orient. Pergentino prided himself that he was no illiterate—he'd gotten through the fourth year of high school. True, he hadn't completed the full six years of secondary education, but that was because his father had dropped dead and he had had to go to work. The work he chose was risky, but it had required paying no income tax, and had no bosses breathing down his back. In addition to being literate, Pergentino was an individualist.

Engrossed in thoughts of Ali Baba's treasure, Pergentino had missed the rest of the information provided by Professor Veiga's illustrated lecture, and he had done himself a disservice. President of the Axé of Opô Afonjá, the *candomblé* of Mãe Aninha and Mãe Senhora, the incomparable mothers, of the *babalaô* Martiniano Eliseu do Bomfim, Edison Carneiro, and Pierre Fatumbi Verger, the wise men—*saravá!* hail!—Carybé is one of the twelve *obás* of Bahia, his name is Obá Onã Xocun; at the temple he sits on the right side of Mãe Stela de Oxóssi, the *iyalorixá*.

Pergentino's eyes were accustomed to peering through darkness—it was a necessity of his trade—and the heedless visitor made out the shape of a naked black woman asleep on a wooden bench. Step by step, he drew closer: she was statuesque! She looked like a goddess. But he didn't recognize Oyá Yansan—how would he have known her? Her unsuspecting breasts swelled in the rhythm of her breathing, and her sovereign derriere hung over the rather broad limits of her improvised bed, a derriere to drive any mortal mad. And Pergentino did go mad—he'd never seen such munificence. He was especially attracted by her purple lips, half-open to reveal biting teeth, and the tuft of pubic hair surrounding the mouth of mercy, how beautiful!

Now with a hard-on, Pergentino forgot about the Goan chest and the treasure of the Orient. He opened the fly of his blue jeans and prepared to go into action. These models who pose naked for painters are easy marks, he thought; they don't make any fuss, they don't raise hell over trifles. Besides, Pergentino was quite aware of his own prowess. He had been the lover of all the blondes and brunettes in Matatu de Brotas.

But he never got to touch the lady, to feel the warmth and softness of her mouth and pussy, because at the same moment that he unsheathed his tool, from a shelf above, a granite Saint George, without even dismounting from his white horse, and followed by the fire-breathing dragon, fell on Pergentino, attacked him, his lance aimed at the cock and balls of the ladies' swain.

With the leap of a cat and as agile as a quick thought—another necessity of his trade—Pergentino reached the door and tumbled down the steps. Saint George pursued him with the evident intent of gelding him. Scorched by the dragon's flames, nearly out of his mind with pain, shouting and pleading for help, Pergentino crossed the garden and reached the street. He only stopped running when he got to the district police station, where he turned himself in. They thought he was drunk, and since they knew who he was, the assistant police chief ordered his men to put Pergentino in the shower and turn on the cold water.

As for the photographer Bruno Furer, as he was going around babbling right and left, Inspector Parreirinha called him in to make a deposition at the Theft and Robbery Division. A sly old fox, he refused to clarify the garbled rumors: If people were bandying them about, it wasn't his fault. Oh, what Furer wouldn't give to discover the figure of Saint Barbara of the Thunder, large as life in Carybé's house or wherever it was, just to be able to photograph her to his heart's content—there was nothing he'd like better. "If you find out where she is, please give me a buzz, Inspector, and I'll come running with my Leica."

Sitting on his bench in the cool garden of the Bahian Academy of Letters, the bard Carlos Cunha, who had heard the gossip, summed up the hodgepodge with a single word: *giroflê*. Anyone who wants to know the meaning of his verse has only to ask the poet for the key to the riddle.

Engagement and Wedding

Promise and Debt

We promised earlier in this narrative to lift the veil with which Adalgisa had covered her married life—to reveal the exact and exacting limitations that religion had imposed on Danilo Correia, a fiery but repressed man in his forties, a clerk in a notary's office and the former hope of Bahian soccer. "Any day now he'll be called up for the Brazilian team," reporters back in those splendid days had predicted.

Now the time for making good on this promise has come, while the police—federal, state, and archdiocesan, each with its own clues and hypotheses—are attempting to find the clues that will lead them to the thieves and the recovery of the statue of Saint Barbara of the Thunder. Will the wily Sherlocks reveal the plot, put those responsible behind bars, and save Dom Maximiliano von Gruden from the perpetual cloistered oblivion to which he has threatened to consign himself?

Dom Maximiliano suffered from claustrophobia; he was born for the wide open spaces, for living among people, for scholarly conversation and merry chats, for controversy, gatherings, soirées, rumors, and gossip, the glow of society. His was one of the names that appeared constantly during July in the society column of *A Tarde,* from which whatever columnist is in vogue can command the days to be sunny or rainy, as she wishes.

The results of all the ongoing inquiries and investigations, the confirmation of any or all of the various hypotheses, will soon be revealed. But since there is nothing concrete to go on, neither the tracks of the thieves nor the trail of the saint, we will take advantage of this break for some flim-flam, some chit-chat, some tittle-tattle, for schemes of loves and lovers, tales of success and failure, anxiety and jubilation, melodramas and happy endings.

The Dreamer

Wearing blue pajama bottoms with pumpkin-colored stripes, his hairy chest bare, Danilo emerges from the bathroom where he has just brushed his teeth. Lying in bed, wrapped up in the sheets, Adalgisa closes her eyes.

On idle afternoons in the whorehouse, while lying beside Danilo on the firm *barriguda* mattress, Goldmouth Isabel would whisper, running her hand softly over the dark hairs, "It's like touching velvet, it turns me on. . . ." Adalgisa rarely touches her husband's chest, and she doesn't know expressions like "turning on" or "getting a hard-on." To know such things is unworthy of a lady.

His glasses placed on the night table, his slippers laid side by side, Danilo lies down. Before he turns out the light at the head of the bed, he lifts up the covers and contemplates with the same appetite as on the first night Adalgisa's behind. It is not quite hidden by her drawers—*drawers,* a word that's completely out of vogue, describing some prehistoric garment, démodé, impossible to find now in any fashionable boutique. Leaning over Adalgisa, Danilo casually makes his request. She declines:

"Not tonight—I've already said my prayers."

Danilo still tries to get close, to move his body alongside, to hug her; Adalgisa moves away, lies facedown, protecting her breasts and her twat:

"If you won't say your prayers, at least cross yourself before you go to sleep. Heathen."

Firmly, she pushes her husband's arm away:

"Get your hand out of there, you degenerate!"

In his dream Danilo plows her behind, but it's only a dream. This has gone on for nineteen years, since they've been married.

The Softy

Nineteen years married, one year engaged (leaving out the months of courtship), makes for twenty years of doing without. Danilo Correia —a good-looking mulatto, pleasant by nature, calm and courteous, whose friends still call him Prince Danilo, not so much because of his soccer playing but because he spoke and dressed well—has had to find solace in drinking and whores, the blessed remedies for ills of his sort.

Why would a cordial and friendly fellow like Danilo tie his destiny to such a harsh and evil-tongued harridan like Adalgisa? Why? Come on! Although she had passed through her thirties by now and was pushing forty, and in spite of her nastiness, Adalgisa was nonetheless an extremely appetizing dish. When she took one of her Sunday dresses out of the closet and put it on to attend the ten o'clock mass at Piedade, to go to her upper-class customers' houses, to have lunch at the home of Dr. Artur Sampaio (a rich friend of Danilo's from their school days), to go to afternoon dances at the Spanish Club—whenever she paraded down the street, she attracted greedy eyes: her hips rocked like a ship on the high seas. A cozy caravel, a truculent clipper, thought the lascivious Professor João Batista as he spied her from his crow's nest up the alley; Adalgisa the buccaneer, threatening to skin her niece alive.

Danilo had less recourse to drink than to hookers. Half serious, half in jest, there was always someone who mentioned, with a touch of either praise or censure, but mostly gnawed by envy, the frequency with which Prince Danilo visited whores. At least twice a week he ended his afternoons, enjoying himself, in the last assignation brothels in Bahia, worthy academies now on their way to extinction.

Danilo's neighbor and his companion at backgammon and on the checkerboard, equally versed in those refuges of bohemia, Professor João Batista was in the habit of comparing impressions with Danilo of the bearing, appearance, and other details, virtues, and skills of these scarlet denizens of various brothels whom they both knew and appreciated. He'd never dared, however, to put to his friend the question that burned on his tongue: why was Danilo seen in brothels so often when at home he had at his disposal a woman in the class of Dona Adalgisa, a dish that could shut down a restaurant, a wonder of a woman. If he, João Batista de Lima e Silva, were married to a catch like that instead of being a bachelor, he wouldn't waste his money on whores. He would gourmandize at home, taking both the plain and the fancy, the appetizers, the main dish, and the dessert. Dona Adalgisa, with her outstanding breasts and sumptuous hips, was a superb female, a rich banquet, an exquisite feast.

But the professor never asked, never found out for sure, although sometimes in the course of various events he came to mistrust the motives that governed the wild sexual life of his proper neighbor—and he was a proper neighbor, in the unanimous opinion of the residents of the Avenida da Ave-Maria.

Damiana considered Danilo a saint, worthy of an altar and worship, because only a saint could have endured Adalgisa's ill temper, her rotten moods—if it were me, Damiana thought, I'd have sent her to rot in the depths of hell. Alina, the neighbor on the other side, found a religious explanation for Danilo's patience: She's the penance that God imposed on him, poor thing. Her own husband, Deolindo, a sergeant in the Military Police and a militant macho, could only criticize Danilo's absurd patience. "What a wimp!" he exclaimed. "His wife wears the pants, she says what to do and what not to do, she does what she wants and what she thinks is right, and to top it off, she tries everyone's patience, that bitch! If I were in Danilo's place, every time she said two words, she'd get two swats. I'd set everything straight. You can't bargain with a woman, give her the least of what she wants: If a man offers a finger, a woman will try for the whole arm. Not with me, no siree."

Deolindo was a determined macho man, a voice of thunder, with few friends. Alina would listen to him in silence, apparently in agreement, apparently resigned, but laughing inside at how her blustering husband was being cheated on. What he said as a blowhard was matched by what he got as a cuckold. He was the biggest fool in Briosa.

A Moment of Silence

At the behest of some of the influential characters in this story—Professor João Batista de Lima e Silva, the journalist Leocádio Simas, the luckless Prince Danilo, and others whose names haven't been mentioned out of understandable discretion—let us pause. These assiduous and satisfied frequenters of the old brothels, doomed to disappear, substituted but not replaced by motels with a fast turnover and massage par-

lors of little imagination, have requested a moment of silence in homage
to those pleasant sites of conviviality and entertainment dedicated to
leisurely indulgence in fornication.

Those who have relaxed in the brothels of the city of Bahia have
been successive generations of rich, poor, and in between, citizens of all
professions and all ideologies, teachers and students, artists and artisans,
bankers, tellers, merchants, clerks, monsignors and humble priests, plantation owners, legislators, important figures in politics and the judiciary,
high-ranking and lower-ranking officers, doctors, dentists, veterinarians,
pharmacists, and engineers—in short, nobility, clergy, people. Democratic and cultural institutions, they made their contribution to education and proper habits. Some of them certainly deserve registration with
the Office of Historical and Artistic Patrimony. Let us preserve the memory of Josette la Rouquine's place, doubling as a *maison close* and a
literary salon, where the poet Bráulio de Abreu once pontificated in
meter and rhyme.

Under the watchful maternal eyes of the wise madams, the girls
would hold court for customers, serve banana candies on round canapés,
and Surinam cherry and chocolate liqueurs, made of roses or violets
distilled through filter paper by nuns in their convents. On aromatic
bedsheets, with skill, fantasy, and kindness, they would run the infinite
gamut of the pleasures and the caresses that prepare one, warm one up,
and lead to the supreme instant where life and death commingle.

Many came in search of the warm breasts of concubines, in compensation for the forbidden delights that moralistic prejudice denied
them in their own matrimonial beds. They would leave refreshed, relaxed, having recovered the joy of living. All this assured harmony for
couples, stability in marriages, solidity for the institution of the family—
the basis of Christian and Western society, needless to say.

An extortionate price has been paid for an ill-conceived progress: a
price in destruction, violence, and vandalism. While growth has been
equated with development, man has been condemned to the solitude of
motels and massage parlors, and the pleasure of life has been degraded.

In brothels, still not too long ago, artists of exceptional gifts, both
native and foreign—oh, romantic French girls, mystical Poles!—plied
their immemorial trade with grace and fancy, priestesses of the voluptuous art, as literary men wrote of them. In today's *hôtels de passe* everything is vile commerce, pornography, and lovelessness; there is an end to
les marieuses and *la delicatesse.*

Not even by saying *hôtel de passe* and *delicatesse* in French, by speaking of bedroom wit and matters of love in the language of erotic practices, not even in that way could Professor João Batista, who was
captivated by brothels, get used to the motels, massage parlors, and
stores where a consumer society merchandised sex to the extremes of

vice and anxiety, despoiled of romance, banana-sweet canapés, of nuns'
liqueur, of parlors with conversation and gallant manners, of poetry.
Alas for days gone by!

The Gambler

The prolix flatterer Sylvio Lamenha, in his column "High Society"
in *Diário de Notícias,* attributed great importance to the "union of the
charming gypsy Adalgisa, genteel ornament of local society, having
stepped out of a poem by Lorca, beloved daughter of our subscriber *el
caballero* Don Francisco Romero Pérez y Pérez, an outstanding figure of
the worthy Iberian colony; and the man-about-town Danilo Correia, the
popular Prince Danilo, a well-known athlete in soccer jousts." In spite of
this fawning, the ceremony was kept simple. It took place in the intimacy
of the bride's father's residence, with no ecclesiastical pomp. The family's
tight financial circumstances allowed for no prodigal spending or waste.

Paco Negreiro was in bad financial shape and was heading from bad
to worse. His gambling habits had separated him from his grocery store,
consumed his stock in the Banco Econômico and the Bank of Bahia, his
last treasury notes. The drought had helped by decimating his herd of
cattle, and Paco had been forced to sell his disintegrating shell of a ranch
for a mere song. The Fazenda Catalunha, or Catalan Ranch, an expensive, hasty, and unsuccessful venture, had been sheer ostentation in the
first place. Vanity had driven him to flaunt himself as a rural landowner
sitting at the poker table at the English Club, as a cotton planter, livestock breeder, and colleague of cacao planter Raimundo Sá Barreto,
landholder Almir Leal, and other plantation owners, the powerful people
in the world. Only very rarely had he even set foot in that backland
domain that he had now lost. The Fazenda Catalunha had had only one
practical use—for Dolores and Eufrásio's honeymoon.

Adalgisa's younger sister Dolores had married quite young, two
years before Adalgisa, amid her family's ostentation and decadence. The
blessing in the cathedral was given by His Excellency the Bishop of Ara-
caju, a friend of the Pérez family, who had been passing through Bahia at
the time. There was music, a chorus of female voices, and Mendelssohn's
"Wedding March." The procession came down the aisle amid bouquets
of natural flowers, preceded by half a dozen little angels, children of the
rich, three girls and three boys, scattering orange blossoms in the path of
the bride, the maids of honor holding the long train of Dolores's or-
gandy gown, embroidered all over, virginal white. Dolores hanging on
her father's arm, her mother Andreza dissolving in tears, the gold rings

—everything was exactly as fashion dictated. Outside the cathedral the onlookers were elbowing each other aside to catch a glimpse. In spite of the bustle, the haste with which the marriage had been decided upon and brought off, Doña Esperanza Trujillo had managed to lend it all that ostentation, that unusual pomp, and no one was surprised: they were familiar with her efficiency.

The haste was owing to the fact that Dolores was two months' pregnant. Even before their engagement, Eufrásio, a consummate serenader, a diligent paramour, had popped her cherry behind the Barra lighthouse—a suitable setting: at the time the Pérezes were still living in their own house, a chalet in Barra whose balconies overlooked the sea.

Now the chalet too had been swallowed by debts, and all that remained of the family's gaudy wealth was a scrap-metal business located in Água dos Meninos. Paco had put money into it as a lark, as a silent partner, in order to help out a young and enterprising follow Spaniard, Javier García. The Spaniard had taken care of the business and made it prosper.

Javier García didn't gamble; he was allergic to casinos, cabarets, bars, and brothels; he climbed up and down the Ladeira de Água Branca twice a day on foot in order to save the pennies that the Pilar Elevator cost. He'd arrived from Tenerife seven years before, emptyhanded, and filled up his bank account by dint of economy and self-deprivation and his agile fingers, leaving his capitalist partner behind. Javier García was not a gambler, he was a swindler.

—§—§

The Sermon

Albeit lacking in pomp, cathedrals, and bishops, Adalgisa's wedding wasn't drab either. No pauper's feast, it kept up the appearances.

There was a table laden with sweets and snacks, and an open bar with Spanish wines and brandies, manzanilla and sherry. The happiness of the newlyweds was toasted with champagne: Amélia and Benito Fernández, who served as witnesses for the bride in the civil ceremony, had brought along with their valuable gift of a fine dining service, half a dozen bottles of *champanha*. Wait a minute—what's this *champanha* business? *Champanha* is a drink manufactured in Rio Grande do Sul. But this was *vin blanc mousseux*, French, so it must be written and pronounced *champagne*, as Professor João Batista de Lima e Silva would teach, so as to avoid any confusion that might arise concerning the family's possible penury or the bastardization of its palate.

The ceremony began at five o'clock on a Saturday afternoon in May, after the fashionable hour-long delay for elegant events had passed. Actually, it might be more correct to speak of ceremonies in the plural: first the religious one, officiated by Monsignor Gaspar Sadock, immediately followed by the civil ceremony presided over by Dr. José Alves Ribeiro, a family court judge. The crowd of people that had filled the cathedral two years before for Dolores's wedding didn't show up, but even so, there were more than enough guests in the apartment in Graça: Paco Negreiro was highly thought of for his good qualities, and not just for the money he no longer had. In addition to being rented, the apartment was small: The guests squeezed into the living room, overflowed into the bedrooms, and chatted in the kitchen, gossiping about the squandering of Paco Pérez y Pérez's possessions. Gambling and ruin are an inseparable pair, the eloquent Father Barbosa would thunder from the pulpit of the elegant Vitória Church on Sundays; there was no better proof than here.

Adalgisa wore an airy tulle dress, Renaissance style, the creation of Maria Zilda and a gift from the Cotrims, Lourdes and Jonas, godparents in the religious ceremony. The veil, garland, and profusion of orange blossoms attested to the bride's virginity—and this time the bride's maiden state was genuine: she wasn't pregnant, nor had the tip of her betrothed's instrument even lightly touched her intact cherry. She'd never tasted the forbidden fruit, which was something unusual in our progressive times, a fact worthy of mention and praise.

Adalgisa shed a tear when Monsignor, in his sermon, recalled two saintly creatures recently deceased: the bride's mother, the good Andreza, and her beloved godmother, Dadá's guardian angel and teacher, Doña Esperanza Trujillo, "sheep of the flock of the Lord, who has called them to his bosom, from whence they bless their daughter and pupil on this her happy wedding day." Monsignor Gaspar Sadock was without peer as a preacher of the marriage sermon.

The Bridal Bouquet

It was too long a sermon, in Danilo's opinion. He had the same criticism of the complicated peroration by the honorable judge. This well-known bard so caressed and praised Adalgisa's "dazzling, sumptuous Brazilian beauty, generated in a crucible where the races mingle," that it seemed more like a declaration of love than a sermon. The bridegroom smelled something fishy—you can't trust poets—and rocked from one foot to the other.

Nor was this foot-shifting merely a figure of speech. Danilo's new shoes, all polished, were squeezing his feet, and he couldn't wait for the moment when he could take them off. He couldn't wait to be alone with Adalgisa in the little beach house on São Paulo Bluff, lent by a friend of his father-in-law, the rich industrialist Fernando Almeida, as a proper setting for their honeymoon.

When the ceremonies were over, the tedium of congratulations began. The line went on around the room—kisses for the bride, embraces for the groom, lots of luck, all the best, wishes for happiness, suggestive chuckles, no end to it. Danilo waited out the vows and chuckles, thanked them all, smiled, hugged them, shook hands, his thoughts far away.

Not really so far. His thoughts were actually close by, within reach of his hand, because he wasn't thinking about anything but Adalgisa's cherry, there beside him. That carefully guarded cherry was now freely accessible to him—he had full rights now that the priest had given his blessing and the judge's signature was on the marriage certificate. At last, God be praised! he was going to devour Adalgisa, cherry and all.

After the congratulations Adalgisa, amid kisses and tears and the sly little smiles of her girlfriends, their envy and drollery, their salt and pepper, went about the room again from guest to guest, from friend to friend. Danilo could barely contain his accumulated sexual drive any longer. But still he had to pose for the pictures: arm in arm, putting on the ring, kissing the bride. At the moment of the kiss he couldn't hold back—he came all over himself.

Adalgisa held up the bouquet of orange blossoms and threw it toward the anxious cluster of restless nubility that awaited it. The one who caught the bouquet would be married within the year.

—&—&

A Serious Girl

During a year-long engagement, the usual things can be expected to happen: a little messing around is inevitable, no matter how chaste and resistant the maiden might be. Hands find their way to breasts, pricks to thighs. But Adalgisa and Danilo's engagement was an exception to this general rule. It lasted a year, almost to the day, from the betrothal to the wedding, but Dadá was a virgin when she arrived at the improvised altar in the living room, and she was almost immaculate, so little messing around had there been.

This was not because of a lack of opportunity: there had been more than enough of that. The two of them would spend the better part of two hours alone together, from eight to ten o'clock at night, during which they would play the part of a betrothed couple, talking about new movies, radio shows, the latest songs, male and female singers—Adalgisa adored Angela Maria, while Danilo preferred Dalva de Oliveira, and both were fans of Elizete Cardoso—recalling brilliant soccer plays by the former Ipiranga star, and making plans for the future. Paco Negreiro would head out to his clandestine casinos, take dubious refuge before roulette wheels and at tables with marked decks. Each evening, as soon as Danilo arrived, they would say good evening, exchange a few friendly words, and Paco would leave. Andreza would stand watch over the lovers for a few minutes, then she too would leave them, she had more than enough to attend to, more than enough.

Sometimes Danilo and Adalgisa would then go out for a stroll in the neighborhood hand in hand, far as the Baiano Tennis Club or the Yacht Club, walking along, admiring the full moon, gazing at the sea from the heights near the Jesuits' residence on Santo Antônio da Barra Hill. It was a good spot for lovemaking, highly recommended, and in the pitch-blackness or in the moonlight, Danilo ought to have been able to pop Adalgisa's cherry with the greatest of ease, with no risk of being disturbed, far from indiscreet eyes—if she'd consented. But Dadá wouldn't consent.

She wouldn't think of giving herself before marriage, she'd rather die. The influence of Dolores, who'd been quick to spread her legs, had not rubbed off on her sister Adalgisa. In that particular as in many others the sisters were like night and day; they thought and acted in ways that were more than different, they were opposite. At the age of seventeen Dolores was with child, and she was pregnant with Perivaldo when she got married. Her son enjoyed the beautiful name he had been baptized with for only a short time—he died of dysentery eight months after his birth.

As elder sister Adalgisa approached the age of twenty-two and the verge of spinsterhood because she had been branded pretentious and haughty; Adalgisa stuck to the principles that she had learned from her godmother, Doña Esperanza Trujillo, a pure and enduring widow. Those principles ruled her conduct; Doña Esperanza had educated her to be a lady. Dadá wouldn't compromise, and the clamor of the sexual revolution left her indifferent. She had no truck with the Pill. "Now that one over there is a proper girl," the gossips in church would nod approvingly.

Hand on Breasts, Prick on Thighs

In matters of messing around, debauchery, whoring, to give it its proper name—their lovemaking encounters had been of the most discreet kind, indeed extremely platonic. Had his beloved, his bride-to-be been a different person, Danilo, a handsome young fellow sought after by womanhood far and wide, would have been treated to custard and pound cake. But Dadá refused to go beyond kissing during their evening meetings; and the closer they got to parting for the evening, the more lingering and ardent became the movie-type lip-sucking as they separated. Adalgisa enjoyed kissing.

She would also allow him to put a hand on her breasts—but only during her moments of greatest liberality, of course. In general, however, his hand had to stay outside the dress and never move under her slip; don't even mention the bra. On the thighs it was allowed to rest only infrequently, almost always over her skirt; on the rarest occasions it could move over her drawers and touch the outline of her pussy, which Danilo's imagination, rather than experience, told him was well-served with hair. On one day when he was more daring than usual and Adalgisa was unexpectedly amenable, he felt its dampness—and it made him flood his shorts. He couldn't wait to get home, as he normally did, for the urgent jerking off, or else to unload in a prostitute. He was popular at the Maciel and the Gameleira establishments—a pretty boy for hookers.

Prick on thighs, he could count on his fingers the number of chances he had with her during that year of urgency and containment. At those times Adalgisa would tremble when she touched his stiff and impatient tool; she would draw back quickly when she felt it pressing against her drawers seeking her pudenda. Danilo never diddled her, nor did she ever jerk him off. Dadá would only heft his weapon in her fearful hand, not really getting to know its caliber and length, its grandeur. She was puzzled by the drop of dew it left in her hand—when rubbed it was like gum-arabic.

The Dialectical Contradiction

It's a difficult and disagreeable task indeed to describe what should have been done but wasn't, to recount the negative, the joyless, requiring bothersome prose, desolate and depressing words. But no chronicler should flee from the truth, hide the sad and the ugly, belch out only the good side and say that Danilo was getting laid when, in truth, the poor boy was treading a rocky road, going through hell, crossing the sands of the desert, suffering hunger and thirst, limited to bread and water, and not much bread and not much water at that. . . .

Adalgisa would loosen up, let down her guard, and let herself go only when she was dancing in the arms of her fiancé at an impromptu party, or an evening affair at the Galician Center, or a soirée at the Spanish Club. Intoxicated by music, especially by the slow and romantic rhythms she liked best, she didn't complain if he put his leg between her thighs; nor did she seem even to be aware of the contact, the slow and persistent rubbing. She would smile, carried away, her eyes half-closed— she loved to dance. But parties at friends' houses and evening affairs at the Galician were not everyday occurrences, while soirées at the Spanish Club were even less frequent. Good things are rare, and they don't last long.

In view of the losses recounted so unwillingly here, then, one can imagine the physical and moral state in which Danilo came to marriage: His tool ached. Impatient and avid, long-suffering and frantic, he had trouble bearing up under the festivities. Tomorrow would be different, he knew; all limits to the full satisfaction of his desires, crazy as they were, would cease to exist. Everything would be accepted, and eventually he'd belch in satiety, on a full stomach.

At this point in the tale, it would be a grave mistake, a capital error, no matter how honest a slip it might be, for anyone to conclude that Danilo, the bereft one, felt nothing but desire for Adalgisa—a censured carnal desire—of which the beginning and the end was a devouring and ephemeral passion. Such a superficial and narrow view would limit and falsify Danilo's true feelings. For he loved Adalgisa deeply, with a true love that was fixed and unwavering.

He was captivated by Dadá's elegance and loveliness, her physical beauty, the perfection of her body: Her well-turned legs, her softly rounded hips, her wasp waist, her proud bosom, her black tresses. Accustomed to speaking in clichés, Danilo was at a loss for the appropriate nouns and adjectives to describe Adalgisa's Iberian face, her African hips. He furrowed his brow, went to the dictionary, the society columns—and came up triumphant: She had the face of a Málaga gypsy, he realized. As for her insolent, stupendous derriere, the popular expressions seemed prosaic and demeaning to him. He practiced meditation and did research: Who would have thought him capable of consulting dictionary entries? Well, he did just that and he was richly rewarded for his efforts, for he finally found the exact expression that described her behind, the opposite of the Málaga face, in fact: She had the buttocks of a Hottentot. Spain and Africa converged in Adalgisa's Brazilian geography.

During his earlier years as a soccer player, Danilo assimilated count-less platitudes, clichés, and commonplaces, endless arcane words and strange expressions from the clamorous radio broadcasts of soccer games, and when he became merely a fan, he'd use them at every turn in his analyses of plays, passes, penalties, and goals in lively arguments with other fanatical fans. When he found less vulgar words that sounded different and gracious to him, he kept them for Dadá and their times of love and madrigals. He would call her brunette, dark-haired, elegant, beauteous, ladylike, Andalusian, callypigian.

He was also a captive of the domestic talents with which his fiancée was lavishly endowed: She was a well-tempered cook, she could make the piano trill with song, she had a way with sewing and embroidery, and she was a first-class milliner. Her character he defined as righteous, un-blemished, sterling: with her, there was room for hyperbole. He was captive too, especially captive, of her moral qualities, her virtues—there were so many of them. And among so many, her greatest virtue, which he appreciated above all the others, was her chastity. He took pride in Dadá's sense of honor, her prudence in their fondling, her strong resis-tance to his attacks: hand on breast, prick on thighs.

It's an explicit contradiction, obviously—there's no way to conceal it or debate it. Dialectical contradictions are an integral part of life, even the ones that seem inexplicable, absurd. Danilo suffered the conse-quences of her chastity in his flesh, but he admired and was proud of the modesty and moderation Adalgisa imposed upon herself and her swain. He couldn't have loved her with such great love now if he hadn't en-dured that year of betrothal. And what can be said of the nineteen years that the marriage had lasted so far?

A Pause for Meditation

Of the nineteen years that their marriage has lasted, nothing will be said for now. No account will here be given of the mad dash of the newlyweds to Valença where they embarked on the launch that took them to their honeymoon on São Paulo Bluff. Let there be a pause in the story of their love—how else can it be described?—as ardent and chaste as it was.

The tale that will be told in these pages is intricate and multiple, as are the places and times where the yarn of life unrolls. To follow it, you have to put your brain to work so as not to get mixed up, go topsy-turvy, or get flustered at the first turn—not go the wrong way when the *ebó* tells you otherwise.

Nobody's the worse for exercising a little patience. Later on we'll pick up the thread of the sexual and sentimental adventures of the former soccer star and his milliner, and we'll tell it with the realism and pacing required in such matters. We'll tell how the wedding night and honeymoon were spent, and we'll discuss further the apparent incongruity of "ardent and chaste love." It's not enough just to recount it—it has to be explicated with a ruler and a compass, as the subject requires. We'll get to all matters in their proper time and give the right voice to each protagonist. If anyone thinks it's easy, let him give it a try.

It's time now to return to the other fronts in this war, pick up threads that have been left hanging, bring equally significant figures to the foreground. Dom Maximiliano von Gruden, for example—he got so little sleep on that night of his afflictions, it's just not right to leave him there waiting for news. Good news, we hope it will be.

But if, by chance, some readers are in a hurry to find out how the nuptial night went, and thirsting after libidinous, titillating details, such readers can skip a few pages and find a complete description up ahead, detailing blow by blow how the maiden fair lost her virginity. No one's obliged to read this book straight through.

The Phone Calls

The Sensational
Journalistic Scoop,
or Shit and Glory

Every morning, even if he had stayed up until the wee small hours hunched over his books in a vigil of study or in a friendly nocturnal debate, Dom Maximiliano von Gruden would get up early, to the crowing of the roosters in the proletarian avenue that ran alongside the convent.

As he brushed his teeth by the window, the director of the Museum of Sacred Art would linger over the morning activities in the neighborhood: men going off to work in sleepy haste, women, already weary, beginning their domestic bustle. A life of fatigue and trivialization, so mediocre, so far removed from his own—Dom Maximiliano von Gruden would never understand it, or feel any solidarity with the troubles of those insignificant people. It wasn't because they were poor that he looked down on them—he wasn't all that rich himself—but because they were common, and were subject to petty vexations and harassment, nothing at all like the museum director's rarefied intellectual worries and cares. On Thursday morning, however, twelve hours after he had received the news of the disappearance of the statue of Saint Barbara of the Thunder, after passing a whole night of insomnia, he felt just like the neighborhood people, even more unfortunate, perhaps. There was no way out, or if there was, it was the narrow gate of dismissal and professional ostracism.

Before he attended to the religious duties incumbent upon his status as a monk, every morning, Dom Maximiliano would read the newspapers left at his bedroom door by Nelito, the "little ox," another of the angels that the auxiliary bishop, the Evil One, had mentioned; this one was a messenger angel, a pitch-black rag doll. Today, not only from force of habit but with the added urgency of finding out any news, he sat down in one of the black leather easy chairs that so contrasted with his white cassock, with the papers piled up on the floor, and read them in the order to which he was accustomed.

He immediately saw a photograph of himself on the front page of *A Tarde,* standing, smiling, leafing through the German edition of his book on the statue. The photograph by Vavá was small but excellent. Vavá was a good fellow—he'd chosen the correct angle and the exact moment to click the camera shutter. Dom Maximiliano would have to send him a copy of the Brazilian edition with a warm and friendly inscription. He took a closer look at himself in the photo and decided he looked quite presentable, with a modest and intelligent smile. He was handsome— why hide the truth?

"Tomorrow, Museum of Sacred Art—Exhibit Opens—Famous Statue of Thunder Saint Arrives": The boldface caption directed the reader to page three of section one for the story on the press conference and information on the exhibit and the arrival of the statue. Taking up three columns at the top of the page, the story couldn't have been better or more thorough. The press conference had been covered and the article written in the usual lively style of the reporter José Augusto Berbert de Castro. Young in years but old in his trade, he'd joined the staff of *A Tarde* while still a boy. In spite of the fact that he'd been excommunicated, Dom Maximiliano thought highly of him—he was precise and capable. During the thirties the late Cardinal da Silva had excommunicated the jurist Epaminondas Berbert de Castro, José Augusto's father, and the whole family *ad aeternum,* but that's another story: It too would make for a delightful picaresque novel, but we can't go into the details here.

José Berbert had left the press conference early, before Edimilson's telephone call had put an end to it, but his article, long and accurate, detailed the events with lots of information, attributing great importance to the presence of the Portuguese poet who had been "sent on a special mission by *O Jornal* of Lisbon to cover the great events: the exhibit and the book." As for Dom Maximiliano's book, he gave its title both in Portuguese, *Origem e Autoria da Imagem de Santa Bárbara, a do Trovão,* and in German, *Der Ursprung und der Schöpfer des Gnadenbildes Barbara, die des Donners,* shooting off high-flying verbal fireworks: "magnificent graphic art, profusely illustrated." As for the content, José Berbert reported the assessment of Antônio Celestino, an authority in the subject, given during the press conference: "A monumental and definitive work," the erudite gentleman had decreed.

Furthermore, *A Tarde* announced that on the following Saturday it would run an article by its distinguished critic, "the learned chronicler of *The Courtyard of the Arts,*" on the book by the director of the Museum of Sacred Art, which was still not on bookstore shelves but already was acclaimed. The title of Antônio Celestino's article would be "Dom Maximiliano von Gruden's Book: A Major Work."

José Berbert's story was accompanied by another shot of the museum director, this one showing him chatting with the poet-journalist from Lisbon. Dom Maximiliano looked great—he mustn't forget to send the book to Vavá.

His chin still drooping but his morale almost lifted and his heart almost relieved, the silence of the bedroom interrupted only by a pair of finches chirping on the windowsill, Dom Maximiliano took himself to task. Self-critically, he blamed himself for being unjust to his friend Celestino. He had imagined Celestino plotting ambushes against himself, awful things, had made snide remarks to him, and used sarcasm, while all the while the good art critic, worthy of all the adjectives in the inscription, had been toiling over his typewriter to exalt the author of the "major work." It *was* a major work—Antônio Celestino knew about such things. Dom Maximiliano felt twinges of glory stirring under his cassock.

He'd also been unjust to the poet Assis Pacheco, the journalist who had come from Lisbon for the exhibit opening. Seeing him in the photograph now, cordial and respectful, he realized that the question that he had asked that had irritated him so much the night before could not have been formulated by his nemesis J. Coimbra Gouveia, hid no double entendres, contained no venom, reflected no conspiracy from across the sea. It had all been imaginary, groundless suspicions, paranoid fantasy, and the press conference really had been what it superficially seemed to be—the best of all possible worlds—or it would have been except for the misfortune with the statue. The end of the news story was of no help; unhappily false, it confirmed the arrival at the museum of the statue of Saint Barbara of the Thunder, after its journey from Santo Amaro: The reporter himself had seen the disembarkation. Well, José Berbert exaggerated sometimes, eager to give his readers good news and then some. Dom Maximiliano, however, was so stirred up by the news story that a ray of hope warmed his heart: Who knew, maybe at that very moment the State Police, the Federal Police, or the Curia itself had solved the mystery, found the statue, and caught the thieves, if there were any thieves. It might just be true.

But, oh! the misfortune that indeed had occurred was there on the front page of *Diário de Notícias,* with another photograph of Dom Maximiliano. How had they gotten it, the wretches? He was standing on the waterfront, his arms open, his face tight, while in the background were Edimilson and the van. The headline ran the whole width of the front page under the masthead: DISAPPEARANCE OF FAMOUS STATUE OF SAINT BARBARA OF THE THUNDER. Under the photo was the caption: "At the market ramp, the director of the Museum of Sacred Art, panic-stricken upon learning of the theft of the most famous statue in Brazil." "Most famous and most valuable" was how the article, which took up half the front page of the morning edition, described the statue. The byline was Guido Guerra's but even if there had been no byline, Dom Maximiliano would have known the authorship of the story. The giveaway was the malicious reference to the loan conditions of the vicar of Santo Amaro. It recounted, step by step, the museum director's running around from the market to the bishop, from the chief of the State Police to the chief of the Federal Police and his return to the museum with the empty litter. It was a sensational journalistic scoop; Guido had thrown the shit into the fan. Were there twinges under the director's cassock now? Dom Maximiliano felt himself splattered all over with shit.

—❦——❦

The First Phone Call

The daily mass Dom Maximiliano said was brief, and he'd only just finished it when he was called to the phone.

"It's the Federal Police, sir."

A university student in his last year, majoring in museum curatorship and serving a training period at Santa Tereza, Oscar Mafra was surprised at the haste with which the director, normally so calm, ran to answer: He was almost tripping over his cassock.

A phone call from the Federal Police, Dom Maximiliano thought. Good news! The night before the colonel had promised him good news in a short time, and now he was keeping his promise with laudable speed, proving the efficiency of the organization he headed. Dom Maximiliano was eager to hear anything that would turn that Thursday into Resurrection Day: Praise the Lord! Hallelujah! He bounded down the stairs, reached his office out of breath, and picked up the receiver:

"This is Dom Maximiliano."

"Just a moment, please. Colonel Raul Antônio wants to talk to you."

Then he heard the muffled, anonymous, coarse voice say, "The guy's on the line, chief," and immediately the colonel of the Federal Police roared into the phone without even saying good morning:

"Why didn't you tell me yesterday that Father Abelardo Galvão had arrived on the sloop along with the statue? You concealed something of the greatest importance from the police! You neglected to disclose a fundamental piece of evidence! Care to tell me why? Answer me!"

"An important fact? I—"

"I what?"

"Since it was a question of a priest, I thought . . ."

"You weren't supposed to think or not to think, just to cooperate with us. You concealed the presence of the priest on the sloop. Of Father Galvão! Why did you do it? Just what were your intentions?"

"None. I had no intentions. How could you imagine that a priest had something to do—"

"Something to do? That priest is the key to the whole plot! If he's not one of the leaders of the gang, he's at least an accomplice."

"Accomplice? Leader of a gang? Good Lord!"

"Don't try to tell me you don't know who Father Abelardo Galvão is!"

"I really don't know, Colonel. This is the first time I've heard that name." As a matter of fact, he'd heard it the night before from the lips of the auxiliary bishop, who had shrouded it in suspicion and censure. "I only knew that a priest and a nun had arrived on the sloop."

"And you said nothing to us, not about the priest and not about the nun. Listen carefully, Dom Maximiliano, because I'm not going to repeat it a second time: Don't try to trick us—it won't get you anywhere."

"I—"

"Don't forget that we know all about you." As he had done the night before, the colonel stretched out his syllables. "Absolutely everything."

He slammed down the phone without saying good-bye. Dom Maximiliano, in his haste to hear good news, had been standing up, next to his desk; now he collapsed into the swivel chair. Oscar Mafra had come with him, and when he saw the monk undone like that, a wax figure soaking in sweat, his hands covering his face, he became concerned and ventured timidly:

"Are you feeling all right, sir?"

The monk reacted to the boy's concern, regained his composure in the chair, and attempted to smile, but couldn't:

"I'm all right, Oscar, thank you. Go about your business and leave me alone. But first bring me a glass of water, please."

Out of his cassock pocket he pulled a little oval box with engraved enamelwork—the miniature on the cover was a reproduction of the Trinity by Andrei Roublex, showing the three angels at Abraham's table. In it he kept the pills that maintained his pleasant vagueness and shook one into the palm of his hand. He reflected on his circumstances, then doubled the dosage: He swallowed two just as the water arrived. What had the auxiliary bishop said about the priest? That Father Abelardo was a scoundrel. That was why Dom Rudolph had ordered him to keep quiet about his presence on the sloop, and that of the nun. It had been a useless bit of advice. They, the federals, know everything, absolutely everything.

The Second and Third
Phone Calls

Dom Maximiliano didn't answer the second phone call. "Tell them I'm not in, that I went out and you don't know what time I'll be back," he ordered Oscar when the student announced an intercity call from Santo Amaro. The vicar was undoubtedly ranting furiously because the lad was repeating mechanically into the phone:

"No, I'm not lying, Reverend Father. The director went out. No, he's not here telling me what to say—he really has gone out." Oscar paused, then opened his eyes wide. "Tell him that? Oh, I can't tell him that, no!"

Oscar hung up and stammered:

"The vicar . . ."

"You don't have to repeat it, Oscar, I can imagine what he said." Dom Maximiliano hunched his shoulders, as if bearing a heavy cross, and tightened his lips as if drinking from a bitter cup.

The third call was from the chief of the State Police; Dr. Calixto Passos, unlike Colonel Raul Antônio, oozed friendliness, his voice all coated with honey:

"A very good morning, my dear director." After an exchange of niceties that went on for several seconds, the police chief got down to business: "I'm calling you to keep you informed, as I promised. I still haven't found the solution to our little problem, but we're working on it. We've already got several clues, and one of them is sensational." He repeated, "Sensational! Maybe you'd like to hear it."

Dom Maximiliano thanked him for his consideration and waited for the news a little less ground down now; it was much better dealing with an idiot than with a torturer. He received Dr. Calixto's reply with no surprise.

"Does the worthy director know that traveling on the same sloop and on the same trip as the—the object of our interest—was Father Abelardo Galvão?"

"Yesterday, when I saw you, I didn't know that yet, but I was given that news this morning."

"Do you know Father Galvão?"

"I don't know him personally, and I'd never heard of his name until today. Today was the first I'd heard of him. The first time." In order to make clear that he wanted to contribute to the success of the investigation, he added, "According to what they told me today, there was also a nun on the boat."

"Yes, we have that information." The police chief's voice withdrew from the telephone. He's looking for the note with the information, Dom Maximiliano thought; then he heard him mutter: "Where is it? That's it, here it is." The voice grew stronger. "It concerns Sister Maria Eunice, from the Convent of the Immaculate Conception. She's going to be interrogated today. She's got a clean record, already checked. But Father Galvão has a long record, my dear director: the man is a dangerous agitator." He suddenly fell quiet, most likely thinking he'd said too much already.

In spite of his curiosity—he had the reputation of a gossip—Dom Maximiliano didn't press the colonel further about the activities and possible crimes of Father Galvão. The auxiliary bishop had mentioned the land business, he remembered, something about attacking plantations—that was it, attacking plantations, stirring up squatters, subversion. Good Lord, what was he getting into, with people of that ilk! Then the well-modulated voice of the police chief interrupted Dom Maximiliano's ruminations:

"We'll talk about that in person. As soon as the investigation shows some progress, I'm going to request, sir, that you do me the honor of a visit, where we can chat and analyze the situation together. Maybe even today, if all goes well."

"I'm at your service, Dr. Calixto, whenever you say. I beg you not to forget the urgency of finding the statue. The opening of the exhibit is set for tomorrow, and we can't postpone it. By then we will have to have gotten back—"

"—the statue," the chief of police cut in. "I think we'll get it back to you in time. This confirmation of my theory has made everything easy. Remember the theory I set forth yesterday?"

"Yes . . ."

"About the kind of criminal activity, remember? It turned out to be quite correct. The authors of the—the act—are always people close by, with easy access to the . . . object."

Dr. Calixto Passos waited for approval, perhaps even applause from the director on the other end of the line, but as silence persisted there, he asked, a bit subdued:

"Are you listening, director?"

"With great interest, Dr. Calixto. But I'm not sure I follow your thought. You mentioned the authors—"

"—of the act. Pay close attention: Father Galvão is the vicar of a backlands parish where he's also caused much talk. Before he arrived here in Bahia yesterday, he had to take a long detour in order to pass through Santo Amaro, on the bay, and then sail on the sloop along with the statue. Doesn't it seem strange to you, my dear director? Santo Amaro—think about it. I'm talking about Santo Amaro da Purificação."

"Santo Amaro da Purificação—what about it? I don't understand."

"Wasn't it from Santo Amaro that that solid gold monstrance disappeared several years ago? It was ever so old, and it reappeared later on among some gifts given to the Pope. Do you remember, my dear director? There was a lot of talk about the vicar's involvement, you remember? Put two and two together. . . ."

⚜

Another Digression for Gossip About the Gold Monstrance

In the anarchic structure of this tale, cut across as it is by comings and goings, and lengthy flashbacks, with all its diverse and disconnected narrative sections, *pleine de longueurs* as Professor João Batista would say if he were to read and analyze it—once again, and it won't be the last time, we now have a digression. We need to satisfy the unhealthy curiosity of the indiscreet who are itching to know what the chief of the State Police is talking about when he refers to a solid gold monstrance—"ever so old, my dear director!"—a fine piece, first rate. Stolen from the church of Santo Amaro, it later turned up among the donations that a high ecclesiastical dignitary gave to the pontiff on a visit to the Vatican.

Dom Maximiliano von Gruden, it must be said, tried assiduously to correct Dr. Calixto Passos's information on this, but the police chief hadn't given him time, had simply hung up after telling him to put two and two together. If by chance there were some truth to his story, however, the details he gave were erroneous. The monstrance in question hadn't belonged to the main church of Santo Amaro, but rather to another parish on the bay, and although Father Teófilo Lopes de Santana, the rambunctious vicar of Santo Amaro, might deserve criticism for his crude and vulgar manners and his inelegant language, he had nothing to do with the magical passage of the holy monstrance from the River Paraguaçu to the River Tiber. Furthermore, as is only too well known, he is also an ardent defender of the patrimony of his vicarate. But just try to convince a chief of police, an absolute master of the truth! In order to explain the thefts of religious artifacts, Dr. Calixto Passos had put forth a brilliant and simple hypothesis, and then confirmed it by everyday practices. Indeed, he himself considered it a work of art, he and Inspector Parreirinha. *Cherchez le prêtre!* he would shout when he learned that a given possession of a church had disappeared, imitating Professor João Batista in his recourse to French, but with what a difference in pronunciation!

Dom Maximiliano wasn't averse to slander; according to his adversaries he himself used it quite frequently. Therefore, whoever wants to find out the rest of the monstrance story—the identity of the parish from whose main church the sumptuous monstrance was taken, the item's weight in gold, its value in dollars, its exact age, the names of the parish vicar and the eminence who presented it to the Pope as a costly and beautiful Christian offering—whoever wants to know all that had best seek out the information from the director of the Museum of Sacred Art, because in these chaste pages, there's no room for slander, gossip, or defamation.

Most likely the story, from beginning to end, is merely the invention of those infamous enemies of Western civilization, those unscrupulous individuals who will use any means to attain their malignant, monstrous objectives. Therefore, let us turn a deaf ear to the barking of dogs, the howling of wolves. We boldly guarantee that the uproar in the press, the news items and insinuations, the revelations and denials, the scoops and abrupt silences, the gossip of loiterers on streetcorners, Clóvis Amorim's epigram and the leaflet by Edilene Matos, were deceptions meant to bamboozle the public and bring on a scandal. Fortunately the federal censor acted in time and put an end to the scheme. It was nothing less than a complot, you could take an oath on it if necessary, a sinister conspiracy to undermine institutions.

No, it's asking too much to stick your hand in the flame—there's a clear difference between taking a forthright stand and acting recklessly. Not even in the defense of sacred interests should you lapse into exaggeration. You could burn your hand.

The Other Phone Calls, Lots of Them

The other phone calls that came in were too many to count, and listing them one by one would be a waste of time and paper. Most were from newspaper offices and radio newsrooms, in search of information. A whole slew of writers, editors, and reporters were eager to speak to Dom Maximiliano or, in his absence, with some museum official, preferably Edimilson, an eyewitness. All morning long the phone never stopped ringing. It's the trumpet of Judgment Day, Oscar thought, but he swallowed his bold words, since the boss wasn't in any mood for facetious remarks. As for Edimilson, he had evaporated: taken a vacation, and where he'd gone to enjoy it, nobody knew. "I'm going to find that horse's ass wherever the hell he's hiding!" Napoleão Sabóia, correspondent for *O Estado de São Paulo*, roared into the phone, breaking the eardrums and fastidious calm of young Oscar—what the poor lad heard him say isn't fit for publication.

Not only had Guido Guerra's reporting provoked an earthquake in Bahia newsrooms, it had immediate repercussions in the rest of the northeast and in the south of the country. Journalists who had never in their entire lives heard the slightest reference to the statue of Saint Barbara of the Thunder now came hot on its trail, clutching lists of possible suspects, determined to give the public a good story. They rushed to unravel the mystery of the theft themselves, which had been as sensational as it was daring, carried out upon the arrival of the sloop at the market ramp, under the very noses of several people who noticed nothing at all. In São Paulo, in Rio de Janeiro, in Recife, the press hastened to interview the most reputable experts.

Even so, not even the Bahian reporters, the director's own acquaintances—not even his friend José Augusto Berbert—not a single journalist had managed to get an interview with Dom Maximiliano von Gruden; but it was he, and no other, who was the main target that the local and national reporters hunted *au grande complet*. In his own arrogance it was he who had made himself so central. They sought after him for his title as director of the museum where the statue—the centerpiece, the high point of the exhibit of religious art—was to be unveiled on the following day, for which reason it had come from Santo Amaro; and he was author of a whopping new book on this red-hot subject. Where could they find an advance copy? *A Tarde* was said to have requisitioned the one belonging to Antônio Celestino, and Cruz Rios, an ace newsman, was even now poring over it and wracking his brains to write the editorial.

But Dom Maximiliano had not supposedly gone on vacation, as Edimilson had; he had gone up in smoke, just vanished. The excited

Oscar repeated the litany over and over on the phone: "The director went out quite early without mentioning where he was going; he'll be back soon, certainly. I have no idea what time"—and he would hang up in a flash to cut off the insults.

As soon as he hung up, he would have to answer another call, from newspapers and radio stations in Bahia and from all over the country. There was even a call from the Brazilian correspondent of *The New York Times*, Edwin McDowell, stationed in Rio de Janeiro. Curiously, unlike most of his Brazilian colleagues, the American knew of the existence of the statue and its value. But Dom Maximiliano didn't even answer *him:* On any other occasion, McDowell would have been fawned over, put on a pedestal, but not at that bitter moment, when the taste of bile was in the monk's mouth, and a dagger had been plunged into his breast. Alas, *The New York Times*—oh, Calvary of his misfortunes, Omnipotent Lord God!

Dom Maximiliano only took the call of the rector of the university, who had phoned from Brasília where he and the cardinal were, but only briefly. A return flight was scheduled for the end of the afternoon after their meeting with the minister. Actually, it was not the minister of education and culture they were meeting on behalf of the rebellious students—he couldn't resolve anything—but the minister of war: now that man could indeed decide the students' fate. It was only this meeting, which had been obtained by dint of great travail, that prevented the rector, now alarmed by what he was hearing over the radio stations, from returning to Bahia sooner; to make up for it, he spent a long time with the director on the telephone.

It was a difficult, even indigestible phone call. Ostensibly the rector and the director exchanged friendly words and praises, declarations of admiration and appreciation. It was all hypocrisy—in reality they detested each other. The rector was a practical man, with clear ideas, and he was confused and annoyed by the monk's flights of imagination. The director complained about the mere pittance allocated the museum by the rector, who refused to double the funding for it in the university's meager budget.

Dom Maximiliano told the rector the little he knew, not attempting to conceal the gravity of the situation, and the rector, for his part, was emphatic:

"A serious matter? Most serious, I would say, with unforeseen consequences for the museum and the university!"

He placed complete responsibility upon Dom Maximiliano's head: "Since you did everything possible and impossible, too, to have the statue, now you've got to act with the same tenacity to get it back. If not, the museum and the university will be the target of the harshest criticism and condemnation, not to speak of the most demoralizing insinuations.

The museum, as you well know, doesn't enjoy the best of reputations. There's been talk of items acquired in a suspicious manner, the return of copies in place of . . . and then there's that tale about Saint Peter the Penitent." Then he reminded him:

"The vicar of Cachoeira didn't even want to loan the—"

"Cachoeira, rector?" Dom Maximiliano took his revenge: "You mean Santo Amaro."

"Cachoeira, Santo Amaro—what's the difference? You forced him into it."

That was how the conversation went, stumbling back and forth. Dom Maximiliano held the receiver away from his ear. With all his babble, the rector was trying to leave him with no way out but to resign if the statue wasn't recovered in time. Should he tell the rector that he'd already made up his mind to do so if the worst came to pass? He held off. Why give the rector that pleasure before the situation passed the point of no return? When Dom Maximiliano finally managed to get a word in, he only sought the rector's advice on whether they should open the exhibit on the date scheduled or postpone it.

"I see no reason to postpone it—after all, the exhibit isn't limited to that statue. There's a lot else to be seen. We haven't got the statue, but we've got the book you wrote about it—one thing can make up for the other, isn't that so?" The reference to the book, a missile that wounded, the rector had held back to the last. Dom Maximiliano swallowed it in silence. "We'll open tomorrow, at the time set. The minister said he'd be there." Now the rector was referring to the minister of education and culture—the minister of war had too much else to do.

The vicar of Santo Amaro called three more times that morning, furious and aggressive, cursing: after an outpouring of Gallicisms, the Hispanicisms began, God save us! They were poorly used, though; because Father Téo shouted his real insults in the language of the people of Bahia, which he had learned from those mouths-of-hell Gregório de Matos and James Amado, a linguistic truncheon for plain truths.

The Siege

The telephone calls were actually the least of it all. Skeptical of Dom Maximiliano's absence, a flock of reporters had camped out in the courtyard by the entrance to the museum and the Convent of Saint Theresa, in front of the door. The door was locked because of the preparations for the exhibit—the collection wasn't yet open to the public. One of the more enterprising reporters had tried to climb in through a window on the second floor, but he lost his balance as he was scaling the wall, injuring himself as he dropped—a nasty fall. When he heard about the accident, Dom Maximiliano gave it its proper appreciation—it was a small pleasure, but satisfying nonetheless.

In the corridors of the State Police and in the Federal Police posts, old hands and cub reporters alike had gathered. The chief of the State Police, wishing to please them and thus preserve his reputation as a competent and cordial official, promised to see them later with concrete news. "Maybe before the morning is out I'll be able to furnish you with some momentous revelations," Dr. Calixto Passos said. "Be patient for the good of society." During this short speech he wore the smile of a circus magician who is about to pull a rabbit out of a hat. Inspector Parreirinha raised his right forefinger to reinforce the momentousness of the promised information.

At the Federal Police, Colonel Raul Antônio had sent down a petty officer to get rid of the reporters. He had nothing to declare, and they shouldn't hang around trying the patience of someone hard at work. The journalists cleared out of the former-warehouse-turned-government-offices, but they hung around the area. They set up their own headquarters at the market, where they picked up odd bits of information: the *Sailor Without a Port* had been towed away to the navy arsenal during the night, Maria Clara and Master Manuel had been arrested early that morning. The reporters were flooded with rumors, listening to frightening stories from the mouth of Camafeu de Oxóssi that concerned a woman from São Paulo and a Nigerian ring. They sipped *batidas* and *lambretas* at drink stands.

All this bustle on the part of the media of communication would lead one to believe that the disappearance of the statue of Saint Barbara of the Thunder was of the gravest consequence, the only really serious event that occured in Brazil in the previous few days. Let it be remembered that events narrated in this chronicle—full of veracity, albeit lacking in brilliance—took place during the worst years of the military dictatorship and the most rigid censorship of the press. There was a hidden reality, a secret country that didn't get into the news. The newsrooms of newspapers and radio and television stations found themselves restricted to covering generally unexciting events. Their editorial pages were reduced to unconditional praise for the system of government and those who governed. There was in place a total prohibition of any reportage that carried the slightest allusion to the daily imprisonments, torture, political murders, and violations of human rights; or that suggested any comment on the censorship of public entertainments and of books; the same for any reference to strikes, demonstrations, picketing, protests, mass movements, and guerrilla attacks. If one believed what one read in the newspapers, nothing like that was happening, and the nation was living happily under the aegis of the generals and colonels. Some papers filled in the blank spaces left by the cutting out of important items with cooking recipes—*O Estado de São Paulo* once printed a recipe for *quitandê*, a not-too-familiar Bahian dish, in the middle of its front page. Sometimes they used poems, ballads, odes, sonnets by classical poets, and stanzas from *The Lusiads*. The readers understood and were consumed with curiosity as to what was going on in the nation.

No criticism was permitted of Franco, Salazar, or any of the other glorious Latin American generals who, with equal firmness and incompetence, exercised power in Argentina, Paraguay, Uruguay, Chile, and Bolivia, colleagues of our own erstwhile glorious warlords—nothing was permitted in the press nor in any other public medium. From his seat in the Federal Chamber, when the deputy Francisco Pinto exercised his mandate and called Pinochet a tyrant, he lost his mandate and was jailed. Two French priests who dared defend the slaves of Amazonian feudalism from their pulpits found themselves behind bars after a summary trial.

Censorship, corruption, and violence were the tools of government; this must be recalled because there are some who may have forgotten it by now. It was a time of ignominy and fear: The jails were overflowing, and there was torture and torturers, the lie of the "Brazilian miracle," pharaonic public projects, and graft. Of course, there are some who are still nostalgic for those days.

Well, it's common knowledge that good deeds, happy events, normality, and joy are not the favorite subject matter of news editors: In fact, the greater the calamity, the better they consider a news item to be. In the suffocation and quagmire of the censored Brazilian press at that time, the disappearance of the statue of Saint Barbara of the Thunder fell like a gift from heaven. Most of the reporters on the police beat assumed it was a theft carried out by robbers who were specialists in churches and abbeys, and they wrote of "gangs" and "fences," but others didn't exclude and even promulgated the theory of the complicity of parish priests and bishops—complicity or authorship.

The head of the local office of the *Jornal do Brasil,* Florisvaldo Matos, was a respected poet—so many poets we have in this blessed land of Bahia, God be praised!—and was so indignant that he was unable to speak to Dom Maximiliano that he even insinuated that the key to the mystery was in the hands of the artful monk himself. Eventually, the statue would reappear, he suggested, catalogued as part of the museum's own collection, and it would be seen there in all its pomp and majesty. In exchange, on the altar of the main church of Santo Amaro, a plaster copy would be enthroned, made to order: Saint Barbara of the Phosphorescent Thunder, in Technicolor.

—⚶–⚶

The Flight

The work of arranging for the exhibit continued under the direction of the architect Gilberbert Chaves, who was joined by another architect who doubled as a painter, Lev Smarchevski. Dom Maximiliano supplied the guidelines and supervised matters: Demanding as always, he was now rather taciturn, with few words and no smile, the opposite of the brilliant conversationalist to whom his assistants and friends were accustomed. When Lev mentioned the items in *Diário de Notícias,* the director replied laconically with a single word: "Irresponsible." Nothing more was said about the matter; only the empty pedestal reminded them of the disappearance of the saint.

From amid other objects on a shelf, Dom Maximiliano took out an exquisite gold chalice encrusted with precious stones, of Slavic origin, for evaluation. He had just set it on a pedestal all by itself when Oscar Mafra came out of the office, from his post beside the telephone, to pass on an urgent message:

"Dom Maximiliano, Father Soares just called." Father Soares was the auxiliary bishop's secretary: "Dom Rudolph wants you to go to the palace immediately. Father Soares asks that you not delay." He imitated the Reverend Father's nasal voice: " 'Tell him to come right away—His Excellency is waiting.' "

At the corner window Dom Maximiliano raised the curtain and examined the courtyard, crammed with reporters and photographers. How could he cross it to get to the street? It looked impossible. Even with his back turned he sensed that work had stopped in the room at Oscar's announcement. Without turning around he said:

"Please keep on. There's still a lot to do, and time is short. Everything's got to be ready by noon tomorrow."

He continued to look through the slit in the window, then finally turned around into the room and took a couple of steps toward Lev.

"Lev, tell me—the car that's parked on the other side of the street, by Roque's shop, is yours, isn't it?"

"Yes, it's mine, Dom Maximiliano. You're welcome to it."

"Thank you, Lev. I'm grateful, and I accept. Listen carefully. Five minutes from now the museum door will be opened and the reporters will be invited to come in and see how the work is progressing. When the entrance is clear and they begin to go up the stairs, you, Lev, go down, pass through them, not in any hurry, and go to your car. Start the engine and wait for me. I'll leave through the church and get into the car, and you'll step on the gas." He glanced around the room. He didn't smile, but the ruse he'd thought of to fool the newspapermen comforted him momentarily.

No sooner said than done, the plan worked marvelously. When Nelito opened the entrance door to the museum, Oscar Mafra made the invitation to the reporters: "Dom Maximiliano wants me to tell you gentlemen that you can come in." They piled in, surprised and triumphant: The monk had given up. As they dashed up the stairs, they passed Lev. The exhibit was coming along fine, the architect volunteered, without answering their questions regarding Dom Maximiliano's whereabouts. The television cameras brought up the rear.

Slipping out through the half-open door of the church, Dom Maximiliano began to cross the empty courtyard with quick steps. At that moment a cub reporter inside the museum went to one of the windows to toss out his cigarette butt and spotted him. He shouted the alarm: "There he goes—he's running away!" Losing his composure, Dom Maximiliano grabbed the hem of his cassock and broke into a run. He headed through the street entrance, got into the car, and Lev sped away down the Ladeira da Preguiça.

The Suspect

As the clocks chimed eleven that morning, the first rumors about Father Abelardo Galvão reached the newspapers, linking him to the disappearance of the statue. Anonymous phone calls told editors-in-chief and managing editors about the trail that the Federal Police and the State Police were following, pointing to the vicar of Piaçava as the number-one suspect. Stay at your telephones, they recommended, because new and more extensive information would be coming. Curiously, the phone calls, it was easy to ascertain, came from no police station, not from the building on the Largo da Piedade nor from the warehouse on the waterfront.

From that moment on, the disappearance of Saint Barbara of the Thunder took on a truly sensational character, an uncommon, unexpected significance. The involvement of Father Galvão linked the theft of the wandering statue to explosive matters: the struggles of the landless against landowners, the attacks on plantations, the reactions of the property owners, the bullet-riddled bodies of the peasants, the actions—proper or criminal, depending on who read and judged—of the priests of the Church of the Poor.

The activities of the vicar of Piaçava were already documented in files and had stood out on the pages of newspapers. On more than one occasion over the past few months Father Abelardo's name had appeared in headlines in big letters: DISCIPLE OF DOM HÉLDER, FATHER

ABELARDO FOUNDS COMMUNITY—PIAÇAVA VICAR LEADS INVASION OF SANTA ELIODORA PLANTATION—LANDOWNER ACCUSES FATHER GALVÃO OF ARSON.

On one tabloid that appeared irregularly—it came out whenever some interested party loosened his purse strings—the headline made the spicy announcement, FATHER ABELARDO, RASPUTIN OF THE POOR. The subhead mentioned the name *Patrícia*.

The Ebó

At daybreak on that Thursday morning, Oyá Yansan moved through streets and in alleys, in the center of the city of Bahia and on the outskirts, going from *axé* to *axé* on a visitation. Those who recognized her by her buffalo horns and her breath of fire showed no fear, made no commotion, didn't throw themselves at her feet or call her name. They each greeted her discreetly with an inward whisper that only she and no one else could perceive: *"Eparrei!"* He who knows the most will speak the least; a parade of strutting words is the recourse of fools and charlatans. Oyá Yansan went along, haughty and beautiful, a cotton shawl thrown over her bare shoulders, wine-colored bracelets and necklaces on her arms and ankles. It was early risers and insomniacs who saw her.

In some way or other something was happening: The rumor was flying about, spreading far and wide. At temple houses, in the bustle of bedrooms, in the quiet of *pejis*, conversations in dialect could be heard, exchanges of whispers, while in the Santa Bárbara market in the Baixa dos Sapateiros several stands opened up with decorations of wreaths, tissue-paper streamers, and crepe-paper flowers, even though Yansan's feast day, December 4, was months away. A reveler without peer, Jacira do Odô Oyá was improvising a modest *caruru* with 12 grosses of okra to celebrate. Celebrate what? She didn't say, and no one asked her.

Oyá had come because of Adalgisa and Manela, to collect what was owed her, to make an example of the one who had denied her, to proclaim the right to life and love. As for a festival, she was content with the one of the night before, when she disembarked and went to Gantois: It was an obligatory one, as Wednesday is her day of the week. But if there were other festivals, she wouldn't turn them down. Still, when the unforeseen happened, it brought her new tasks; a doting mother, Oyá couldn't refuse her daughters. She hadn't come for festivities, but with so many things to do, a celebration was in order.

It is said that Oyá probably started that morning at the Axé of Alaketu, near Carybé's house—from Boa Vista to Matatu is only a hop, skip, and jump, they're both in Brotas. Some people swear she spent the night in jolly company there: As proof they point out the canvas showing a black woman dozing in mystery and poetry, while all around her large lean body lies the landscape of Bahia—mountain, sea, people. If you look closely at the figure's features, it's easy to catch her resemblance to Olga, a powerful *iyalorixá*, Olga of Alaketu, Olga of Tempo, Olga of Yansan.

At the Axé of Alaketu, the priestess Olga began her daily tasks that morning by casting the conch shells to invoke the enchanted one and making an offering to the *ebó*. She passed on a strange girl's requests and prayers, some easy, some difficult to satisfy.

When Oyá showed herself and lit up the dawn at the foot of the slope of Alaketu, Olga smiled: My mother has come in person, hail the blessed day! she told herself. A goat tethered behind the shed bleated mournfully.

Crouching over the trough of bean *acarajés*, the strange girl could barely make out the light of dawn as it broke through the shadows, but she saw quick flashes and wine-colored stripes and took them as favorable signs. The *acarajés* were for the one who came loaded down with cares, ambitions, needs, a whole sackful of them. For a large and varied request like this one, for so much need and urgency, would two dozen *acarajés* along with a young goat brought from the interior be enough? the girl asked the priestess Olga.

Never had the girl felt so agonized, because that day had suddenly become decisive for her incipient theatrical career. The girl was ambitious and persevering, as befit a daughter of Yansan. Soon she would complete her three years as an initiate; having started on her name day, she hadn't missed a single obligation since, had fulfilled the calendar of the *boris* to the letter. Yansan had helped her with her entrance exams and even with the debut she had made as an actress on the stage of the

Castro Alves Theater. There, with elegance and praise, she had played the role of Pata in a children's play by Joã Jorge—that rascal. Adorned with the hair of an Indian, straight and black, the blue eyes of a white woman, and the fleshy lips and dark color of a black woman, the girl now presented her requests.

The young actress wanted justice for the exploited, she wanted courage and art in front of the cameras, and she yearned to hold in her arms a certain man for whom desire was consuming her blood. A young university student in sympathy with forbidden causes; an apprentice actress treading the boards of theaters-in-the-round, poor, provisional, and persecuted; a nanny goat in heat moaning with fire and repressed passion. Onto the same bundle of requests that she gave to Olga at the *Axé*, she'd heaped the television program, the famous Frenchman, the handsome but chaste priest, and three corpses that she'd seen rotting from a distance. The other nanny goat, the one she'd brought as an offering to Yansan, as food for thought, she'd stolen from the landowner's flock, which made it all the more valuable and worthy.

While Olga listened to the young supplicant's fervent harangue, Oyá flew away in the voice of the actress, soared over the plantation and village, took up the burden of the unfortunate people, became aware of evil intentions and diabolical schemes, and learned of death sentences. Oyá knew Father Abelardo—he had been her traveling companion during the crossing along the Paraguaçu; he was a good-looking young fellow with a generous and tormented heart. The rest of the girl's requests—the business of the famous Frenchman and the performance—required no effort at all. She would take the parallel lines and draw a circle.

By the time the girl came to the end of her petition, Oyá had returned and made up her mind. She mounted Olga, her favorite steed, gripped her saber, and came out dancing. Three times she spat fire, then took the supplicant to her breast and accepted the *ebó*. The trough with the *acarajés* was put in the *peji*, but when the blood spurted, hot and red, from the neck of the goat, Oyá sucked it up avidly. She ordered the pieces of the animal cooked and her portion set aside with the rest, to be served as a meal for the people of the *axé* at sundown. And that was how it was done.

The Events of Thursday Morning

---~&~--~&

Haphazardly, So Be It

Beginning Thursday morning, the day before the scheduled opening of the exhibit of religious art as is all too well known, events began to pile up, to bump into each other, apparently disconnected, rendering the existing entanglement all the more confusing, a veritable labyrinth.

The characters we already know were joined by new figures, both Brazilian and foreign, some slipping in among the lovable creatures with sinister skill and rubbing elbows with the famous. Not to mention the rabble, who joined in upon no invitation.

These complications make it all the more difficult for us to unsnarl the ball of yarn and tie the ends together: the only way to do it is haphazardly, "letting the pen run on," as they used to say in the good old days. It may become necessary to mix up time and space in the sequence of the episodes, breaking the classical-sequential harmony in the telling of a tale. Who knows, in the midst of the turmoil and confusion, a plausible trail may yet be blazed that will lead to a conclusion of the adventure.

The Twins

On Thursday morning, Father Abelardo Galvão, wearing lay clothes but a collar as an insignia of his status as a cleric, approached the entrance to the archepiscopal palace. When a tall, slim black woman dressed in colorful garments passed him, she smiled at him boldly.

Even though he only caught a glimpse of her, he thought he knew her but he couldn't remember from where. He turned to get another look so he could figure it out, but she was nowhere to be seen—she must've disappeared into the crowd, into the hubbub of Cathedral Square. Deep in his thoughts, wracking his brains to think where he'd seen her and who she reminded him of, he didn't hear the street urchin calling to get him to buy a newspaper, hawking his stock:

"Get the latest news about the statue that disappeared from her church!"

The auxiliary bishop let Father Abelardo cool his heels for a good half hour in the anteroom, in spite of having told him the exact day, hour, and minute he was expected—ten-thirty sharp—and recommending that he not be late. The seminarian who greeted him and then withdrew to announce his arrival didn't even bother to come back. Sorry that he hadn't bought the newspaper to pass the time waiting for his appointment, Father Abelardo gave himself over to his thoughts and drifted back into the backlands of Piaçava. If not for the sounds from the square that penetrated the old building—music, the calls of vendors—he would have been wholly transported to the barrens of the rough back country, a field of palm trees, stands of *piazava* and dendê palms, the squalid little village, the unprotected people.

In the anteroom a chime tolled the hour. That was the same time of day that, give or take a minute, Patrícia used to ride across the small square in front of the church in Piaçava at a gallop that would take her to the bed of the river, left empty by the drought. She would return at a slow trot, dismount before the vegetable stand of Milá, the Indian woman, behind the bandstand. She would lay the reins over the saddlehorn and loosen the harness, and the horse would withdraw by itself into the shade of the shed.

Father Abelardo, who watched her from the door of the church, followed every movement, every gesture of the equestrienne; instead of culottes, she wore blue jeans; instead of boots, a pair of tennis shoes. Recollections of his childhood on the pampas flooded his memory; his grandmother by the corral gate, the Indian woman and the animal, images that were unrelated but that gave him the feeling of a full life. Patrícia would repeat her errand each day—alas, so few!—during her visits to her parents' home, visits that had become more frequent and prolonged, or so it seemed to him. Or was he fooling himself? Father Abelardo Galvão, balanced on a knife edge, was carrying the weight of the universe on his back.

No sooner had he begun pondering Patrícia's behavior, her old habits of coming and going and staying, than Father Abelardo was taken with an unexpected daydream: The black woman who'd passed him before the palace—where had he seen her before? Coal black as she was, she reminded him of Patrícia. Patrícia—yes, it must be she and no one else. They were physically similar, a similarity that grew greater with each minute in the silence of the anteroom, but how exactly were they alike? Alike in what way? Their bearing, their features—who could say? Perhaps it was the slimness, the height, the verve, the ambiguous smile, confident and evasive. But there was something else, he didn't know what: He'd only seen the black woman briefly, but he'd seen her thoroughly and forever.

She was just like Patrícia, as if they were twin sisters, but of different family, race, and lineage. The vague identification with Patrícia made him recall where and how he'd first seen the black woman—for he'd seen her once before. It had happened last night on the market ramp, as the sloop had docked. It came back to him; mulatto and dressed as a Baiana, she'd winked at him. The height, the smile, the elegance, the face, the bearing were all Patrícia's. But what else? He hadn't realized it at the time, worried as he was by the auxiliary bishop's summons, but now, in the anteroom of the archepiscopal palace, he identified them as twin sisters. Two, or were there three? How many more? Surely it was a fable! But fable, nonsense, or daydream, the tormented vicar of Piaçava got no further. For he looked up and saw standing before him, hands crossed over the mass of his belly, Father Soares, examining him up and down. His voice nasal, Father Soares announced that His Excellency was waiting for him.

The Bishop at the Window

As he entered the room where Dom Rudolph received and dismissed people, Father Abelardo saw him standing by one of the windows that opened onto the square: up on his clogs—being short in stature, he wore high heels—his head topped by a red skullcap, his stance was martial. Father Abelardo had always mentally dressed the auxiliary bishop in a military tunic. But it wasn't the stars of a general, victorious on the field of battle, that he conferred on him; only the stripes of a bossy and intolerant lance corporal. The vicar of Piaçava stopped beside the desk and cleared his throat to show he was there.

Dom Rudolph paid no more attention to the clearing of the throat than he had to the footsteps. He remained distant, peering off: the velvet drape veiled him from the curious glances of passersby. He too was taken by the figure of a black woman standing in the center of the square in the gleaming sun—a veritable statue. In spite of the distance, Dom Rudolph could see, as if he was standing face to face with her, that the black woman's eyes were sparkling like two lighted coals, two embers, and that it was he whom she was obviously laughing at—mockingly! So much the worse—nonsense like that didn't bother him, although it did leave him uneasy, perturbed by its meaning.

Behold, the black woman disappeared suddenly. Even as he was staring at her, she disappeared. It wasn't that she left her place—she didn't move; she didn't go up in smoke, she just stopped being and being there. The place where she had been was empty.

As Dom Rudolph turned his eyes away, they chanced to rest on a fellow in the square who was staring up at the outside of the palace: shabbily dressed, wearing backlands rope sandals, a wide-brimmed hat covering his face, and in spite of the burning sun, a raincape. Not interested, the auxiliary bishop moved away from the window, made his initially hesitant step firmer, and walked over to his desk. Before he sat down he poured himself a glass of water, took two swallows, and wiped the sweat from his face and neck. He put away his handkerchief, not concealing his annoyance with the fatal tropical heat, the sticky, awful humidity, and the difficult priest standing before him. He felt his annoyance on the back of his neck, as his forehead still frowned.

Christ's Army, Which One?

Father Abelardo hadn't counted on getting a warm reception from Dom Rudolph, not even a cordial one—he was familiar with the auxiliary bishop's position on the questions affecting the parish of Piaçava, questions of social problems that divided the Brazilian clergy. He hadn't imagined, however, that the meeting would become steeped in so much acrimony as it did. Instead of participating in a thorny but civilized dialogue, with quotations from Scripture, references to Vatican Council II, to the Pastoral on land, and to recent books on theology, the priest found himself seated in a prisoner's dock listening to a sharp, accusatory bill of indictment. Hardly any defense rights were given him—His Excellency imposed silence at every attempt he made to tell the truth.

Hypocrisy was not one of Dom Rudolph's defects: He wasn't in the habit of concealing his thoughts, pretending esteem when he actually had small regard for a person. So when he first sat down, he only nodded in the direction of Father Abelardo. He didn't take him to his breast in a fraternal embrace, didn't shake his hand, didn't give him his ring to kiss —he was a warrior, not a diplomat. He indicated the chair on the other side of the desk, his finger pointing, gripping his lance:

"I see you've forgotten, Father, or that you haven't followed the recommendation I made to you the last time we met, about the dignity of priestly dress."

"I've followed it exactly—I've dressed as a clergyman in obedience to Your Excellency's orders."

In this proper response, with its respectful inflection, Dom Rudolph sensed signs of irony, so he raised his voice: "I said, in a cassock. In plain and simple Portuguese. The next time, I want to see you in a cassock. Or is it that a cassock is too heavy or restricts your movements?"

Dom Rudolph's Portuguese wasn't always clear and simple, while his guttural accent made the reprimand all the sharper, the order all the more imperious. Between the auxiliary bishop of the archdiocese of the primate of Brazil and the obscure parish priest from Piaçava, the Army of Christ stood drawn up in battle formation. The army—or armies. Each was quite different from the other, the bishop's and the vicar's: on opposite sides, they were enemies.

Dom Rudolph had no doubt whatever, and he would affirm it in an authoritative way: Christ's army had a centuries-old mission to uphold over five continents the property rights of the ruling classes. Such abuses as existed would be corrected with charity: that was what charity is for, Father Galvão, it was one of the three theological virtues. The Church supports order, it doesn't promote disorder. Exercise charity, Father.

Father Abelardo, on the contrary, considered that the Church required submission and blind obedience of its faithful, in the service of the rich and powerful—to the rich went the goods of this world, to the poor, the hope of the kingdom of heaven. It was the very negation of the words of the Savior: The Church had been intended to administer justice to those in need of it. The true Army of Christ, Father Abelardo believed, should be recruited in the slum shantytowns of the cities and in the poverty of the countryside of a Third World desperate for priests and bishops who bore new preachings; it should uphold defiant action, resistance, and struggle.

The two military formations stood face to face, both wearing the uniform of the traditional cassock, and it would have been impossible not to distinguish between the old and the new, the contradiction that will lead inexorably to the advance of society. But enough speechifying— a succinct and impartial record of the controversy between the auxiliary bishop and the vicar from the backlands will suffice, without our taking sides or trying to influence the learned discussion. At one point Dom Rudolph defined the vicar's heresy:

"You, Father, are an ochlocrat. No heresy in our time is more noxious than trying to implant ochlocracy in the Church. And that's what you're trying to do."

Dom Rudolph was a font of knowledge; but not only was Father Abelardo an ochlocrat, to top it off, he was unfamiliar with the term or its meaning. All he wanted was respect for the rights of tenants and smallholders. But he, too, had written treatises, he'd been an exemplary seminarian, they'd called him brilliant and seen a solid future for him, showered him with honors. Father Abelardo quoted Saint Ambrose, with the customary accent from the southern part of the country: "The land has been given to all, not just to the rich, the good that you claim has been given to all for the common good—" But before he got to the end of the sentence, Dom Rudolph cut him off, deflowering him with Scripture, silencing him with Latin: *"Redde Caesari quae sunt Caesaris, et quae sunt Dei Deo."*

The Ultimatum

When the owner of Santa Eliodora plantation, Colonel Joãozinho Costa, requested the removal and the immediate replacement of the vicar of Piaçava, the auxiliary bishop hadn't acceded to it. Even though Dona Eliodora Costa was a pillar of the church, a majestic one, the cardinal simply wouldn't have agreed to it.

In the opinion of the cardinal, the conflict in Piaçava, like so many others around the country, had its origin in the extreme and offensive poverty that existed there, and he couldn't avoid that fact. The Church should proceed with prudence, of course, but it must also recognize the facts. That was what the cardinal had told the auxiliary bishop when they decided to summon Father Abelardo Galvão to "clip his wings, but not cut off his head."

Dom Rudolph had promised, for his part, to put a damper on the priest's subversive activities—they were subversive, of course, according to Joãozinho Costa, the landowner. During a quiet conversation after a regal Sunday lunch that had brought the Costa family together to celebrate the confirmation of the youngest daughter, Marlene, the auxiliary bishop had preferred to characterize the vicar's activities as imprudent and impetuous rather than subversive. Joãozinho Costa had mentioned in passing that the Reverend Father was suspected to be involved with a certain young lady, the daughter of the state tax collector, who lived in Piaçava. This little fox, no doubt a busybody, would show up in Piaçava at the drop of a hat on the pretext of visiting her parents, to meddle in plantation matters, visiting tenants' homes—that is, when she wasn't visiting with our holy man behind the locked doors of the church. Her activities were already attracting attention.

Now that Dom Rudolph had finished with the ochlocracy and the Latin, the time for giving the ultimatum to Father Galvão had come: "Listen carefully, so that later on you won't say I didn't warn you, Father Galvão."

If the priest wanted to continue in the Lord's service in Piaçava, the auxiliary bishop told him, he would have to cease using His name in vain and stop his subversive activities once and for all. "Subversive" rather than imprudent, he called them—alone there with the vicar the conversation was different, he didn't moderate his adjectives. Father Abelardo would have to cease his Marxist preaching, unworthy of a man of the cloth, and go back to saving souls, not leading a gang of outlaws. God and the archdiocese had appointed him vicar; it would depend only on him, Father Galvão, whether he would continue in Piaçava. His activities would be observed step by step. Look after souls and practice charity— Dom Rudolph spoke with vehemence and conviction, the voice of command: He wasn't giving advice, he was issuing orders. He paused, then added:

"I also recommend that you exercise reserve in your relationships with women. They're beginning to arouse notice."

"Relationships with women? What relationships, tell me! I want to know!"

"It doesn't matter when or where, I'm not asking you and I'm not going to answer you. No, don't get up yet—we've got another matter to deal with." The explosive work was done, the wings clipped, but the neck not yet—the auxiliary bishop's voice lost its aggressive tone:

"Do you know anything regarding the whereabouts of the statue of Saint Barbara of the Thunder? It came Wednesday evening on the same boat—"

The question hung in the air unfinished. At the door to the anteroom, Father Soares asked permission to come in, waving a sheet of paper.

The Accusation

Father Soares placed the message in front of Dom Rudolph and stood waiting, his hands crossed over his stomach. When the auxiliary bishop finished reading, he raised his eyes:

"Is he on the phone?"

"Not yet. He had them call."

"Tell them I'll be right there."

Father Soares returned to the anteroom, and his voice could be heard announcing, "His Excellency will be on the line—you can put the call through." Dom Rudolph picked up the telephone on the corner of his desk, and sat waiting. It wasn't long before his voice became solicitous:

"Good morning, Colonel. How have you been? To what do I owe the pleasure of hearing your voice?" He listened, frowned: "Important and urgent? Tell me, please." He interrupted the party on the other end immediately to confirm: "I'm aware of it, yes. I was the one who advised him to go see you, Colonel. Don't you remember that I asked you to see him?" He smiled with the expectation of some good news, but the smile disappeared almost immediately. "What did you say? Yes, I know him, of course. . . ." He raised his eyes, fixed them on the vicar of Piaçava. "One moment, Colonel—I can't hear too well. I'm going to try another phone."

He got up and went into the anteroom. As he passed Father Abelardo, he said, "Wait for me, I won't be long." But he was long—the phone call went on and on. At a gesture from the bishop, Father Soares hung up the phone on the desk and closed the door between the two rooms.

The priest, now by himself, thought about the orders he'd received. The landowners had a long arm, a heavy hand.

Suddenly he was startled to see the auxiliary bishop in front of him, his fists clenched, still asking about the statue, as he'd started to ask before being called to the telephone. Now, however, Dom Rudolph's voice was choked and furious, and he was no longer asking a question but making an accusation, a most peculiar one:

"And the saint—what have you done with it?" He didn't even give the priest time to be startled, but ranted on: "The statue of Saint Barbara of the Thunder that came from Santo Amaro under your care—where did you take it? What have you done with it? Why did you steal it? Who are your accomplices? You've gone too far, Father Galvão."

A Snapshot of Patrícia in Daylight

Anyone who takes the trouble to look back to the beginning of this tale will remember that all Father Abelardo Galvão knew about Patrícia was her crystal-clear voice, her enigmatic smile, and her flirtatious eyes. Beyond that, little more has been said or learned about Patrícia. It is therefore incumbent on us to make up for this inept omission, dispensing with any attempt at justification as useless, any request for pardon— it's impossible to explain such negligence without recourse to wiles or treachery.

Perhaps some readers recognized her at the Axé of Alaketu, offering an *ebó* of blood to Yansan, mistress of her head. She'd closed her eyes at the moment the dagger, wielded by the *axógun*, had cut off the life and bleating of the goat. In fact, the strange girl had been Patrícia, and the goat had come from Colonel Joãozinho Costa's flock.

That was the same Joãozinho Costa, feudal lord, who had not cited her name but had furnished precise details that identified her quickly and unmistakably, in that quiet conversation with the auxiliary bishop of the archdiocese on that festive Sunday when His Excellency had confirmed Marlene Costa in the cathedral after the eleven o'clock mass. In his sermon Dom Rudolph had lauded the virtues that graced that Christian household.

Riding at a gallop, this was the same Patrícia who had come to Piaçava to visit her parents, dismounting near the little church of Piaçava before Father Abelardo's eyes, dim and eager. Because of the priest, Patrícia's name had appeared in the newspapers, outside the usual section for theater news and commentary.

But apart from these few references, nothing else has been said about her so far in this tale: maybe a few adjectives scattered here and there—beautiful, elegant, haughty. These generic adjectives are well deserved but they don't begin to portray her, to describe her, not physically and even less morally.

Was she tall or short, fat or thin, serious or smiling, large or small breasted? What was her behind like? Not even the color of her skin has been made clear—a mixture of Indians, blacks, and whites, a dusky color was mentioned—but what precisely was meant by that? Now the time has come, albeit a little late, to present the strange Patrícia in the full light of day, a day of offering, after the morning fog has lifted but before she's gotten dressed up, her hair combed, her face made up, and is under the glare of the spotlights.

As for the dusky color of her skin, it should have been transcribed as dark—the dark color of a jambo fruit—pardon the cliché, but there's no better comparison. Her long straight hair, black and shining, her shield-shaped, oriental face—these are the heritage of her Pataxó ancestry: prominent cheekbones, slanting eyes. Although slanting, they are light blue, aquamarine—and there stands another key: she had the eyes of a gringa, a European. Flirtatious eyes, Father Abelardo had defined them, his words hitting the mark in spite of his limited authority on the subject of women—the result of his vow of chastity, let it be assured at once, so as to avoid any misunderstanding. Had he been a bit more expert, he would have seen that Patrícia's flirtatious charms extended beyond her eyes to her whole body, that they were obvious in the swing of her breasts, in her nipples pressing against her cambric blouse, clearly visible in the sway of her derriere, barely covered by her miniskirt. Her behind was that of a black woman, *Deo gratia!*

She'd finished her course in French literature at the philosophy department, but she hadn't left the university because she'd gone on to enroll in the school of drama, where she was the favorite of the director, Nelson Araújo, the playwright and novelist, who discovered her true vocation, changed her name, and foresaw a brilliant future for her: She had been born for the footlights.

Patrícia had made her stage debut two years earlier, in a children's play; from that moment on she never stopped acting. In those two years she'd done everything—more children's plays, musicals, soap operas, tragedy and comedy, slapstick, Brazilian and foreign authors, she played any role that came along—the scant theatrical activity in the city left her no room for choice. In the movies she'd obtained—through the intervention of Nilda Spencer, another mentor who saw her talent and looked after her—a tiny role, a bit part, in a film by Nelson Pereira dos Santos, adapted from a Bahian novel. According to what Walter da Silveira, the big gun of movie criticism, had written, Patrícia stole her scene: If her part had been more important, she would have stolen the show.

With colleagues from the university who were intent on resisting the military dictatorship, she'd helped found the Arena Theater of Bahia, a dynamic but short-lived effort—one day the police came and put the whole troupe into a paddy wagon and drove them straight to jail. The girls were let out a few hours later, the boys in the middle of the night. The arrest had been brought on by the students' insistence on performing a play that was prohibited by the censors: They kept on rehearsing it anyway and put up a malicious poster on the front of the theater announcing the date of the opening. The poster was torn from the wall in shreds and reduced to scraps, and the young people had lived their moment of heroism, earning the right to a dossier in the Delegation for Political and Social Order, the DOPS, and the accompanying threats.

Patrícia frequented the Alliance Française, recited poems by Eluard —*"Liberté, j'écris ton nom"*—and dreamed of a fellowship to Paris when she wasn't dreaming about Father Abelardo. She chanced to bring the priest and Paris together in the same dream. She saw herself holding hands with him walking through the snow down the Boul'Mich amid the mad inhabitants of the Latin Quarter. *Des tourtereaux,* Professor João Batista would have said—the turtle doves. Speaking of Professor Batista, what's happened to him? Why has such a pleasant figure been permitted to disappear from our tale? Let us just point out that the professor knew Patrícia and figured among her admirers, praising her French pronunciation, her *charme,* and her gifts as an actress. He prophesied that one day yet, she'd be performing Racine's *Phèdre.*

Patrícia in the Dressing Room

It was not because of any scruples, bashfulness, or negligence on Patrícia's part that Father Abelardo knew only her crystal-clear voice, her enigmatic smile, and her flirtatious eyes. Oh, if it had depended on her, on her alone! The voice that broke off midsentence, the lost look, the ambiguous smile, the thoughtfulness, and the sigh—she had tried everything.

She herself had never been an easy conquest, had demanded to be courted, made love to, seduced—she wasn't the kind who went straight to bed. On only one occasion had she felt herself consumed by desire, aroused, unable to think or reflect. That passion, just like the one she now tendered for the priest, had lasted during the Bahian run of a play by Boal: besides being nice-looking, however, her old swain was stuck-up. Abelardo, on the other hand, was not only just as nice-looking, but was a marvelous person. Patrícia didn't know anyone who could compare to him. He had a pure and generous heart, lucid intelligence, and in the struggle to eliminate the causes of poverty, there was no firmer, or more compelling voice. And his southerner's hair—she had a perpetual urge to run her fingers through his blond, wavy locks, to stroke him behind the ears. But her beloved, alas, stayed cold and distant—he didn't perceive the fever that was devouring Patrícia's womb.

The relationship between student and priest had been born of their shared interest in improving the living conditions of tenants and small-holders and the landless; it had been fed by endless conversations about politics and literature, music, film, and theater; by discussions of world events and the sufferings of the Brazilian people, of the imprisonments, torture, resistance; of the preachings of the archbishop of Recife and Olinda, and the deeds of the urban guerrilla fighter Carlos Marighela. They had become intimate and affectionate, but it was the intimacy of brotherly affection. They were kindred souls, he would say.

Sometimes, for a few fleeting moments, Patrícia thought she caught glimpses of desire, sparks of an urge in the priest's eyes, in the quaver of his voice, most of all in his sudden silences. Yet these were brushfires, and not long-lasting: he would immediately get back on the track of brotherhood. He seemed not to have noticed the heaving of her breasts, or seen the curve of her open neck line, or felt the contact of her knee, the quickened rate of her breathing. Didn't he understand, or didn't he want to understand? Was he indifferent, insensitive to her womanly charms, or was he timid, fearful of the forbidden?

Patrícia had never believed priests could really be faithful to their vows of celibacy, much less modern priests in blue jeans and flowered shirts involved in social problems, heading up communal actions, rising up in wrath against landowners and the bourgeoisie, men of the left. Celibacy? That was something out of a long-dead past, like a girl's virginity before marriage, based on prejudices.

In her dressing room, sorting out skirts, blouses, slacks, and the white dress of a Baiana—clothes that she would wear during the five upcoming days of filming with a French crew—she felt a coldness in her womb when she thought of the television program. On that Thursday morning, at the same time that Father Abelardo Galvão was discussing doctrine with the auxiliary bishop, Patrícia was bringing his name up in a conversation with Sylvia Esmeralda, a fellow student, friend, and confidante.

Sylvia Esmeralda was the *nom de guerre* of an outstanding social butterfly who had been bitten by the theater bug; she followed the episodes of suffering passion that Patrícia related with amused curiosity: Indeed, Patrícia couldn't talk about anything else but Father Abelardo, as if the priest were the last man on earth. And this was just when she had a whole crew of Frenchmen at her disposal: To have had the director, who was quite famous, would have been a crowning glory for her, a plum!

For his name alone he was worth a try, and the affair could have built up the biography of a star of stage and screen.

"As I figure it," Patrícia told her confidante, "he must have arrived in Bahia by now. He promised to look me up when he got here. It could be that right here—"

"What?"

"You've got to know, Sylvia, I'm going to get that priest even if I have to drag him along by the wrist. I've never run across a more dogged fool!"

Sylvia Esmeralda held her hand out under the light and examined her nails, painted dark red:

"Not *dogged,* my dear—*dogma.* The dogma of chastity. He's locked up, there's no way out. You'll see—he's still a virgin."

"A virgin?"

It seemed impossible. A man like that—why, he must have been pushing thirty! But now that Patrícia thought of it, it might just be; unbelievable things happen when you least expect them. Patrícia bit her lip, her eyes distracted, pensive.

"Virgin, the poor thing—" her voice faint, breaking: "Well, if he is a virgin, he won't be for long. I swear it on the salvation of my soul!"

She made a cross of her fingers and kissed it.

"God will help me."

"Heretic!" Sylvia Esmeralda said in order to say something intelligent; her mind was on the Frenchman.

La Chanson de Bahia

The famous Frenchman in question, the old guy who was in such great shape that he disturbed Sylvia Esmeralda's thoughts, was Jacques Chancel. Strolling through the byways of the historic city, collecting the final details for the filming of another segment of *Le Grand Échiquier:* He would begin filming it that Thursday afternoon. The broadcast would last two hours and fifteen minutes, all of it devoted to the life and customs of the city of Bahia: *candomblé, capoeira, samba de roda, blocos,* and *afoxés,* the sea, the people, and the music. *La Chanson de Bahia—* Chancel had announced the segment title at a news conference upon his arrival.

Three years before, Chancel had traveled to Brazil with a group of stars of the RTF—Radio and Television of France—to take part in the presentation of the Molière prizes in Rio and São Paulo. On his journey back to Paris he had stopped off in Bahia for a short stay of two days to interview Vinícius de Moraes, who was living in Itapuã at the time, for another of his programs, this one on radio. At the home of the poet he'd met Dorival Caymmi, listened to his sea songs and sambas, and fallen in love with them.

When Chancel learned that Caymmi was the patriarch of a whole flock of songwriters, he asked Nilda Spencer, at whose home he was eating a lunch of native dishes, to help him get to know some of those Bahian songs that everybody was talking about. Nilda picked out a dozen LPs, and both before and after the *caruru* and the *vatapá*, the guest of honor sat by the stereo listening to a fabulous songfest with the voices of Maria Betânia, Gal Costa, Maria Creusa, and the composers themselves.

Those who had been invited to lunch to chat with Chancel had to forgive him his lack of attention to them; at the end of the afternoon he would leave for Rio, where he'd change planes for Paris, so he had to make good use of his time. The brief moments of conversation, nevertheless, were worth the trouble because the celebrated director made a heartfelt declaration of love for the city that had so dazzled him with its ancient beauty, its magical atmosphere, and the power of the life of its people. He marveled at the music he'd just heard and revealed his intention of showing the city and the people of Bahia to French audiences; he would devote an upcoming segment of *Le Grand Échiquier* to them—and the program had a record-breaking number of viewers, as his friends were no doubt aware.

Intention, no—an irrevocable decision, made there, on the spot: As soon as he got back to Paris, he would quickly make the necessary arrangements to return immediately for the filming. Nilda Spencer clapped her hands enthusiastically, and the Frenchman gave her a list of chores. To begin with, she was to meet with Vinícius de Moraes so that he, with the necessary urgency, could prepare the script for the program in all its details. Having spoken, the heralded visitor took his leave amid kisses and embraces: *à bientôt!*

The following day, when Nilda hurried to see him to give him the job of writing the script—"The man wants it as quickly as possible, dear poet!" Vinícius laughed at her innocence. "My darling Nilda, forget all about it, don't follow up on anything, don't make any promises, don't waste your time, don't put your prestige on the line. If you do, you'll be sorry for it." He took her hand and kissed it affectionately, then continued.

Didn't she know how things were with these foreigners? They come to Brazil, they get all enthusiastic, they land in Bahia, they fall in love with it, they decide to do all kinds of things, they announce musicals, television programs, movies, the devil knew what else. The enthusiasm is real, the intentions are good. It's just that after they climb aboard the plane back to Paris or New York, our old friends are into other things, and we never hear from them again. Jacques Chancel had flipped over Bahia, and he'd genuinely love to make a program with the music of people from here, he wasn't bluffing when he said that. But right now, in Paris, he doesn't even remember yesterday's conversation. Even if he did remember, he wouldn't have time, busy as he is with a thousand different things, my lovely Nilda.

Nilda mentioned *Black Orpheus*, the film by Marcel Camus adapted from the play by Vinícius. What about that? It was the exception that proved the rule, Vinícius replied: There'd be no repetition. "But don't be sad, sweet—listen to this song about Itapuã that Toquinho and I just put together." He took a sip of whiskey, picked up his guitar.

The actress followed the poet's advice, although she did so with a deathly sad heart: A program dedicated to Bahia on a show as important as *Le Grand Échiquier* seemed like the greatest of projects to her, and the fantastic idea had been born at a lunch in her own house—she felt it belonged to her, and she wanted to see it carried out. But Vinícius had had more experience, he was shrewd, and Nilda didn't take long to acknowledge her mistake: She got tired of waiting for word from the Frenchman, who showed not a sign of life.

She'd gotten over her disappointment and completely forgotten the matter when, lo and behold, three years after the lunch, she received a telegram from Paris signed Jacques Chancel, announcing the arrival in Bahia four days thence of one Guy Blanc, a movie and television producer and technician, whose job was to set up the show for *Le Grand Échiquier*. Chancel himself would arrive a week later with the rest of the crew. The long telegram talked about the program as if only a few days and not three years had passed since the lunch and the initial conversation: He asked her to get in touch with Vinícius and let him know, and to pick up the script from him. Nilda was floating on air, happy as could be —she often liked to say that life is surreal. There was only one thing wrong: Vinícius wasn't in town, he'd left on a trip to Argentina and Uruguay, so they couldn't count on him for the script.

A competent and efficient producer, Guy Blanc lost no time; as soon as he landed, he started the project up at full speed. He flew about the city in Miro's taxi, which he hired for the use of the crew. As popular and well-liked as Nilda was, her connections were most helpful to him: the governor, the mayor, the cardinal, and the *mães de santo* all pledged their help; artists and composers became his pals; she got him everything he needed and then some. She made two suggestions, that Guy Blanc immediately accepted: hire Nelson Araújo for the script, and hire Patrícia da Silva Vaalserberg as translator for the crew.

When he arrived, Jacques Chancel approved all the producer's decisions, except for the one concerning Patrícia. As soon as he saw her, a
dark girl with blue eyes, Pataxó and Dutch, and heard her speak a
healthy French with an irresistible Brazilian accent, he promoted Patrícia
das Flores to be his assistant. Her sensual and exotic beauty, seen and
unseen, he recognized, and he proclaimed that no one else was so perfect
to serve as *partenaire* in the presentation of the program: *"tout le monde
sera envouté,"* everyone would be spellbound by her.

The Virtues of Olímpia

A simple soul, an upright man, Colonel Joãozinho Costa is the
owner of the Santa Eliodora plantation, not to speak of other rural and
urban properties that we shall not mention here out of regard for discretion. Because of his natural modesty—or perhaps because of an understandable prudence about income taxes—he doesn't like to see any
public mention of his holdings.

The one who described him so rigorously was his esteemed son-in-
law and counselor, Dr. Astério de Castro, a successful public works con-
tractor and the happy husband of Olímpia, Joãozinho Costa's eldest
daughter. Olímpia was monumental in size, yet nimble. When the journalist Augusto Bastos, better known as Gugu Bosta ("Gooey Crap") met
her at a lively cocktail party held in honor of the new headquarters of
Castro Real Estate and Construction, Ltd., he had lost his bearings,
thrown caution to the wind, and came away proclaiming, "She's just like
an airplane, an airplane!" On assignment for Dr. Castro, the journalist
wrote small pieces in praise of the government; Dr. Castro signed them,
and they were published as letters to the editor in newspapers. These
pieces and Olímpia's unselfishness were the two master keys upon which
Dr. Castro relied to open even the most tightly closed doors—and coffers
—of the state.

Since Olímpia has taken a jet flight and landed in this tale, we will
speak of her forthwith, but we will postpone the details of a conversation
that occurred a week before between her father and her husband, even
though it is a leading thread of the plot. Because she's a woman and
because she's so impetuous, knowing how to get what she wants,
Olímpia warrants preference, the primacy in the sequence here. When
Dom Rudolph gave his sermon at Marlene's confirmation, he didn't go
into detail about the personal virtues of each member of the Costa family; had he done so, we would already have known about Olímpia's

altruism, her spirit of personal sacrifice, and her limitless dedication to her husband.

Being an airplane, a big woman in all respects—she favored her father—with her tall stature, her showy facade, her spectacular body, her fearless character, Olímpia marched around surrounded by desirous suitors—not after her hand, obviously, she'd been married for over three years, but rather desirous of her queen-size pussy. It was known that she put out and that her husband covered his ears, closed his eyes, unperturbed by it. Olímpia could choose from among all the young and ardent studs the one who seemed best to her. Witnesses, however, emphasized the care with which Olímpia selected her lovers. Disdaining pretty boys and gentlemen alike, she favored those at the highest reaches of power: and of those she had a wide range of the shining lights—a governor, a minister, a general on active service, and a troop commander.

Let no one raise any false morality here, or deny the virtue of her selectiveness. A devoted wife, Olímpia sacrificed herself in bed to ensure her husband the blessed contracts, the ones that made for so much talk among his envious vilifiers. It was a sacrifice, yes, because going to bed and engaging in coitus with some of those disgusting specimens demanded a strong stomach indeed. A strong stomach, and a strong character: Olímpia had them both, it was a proven fact. She'd married Astério de Castro with full knowledge of what she was doing. Astério, not being what you would call a handsome man, boasted of being an ethical man, that is, one capable of accepting and digesting anything that served his ambition.

In order to compensate for her repeated martyrdom, Olímpia developed a taste for adolescents. She liked boys in school uniforms—except that school uniforms no longer exist, let's correct that right now —boys *al primo canto,* youngsters. She had talents as a teacher, and she understood her subject matter. Olímpia, an airplane.

The Holy Missions

Dr. Astério de Castro fastened his puffy frog eyes on his father-in-law, who was a simple soul, an upright man.

"Call off your gunman—buy his silence, send him away," he said.

The son-in-law's influence took over. His bulging eyes and the chiding tone of his voice silenced the upright Joãozinho Costa in the middle of his outrage. Dr. Astério, for his part, got the meaning, the significance of these words confused: He saw no difference between *upright* and *right,* maybe because of their similarity. In any case, he wanted to temper the plantation owner's impulsive manner, the haste with which he took recourse to extreme measures. It was more a defect than a virtue, and Dr. Castro's esteem for his father-in-law was tempered by a touch of disdain. Between the two lay an historical era: Joãozinho Costa was still living in medieval, feudal Brazil, where strength and command were enough to come out on top. Dr. Astério Castro, on the other hand, worked in industrial, modern Brazil, undergoing the process of development: for him, in order to win, you had to work with your head and use your fists only as a last resort.

"Only as a last resort—remember that! Otherwise, you'll be creating a martyr, when what you want to do is unmask him as a hypocrite, a scoundrel. Use your head." He blew a puff of smoke from his Cuban cigar, a costly bit of contraband, the privilege of fat cats and high governmental officials: "Didn't you tell me that the priest is involved with a girl, the one who works in the theater? I even got her name coupled with the little priest's in Gugu Bosta's scandal sheet: you asked me to, remember? That the Reverend Father was shacking up—I saw the girl onstage the other day, she's not bad. She pronounces every dirty word with the sweetest face in the world—and has she got a body, boy, I can't begin to tell you. She came on half naked." He stuck his tongue out of his flabby mouth, squinted his frog eyes, and put on an indecent, pornographic face. "Call off your gunman, Papa Joãozinho. Leave the priest to me."

Joãozinho Costa had seen no other way out after his conversation with the auxiliary bishop had convinced him that Father Galvão wouldn't be removed from Piaçava. Added to that, the priest had taken a trip to the capital where he could easily be bumped off, and the event wouldn't take place in the backlands, let alone inside the boundaries of his plantation. It would be that much harder to accuse him of having ordered the job. In lower-class church circles, at mass, during the sermon, red priests already blamed him for the deaths of the three bandits who'd resisted expulsion from Santa Eliodora plantation. So a gunman seemed his only alternative, and he'd sent to the backlands of Pernambuco for Zé do Lírio, an old acquaintance, a man of trust, who carried impeccable credentials.

"Have you thought, Papa Joãozinho," Dr. Astério said, "about the look on Dom Rudolph's face when he gets a photograph of the Reverend Father and the girl naked in a motel room? Think of his face and the cardinal's—make no mistake about it, he's the pismire who's been giving a free hand to those subversive priests." He laughed through the cigar smoke, savoring in advance the cardinal's reaction once he found his back against the wall. "He won't have any other way out except to bury the priest in some monastery, send him far away. If necessary, I'll have the picture printed in Bosta's paper—on the front page, Papa Joãozinho, for everyone to see!" He kept on laughing with his flabby mouth: described in his whining voice, the predicted nudity took on an obscene, filthy character.

"And who's going to get those pictures? How are you going to get the priest with some dame into a motel? They're not dummies."

"What you lack is a little imagination, my dear friend and father-in-law. Leave it up to me, as I said, and don't worry. For this holy mission, I've got competent people at my disposal, people with experience."

Joãozinho Costa swallowed his questions—he preferred not to know. He was afraid to get mixed up in certain activities of his son-in-law, in dark, upsetting areas. Rumors circulated constantly about the businessman's connections with the SNI, the National Information Service. What were his connections in the underground chambers of the highest, most secret power? Was he a big wheel, or just an informer? Joãozinho Costa didn't want to know, it was better that way.

Mafioso and Informer, without quotation marks, printed in big letters, was the title of the article on Dr. Astério de Castro that Ariovaldo Matos had run on the front page of his weekly some time ago. It had covered his political career, from his renegade Communist youth to becoming a supporter of the military coup, one of its brain trust in Bahia; his lucrative business deals, his public life. Of bribery, corruption, and the public works mafia, there was proof by the carload: It had been a true horror story. No direct reference had been made to the SNI—Ariovaldo was crazy, but not that crazy—nor was it necessary. Whom did the informer work for, who employed him? The answer was obvious to any reader. Nor was any allusion made to Olímpia, directly or indirectly, not even the shadow of an insinuation: Whether his subject was a commie or a full-fledged loony, after all, Ariovaldo was a gentleman of the old school.

On that occasion, Joãozinho Costa, indignant over the exposé, had announced to his son-in-law that he intended to see that a few lumps were delivered to Ariovaldo Matos, who had both written and published it. Astério had thanked him but refused the favor: Even back then he'd told him, "Leave it to me." It wasn't long before Ariovaldo's weekly found its circulation cut off. This should have caused no one any surprise, because for some time beforehand, Dona Norma Martins, in conversation with Adalgisa, had been predicting it. But she'd not foreseen the prison sentence handed down to Ariovaldo, or even his being put on trial. The charges brought against him didn't include writing the explosive article on Dr. Castro but included Ariovaldo's involvement in the outlawed student Congress and his coverage of bloody repression; also, he had incited city transit workers to strike, which was quite illegal. Still, Joãozinho Costa wasn't fooled—he saw Astério's hand in the closing down of the rag and the imprisonment of its editor: a heavy hand, a cat's paw.

But, once again his son-in-law was intervening to hold him back, to curb his actions, veto them. But this time it wasn't a matter of lumps— the sentence he wanted to carry out was appropriate to the crime the priest had committed. Still, although he was not entirely convinced that the strategy would succeed, Joãozinho Costa finally agreed to it; he, too, enjoyed the prospect of the cardinal's face, known to be prissy, when he got the photograph. "Save a copy of it for me," he told his son-in-law. "I want to show it to the people of Piaçava. Those louts are all set to pull their statue of Saint Joseph down out of his niche and put the priest up there in his place."

The Underlying Reason

Even though he'd agreed, Joãozinho Costa didn't consider the holy mission that he'd entrusted to Zé do Lírio dropped. He left it in abeyance for the time, waiting to see how Astério's crazy plan worked out. He told the gunman to wait for new orders, and Zé do Lírio reported to him that he would take advantage of the postponement to memorize the face of the doomed man, engraving it deeply in the pupils of his eyes. That he wasn't good at faces was his only professional deficiency.

Mixed in with Joãozinho Costa's esteem for his son-in-law there was also a touch of disdain. He recognized his virtues, and he praised those that were laudable to all comers. It was better, however, to remain silent about others. For his tastes as an upright man and a simple soul, a backlands boss and a landowner, Astério de Castro was too spineless: an ass-kisser, a bootlicker, a doormat. The major reason, however, for his disdain toward his son-in-law was so delicate that he kept it deep in his breast, never referring to it. In spite of the commitment to truth that presides over this chronicle, we hesitate to proclaim it even here. The fact is that Joãozinho Costa despised cuckolds, passive husbands; they were the favorite targets of his derision and mockery. But as it was, the horns in his own family were plunging into his throat, choking him. He didn't blame Olímpia: she'd inherited her stature and promiscuity from him. He blamed her dunce of a husband, incapable of satisfying and restraining her.

In the exposé, Ariovaldo Matos had used burning words to describe Astério: terrifying, sinister. He had the terrifying physique of a bullfrog, the sinister character of a vampire. When the columnist of the *Semana do Jet-Set* had asked Olímpia to describe her husband in one sentence,

"A man of honor, a knight in shining armor," the faithful wife had replied. "A man of ethics," he'd described himself. Dr. Astério de Castro —quite a character!

The Curtain

In the empty room on the second floor of the palace, Dom Rudolph was wholly absorbed. When he came to, he found himself looking out the window: There was the black woman again, in the same spot, a statue, baring her teeth, laughing at him. His Excellency drew the curtain and shuddered as drops of sweat dampened his forehead. It had been a disastrous morning, full of all sorts of problems: the statue that had disappeared, the scandal in the newspapers, the suspicions of the police, the priest's indignant denial of his involvement, the prospect of a meeting with Colonel Raul Antônio—the auxiliary bishop was caught between the devil and the deep blue sea, no doubt about it. How far could a cleric like Father Abelardo go on the road to heresy without being stopped? In the headiness of his temptation, sipping the poison of Marxist doctrines, would the priest still respect the sacred commandments? Although he prayed according to the catechism of ochlocracy, however, Father Galvão did possess one virtue: He didn't hide his ideas, he didn't conceal his actions, he kept his position out in the open. He didn't lie.

After Father Abelardo left, His Excellency had sent for Dom Maximiliano. When all was said and done, the director of the Museum of Sacred Art was the one responsible for the statue; since if it hadn't been for his whims, dictated as they were by vanity, Saint Barbara of the Thunder would have peacefully remained in Purificação Church in Santo Amaro. Slowly, fearfully, Dom Rudolph lifted the corner of the curtain again and peered out. The black woman stuck out her tongue at him. Get thee behind me, Satan!

The Procession

Father Abelardo Galvão left the Archbishop's palace through the same door through which Father Eliseu Madeira of the Works of Piety entered, hurried but smiling broadly. They nodded in greeting although they didn't know each other. In the immediate vicinity of the palace, only a few people stirred when they saw the vicar of Piaçava pass. Elói, the seminarian on watch duty, took advantage of the coming and going to take a peek at a movement he saw on the square: What a pretty black girl, wow! Bené, the sexton, whispered that black women are the hottest . . . The urchin approached, on the run.

Still steaming from Dom Rudolph's accusations, Father Abelardo changed his clothes, then went to look for Patrícia. "I'm easy to find at the drama school," she had said. He set out for Misericórdia.

As he walked, five people followed in his path, keeping their distance more or less, yet dogging his heels in a ridiculous procession.

Inspector Parreirinha led the group, picked his teeth casually so as not to be conspicuous, but the bulge of his revolver lifted the hem of his jacket and the butt was showing. "There goes Inspector Parreirinha on the trail of some poor devil," a marijuana pusher pointed out to his chum as they headed down around the curve in the sloping street.

Next in the parade came two cops from the Federal Police, one seedier-looking than the other. They kept apart from each other so as not to attract attention, but stayed in touch by means of sophisticated Japanese walkie-talkies, the last word in surveillance equipment. They made a surprising amount of fuss nevertheless, startling passers-by. Bringing up the rear, came a character in a raincoat and wide-brimmed hat, with dark glasses added to the classic getup of a gunman. On the trail of the priest to get a closer look at him, Zé do Lírio didn't want to run any risks once the orders finally came for him to carry out the contract.

The fifth in the parade, the black woman, sometimes took the lead, passing the priest, and sometimes kept pace with the Federal Police cops, the static crackling on their tiny walkie-talkies. In one encounter, she almost knocked Inspector Parreirinha over. It was easy to see that she was having great fun. When Father Abelardo stopped for a moment before City Hall, she rushed ahead and waited for him on the terrace by the Lacerda Elevator, sitting at a table in the bar that overlooked the bay, savoring a cherry sherbet.

While the vicar of Piaçava was admiring City Hall—such perfection! —the rest of the paraders waited too: The cops stood at attention, the gunman rested, the inspector shifted from one foot to the other. The police were following the vicar to find out where he was staying, where he was going, and whom he was meeting and to pick up any new leads before they arrested him. The gunman fixed his face firmly in his mind so as not to err with his shot.

The black woman went over to the balustrade and opened her arms out over the sea and the city. As she did so, on that sunny, clear, splendid morning, a strange flash of lightning broke, a dagger strike. The sky became tinged with purple from the paint on Oyá's necklaces and bracelets, then filled with shadows, thick and heavy. The black woman dissolved into the darkness.

The roar of thunderclaps rolled over the palace, deafening the world. Behind the priest, night closed in: He disappeared in the blinding light. Poof!

Nuptial Night(s)

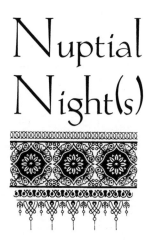

Invitation to the Hymen

In the confusion reigning at City Hall Square, in the pitch blackness, Inspector Parreirinha is knocking down pedestrians, the Federal Police cops are trying to turn on their Yankee flashlights (a gift from the CIA, they aren't working because they'd forgotten about batteries), and the gunman is reciting a prayer of exorcism. Let us take advantage of this darkness at noon to pick up on the newlyweds Adalgisa and Danilo again. On the Valença wharf they are nervously waiting for the boat, holding hands. Night falls at its proper time, a moonless night, a widow's night.

There may be some readers who have been waiting with uncontainable impatience for this chapter of intrigue, on the hymen. If others find the following description of the wedding night too overblown, for the same reasons it will please still others. History isn't made up only of priests and bishops, it doesn't feed only on theological questions. A nice story where sex doesn't exist, either openly or disguised, as a motive for joy and suffering, as the fountain of life, has yet to be written—not even the Bible escapes it. Quite the contrary.

Since this part of the story goes on longer than we had originally foreseen, the writing will be slow. But the blame for this rests on Adalgisa, who didn't want to fulfill the ritual in its proper time, and to Danilo, who didn't know how. The ideal would have been for them to do it before the wedding, at the time of their betrothal. We have already pointed this out, and there's no reason to repeat ourselves here. Puritanism took over and prevented it, and that was that. Now, however, Danilo and Adalgisa are married, with a certificate and a ring, and the long-awaited ceremony of the hymen is about to begin. The invitations have been sent out. Anyone who doesn't care to attend can skip these pages.

The Transistor Radio

Luckily, Danilo had brought his battery radio to the island of São Paulo Bluff, the little transistor set he had taken along to soccer games ever since his high-scoring career had ended. He would watch each match while listening to the heavy-handed baritone commentary of França Teixeira; in those days gone by, the young and already popular but still impecunious sportscaster was still a dyed-in-the-wool Ipiranga rooter. A fan and friend of Danilo's, he'd always given him his best and had contributed in great measure to popularizing his name: He grew ecstatic over Danilo's plays, credited him with wins, and even invented the celebrated nickname of Danilo, Prince of the Playing Field.

Reduced to the essentials, Danilo's honeymoon necessities fit into a hand satchel: swimming trunks, two pairs of shorts, two T-shirts with the Ipiranga emblem for strolling in the village and mingling with the vacationers, pajamas, and a pair of Japanese sandals. To make up for her husband's simplicity, Adalgisa had filled one of her father's large suitcases, as if the honeymoon were going to last a month and were to be in Copacabana or Honolulu: a batch of dresses for morning, afternoon, and evening; three pairs of shoes, one with high heels; two brand-new bathing suits and a bikini, a gift from Dolores (she didn't want to be square, nobody wore one-piece suits anymore); a variety of drawers, slips, petticoats, blouses, and skirts; half a dozen nightgowns—even though he wanted her naked in bed, without a shred to hide the smallest detail of her magnificent body! At the last moment Danilo had packed his radio in the hand satchel along with his clothes, an inspiration from heaven.

Having brought the radio on Saturday was what enabled Danilo to get through Sunday afternoon: listening to the interstate game between Bahia and Santos. Pelé had broken things up, with three goals, each more improbable than the one before, the third one impossible to describe. França Teixeira had lost control of what he was saying. So remarkable in fact that they kept Danilo glued to the radio, so he didn't go over and interrupt the deep sleep that Adalgisa had succumbed to after lunch. Asleep on the couch, she breathed sensually, her breast rising and falling: her bra and blouse concealing the mark left by his avid lips, a purplish-blue blemish starting at her left nipple.

King Pelé's maneuvers were such works of genius that they diverted Danilo's thoughts from the events of the night before. The events of the night before, the nuptial night—oh, woe! Alas!

Roundelay on the Ferry

Darkness had fallen over the sea on Saturday evening by the time the ferry from Valença reached the small dock at the base of São Paulo Bluff—the bluff that gave the enchanted isle its name—and the newlyweds disembarked.

Pitch-black, a new moon, Adalgisa and Danilo were barely able to make out their fellow passengers, crowded together inside for the day's last trip. All of them were weekend habitués of the homes along the beach, the miles of fine, white sand, beaten by the waves—it could only be compared to paradise. They all knew each other and had lively conversations as they made plans to get together on Sunday. Danilo isolated himself with Adalgisa on the stern of the ferry. A woman nudged her neighbor and whispered, "Newlyweds," and they both laughed.

The May breezes grew stronger after dusk and caused Adalgisa to seek shelter nestled beside the athletic chest of her boyfriend—no, boyfriend no longer, husband now, with a sealed document and a ring on the fourth finger of his left hand. She reclined against her husband's masculine chest—her husband, her master, her lord, her man, she thought—in search of comfort, warmth, security. Her head rested on Danilo's shoulder, so recognizably a new bride, and she closed her eyes and tried to calm herself down.

Danilo wrapped her trembling body inside the jacket of his brand-new blue tropical suit, which had been cut and made to order for the wedding by Gustavo Reis, the tailor for the Sampaio family, who had a large clientele. It was quite expensive: the one who paid the bill was Dr. Artur Sampaio, a patron of sufficient wealth. As Danilo made her comfortable with the jacket, he took advantage of the moment and rested his hand on the breast that stood out beneath the silk blouse: Adalgisa had changed clothes before they departed, leaving her bridal gown behind on her spinster's bed. She jumped at his touch and shook her bosom as if she'd received an electric shock. Was it only the cold, or was it fear that was making her tremble? Adalgisa squeezed Danilo's arm.

Slyly, he grasped her hand and pulled it along to his crotch, placing it, palm down, over the lump that was threatening to break the buttons and free itself, so anxious and ready was it. Adalgisa didn't realize immediately where he'd placed her hand—she even felt comforted by the concentrated warmth emanating from there—but when she felt a nervous throbbing under her fingers, she understood that something else was under his pants besides his thigh. She quickly withdrew her hand and brought it up to her mouth to muffle her exclamation—a wail, ooh! —less of revulsion than of fright. Danilo, incorrigible, took advantage of her frightened movement to put his tongue in her ear, inside and out, an unprecedented bit of boldness. A shudder ran through Adalgisa's body from top to bottom, and her voice broke:

"Please! People are watching—"

"Come on! Nobody's looking."

But she looked at him with such pleading eyes that Danilo gave up, and for a few minutes nothing noteworthy happened. He was reduced to delivering a sincere and passionate discourse, with eloquent, seductive words, a string of romantic and radio clichés to which his bride listened with obvious pleasure and growing temptation: "Dadá, you're the high-noon sun of my day, the pole star of my night," he recited in a warm, enveloping voice.

When the ferry pulled up at the dock of the island, Adalgisa, melting with emotion, laid her head on her husband's chest again and put her arms around his neck. Danilo kissed her softly on the face and moved along slowly from kiss to kiss until he got to her ear. He used his tongue and took the lobe in his mouth, a trick. Dadá didn't stop him or protest, even as he slowly bit her lobe.

The ferry bumped alongside the dock, and the passengers got up. Adalgisa straightened herself, embarrassed. Danilo extended his hand to help her leap off. She held out her fingers, smiling confusedly. The time of the crossing had seemed so short.

—&—&

The Discord

Indeed, it had been a short trip, full of daring and caring, the difficult apprenticeship of a wife's obligations, of the conquest of pleasure. Adalgisa sighed as they disembarked.

For Danilo, it had been forty dull minutes in the solitude of the sea in which he had had to hold back his desire. He'd chewed on the reins, so to speak, to avoid taking the bit in his teeth; he'd killed time making declarations of love, eager to claim his newly acquired rights, to take possession of Dadá's charms and pudenda, to break her in, make a woman of her—his woman.

Once the two of them found themselves all alone in the bedroom, he thought, there would be no more witnesses, limitations, complaints, or pleading looks. His small successes on the crossing he didn't even consider an appetizer, an antipasto; he could do without tidbits on the menu—he wanted to start right in on the main course, which was nothing more nor less than Adalgisa's cherry. It wasn't that he disdained refinements, the quintessences, the niceties, or wished to abstain from them: On the contrary, he appreciated them very much and practiced them faithfully. But there was more than enough time to enjoy them with Dadá—they had their whole life ahead of them.

Acceding to his bride's bashfulness and prudery, yielding to them, even valuing them, he'd waited for over a year now, eating the bread the devil had kneaded, anticipating the moment when he could "pluck the flower of maidenhood in the garden of beauty and innocence," as a poet he knew put it, or as it were, gobble up the pussy of the most beautiful and chaste damsel in Bahia. His commitment had cost him, along with bitter abstinence, the freedom of his bachelor life. He'd taken a job, become a serious person, assumed responsibilities, said goodbye to carousing, to the good life, to bohemia. Now he could claim what was his, and he was in a hurry to do it.

What would finally happen when they confronted each other in the boudoir at the moment of truth? Dadá had wondered as the boat rocked. Her godmother, Doña Esperanza, had explained some of it to her after Danilo had gotten the job in the notary's office, and they had decided on a date for the wedding. Then there'd been a postponement of the wedding announcement caused, as a matter of fact, by the sudden death of her godmother—oh, what a misfortune! It was inexpressible how much Adalgisa missed her.

Doña Esperanza had recommended that Adalgisa submit patiently at the crucial moment; moreover, physical pain would worsen her shame; a woman must prepare to suffer, *hijita mía*, when she renounces the most valuable thing she possesses in the eyes of God—the purity of her body, her virginity. The possession of the wife by the husband isn't listed in the roll of sins because the sacrament of matrimony has sanctified it, but nor does it cease to be a cruel and obscene act.

Adalgisa should be especially watchful of the prohibitions and limitations that Holy Mother Church imposes on the sexual relations of married couples, so as not to break them and run the risk of seeing herself suddenly excommunicated, Doña Esperanza told her. "There are depraved men—*la mayoría, mi niña*—who abuse the innocence of poor creatures and are not ashamed to drag their wives down paths of lust and licentiousness as if they were prostitutes! Those are the paths of ignominy and perdition! Think of your guardian angel, always by your side, to witness your every action." Her godmother didn't clarify what was permitted and what was prohibited, and Adalgisa didn't dare ask; she was too shy.

She did know some things, however. Marilu, one of her more knowledgeable classmates, an amusing and gabby girl, had tried to tempt her with the pleasures of smoking grass and suggested introducing her to some generous executives who paid big money to be jerked off or sucked off. The artful Marilu flaunted her worldliness, both theoretical and practical. Not only was she familiar with a crude version of the *Kama Sutra* published in a cheap edition, she'd read the hottest pages of a translation of *Sexus* by Henry Miller, and she'd even heard of Freud. As for practice, she had plenty—enough to give away, and more to sell.

Adalgisa wasn't corrupted by marijuana; nor did she put out. She tried tobacco just once but didn't like it, and no business magnate ever saw her face, much less her body. But she did continue to learn from her classmate what such things were and how they were done. She listened to Marilu's gibes about couples who limited their sexual encounters to the pure and simple "mama and papa" position, so ridiculed by distinguished sexologists, specialists in the matter, on radio programs with large audiences. It was the classic position, according to authorities, and furthermore, it was accepted by the canons of the Church, which accepted and even blessed fornication. "Fucking," Marilu corrected, dispensing with erudition. Yet it was only accepted if practiced with the exclusive aim of reproducing the human species—everything else was sin and infamy.

Two halves of the same orange was what people said Adalgisa and Danilo were, because of their identical tastes, because as many sweethearts did, they always seemed to think and act alike. As far as sexual relations were concerned, however, their disagreement was total and complete. They had two different conceptions of life and love—an ancient, age-old controversy.

There was no craft, no hypocrisy in Adalgisa's behavior, her godmother had reared her as a puritanical Spanish woman. Nor was there hypocrisy in the conduct of Danilo, the product of the prevailing *machismo*. What for Adalgisa was nothing but the painful duty of a wife, for Danilo meant the fulfillment of the marriage bond: The rest of it— marriage, nuptials, matrimony, engagement—all seemed secondary.

When they got to São Paulo Bluff, misunderstanding took over, and the idyll gave way to discord. The wedding night that had promised to be sweet and pleasurable in the darkness of the ferry shifted from seduction into violence. Danilo was in a fury, while Adalgisa's timid smile changed to convulsive sobs.

The Dame

The blond dame with a twisted mouth and a streetwalker's look was quick to show Danilo and Adalgisa where Dr. Fernando Almeida's house was. As she walked with them along the road, she joked:

"Dr. Fernando is always lending his house out for honeymoons. They even say that a wedding night spent here means a sure child nine months later, counting day by day."

She stopped and looked Danilo over from head to toe in the almost nonexistent light of the flashlight. Recognizing him as the former soccer player, she congratulated Adalgisa:

"Yes, ma'am. The star dribbled up and made a fine goal! Congratulations."

The blonde went on ahead and showed them where the path was that opened up between the rocks; other passengers from the ferry watched them curiously. At the end of the trail that had been cut through there, she said, they could hear the murmur of the sea, the waves beating down on the expanse of the beach, of which no beginning or end could be seen. Then the blond woman pointed to the house off in the distance. Danilo and Adalgisa could make out a two-story house—it didn't look at all like a cottage. The woman halted, lamenting:

"Too bad there's no moon. I've been all over the world, but I've never found a nicer place than São Paulo Bluff. Ideal for a honeymoon." A brief pause, then: "Even better for adultery."

She paused, looking and listening, withdrawn, then she addressed Adalgisa:

"I don't have to wish you a good night, it certainly will be a night you'll never forget—that's what I wish you, my pretty." She looked Danilo up and down again, bit her lip. "And you too, sweetie pie."

The dame laughed, accelerated her pace, and left them. A tinkle of seashells, her laughter died out along the beach.

Dinner

A strong mulatto woman with graying kinky hair, the maid, met them at the door, smiling and attentive:

"My name is Marialva, I'll show you the bedroom. While you're washing up, I'll put dinner on the table."

"Dinner?" Danilo was concerned. "We weren't thinking—"

"Just something light. You can't go to bed on an empty stomach!"

Go to bed: had she emphasized the phrase, he wondered, had she said that on purpose? Puzzled, Danilo took a close look at the woman, but he couldn't catch anything malicious on her pleasant face, in her cordial attitude. Instead, solicitous, she took them to their room, on the upper floor. She set the suitcase down on a bench, opened the empty dresser drawers, pointed to the closet where the dresses could be hung, showed them that there was running water in the faucets, left one of the kerosene lamps beside the vase of flowers on the sideboard, and took the other lamp into the bathroom. After a last look around she went out, closing the door; her steps could be heard on the stairs. Danilo took Dadá in his arms and covered her with kisses. He interrupted this pleasant activity only to say:

"I'm not going to have anything for dinner. I don't even want to hear food mentioned."

But Adalgisa disagreed, claiming that it wouldn't look right to let the plates get cold on the table; after all, the maid had gone to the trouble of preparing it, they had to do something, even if it was just to put in an appearance.

"And I'll tell you something else," she said. "I'm dying of hunger, the sea air has given me an appetite."

Danilo had a different kind of appetite, but he didn't want to cause any problems. Dadá was right, he recognized it: They shouldn't be rude, or leave an opening for gossip and wisecracks.

"Let's go, then. But no hanging around down there for long, do you hear?"

He sank his hand into the mattress to test its strength and softness: first rate. It was going to be quite a party. He gave his arm to Adalgisa, and they went downstairs together, where Marialva, stationed down below, was waiting for them with her maternal eyes.

Resting on the linen tablecloth—an extravagance for a beach house, even if it was the property of a rich industrialist—the *moquecas* of fish, oysters, and shrimp offered themselves in an appetizing way, seasoned with coconut and dendê oil. There was manioc mush, hot red pepper sauce ground with lime, onions, and coriander, and a bottle of Portuguese sparkling wine cooling in a chrome ice bucket. Danilo feasted his eyes. The extravagant generosity of the owner of the house was proof of the prestige that Francisco Romero Pérez y Pérez enjoyed among his friends: It was as solid as ever, in spite of the ups and downs of his fortunes.

Adalgisa had said she was famished, but yet she served herself sparingly: She was on a diet so as not to get fat, she said, and she was afraid of eating too much food cooked with oil, especially at night. Danilo, who'd resisted even sitting down at the table, didn't hold back: He pounced on the *moquecas* voraciously and added lots of pepper, ate his fill, finished off the bottle—Adalgisa barely tasted the wine—and when Marialva, smiling, displayed a porcelain dish with the crowning glory, coconut mousse with chocolate sauce, he couldn't hold back, he clapped his hands to welcome his favorite dessert, and loosened his belt. Oh, boy!

The Rubber Girdle

After they returned upstairs, Danilo circled around Adalgisa, trying to undress and dominate her, like the principal clown in a comic pantomime. His female lead was getting away from him—she fled from his hands, busying herself going from the suitcase open on the bench to the dresser or to the closet, to the bathroom, drawing back and keeping the minimum distance away from him. The two of them were laughing, characters in a burlesque.

Danilo alternated between raillery and spite, cursing and flirting, adulation and complaint; he snorted interjections, his arms outstretched trying to grab her, with the intention of flinging her onto the bed and having his way with her. Dadá was getting excited, between derision and fear, worked up, having fun, just barely avoiding the clutches of her pursuer. She'd already lost her blouse, torn violently away, one of the buttons leaping off and disappearing under the dresser.

At one moment of greater risk, when she barely slipped away in time from the fingers attempting to pull off her skirt, as if to make fun of her husband's fiasco, she stuck out her tongue at him as a challenge. She mocked him, seeming to be enjoying that game of blindman's buff, but inside she was trembling with fear of what could eventually happen if he succeeded in stripping her and laying her down on the lavender-scented sheets. During dinner the maid had removed the crocheted bedcover with its satin lining, leaving the prepared bed ready and waiting.

The third acrobat didn't let himself be seen, but Adalgisa knew he was present and active: her guardian angel. He was responsible for Dadá, for the purity of her body and the salvation of her soul, alert to the countless threats that hang over a poor maiden on her wedding night, a fatal night. Ready to guard her honor and virtue, the good angel caused Danilo's feet to stumble, made his hands miss, made him tumble when there was nothing there, as if he were drunk. During her most difficult moments, when she had no strength left and could no longer see any way out, Adalgisa would have recourse on high, would murmur: "Help me, my guardian angel!" Then she would get untangled and be left untouched.

Untouched to a degree. Overcoming obstacles, both visible and invisible—Dadá was agile, while he felt a torpor in his leaden legs—Danilo managed to get her skirt off, albeit a complicated and laborious maneuver. At his threat—"I'll rip off this crap!"—she lifted her arms and allowed the slim skirt to pass over her head. All that was left to him now was to free her of her slip; the bra and stockings would be no problem once he got hold of them. He tried to salute the decisive act, but instead of an exultant exclamation of victory, a crude belch came up out of his insides. If Adalgisa had heard, she didn't show it. For a moment Prince Danilo had been brought down a peg.

Recovering, he grasped the hem of her slip firmly. Since his next threat hadn't induced Dadá to cooperate, Danilo, more indignant now, resolved to carry it out. He tore this brand-new, elegant item of her trousseau from bottom to top, into pieces. The shreds curled round the virgin's feet, revealing the nudity of her midsection. Her tiny waist, her breasts visible through the transparent lace brassière, her stomach smooth and round like a clay jug, the dark mystery of her navel. But she hadn't shown him her derriere, alas, not that!

But starting just above her knees, going all the way to her waist, subjecting and compressing the two divisions of the universe, denying Danilo the dreamt-of and yearned-for vision—after such a long wait he had thought he was finally going to feast his eyes—a monstrous rubber panty girdle spread out like a desert. A chastity belt, Danilo had felt it under his fingers during the last few months of the engagement, felt horror and revulsion at it. All he had to do was touch this definitive barrier against lust, and he would lose his erection.

Adalgisa had convinced herself that wearing the panty girdle improved her beauty, gave her a slimmer shape, and especially diminished the malevolent volume of her hips. In the assurances in a full-page ad in a São Paulo magazine, high-society ladies, the chic-est of the chic, had expressed the identical opinion. The advice of Madame Nadreau, a well-traveled Frenchwoman, had been decisive in having Dadá hurry out to Mr. Miguel Najar's shop for a rubber girdle; she immediately bought two. From then on she never failed to wear one.

The desolating, hateful sight of the panty girdle defeated Danilo.

Suddenly despondent, the prince of the soccer field shook his melancholy head, raised his arms, sat down on the bed. The bride took advantage of the moment to lock herself in the bathroom, taking her gown with her. Not just any gown, but the one that she separated from the rest by calling it her "nightie," for her wedding night. A work of art in Chinese crepe, its white froth light, fluttering, and transparent, with lace on the hem and neckline, the hem just below the knee, and open on both sides, Adalgisa's "nightie" had been sent from the Laura Alves boutique in Ipanema, in Rio de Janeiro, with compliments of Dona Glória Machado, who would be unable to attend the wedding because she was traveling to Thailand with her husband, "Big Boss" Alfredo.

Danilo took off his shoes and sighed with relief, massaged his aching feet. He took off his clothes, piece by piece, and stretched himself out naked on the bed, waiting for his wife to come out of the bathroom, when he would finally get to screw her. His head resting on the pillow, his natural attributes at half-staff, he closed his eyes to better envision the box of her twat, where her hymen was inlaid, hiding, a beautiful thing. He fell asleep.

----&----

Made Up

It would be a complete misconception, totally off the mark, bordering on the ridiculous, for anyone to laugh at Danilo's expense, making him the butt of bad jokes because he fell asleep and slept soundly until the following morning, losing both the moment and the occasion. Of course, we should have used the expression "dozed off" here instead of "fell asleep," as we did, so as not to give occasion for hasty and mistaken conclusions.

Danilo dozed off, then, without falling completely asleep, his thoughts on what, we well know. Nevertheless, from time to time he would open his eyes, check the bathroom door—still closed—and shut his eyes again. He shut them several times, because Adalgisa took a good half hour to pretty herself up, and when she came back into the room— or "came out onto the grass," as soccer writers say when referring to the triumphant entry of the prince onto the field of battle—she was simply dazzling, a princess out of a fairy tale, or perhaps from the Principality of Monaco, let each choose his or her own comparison.

She was made up from head to toe. She'd removed the makeup she'd worn for the ceremony, taken a shower to get rid of the sweat, cooled off her face with toilet water, and perfumed her body with cologne water—*l'original eau de cologne* from Köln-am-Rhein, she'd been given a flask as a gift from a high lady, Doña Eva Adler, wife of the Austrian consul and a customer of Doña Esperanza's. She had loosened the curls of hair around her neck in the manner of certain medieval statues, taken off her bra, taken off the rubber panty girdle, thereby freeing her breasts and hips, and washed her privy parts, including her pussy, with a deodorant made specially for "intimate hygiene" that Dolores had recommended: "To bathe your pussy, girl—there's nothing like it." Adalgisa's foul-mouthed sister was absolutely right: It was clean, sweet-smelling, smooth—heady! The luxuries of Dolores, her sister who had devoted herself to such allures ever since she was a young girl.

Putting on makeup is just the opposite of what was described above —such ignorance! Making up is making use of sophisticated items — purple eyeshadow, mascara on the lashes, eyebrow pencil, red lipstick, rouge on the cheeks—a voluptuous mask! It's displaying an unusual hairdo, invented and sculpted by an expert like the great Severiano or some *coiffeur des dames* of equal finesse. It's perfuming oneself with science and art, using a French fragrance, expensive and exciting, sexy: one drop redolent with lasciviousness on the pubic fluff. Such ignorance! One who ought to know better accepts censure and reproof—let him practice self-criticism, put together a respectful request for pardon! But one way or another, be that as it may, made up or simply cleaned up, free of artifice, Adalgisa had become even prettier, even more appetizing. No princess from a fairy tale, or from the Principality of Monaco, could hold a candle to her.

She'd hesitated about putting on the nightie, short, fluttery, and transparent, open on both sides up to midthigh, the gift from Dona Glória: She was afraid of looking provocative, of offering herself shamelessly. She didn't feel right. But the other nightgown, sewn by Doña Esperanza, had been put away in the dresser: It was of rich satin, with insets of English embroidery, circumspect, closed at the neck, a wide sash at the waist, long, down to her feet, accompanied by a robe and drawers in the same style, decorous accessories. Dona Glória's was just a single piece with no panties, much less drawers and a robe.

When Adalgisa got the three gift-wrapped pieces from her godmother, with Doña Esperanza's permission she unwrapped the package and held the gown over her slip to see how it fell along her body: perfect! Then she held up the drawers and measured them with her eyes—she didn't have to try them on—they were perfect too. Interrupting her godchild's praise and thanks, Doña Esperanza uttered a sentence whose meaning escaped Adalgisa: Her Spanish accent grew even thicker than usual when she referred to certain topics between clenched teeth. She must have meant, surely, that the nightgown would be the last moat protecting the bastion of Adalgisa's virginity on her wedding night, the conquest of which must come about as the result of maneuvers and ruses on her part that would transform the surrender of the fortress into a victory and not a defeat. It was the sibylline language of a prudish widow. Dadá, uncomprehending, had remained ignorant of the maneuvers and tricks in question, of where the victory would be and whom it involved. But she pondered it while she was slipping on the sheer nightie, the gift of the moneybags in Rio, instead.

The movement of the latch as the bathroom door opened awakened Danilo, and he spotted his bride in the dim light of the lamp, an unreal vision, something out of paradise. He thought he must still be asleep and rubbed his eyes to make sure he was awake. Then he sat up with a roar, leaped out of bed, his natural accoutrement extended like a lance, powerful and aggressive, a battering ram. So arrogant was it that Dadá's guardian angel spread its wings and, there being no doubt what was going to happen, took flight, never to return. The angel fled through the cracks in the window just as a sea breeze idly entered the room and lifted the hem of Adalgisa's nightie.

The Breeze

The night breeze was having fun lifting Adalgisa's nightie, raising it above her knees, showing off a piece of her thigh. With an unexpected flutter, it lifted the nightie as high as the furrow of her derriere. Seeing her even faintly in the dim light of the kerosene lamp, Danilo's chest thudded, and without fear of consequences, he let out a war cry, a vibrant bugle call.

The bride tried to govern the breeze, hold down her hem, cast her eyes downward and smile timidly, not knowing how to act or what to do. She'd never seen him like that, completely naked: on the beach she'd admired him in his bathing suit—trunks, a new and daring style—and she would lightly touch the muscles of his chest and arms. The newspapers praised the Ipiranga soccer star's athletic build, and she was proud of it. But now there she was, seeing him without his shorts on, without even any trunks, stark naked—and that weapon all triggered. Save me, oh, Our Lady of Purification!

It wasn't right to call on the Most Pure Virgin, the Immaculate, in the presence of this shameless nudity, she thought, all the more confused. What had Doña Esperanza told her about the nightgown—the other one, not this indecent filmy trifle that, instead of covering her, exhibited her? The breeze was running about her legs, climbing up between her thighs, wafting through the curls of her pubis, a delicate tickle. All gooseflesh, she tried to convince herself that it felt disagreeable, but failed.

On the other side of the moat, the conqueror was making ready to transform word into deed, when he suddenly had to postpone the thrust of his attack in order to rein in a belch and let it out with prudence and discretion. Digestive troubles, a lump in his stomach—shit!

Still, no small stomach upset could lessen his enthusiasm or lower the intensity of his desire. He hurled himself into the fray, more than determined and impetuous—uncontrollable, as when he had run for the cage to make a goal. It was now or never. He didn't expect to find any difficulty, resistance, opposition. The obstacle—but the obstacle was the goal he was aiming at, the best there was, the coveted trophy: Adalgisa's cherry.

—✥——✥

The Stud's Points

Danilo had already had a little experience; he had two cherries to his credit as a big macho man, collected during the glory of stadium days. Back then, his picture in the newspapers all the time showing his Latin profile, while radio programs gave him wholesale praise, Homeric descriptions of his goals, called him prince here, prince there—he could have conquered the heart of any virgin he wanted had he not feared scandal, headlines in the newspapers: SOCCER IDOL UNDER FIRE: SHOTGUN WEDDING AT CITY HALL. That would have been good material for Armando Oliveira, a humorous columnist whose faithful readership numbered in the thousands; there couldn't be a better subject for their titillation. Besides, the position Danilo played on the team, the leading forward—called "tip of the lance"—lent itself to wordplay, an outright gift for Armando Oliveira. God protect him from bigger mess! He took no chances: When the possibility of doing something foolish seemed an imminent threat, he would break off the affair, disappear, head for the hills.

The cherries he popped had been ripe, both of them easy and peaceful. Albertina had been at least twenty-one, a civil servant with a good salary, her own income. Why she hadn't given in to anyone before was a mystery. But having started with Danilo, she forged ahead like a champ, breaking records. When Danilo took her to bed, he assumed she'd been drilled long ago, and he was much surprised to find her still a virgin, bearing a cherry. When he felt the unexpected block in the entranceway, he suspended the holy task and pushed her away in confusion. "Don't tell me—"

Albertina admitted, part proud and part downcast, "I'm a virgin, yes. You're the first one—I swear."

The wholeness of her ripe cherry was evidenced by the blood that now crowned the tonsure of the reverend confessor. It was a glorious afternoon, a red-letter day: The heavy summer rain was washing the streets of the city of Bahia while, snug in this room in a house of assignation, Albertina Carvalhaes, until now a simple administrative official working in the labor court, was beginning a career as one of the most competent and successful "scorers" ever known. And she began under the aegis of Prince Danilo, to whom in the lassitude of bed she purred, thankful, "Oh, my Clark Gable, you're simply too good!" Albertina Carvalhaes; her face homely, her body a monument.

A little less peaceful and much less intact was Benzinha's cherry. Danilo had no cause for vainglory in that event: Benzinha had offered herself, had given herself, had opened her legs without his having asked, at the Pedra do Sal, the salt rock, near the summer home of Miss Switt, the American cultural attaché where Benzinha was working as a maid. Theirs was a disturbing love affair because this temptress was already engaged to Isaías Formigão, a veteran goaltender who was about to hang up his spikes, a wellspring of jealousy, and a tough athlete as well. Formigão kept a close watch on his fiancée, whose fidelity to him he had more than enough reason to doubt: Benzinha was, after all, a popular hanger-on at the Baron's Dive.

Fed up with stolen moments, tired of running around on the sly and knowing that Isaías was tied up in practice on the eve of an important game, Danilo and Benzinha rushed off to the solitude of the beach in front of the cardinal's mansion retreat, an ideal spot for a whoring session. Whoring was what Benzinha, aroused to the point of losing her bearings, wanted to give away for the asking. She lay down in the sand and pulled up her dress—she didn't wear panties—thrust her legs apart: "Take me, prince, I don't want to keep it for that cuckold Isaías!" Danilo pulled down his pants and satisfied her wish with his own pleasure, but as he recalled the conquest later, he played it down. The heads of a lot of lovers had already widened her entranceway, and if none of them had actually entered, leaving behind only the small remnants of virginity, it was because of their fear of Formigão, a giant and a blowhard, and his huge hands. Off in the distance, nuns on retreat were taking advantage of the half hour of evening recreation to play on the beach and get their feet wet in the waves. To the echoes of their innocent laughter, Danilo gobbled up what was left of Benzinha's cherry.

He'd lived in apprehension when Isaías married Benzinha, shuffling from one foot to the other, afraid the cuckold Isaías, notorious for attacking referees and opposing players, would find the path open, raise hell, and come and collect his price from Danilo for his bride's cherry. Price? Her cherry couldn't have been worth more than a couple of pennies! Benzinha, Rita Benta de Lima, was a high-spirited girl with a dark face, provocative laugh, and haunches like a ship under sail.

A Poetic Pause

Now that Danilo has released his belch, and now that we have ended our digression concerning the previous deflowerings that our hero had already managed almost inadvertently, let us pick up the thread of our story again at the precise moment in which Danilo heads toward Adalgisa and takes her in his arms—a crucial moment! In this case it was not a question of a ripe cherry, well seasoned in the practice of promiscuity, reduced to half its size from contact with fingers, tongues, pricks. Never yet touched by a sinful finger, an adroit tongue, not to mention a penis—Danilo's or anybody else's—Dadá was truly virginal.

Under the circumstances, if our prince had been a lover of poetry, like the columnist Lamenha, he might have given himself a romantic aura by reciting that commonly quoted line from Lorca: *"verde que te quiero verde."* Or perhaps less of a cliché, such as *"en la concha de la cama / desnuda de flor y brisa."* Either of them would have been most suitable for the present ceremony. But in deference to the truth that strictly governs this tale, we must reveal the bridegroom's noteworthy ignorance of poetry, and of the poetry of the Iberian peninsula in particular.

Haste and Off-Side

When last we saw them, Danilo had taken Adalgisa in his arms, raising the nightie up to her shoulders in the same movement. An excited kiss, his hands grasping her breasts, their bodies close, thigh against thigh, stomach against stomach: His Highness was pressing against the Princess's curly mat of hair. With a brusque movement, Danilo dropped Dadá atop the bed and laid down on top of her. Withdrawing his hands from her breasts, he ran them over the curves of her hips and, tightening his grip on them, pulled her thighs apart, trying to position himself at the right point for the attack. Not fitting in the narrow space, he increased the pressure of his fingers to make her open her legs more, leaving the path to her cherry clear.

Adalgisa moaned, and Danilo muffled her protest by smothering her with kisses, devouring her mouth with an endless sucking of tongue and teeth. Feeling herself asphyxiated, she struggled, held down only by the pressure of his body. He pinned her wrists to the mattress, but in order to hold her wrists down and keep her arms still, he had to release her thighs. Ever so quickly, Dadá crossed them, one over the other, blocking the entrance goal, leaving the eager point man—the lance tip—with no room for play. Several times França Teixeira at the stadium microphone had criticized the star's boldness, to the delight of the fans of the opposing team. Prince Danilo often got ahead of himself without waiting for the pass, in which case the referee would whistle for a penalty and call him off-side.

—❦—❦

The Doubts

That was how the atrocious night began, and that was how it continued, with combat and massacre, attack and repulsion. It was a declared war between archenemies, and not, as it should have been, the loving discord, the tenderness of lovers. Danilo tried to hold Adalgisa immobile with her legs open; she struggled, resisting. The arduous, mortifying battle grew in violence and fright, till all calm was lost, all clear thinking exhausted, harsh talk replacing gallantries, orders replacing pleas, anger replacing tenderness, force replacing seduction.

Teary-eyed, her heart twisted in agony, Dadá wondered if he loved her or if he just wanted to make use of her body. Why did he want to take her by force? Why didn't he have the patience to wait? Her lips hurt, both the upper set and lower, the upper set bitten, the other set molested, kicked about, abused from the constant rubbing, his incessant attempts to break her resistance and her hymen. She was weary, depressed, her strength beginning to give out, and she was trembling with fright.

But how could a citizen of Brazil, who had just been married before both a priest and a judge in a simple but decent ceremony after six months of loving and an engagement of over a year spent with tenderness and understanding, how could Danilo be expected to understand why his wife refused him on their wedding night? During their engagement, Danilo had accepted the limitations imposed by Dadá, whose fanatical godmother had reared her in the rigid canons of the Church, and he had even taken pleasure in her principles as proof of his fiancée's uprightness and honor. But everything in the world has its limits. They were now husband and wife, the certificate said so, and notions of immorality and dishonor had become inappropriate. Could it be, he thought, that he was mistaken and that she didn't love him, that she had smooched with him and had gotten engaged just for the vanity of strutting down the street on the arm of a soccer star, the prince of the playing field, the idol of the crowd?

To complete his displeasure, increase his humiliation, his belly was bloated, his digestion was off, his stomach was swirling, his mouth was sour, his insides were on fire, and the threat of another belch paralyzed his initiative, facilitating Adalgisa's stubborn resistance. Sweaty, irritated, and sad, Danilo saw that it was time to forget about his head and use his palm.

Pain Without Pleasure

Late in the evening, after some painful discussion, there was a brief period of reconciliation: Adalgisa seemed to agree, she consented to take her nightgown off, to let herself be seen, and she asked him only for care and calm: go slowly, in God's name. "In God's name, I will!" he swore.

But stronger than her resigned willingness to fulfill her duties as a wife bravely was the fright that came over her when she felt Danilo's immense bulge forcing its entry into her narrow slit, so small, so tightly closed, it would surely be permanently damaged. The tighter, smaller, narrower it was, the more tempting and desirable it was for Danilo: It was the opening to a world that his eyes had only glimpsed and that his prick was badgering him to pass through to a universe of pleasure, an ocean of delights. Somewhere between depressed and excited, with a sudden lurch Danilo tried to force the barrier. Adalgisa cried out: Ow!

She was tired, frightened, her strength was failing. Her fright was such, however, and the pain that seized her was so sharp, that she succeeded in freeing herself from under Danilo and leaping out of bed. The pain that went through her and filled her hadn't originated in her privy parts because Danilo hadn't gotten to complete his thrust: he'd missed the boat, he was standing at the dock.

A headache had tormented her ever since adolescence, returning insistently on certain occasions, growing unbearable. Now it tore through her scalp like a flame, while a tongue of fire cut through her eyes, blinding her, threatening to drive her mad. Her migraines had attacked her ever since she was fourteen when she had had her first period. No doctor had ever been of any help, and old wives' remedies were useless. "When you get married, all that will stop" had been the prognosis of Dr. Elsimar Coutinho, the family doctor. Evidently the prescription of matrimony wasn't working.

The impetus of her flight carried Dadá into the bathroom, where she locked herself in; her loud, piercing sobs echoed through the bedroom. Danilo pounded on the door, shouting: "Come out of there, come out of there before I do something I'll regret!" At length he dropped his arms and stood there naked, pathetic, idiotic. His dick was limp, shrunken into a useless thing, flaccid and foolish, and on top of it all, bruised and aching.

The Bathroom Door

Reconciliation came through the locked bathroom door; the two made peace, swore eternal love. At first they spoke in tones of weeping and loss, in hesitant voices, disappointed and dissatisfied as they were with each other. But then the scruples of commiseration and pity prevailed, disposing them to mutual forgiveness and hope. When Danilo's pounding on the door ceased, the sobs lessened, grievances and threats were no longer exchanged, the words softened, the threats dissolved into complaints, the demands into pleas.

"I can't take it anymore. I've got a splitting headache. If you love me, wait till tomorrow."

"If I love you? Do you doubt me? Silly!"

"Then let me have my way, you brute! Be patient with me!" She repeated, "Brute!"

She was pleading humbly, and Danilo knew that her headaches made her suffer. But she'd called him a brute, and he reacted:

"You're the one who doesn't love me—you were just stringing me along—"

"Don't say nonsense like that. Why do you think I married you? Please!"

"What about tomorrow. Will you let me? It won't be like today, will it?"

"I swear I'll let you—tomorrow! I swear!" More than any affirmation, it was her pained voice that won him over. "Have pity on me, my sweet."

My sweet gave in:

"That's fine, Dadá. We'll leave it for tomorrow. You can come out."

"You won't grab me?"

"I already said we'll leave it for tomorrow. But tomorrow without fail, eh?"

She demanded a final guarantee:

"Do you swear on the soul of your mother?"

"On the soul of my mother."

Even so Adalgisa didn't come out right away, and he found himself obliged to pound on the door again:

"Come out! Come out right now! Let's go!"

"Why all the rush?" She was fearful despite his sacrosanct pledge.

"Because I've got to go in, Dadá. Hurry up!"

He had just enough time to bend over the toilet bowl, and even then the uncontainable gulp dirtied his chin. He stuck his finger down his throat, vomited up the *moqueca* and the chocolate mousse, manioc mush and wine. Adalgisa curled up in bed and disappeared beneath the sheet, wrapping herself up in it, playing dead. Danilo opened the window, breathed in the night air avidly, a lost soul in the solitude of his nuptials.

The Unforgettable Night

Alas, it should have been the best night of his life, a celestial night, sublime, gratifying, cause for exaltation and pride—greater even than winning the Bahian soccer championship, a championship that Danilo had won for Ipiranga, as those in the know mostly agreed—a delightful memory, an unforgettable night! Alas, it was the worst night of all, the most unfortunate. He wanted to erase it from his memory. It was disastrous and bitter, it was unfortunate and humiliating, a night of wrath and violence, deception and ridicule. Unforgettable!

Leaning out the window that opened over the beach, Danilo watched the transparent dawn being born out of the shadows on the horizon, and even when he finally lay down again, he closed his burning eyes and sleep overtook him until well into Sunday morning. As he fell asleep, he was no longer bloated, but he was demoralized, filled with shame and disappointment, completely, from head to toe.

From toe to head, completely wrapped up in the sheet at the edge of the bed, Dadá didn't even show a tip of a fingernail, a single hair of her head—she was a huddled bundle of fear. Had she managed to fall asleep, or was she pretending to be afraid so he'd feel sorry for her and leave her alone? Adalgisa at least had her fear to feed her, but Danilo was completely empty, desolate, stark naked, a figure worthy of laughter and mockery. The absence of witnesses didn't matter; misfortune needs no witness to sting.

The Love Birds

Danilo opened his eyes with the feeling that they'd been closed for only five or ten minutes; a bitter aftertaste was still in his mouth and the feeling of shortness of breath in his chest. He was startled: Sunlight was flooding into the room, the bed was empty—where could Dadá have gone? He quickly looked at his wristwatch on the night table: nine twenty-five. He went into the bathroom and closed the door. As he relieved his belly, shaved his beard, and pulled on his trunks, he watched the bathers moving on the beach. A dive into the ocean would give him a physical and moral boost, but he couldn't imagine Adalgisa being up for beach activity or swimming after what had happened. Where could she have gone off to?

On the stairs Marialva was polishing the banister. She said good morning and, in answer to his apprehensive question, informed him that the little bride was waiting for him downstairs—the lady, she corrected herself, smiling. She'd gone down early, had had some *café au lait,* eaten some corn couscous and sponge cake, and was sitting on the balcony. It was a nice day for a swim, she said, a nice day for lying in the sun and relaxing. Danilo bounced down the stairs two at a time.

There she was, stretched out on the chaise longue. Beautiful, my God, she was so beautiful! Her feet were bare, her legs were crossed, her thighs were wrapped in a flowered scarf, the shape of her breasts showed under her bathing suit, a silk kerchief held in her hair, she wore sunglasses. When she saw Danilo she took off the glasses and smiled, showing bruised eyes and puffy lips. Danilo went to her with his heart pounding; he kissed her softly on the mouth, and out of the corner of his eye he spotted teeth marks on her lower lip. His fingers touched her face delicately, and he asked, leaving the decision up to her:

"Do you want to go to the beach? Or would you rather not?"

Adalgisa nodded her head in assent. As Danilo leaned over her, she pulled him to her and offered her mouth for another kiss—she was really the one who kissed him. She did it slowly and forcefully, as if she were doing it for a purpose, as an affirmation, unconcerned about the state of her painful lips, the swelling and the bruises. It was a proof of her love.

Danilo caught on and didn't take advantage of the moment, in spite of the quiver that ran through him when he felt the tip of Dadá's tongue touch his teeth. He held out his hand to help her up:

"Let's go."

"Have some breakfast first."

Standing beside the table, he downed half a cup of coffee and nibbled a slice of sponge cake. He didn't try the couscous, even though it was his favorite dish. The veranda opened onto the beach that extended out of sight; the sand was white and clean, the beach was wide in front of the house. They went out holding hands, and Adalgisa seemed free of cares, self-assured, and lively.

"Your headache better, Dadá?"

"It's all gone, thank God."

Danilo wasn't surprised. Unexpected and terrible as her headaches came and took over, they would disappear all of a sudden, vanish, just like that. The newlyweds walked along amid the looks and smiles of other sunbathers, leaving a trail of whispers, in search of a quiet place where they could set their mat down: running, Marialva had caught up to them with towels and a straw mat. Although he had stopped playing soccer more than a year before, his fame aroused the curiosity of the sunbathers. Nor could they fail to notice the opulence of Adalgisa's figure, even in her unfashionable bathing suit, although they regretted that someone with so many treasures was so parsimonious about showing them.

They walked a fair stretch to a spot where there weren't many bathers. They stretched out their mat on the sand, far from the agitation and the tumult, the curiosity and the attention. They lingered in the sun, then confronted the waves; Danilo, a good swimmer, took off in the direction of the motorboats and sloops anchored in the distance, while Dadá contented herself with a few strokes close to the beach.

It was a peaceful morning for speaking of love, amorously, and other pleasant subjects. They exchanged kisses: "I've got the lips of a black woman," she said, but she didn't say it as a complaint; she was even smiling. She looked around, then pulled down the neck of her bathing suit to show him the purple mark, the result of his sucking. When she said, "Look what you did to me, you brute!" her voice was flirtatious.

As they were enjoying that morning of sun and tenderness, Adalgisa, momentarily saddened, spoke in passing about the events or the nonevents of the night before. She begged his forgiveness and patience. Danilo did no less—he confessed that he'd gone to the well too thirsty, had been crude, and he asked forgiveness himself. Forgiveness? was her reply. The one who should beg forgiveness was she, because she'd acted like a coward and a fool, incapable of assuming, as was proper, the status of a married woman, for which her godmother had prepared her. But if he understood her and had faith in her, she said, she would turn out to be a good wife to him, and the home they would build, with God's blessing, would be a happy one, she was sure of that. Yes, Danilo assured her, that was just the way it was going to be. Then she purred, more flirtatious than ever:

"Do you swear that you love me?"

Danilo didn't get to swear because suddenly a pleasant couple came over to greet them, interrupting his affirmation. Laura and Dário Queiroz lived in Valença, but they had a house on São Paulo Bluff, where they spent most of the year. Although Dário, a soccer fan, rooted for Vitória rather than Ipiranga, he knew all about the career of the former prince of the playing field and started up a conversation. Why had he hung up his spikes when he still had several years of soccer left in him? Dário wanted to recall some classic plays and goals, but Dona Laura wouldn't permit it:

"Let's go—the lovebirds want to be left alone!"

The Headache

Danilo wasn't surprised, and no readers should be surprised, that as unexpected and terrible as the appearance of the headache had been, it would disappear so completely just like that, suddenly go away. It's worth emphasizing this so no one will suspect that it had been a trick by Adalgisa to avoid the branding iron.

Whenever Danilo found her prostrate from a migraine—and it happened frequently—he always wondered whether Dona Teodolina had been right when she said it was a matter of a hex—that is, some laggard spirit had gotten inside the poor girl. Since the problem was of supernatural origins, Dona Teodolina had told Doña Esperanza, the attacks could easily be cured: with a few sessions at the Waters of the Jordan tent, with prayers, seances, and positive thinking, Sister Fátima, that saint, would expose the disturbed spirit and send it off to the circles in space whence it had come.

Doña Esperanza had listened in silence to Dona Teodolina's babbling in deference to her wealthy customer, but she had rejected both the advice and the saint. Not only would it be a mortal sin to take her goddaughter to a spiritualist session, to a medium, it was ignorant and backward. Doña Esperanza strongly condemned such superstitions and myths: the only thing worse than a spiritualist session with a medium was the clapping of a *mãe de santo* at a *candomblé*.

Without referring explicitly to marriage, she shared Dr. Elsimar Coutinho's opinion that someday this would all pass away.

The Wait

Danilo asked Marialva to serve them only a frugal snack that night. The lunch had been too much, with fresh lobster, fish and manioc mush, and fried shrimp, not to mention the appetizers of crab legs, all washed down with beer and guaraná soda. Returning from the beach famished, the newlyweds had done proper justice to the meal. Danilo had attempted an invitation to the bedroom, but Adalgisa stretched out on the couch and immediately dropped off, sleeping all afternoon.

Marialva had promised:

"Leave it to me, I'll prepare a quick meal—something light." The attentive smile on her affable face was unchanging.

Marialva had very idiosyncratic ideas as to what constituted a frugal meal. It would be a simple serving of café au lait, she'd said, but to accompany the simple café au lait she had cooked up some sweet cassava, yams, and corn on the cob, and she prepared a tapioca couscous with coconut milk that was hard to resist. Beforehand, however, she served roast chicken with white rice. Everything was light, there's no denying it. Nervously, Dadá barely nibbled, while the memory of the night restrained Danilo's gluttony.

Adalgisa's restlessness had been building to a crescendo ever since she awakened from her afternoon nap at sunset. She had rubbed her eyes, seen Danilo standing before her—on watch, she thought with a shudder. A game of cat and mouse then took place, with long pauses, heavy with hints but short on words. Rising from the sofa, still drowsy from the beach and her siesta, Dadá headed for the stairs, and he made as if to accompany her.

"I'll be right back," she cut him off, as if asking him to wait.

She took a rather long time, but she came back all fresh, wearing a simple house dress. Taking a shower had freed her of her lassitude but not of her nervousness. Night had fallen completely over the hill by now, and the overloaded ferry to the mainland was pulling away from the dock. Marialva asked if she could serve them the snack.

"Yes, you may," Danilo answered, unable to hide his bewilderment, disoriented, unable to keep his chair warm.

If it had been up to him, they would have gone right up to the bedroom as soon as they laid down their knives and forks and left the table. But Adalgisa proposed that they take a stroll past the houses—to help her digestion. What digestion? She'd hardly eaten anything! But since she had made the suggestion in the presence of the servant, Danilo held back his impatience, didn't argue, and gave her his arm. They stepped out onto the porch.

"I'll go turn down your bed." The innocent voice of Marialva saying good night renewed Danilo's anxiety. "When you come back, just bolt the door," she said. "We don't have any thieves here."

Out on the street there wasn't much activity; only a few strollers, some couples, nodded and said good evening, recognizing the lovebirds, following them with curious, kindly eyes. The wind was raising small whirlwinds of sand and bearing the sound of music from some of the houses; dancing and tables of canasta and poker, the maid had explained, filling them in on the customs and manners of the summer people. Under the stars, the powerful motorboats of the wealthy were skimming along the sea at high speeds, with whiskey and merriment.

The silence was interrupted only by friendly greetings or the sound of passing motorboats. "These people know how to enjoy life!" Danilo said enviously, trying to start up a conversation. Adalgisa didn't answer, her teeth clenched. They walked as far as the steps of the dock, then returned at the same pace. Although he tried to accelerate it, Adalgisa maintained a slow step. When they got back to the front of Dr. Fernando Almeida's house—the lamp in the living room was left lighted by Marialva—Danilo stopped and said:

"Let's go inside." He didn't ask for any agreement. He was collecting his due.

Adalgisa lowered her eyes to the ground—her godmother had recommended submission and courage during the crucial crisis—and stammered:

"Let's go."

Suddenly out of the shadows emerged the soccer fan Dário Queiroz, ready to talk about Pelé's goals. As Danilo tried to excuse himself—"Wait till tomorrow, we'll talk tomorrow for sure"—Dadá took advantage of his predicament and slipped away to the bedroom. When Danilo finally got there, out of breath, she'd just gotten into bed under the sheets. She was wearing the sacrificial nightgown her godmother had sewn.

―❦―❦

Finally, Uff!

Danilo turned down the wick on the kerosene lamp, and the darkness blended with the silence. Under the sheet, Adalgisa closed her eyes tightly. She had dreamed that afternoon that her guardian angel had covered her with his wings, protecting her. But the guardian angel, when all was said and done, was Danilo himself—the husband is the guardian of the home, the defender of his wife. Good Lord, she'd never been so confused.

In the bedroom she couldn't even think, so cowed by fear was she. Now the bright blazing angel, the flaming demon, tore off the sheet and threw it far away, then began to pull her nightgown up over her body. The brute demanded that she lift her derriere to free the gown—he was giving stern orders, and there was no room for discussion.

Dadá lifted up not only her derriere but also her arms and raised her head: The slightest hesitation on her part would have turned his determination into roughness. Prepared to follow her godmother's advice, she obeyed, and her nightgown went trailing off after the sheet. Just as she had been the night before, she was naked, and the time had come: She gritted her teeth.

Danilo moved her legs apart, opened her thighs, lay down on top of her, and kissed her mouth ardently albeit not furiously, in deference to her sore lip. Momentarily distracted by that sign of consideration, Adalgisa let him move freely, and he took advantage of this to position satisfactorily the tip of his lance: flamboyant, ostentatious, gleaming, flashy, glowing, delectable, fabulous—I leave the choice of adjective to the ladies, since only those who have been served and glutted by it are qualified to celebrate it. Lance at the ready, its point at the virginal lips of her pussy, Danilo pushed on with force and decision.

When Adalgisa had felt the red-hot stake approach her, she had readied herself for the assault and waited, her nerves tense, her heart in suspense, ready to bear anything, as she had up till then, with resignation and stoicism, without a single moan, any protest. But when he thrust and the pain became fearsome, she forgot her decision and shouted and floundered. She scratched his back, tried to bite him.

But unlike the night before, she wasn't able to free herself tonight. He held her, squashed and open, and attacked again, violently, out of control. She said, amid roars and sobs, "Oh, stop—stop for the love of God, stop, I can't take it I'm going to die, oh, I'm going to die!" He gave another shove, definitive and atrocious, and penetrated inside her cunt.

Any fool who thought Adalgisa's shouting "Oh I'm going to die" meant she was fainting with pleasure deserves a punch in the nose. Torn, lacerated, Adalgisa felt only pain, pain, and nothing else. She moaned ceaselessly, while Danilo lorded it over the stronghold, took possession, installed himself, moving impetuously, faster. He was moaning, too, and the *ohs* that came out of him were of pure pleasure. His sighs of pleasure were mixed with howls of triumph. He too said he was going to die as he poured out inside her and, exhausted, collapsed on top of Dadá and kissed her. He raised his head to announce "My woman!" to her and to the world.

Then the warrior withdrew from the conquered redoubt, from the fortress that had finally fallen. Adalgisa moaned aloud, in a wail. Danilo wiped himself on the sheet. If the maid, the deceptive Marialva, had been startled during her cleaning of the room that morning to find the bedsheets in immaculate condition, with no trace of deflowering, she would have no reason for suspicion or doubt tomorrow: The proof of blood was there, sacred and sacramental, blood in profusion. At last, uff! It was about time, a most difficult cherry.

Postscript

In order to gain a better understanding of what has been reported relative to the event and its consequences, about which we shall say more later, it would be useful at this juncture to make reference to two details, no matter how irrelevant they may seem initially.

Let us mention first, briefly and without comment, that Danilo, unsatisfied with the entry—difficult for him, excruciating for Adalgisa — returned to his task, paying no attention to the pleas of the one just raped, penetrated her, and found delight in a slow and prolonged possession. He even took a third go at it. Adalgisa was tight and narrow, a gift of God.

He stopped after the third time, not because he was sated or had lost his erection—let no one cast aspersions—but to allow Adalgisa some rest. There was no hurry; they had a week of honeymoon before them to enjoy on São Paulo Bluff: There would be lots more beach and bed.

Let it also be mentioned that Dadá, stretched out between the sheets, her strength gone, incapable of resistance, was still moaning, but among the moans was mingled an imperceptible humming. Danilo moved his ear closer: Her eyes closed, her hands crossed, Adalgisa was moving her lips in prayer. Dadá was praying. Danilo smiled to see her thanking the Lord for making her a complete and fulfilled woman, a wife and lover. A prayer of thanks, it must be, he thought, that was all it could have been.

Then, too, it was also possible that she was offering God Almighty a sacrifice in payment for her sins, the sins of the flesh she had committed during the year of her engagement, and that she was promising now not to fall into temptation again. One way or the other, this is the postscript.

Adalgisa's Altar and Bed

Nineteen years had passed, as is written in the best serial novels, since the honeymoon, since those unforgettable days on São Paulo Bluff. The situation today has already been described: Danilo enjoys himself in brothels to compensate for what's missing in his married life, to relieve his erection, aroused and repressed by his wife. Nineteen years after the unforgettable events, let the adjective unforgettable be repeated, since it applies to him as much as to her, the ex-prince of the playing field continued to find only bitterness in his barren bed; parsimonious pleasures, scant variety. He is limited to a rare and modest kicking up of the heels at a frequency of once a week, in the classic mama-and-papa position only. The know-it-all Marilu, who is today the very worthy Mrs. Liberato Covas Albufeira, a paragon of virtue, the patroness of pious works, is no longer present to mock the mama-and-papa position. The occasion has now arisen for us to seek out the data with which to establish the moral of the story, the high point of any tale worth its salt.

The second night after the newlyweds had stepped off the launch to take over the nuptial bedroom in Dr. Almeida's house, the prince had dispensed with the appetizers and dived exclusively into the main course. He had eaten it all covered with blood, with the greediness of a starving man and the boorishness of a savage. Nineteen years later, he still wasn't aware of the error he'd committed.

Appetizers, antipasto, dessert, rare delicacies, pleasing to the palate, delightful to the tongue, sugar, ginger, and pepper—the delicacies of the bed, not having been tasted on the honeymoon, were not forthcoming in the marriage bed either. No matter how much he tried to convince her with cantatas and wiles, wheedling words and wrathful imprecations, he never succeeded in getting Dadá to accept her participation at the banquet festivities, even if he served caviar or *fromage camembert bien fait— merci*, my dear Professor João Batista! Strictly, she neither served nor consumed anything beyond the bare necessities, without *la sauce au poivre—merci* once more, Professor Batista!—of the cherry to provoke the appetite.

Her obstinacy proved difficult, especially during the first months. The initial loving honeymoon climate soon deteriorated into a clamor of quarrels, recriminations, complaints, and censures, and as a consequence, the migraines returned. The celebrated harmony of bride and groom went down the drain, and nearly took the marriage along with it. Even while they were still on São Paulo Bluff, on one very bad day, Adalgisa had threatened, sobbing:

"You really don't love me! I think it would be better if I left, went back to my father's house. All by myself!"

Danilo came to, bent over backward to ask forgiveness, and swore his love. How many times, on the beach or in bed, had they made up or kissed at the height of passion? At the height of passion, in the heat of kissing, confusing peacefulness for docility, he went back to asking, and she went back to refusing:

"If you love me, get those ideas out of your head. That's not love."

The disagreement that started on the bluff grew upon their return to the city, and even then the situation was close to the point of no return. Pledges and hedges, headaches and heartaches, Adalgisa ended up winning the dispute back in Bahia, in spite of Danilo's refusal to accept his defeat as final. She managed to keep him within the limits that her godmother and her father confessor permitted, without giving him the slightest margin for abuse. Her godmother had warned her of the danger of the first step on the slippery slope of indecent behavior: *"El primer paso es fatal, hijita."* Father José Antonio, in the confessional, tried to keep her on the alert: Nothing beyond the relationship necessary for the reproduction of the human species should be allowed. The voice of Father José Antonio, normally discursive and powerful, became thinner, lower, hoarse, and quavering when it took up the delicate theme, out of embarrassment, no doubt.

The Doll

Quite properly, then, Adalgisa had not refused to fulfill her wifely duties. During the honeymoon, every night without exception and on some extra afternoons, in order to avoid discord and quarrels—Danilo was a madman with his demands—she'd surrendered and received him. Little by little it became easier, less uncomfortable with every entry. It was no longer the extreme suffering of rape, although only after a month would it stop hurting.

Danilo was not content to have only one orgasm, he always had seconds, and occasionally he would even repeat the seconds. Adalgisa would put her thoughts elsewhere. Dadá had heard the word *orgasm* and learned its meaning from the mouth of Marilu, who else? But her old classmate, the incipient sexologist, hadn't told her that women, too, are capable of orgasm and pleasure.

Dadá subjected herself to her wifely duty if not with pleasure, at least without resistance and even with a breath of hope. It was not the hope of someday getting to enjoy the penetration or the rhythm, because she had no idea whatsoever that the woman too could find pleasure in sexual relations; it was the hope—and desire—of becoming pregnant, immediately, if possible. The night they had stepped off the launch, the woman's pronouncement had been auspicious: A honeymoon at Dr. Almeida's house meant a baby nine months later to the day.

The greatest dream of Adalgisa's life was to have a child, preferably a girl—that was why she'd married. While the hip Marilu was going out on dates and visiting boys' apartments, Adalgisa, the booby, was still playing with dolls. Enormous, spectacular Spanish dolls that walked and talked, brought back from trips by her doting father in his days of plenty. It was to the daughter she imagined, blond, pink, and beautiful, just like her favorite doll, that Dadá, aching, turned her thoughts when, in order to conceive her, she gave in to copulation. *Copulation*, an ugly word— *fucking*, Marilu would have said.

But Adalgisa's period started on schedule the last night of their honeymoon, much to her disappointment. The dame had been mistaken in her prediction this time.

The Fanatic

Adalgisa knew without doubt that in order to become pregnant, to have a child, nothing else was necessary in bed beyond what she had been doing daily; everything else only served the diabolical satisfaction of the flesh. During their engagement and even during the crossing from Valença to São Paulo Bluff, she'd been on the verge of succumbing to temptation, of falling into error, of letting herself be corrupted. But she had redeemed her sins with the sacrifice of her body on her wedding night, or on the second one, rather, since the massacre had gone on for two nights. How could she have withstood it? The Lord, who had protected her, giving her strength and courage to fulfill her duty as a married woman, would help her, give her the strength to fulfill her obligations as a practicing God-fearing Catholic.

During the honeymoon Danilo had had to content himself with the main course: apart from that, total abstinence. When they returned to the city, it got worse right away. As long as she had hope of getting pregnant, Adalgisa gave in without being begged. But then Dr. Elsimar Coutinho, from laboratory tests made by Dr. Brenha Chaves, diagnosed Danilo as sterile. Danilo explained to her that it was most certainly the result of his soccer playing, a blow on the nuts; while Dr. Elsimar confided to the weeping wife that it was congenital, incurable. In any case, Dadá immediately reduced the frequency of their already modest sexual relations.

Unhappy situations such as this one, not as rare as is generally thought, often lead to religious or political fanaticism. They limit, deform, debase, castrate the spirit. Is this the moral of the story? In part, yes, but it still isn't finished. With a little patience, please, we'll reach the end of these mundane matters together.

The Stud

Without minimizing the impact of the Church on the troubled life of this couple, if we are to establish the moral of this story completely and correctly, we must ask whether Danilo himself, that Brazilian stud, doesn't also have a place in the moral archive.

Given its antecedents in the engagement, Adalgisa hadn't imagined that the honeymoon could become such a disappointment, or that back in Bahia the conflict would stretch out into tears, ill humor, reproaches, and threats, threatening even to end the marriage. Convinced that her husband didn't love her after one painful scene, her head bursting, her finger pointing, Adalgisa was ready to put an end to the untenable situation once and for all:

"What could you have been thinking? How dare you propose filth like that to me! Do you think I'm a common whore, a prostitute? The only ones fit for disgusting things like that are sluts in their bawdy houses! No woman with regard for herself would lower herself to such things. No, everything's all over between us. I can't take it anymore. Pack your things and leave!" They were living at this time in the apartment in Graça, along with Paco, her father.

Without knowing it, Adalgisa had just saved the marriage. Danilo remained thoughtful, stunned, his eyes far off:

"But I—I'd never thought about such a thing."

They didn't break up. Danilo promised to behave, he always did, vehemently, swearing oaths—it was no trouble for him to promise. They were reconciled at the movies, watching one of those tearjerkers that were Adalgisa's favorites.

Despite the limitations that the laws of the catechism imposed, the frigidity into which Dadá locked herself also had its origins in the way she'd been first possessed on her honeymoon: the violence, the butchery of losing her cherry. Butchery, a clumsy word here, is taken from the notable essay by Dr. Graciela de la Concha Carril, an Argentinian psychoanalyst to whose wisdom we have had recourse—it's always advisable to look for support from someone in possession of authority and competence. "The audacity," the celebrated sexologist writes, "the ignorance, the imposition, the tyranny of the male and master, impatient to take possession of the hymen purchased with matrimony, are responsible for the large group of women who, in the marriage bed, go through life without ever experiencing, without ever tasting the pleasures of sex."*

The scientist is absolutely right: There is an immense legion of Brazilian women for whom encounters in bed don't go beyond the monotonous wifely duties. They never reach an orgasm, never have pleasure. They end up dry, apathetic, sad, afflicted, ill. Objects of pleasure, they are victims of puritanical dogmas and *macho* violence.

Alarmed, Adalgisa had mentioned that on the ferry during the crossing—do you remember?—she'd been on the point of giving in to temptation. Had Danilo continued his conquest, softly and pleasantly, who knows, he might have knocked down the walls of her puritanism: Such things have happened.

Reflected in the two faces of tragic reality, the moral of the story may be of some use to us today, in spite of the fact that nowadays, with the contraceptive pill and the hippie revolution, there aren't many virgins left for official wedding nights. When today's bridegrooms knock down an open door, they eat a warmed-over meal. In any case, here's the lesson, and it's worth one's while learning it: Virginity must be taken without rashness, with grace, love and courtesy. So let us consider this chapter of the tale closed, a chapter on a wedding feast that was meant to be merry and pleasurable, full of the caresses and moans of love, but one that turned out to be something completely different.

---

* Dr. Graciela de la Concha Carril, *The Frigid Woman: A Crime of Machismo*, trans. Fanny Rechulski (São Paulo: Diaulas Riedel).

An Obvious Explanation

Is there anything left to be explained? What? Well, for example, how Adalgisa saved her marriage when she had threatened to break it up forever? But the explanation is obvious—it's right there, only too simple. How is it possible that nobody has caught on to it?

In her indignant accusation, Adalgisa had said, word for word: "The only ones fit for disgusting things like that are sluts in their bawdy houses!" Right? So? Without knowing and without intending, she had pointed out to Danilo the safe harbor where he could anchor the ship of matrimony that was about to founder.

In the afternoon of the following day, after four months of absence, the prince of heartfelt memory returned to Fadinha's townhouse on the Ladeira de São Francisco. Couples in the delights of their play could look out through the open windows and see the church biddies and tourists going into the church of São Francisco, all covered with gold.

"Anyone who's alive and kicking will always show up here," Astrud exclaimed, falling into his arms.

Nota Bene

We've now had a digression and a postscript, so all that's lacking is a *nota bene*, and here it is. At the whim of the plot, we have mentioned some of the presents that the bride and groom received and the names of the friends who sent them. We have alluded to gifts given by the Fernándezes, Cotrims, Machados—who sent the indiscreet and, why not say so, exciting nightie, the choice and memento of Dona Glória—Frau Consul Adler, the merchant Artur Sampaio.

The gifts received, however, were not limited to those few. There were other gifts, expensive ones. Notably pricey were those of Lúcia and Paulo Peltier de Queiroz, Ana and Angelo Calmon de Sá, and Regina and Newton Rique: particularly quaint was the *berimbau* given by Master Pastinha, with whom Danilo had been taking *capoeira* lessons.

It was a long list, too long to include each person's name here, but to each one of them Adalgisa sent a gracious card of thanks—the front showed two hearts run through by an arrow shot by Cupid—thanking them for the present and opening her home to them. The address was Paco Negreiro's because the young couple didn't have enough money for rent and had to stay with her father. At the notary's office, a mere clerk, Danilo earned a miserable salary. So much the better that Dadá had learned the trade of milliner from her godmother.

The Events
of Thursday
Afternoon

The Cloister
of the Penitents

Six hours, measured on the clock on the Largo São Pedro, barely passed between the discovery of the note and Manela's internment in the Convent of the Immaculate Conception in Lapa, the Cloister of the Penitents.

In days of yore, as well as in more recent times, the father of a maiden who had taken the wrong step, dragging the family name through the mud of dishonor, would lock his unnatural daughter up there in the convent for the rest of her life: It was an abbey of gloomy renown. Dead and buried to the outside world, without even visits from her weeping mother permitted, even her memory would be wiped out: Her portraits were done away with, her face vanished, her memories were extinct, and mention of her name was forbidden, as if the infamous girl had never been born, had never existed.

As absurd as it may seem, life imprisonment in the convent was a liberal advance over the previous penalty, a sentence still current in cities and obligatory in the backlands: death. Only the proven execution of the criminals—the accursed daughter and the vile seducer—would cleanse the honor of the family, restoring its dignity and pride. Certain spirited fathers, diligent in the pursuit of justice, would cut off the seducer's balls before cutting off his life.

It still happens today, even if the more usual denouement in our progressive times is that the attentive father receives the lover of the day into his house, feeds him opulently, and escorts him to his daughter's bed, without assistance of priest or judge. Times and customs do change, but the exceptions persist, and to serve these remaining parents and guardians who seek proper justice, the Cloister of the Penitents at the Convent of the Immaculate Conception remains available. Manela's case had not reached the irremediable stage, so her internment was preventive, not perpetual. She would return home as soon as she got the devil out of her head, no longer wanted to hear anything about that chimpanzee of a boy, her aunt Adalgisa told the mother superior.

When the main door of the convent closed, a tear crept into the corner of Adalgisa's eye. But she quickly wiped it away before Father José Antonio noticed that sign of weakness.

The Torn Note

It need not have turned out this way. Guided by the hand of God, Adalgisa had seen and picked up a little scrap of paper in the bathroom behind the toilet bowl, the mere fragment of a note, crumpled but still legible. It must have dropped from Manela's hand without her noticing after the wretch had crushed and torn up the message and thrown it into the toilet to flush away.

"Good Lord in Heaven!"

Adalgisa had recognized that devil's handwriting. In repeated searches she'd gone over her niece's room with a fine-tooth comb looking for clues, and she'd found many letters and notes from the chimpanzee. *Devil* and *chimpanzee* were how Adalgisa referred to Miroel da Natividade, Miro to everybody else, who, in his correspondence with Manela, signed himself, "Your future husband, Mirinho the Ever-Loving." Convinced that the lovers had conceived a plan to run off, with the help of Damiana and other neighbors and with the obvious participation of Aunt Gildete—the list of suspected accomplices was endless—Adalgisa devoted herself fully to the finding of traces and proofs, ready to do anything to stop the execution of the diabolical plot.

Finally, she'd lost hope. Chats, warnings, advice, moral lessons, not even pleas had gotten her anywhere: Manela would listen in hostile silence, wouldn't open her mouth even to reply, let alone to argue. Only when her aunt got all worked up against the "devil," the "chimpanzee," would Manela repeat, "I love that devil. I'm going to marry that chimpanzee, whether you like it or not, Auntie." Rent by one of her piercing headaches, taken over by her migraine, Adalgisa was foaming at the mouth in rage. Manela, overcome by pity, embraced her: "Ask me to do anything you want, Auntie, anything but that."

It was the worse because she could no longer make use of the leather strap. After that fateful Bomfim Thursday she'd tried to use it on her errant niece to frighten and correct her, to put things back in order, but she hadn't been able to pick it up again. As if she'd unlearned how to manipulate the whip, when she took it in her depraved hand, she couldn't grip it; her arm was like lead. Deprived of the leather strap, she did only the little that was left to her to do: She locked Manela up in the house as punishment, forbade her to go out with classmates and girl-friends, chaperoned her or had Danilo accompany her to the door of the school, and went to wait for her there when she came out. Adalgisa had become a slave to her obligations to guard Manela's honor, before God and the juvenile judge. As long as Manela was under her care, Adalgisa wouldn't allow her to go astray, or worse, elope with that chimpanzee, a black man of low origins, a taxi driver! She couldn't marry anyone without the consent of herself and Danilo, under whose guardianship the orphaned girl had been placed.

Miro was the owner of a secondhand car, but so what? He was still nothing but a pauper. Adalgisa wanted a proper husband for her niece, someone with an education if possible, someone successful in life or at least embarked on a promising profession that would raise the prestige of the family. That was the reason Adalgisa had reared her so strictly. While she waited for a suitor of that level to appear, she had tried to keep Manela away from the sexual promiscuity of adolescence, the libertine ways that were transforming innocent schoolgirls today into gangs of depraved whores. Adalgisa had periodically rummaged through Manela's dresser drawers and purses in search of birth-control pills.

Now, holding the shred of paper in her trembling hand, Adalgisa wondered whether there was still time to intervene, to avoid the irreparable. Maybe there was, if she acted with speed and efficiency. It hadn't been luck but divine providence that had saved this scrap from the toilet and given her precise indications concerning the elopement, its day and hour: The devil would be waiting in his car, at seven in the evening that very day! The chimpanzee hadn't beaten about the bush: "Today you're going to enjoy the best of the very best, it's going to be a wonderful night, my love. You can't go on under the thumb of that . . ." That what? It wasn't hard to guess how Miro had finished, describing Manela's conditions of life as slavery, her aunt and guardian as jailer and torturer.

To whom could Adalgisa turn at this decisive moment except God? Hadn't He been the one to show her this piece of the note? For Adalgisa, God's personal and accredited representative in the city of Bahia was Father José Antonio Hernández, her confessor of many years, the director of her conscience. She dressed hurriedly and fixed her hair. So vexed was she that she forgot to take her cup of boldu tea to lessen the migraine that had implacably taken over.

Adalgisa was working to fulfill two dreams. One was the old one of having her own house. In order to bring that about, she deposited what she could put aside from her millinery business every month into a savings account. The other dream was one she'd had since January: She dreamed of seeing the devil, the chimpanzee behind bars. To that end, she said a Hail Mary and an Our Father every night. She had faith in deposit slips and in the infinite goodness of the Lord.

The Juvenile Judge

Early that Thursday afternoon, accompanied by Father José Antonio, Adalgisa was received by His Honor Dr. Liberato Mendes Prado d'Ávila, the juvenile judge, where she laid out the matter and obtained satisfaction.

In Rio Vermelho, in the pompous sacristy of the recently built Church of Sant'Ana—"So marvelous!" the church biddies exclaimed in ecstasy: "A monstrosity!" artists retorted—Adalgisa confided to the priest her fears that the worst might happen, irreparable harm, and asked for his advice and help. The honor of her ward and her responsibility as guardian were at stake.

Father José Antonio listened with his head down and his eyes cloudy; sins of the flesh affected him to the point of causing changes in his face and voice. "Do you think she still hasn't given in?" he asked. "How far can she have gone along the path of sin?" "She certainly hasn't given in and she can't have gone far into shame," Adalgisa replied. "I keep her on a tight rein, I don't give her a chance. What shall I do?" Preventing the elopement set for that very night was easy: All she had to do was lock Manela in her room, stop her from showing up at the rendezvous, and the plan would come to naught. But what about after that?

Even if she took her out of school—and Adalgisa was prepared to take that extreme measure—she wouldn't be able to keep her in her domestic prison forever, considering what the neighbors would say. Gildete would intervene, protest, raise a row and a scandal. What could Adalgisa do to keep her niece far from temptation and danger and prevent further plotting, until she finally broke off the love affair, dumped the taxi driver, forgot the black pauper? In freeing her niece from error, Adalgisa would also free herself from a situation that had transformed her life: If she continued on like this with Manela, she'd end up in an insane asylum.

Unable to give the kind of answers that would allow a quick judgment, the priest raised his shoulders and his eyes, a bit disappointed; then he recovered the solemn and harmonious voice that so enraptured devout ladies and spoke of consolation and providence. God, on his throne of light in the high heavens, he assured her, had witnessed the zeal of the good sheep from his flock who had made so many sacrifices in order to see the precepts of Holy Mother Church fulfilled. She mustn't despair because he, Father José Antonio, was there, under the Lord's command, to help her get through the crisis, to foil the designs of Satan, defeat him, save the maiden's innocence or what might be left of it, it probably wasn't much—he thought that but didn't say it, there was no reason to. In the tragicomic battle against the forbidden love of Manela and Miro, Father José Antonio Hernández, in the name of God, assumed operational command. A militant of virtue, he wasn't content with theory, he practiced it.

"*Quédate tranquila, hija mía, el honor de Manela está en las manos de Dios.*" He spoke to Adalgisa in Spanish, and were it not for her Saracen endowments, a more classic Valencian woman couldn't have existed.

In fact, God had just inspired him with a solution. In the convent in Lapa, Manela would be safe from any danger, far from temptation. In the peace of the cloister, living with the holy sisters, in intimacy with God, as the fiancée of Jesus, she could reflect calmly and realize how much her deviation was harming her. In a short time she'd give up both love affair and lover, would thank her aunt. She'd return home with a clear head and a pure soul; she'd cease being any trouble.

"In the Cloister of the Penitents?"

"*Sí, mi hija, el local propio para la peniténcia y el convencimiento*"— just the place for penance and conviction.

He, Father José Antonio, would take it upon himself to speak to the mother superior immediately. But since Manela was a minor, it would be necessary to obtain the authorization of the juvenile judge to place her there. The judge would be no obstacle: Dr. d'Ávila, the priest guaranteed, would understand Adalgisa's reasons and approve her decision. He was a Spartan, a bastion of morality, the priest told Adalgisa.

Spartan, bastion of morality, educator, and disciplinarian of wayward youth, that scourge of our time, His Honor, didn't use his hand to tousle the hair of delinquent minors; he used it to sign orders of internment in reformatories, thereby furnishing boarders for those exemplary schools of crime and vandalism. Another His Honor, Dr. Agnaldo Bahia Monteiro, a colleague in family court, who was in many ways Dr. d'Ávila's opposite, didn't mince words: He described him as retrograde, prejudiced, reactionary, fascist. His own wife, Dona Diana Teles Mendes Prado d'Ávila, known to us under the *nom de guerre* Sylvia Esmeralda, a negligent student of theater history and an amateur actress, confided to her intimate friends that apart from his touch of aristocracy—the bay area family, now down at the heels, was descended from Garcia d'Ávilas —her husband's two major qualities were stupidity and discipline. Everything else was derivative from those two, including evil, hypocrisy, toadying to the powerful, his overbearing demeanor with subordinates and the poor in general, empty rhetoric, strutting, and cuckold's horns.

Father José Antonio introduced Adalgisa to His Honor and praised her warmly to him: "A dedicated and pious sheep from the Lord's flock, exemplary in her virtues, she bears the cross of a rebellious niece whose guardian she has been since the death of the girl's parents." The judge asked her to present the facts, listened gravely, showed himself to be on her side, and signed the order. Interned by order of the juvenile judge, Manela would remain in the Convent of the Penitents for the time determined by her guardian, and no neighbor or relative, no matter how close, had any right to protest or intervene.

As for the satyr—the taxi driver—if he'd harmed the minor, Dr. d'Ávila would be happy to send him to jail. Since this was not the case, he promised instead to summon Miro and inform him that the court was keeping its eye on him. They would familiarize him with the punishments to which corrupters of minors and rapers of virgins are subject— and squeeze him a bit, take him down a peg.

The Falangist

How wonderful it was that God had put Father José Antonio in Adalgisa's path a short while before Doña Esperanza died. The priest had taken charge of completing the task that the godmother had begun: to rear Adalgisa in all the fanatical and puritanical rigidity of Spanish Catholicism, so as to make the daughter of Francisco Romero Pérez y Pérez a servant of Christ, a flawless Catholic, a first-rate Spanish woman invincible to dissoluteness and idolatry.

José Antonio had been almost thirty when he came to Brazil in a levy of priests that the Vatican was sending to Latin American countries where Church doctrine was being corrupted, its principles weakened, and pagan rites were overcoming devotion to the saints. He was a fervent Falangist, an impetuous bearer of the Pope's infallible word to heathens in general, and bearer of the orders-of-the-day from Generalissimo Franco to the Spaniards of Bahia, whether they had been born in the homeland or in the colonies. After the end of the war, with the demise of Hitler and Mussolini, those unforgettable heroes and martyrs, the confidence of certain fellow countrymen in the Falange had vacillated, their faithfulness and contributions had grown smaller, and Republican swine were lifting up their heads. In his luggage Father José Antonio had brought along the Falangist banners that he'd carried through the streets of Valencia: *!Viva Cristo Rey! !Arriba España!*

In his Bahian curriculum vitae he counted eloquent victories, while the defeats he had suffered didn't discourage him whose soul was tempered in Francoist ranks. Among the campaigns he undertook against his powerful enemies, two deserve notice, citation, and commentary in these pages. Therefore, as we give information on him, we shall take advantage of any opportunity to narrate events that took place in the city of Bahia: Everything that happens there is of universal interest.

The construction of the new Church of Sant'Ana in Rio Vermelho was an epic event! A splendid victory! He'd succeeded in building the large, imposing church dedicated to Mary's mother, whose worship had hitherto been reduced to a miserable chapel traditionally connected to street festivals and *candomblé* ceremonies. It was a splendid victory, the culmination of an insane campaign that had taken six years of drive and pleading. Even so, the victory wasn't complete, however, because Father José Antonio had wanted to erect the new church on the ruins of a popular syncretistic chapel located in the middle of the Largo de Sant'Ana.

He'd sought the explicit support of the cardinal for the necessary demolition but hadn't obtained it. A band of irresponsible intellectuals in the service of Moscow had taken over the pages of the press to protest the project. Pedro Moacyr Maia wrote an article documenting the traditions of the square and the chapel, and the poet Wally Salomão published an "Indignant Invective on the Chapel of Ana Yemanjá." Many had defended the preservation of the little chapel, so dear to the inhabitants of the district, reproduced in paintings by José de Dome, Willys, Cardoso e Silva, and Licídio Lopes. It hadn't mattered much that it had no historical value; it was a possession of the people of the city; it was poor and simple, just like they were. The archdiocese hesitated, the cardinal washed his hands of the matter, and in the end, the little chapel had stayed where it is today on the square, drawing in devotees with its simple grace on the festival of Our Lady Saint Anne and during the procession for Yemanjá.

The majestic new Church of Sant'Ana, of the dimensions and architecture that Father José Antonio had planned, had been built instead in between the Largo de Sant'Ana and the Largo da Mariquita, right next to the Colônia de Pescadores, the fishermen's colony. This site was also appropriate, for as tall and broad as the church was, it would smother—that was how the priest had imagined it—the Peji de Yemanjá located in the Casa do Peso. There the people left their presents for Yemanjá, the queen of the sea, and it was from there that the sloops departed on February 2, a day dedicated to Dona Janaína: Janaína, Inaê, the Siren Mukunã, Dadalunda, Kaiala, Dona Maria, the Princess of Aioká—many and varied are the names and nations of Yemanjá, fiancée and wife of fishermen.

Father José Antonio had dedicated his church with all the pomp and solemnity of a *te deum,* presided over by the cardinal in the presence of the regional commandant, the admiral of the naval base, the brigadier of the air base, the governor of the state, and the mayor, as well as prominent people in the city and large numbers from the Spanish colony. A ceremony worthy of Franco's redeemed Spain, it had been. Adalgisa, on her husband's arm, a black mantilla on her head, was exultant. She had won a mother-of-pearl rosary as a prize in a contest to collect gifts and donations for the building of the church, which the priest had set up among the ladies of the parish; they'd conducted raffles, held drawings, and run bazaars and fairs.

A week later on the invitation of the inhabitants of the district, the common people, the black masses, led by Flaviano, the president of the Colônia de Pescadores, had assembled to the sound of drums and Yoruba songs to dedicate a statue of Yemanjá erected between the church and the Casa do Peso, the work of Manual do Bomfim, a sculptor in the area. It was an unheard-of bit of insolence, frightful! In his Sunday sermon Father José Antonio, burning with anger, inveighed against sacrilege and barbarism.

At the time of Manela and Miro's insubordination, the priest was involved in an equally fierce and equally opportune campaign. He was planning to extinguish the Engenho Velho Candomblé, the Ilê Iya Nassô, the most ancient and venerable fetishist temple in Bahia. Scholars date it to 1830, but others give it three hundred years of life or even more, no one knows for certain. Father José Antonio appealed to the interests and greed of the property owners and the real estate magnates: On the top of the hill, he pointed out, was the temple, then the White House, and below on the Avenida Vasco da Gama, the Barco de Oxum—Oxum's Ship—with its magical cargo of *fundamentos* and *axés*. So much money was being lost, he said, so much space was going to waste in a place where a good dozen high-rises could be built.

Then a gas station appeared in front of the Barco de Oxum, hiding the ship from the view of passersby, and there was already talk of subdividing the rest of the land, tearing down the *candomblé* temple and the houses of the enchanted ones, even those of Oxalá and Exu. Alerted, the intellectuals, those thinly disguised agents of the devil and the Kremlin, once more spread the word. Not content merely with halting the operations underway, they dared propose to the Historic and Cultural Landmarks Commission that the whole area be registered, houses, shed, temple, the Barco de Oxum, as a holy place, filled with history, the symbol for blacks of the fight against slavery. Such effrontery was unheard of, and Father José Antonio was astounded—as if the *candomblé* temple were the Church of São Francisco, the Carmelite convent, or the Cathedral Church! Father José Antonio Hernández wrote letters of protest to the newspapers, went to the civil and military authorities—the military especially—and declaimed in his sermons, trying to keep the banners of the Falange flying in Bahia—though they seemed to fly at half staff in this land of mirages and illusions.

He didn't have many sheep in his flock of fanatics and puritans, but he showered them with attention. We are living in a time of negation and permissiveness, he believed, when priests trade in their cassocks for blue jeans, their Latin for Portuguese, the rich for the poor.

In a time when priests were demanding an end to celibacy and getting involved with Communist guerrilla fighters, Father José Antonio remained faithful to fascism and dogma. He maintained his vow of chastity, a difficult chore, with much bravery and valor. But when he dreamed about Delilah, Salome, Mary Magdalene, Lot's wife, and the Queen of Sheba, he polluted the sheets of his bachelor's bed. Lately, he'd begun to dream about Adalgisa.

The Abicun

The deaths of Adalgisa's mother and godmother followed one after the other in the year preceding her wedding. In his sermon to the bridal couple Monsignor Sadock had recalled the deceased, two saintly creatures. Doubly orphaned now, with her hand clad in a white glove, Adalgisa wiped away a nostalgic tear, mourning their absence—that of Doña Esperanza even more than that of Andreza.

Not that she was a bad daughter, or was unfeeling about the death of her mother. Beside the inert body she'd had a terrible and strange attack in which she was smothered in sobs, as if she were to blame for the death. She was like a person possessed, foaming at the mouth.

But Adalgisa's despair was different when she faced the equally unexpected death of her godmother. She wept for her with rosary in hand, fingering the beads, kneeling beside the coffin, lifting from time to time the handkerchief that covered the dead woman's face, to stare at her, tears running down her cheeks. From the time she'd carried Adalgisa to the baptismal font, Doña Esperanza had taken charge of her and taught her how to make the sign of the cross and recite the Our Father. Later on, she'd instructed her in the art of making hats, sewing fabrics, putting floral bouquets together, adding lacework. But most of all, she'd shown her what direction to follow, reared her, made a lady of her. Even though she was poor, living on the Avenida da Ave-Maria, Adalgisa was a lady. She saw herself in Doña Esperanza's mirror: Her godmother had known how to keep herself above and apart from the riffraff—*!la señora!*—in spite of being obliged to work in order to eat. She owed everything to her godmother, the goddaughter would repeat to herself when she thought of her. She was grateful to her mother for having given her life—she'd done it twice, but Adalgisa didn't know that she'd been born and reborn.

Between Adalgisa and Andreza there had always been distance, and their divergence had gradually been accentuated with the passage of years. Dolores wouldn't let go of her mother's skirts and was always helping her with domestic chores, accompanying her on visits to relatives and friends and in a broad range of involvements and friendships, tendering obligations to saints, *amalás* for Xangô, *carurus* for Cosmos and Damian, *doburus* for Obaluayê, *boris,* leaf baths, temple festivals— Dolores had been Andreza's constant companion, her devoted daughter, most certainly her favorite. Through it all, Andreza had maintained an uncommon attention for Adalgisa, a kind of consideration and deference, as if for some reason the elder daughter deserved special devotion.

Adalgisa had spent most of her time in her godmother's small apartment, a residence and millinery workshop carved out of one of those buildings set against a hill, four floors up and four floors down from the street. Doña Esperanza lived and labored in the lowest part, where only a strip of sunlight could be seen in the morning. On the other hand, the building was in the Graça district, the most aristocratic address in the city.

Andreza and Paco Negreiro had gotten married without any guests, without any announcements in the papers, in the presence of their sponsors and a half-dozen friends. The ceremony took place after their two daughters had already been born, after more than ten years of living together, the pretext being that Paco had recently escaped from an automobile accident and was afraid of dying suddenly and leaving his mistress and girls with no rights of inheritance, in poverty. In truth, he was crazy about his daughters and Andreza, whom he'd met when she was quite young, a dazzling shepherdess in the Flower of Solitude Epiphany procession. He fell passionately in love with her in an instant. Paco Negreiro was a man who normally hovered darkly like a vulture, a hawk, a bird of prey, hunting here and there without rest or respite—when his urge was satisfied, he would release his prey. But with Andreza, just the opposite occurred: He sweated to possess her, she was a virgin when he discovered her, all done up with crepe paper, carrying the lantern for the Three Kings. She tried to give him the brushoff when she saw him with his eyes on Esmeraldina, an adept of Omolu, wild and loose in the samba circle, a ship in a storm.

Even when she was finally shacked up with her rich Spanish white man, Andreza didn't forget her poor black friends and family; she kept on going to *candomblés*, fulfilling the saints' obligations and the norms of friendship. When she met Paco, she'd just arranged with Mãe Aninha of the Axé do Opô Afonjá that she'd be on the next *barco* of *iaôs* to shave their heads, and receive Yansan, their *orixá*, face to face. That was what she did, leaving him to daydream while she was gone, counting the days of her initiation on his fingers. She didn't know, however, that at that moment in her womb she was carrying the result of her affair with the *gringo* who'd seduced her and set her up in a house: She was pregnant with Adalgisa. When she found out, it was too late: She was already a thoroughgoing *iaô-de-éfun*, her head shaved, her body painted and seeped in *maionga* baths; the enchanted one was inside her along with the *abicun*. The child growing inside her wouldn't belong to her, it belonged to the saint. On the day of the *órunkó*, the festival of her name, Andreza had leaped up twice and given two names; one was hers, the other that of the *abicun*.

When Adalgisa was still a young girl (she'd just passed the first stage, that of the age of seven), Andreza told her about the event in abundant detail, informing her of the special status of *abicuns*. In later years she returned to the subject and repeated that an *abicun* belongs to the enchanted one, and if it wishes to live, it must fulfill an inordinate number of obligations. Adalgisa didn't want to hear about it; she swept the facts from her memory, the name, the details, the threat. Having paid the passage of the fourteenth year at the cost of vast sacrifice, Andreza tried once more to explain to her daughter the risk she was running. Adalgisa refused to listen, her beliefs were otherwise, her saints were others, as were her beliefs, her duties, her principles. It was of no avail to reveal to her the price Andreza had paid by replacing the *abicun* at the two thresholds, that of the age of seven and that of the age of fourteen: At the last one, at the age of twenty-one, the price would be death.

Adalgisa, who thought of herself as a Spaniard, had other burdens to bear, the crown of thorns, the cross of Christ; she looked down on superstition and fetishes.

She hadn't learned all this by the eve of her fateful birthday, so that when the sentence was carried out, it wouldn't destroy the *abicun*. Andreza had proposed a "swap of heads" to Oyá: On the day of the festivities of her elder daughter's coming of age, she herself would be found dead. Adalgisa didn't know what a "swap of heads" was, and the word *abicun* meant nothing to her.

On certain occasions, however, Adalgisa felt an invisible presence beside her, an afflicted, desolate shade. On the afternoon of that Thursday, while she was walking with Manela to the Lapa convent where Father José Antonio was waiting for them—Manela suspected nothing since her aunt often took her to customers' houses to show her what wealth and good breeding were—Adalgisa had the feeling that a shadow was accompanying her: It touched her face, took her hand, made it hard for her to walk. Was it her mother, Andreza? But who else could it have been? It couldn't have been her godmother, Doña Esperanza, who would have held her back on the dutiful path: "Pull out evil by the roots when there's still time, *hija mía*."

Even after a "swap of heads," the freedom of the *abicun* is limited and dependent. If the *abicun* fulfills its obligations rigorously in its zeal for the greatness of the *orixá*, it will be a person like any other, with rewards and rights. If, however, it doesn't recognize its condition, denies it, doesn't follow its precepts, and eats and drinks forbidden things, the enchanted ones will not save it, will not offer it the *ossé* and possession; it becomes clandestine, subject to discomfort and ill health, has no rest, no peace or happiness, hears only what is bad, notices only what is ugly. A male will give out while he is still a young stud, and his dick will be limp, a useless scrap of meat; a female will never feel the damp pleasure in her moist cunt. The *abicun* who forswears the *orixá* and ignores it will go through life as if blind, deaf, and nonhuman, clandestine: a robot, a monster, a zombie. Instead of a heart, it will have a stone in the hollow of its chest.

The Ladyloves

Father Abelardo didn't pass through the door of the school of drama. Patrícia was just coming out, and when she saw him, she threw her arms around his neck, pecked a kiss on each cheek, and stroked his face lightly with her hand. Turning to the friend accompanying her, she cried,

"Didn't I tell you he'd come, Sylvia?"

She held him tight in her embrace, her breasts visibly loose under her cambric smock, pressed against the priest's throat, which was free of the celluloid collar, his shirt now open. From the car, Nilda Spencer was urging them to hurry up, saying they were very late, the lunch with the French film crew was set for one o'clock, and most of the guests had probably arrived already. Patrícia pulled Father Abelardo by the hand:

"Come with me. Get in the car!"

The car, Miro's taxi, was idling with the motor running. Besides Miro, the front seat was occupied by Nelson Araújo, who was gripping a bundle of typed pages, and a petulant hippie girl with thick, unruly hair wearing a short Indian-print tunic that showed off her thighs. Sylvia was climbing into the back seat next to Nilda. Patrícia urged the priest:

"Get in, hurry up! We'll be a little squeezed, but it's a short ride. Close your legs, Sylvia—there are two more people to come."

The four of them squeezed into the back seat, Patrícia on the edge, barely sitting down. Miro, his hand on the enhanced horn—it played the refrain from "La Cucaracha"—gave the hand signal that he was pulling out. He maneuvered the car away from the curb, waved good-bye, and took off like a jet. Entering Campo Grande, he swerved suddenly to avoid a pothole. Patrícia fell on top of Father Abelardo, just as she was making the introductions:

"Father Abelardo Galvão, the Robin Hood of the wilds—this one here, Abelardo, is Nilda Spencer, you know who she is."

"Your blessing, Father," Nilda joked, holding out her hand.

"The woman next to you is Sylvia Esmeralda, a classmate of mine at the drama school; in front are Master Nelson Araújo, our director and my second father; beside him Arlete Soares, a friend who lives in Paris. The driver is Miro, a local celebrity."

"How are the barricades coming along? Invaded any properties lately?" Nelson Araújo joked pleasantly without ceasing to thumb through the film script; then he changed the subject: "Nilda, what do you think? Should we alternate celebrity interviews with musical presentations, or what?"

"It's better if Jacques decides himself, don't you think?"

The Soares girl, her head turned to the rear, her fingers running through her hair trying to spread it out even more, was looking the priest over, openmouthed:

"Tell me, friend, you couldn't be related to Father Herbert in Munich, could you? Herbert Heuel—I never saw two people look so much alike, same face, exact same features. I met him in Paris," she explained to the whole group. "A crazy guy. He's doing his doctorate at the Sorbonne. Do you know what his thesis is on? Brecht's theater—can you believe it? When he comes to Paris he stays in the Cité, lives a student's life. Wild!"

"Does he stay at your place, dear?" An innocent smile broadened on Sylvia Esmeralda's well-scrubbed face: "He's your *petit ami,* isn't he?"

"And so what if he is? What's that got to do with anything?"

"I haven't got a drop of German blood in me, or even Spanish," Father Abelardo explained, "in spite of having been born on the Uruguayan border. I've heard about the worker priests over there, and I know a little bit about them. Good people."

"Tell us more about your lover, Arlete," Sylvia went on insistently.

When Miro took a curve at full speed, Patrícia, without any support, slipped off the seat. When she got up, she sat on the priest's lap, as nice as you please, as if it were the most natural thing in the world to do. No one paid any attention, unless it was the priest himself: God was putting him through an awful test! But then, could *awful* be the right word?

Within the speeding taxi Patrícia leaned back against the vicar of Piaçava, settled in, and took his hand; her long hair cascaded down over him and tickled his face. The high-society woman, all aroused, was talking about lovers, Nelson Araújo continued leafing through his papers, and Miro peered over the steering wheel at the Ladeira do Contorno, while the priest sat silent and immobile. *Awful* wasn't the exact word to express everything, the cold and the fever, the panic and the disorder, the precipice—alas, no.

The Morning Chat

Sylvia Esmeralda had answered Olímpia's phone call—it was unusual for her to call at that hour—in the faculty lounge, away from indiscreet witnesses. Any chat with Olímpia de Castro, that high-society locomotive who was her bosom friend, accomplice, and confidante, mustn't be overheard by third parties—there was always risk involved. Sylvia herself had been born to be a confidante; she loved to hear tales of love affairs, passions, of first meetings and last meetings, of voracity and the subsequent distaste.

Every morning, before they took the measures and pleasures of the day, the two of them would linger on the telephone, raking over other people's lives, exchanging slanders about scandals that had just come to light and others that were still in rough draft. What they didn't know, they'd guess—formulating opinions, offering hypotheses, dissecting the upper crust day by day. Colleagues in the licentious and sentimental, they would whisper secrets about the latest adventure each of them had had—Olímpia's whims, Sylvia's passions—amid laughter, exclamations, sighs. Sizzling and exciting themes, from confidence to gossip, were explored, along with the various specialties, aptitudes, and attributes of their partners, the physical and moral details, all discussed in the precise language of teenagers and ladies; they would laugh till they burst. They exchanged advice: "If you get a chance, girl, don't miss Telésforo's tongue—it's divine! That's why they call him honeysuckle, the sucker of the century." And: "Gilbertinho, kid, is colossal! He's got the dong of a donkey. I thought he wasn't going to be able to get it in." "Did he, girl?" "Every little bit, kid, right down to his balls." That was how it went in their instructive morning chats, "girl" here, "kid" there, tongue, dong, asshole, cocksucker.

At one end of the telephone line was Olímpia the airplane; on the other end was Sylvia, "a lighted carousel," to use the metaphor of the poet Joca Teixeira Gomes, one of her first lovers. At the time Sylvia was a newlywed, and he a high school student. Nor is the carousel metaphor entirely lacking in sense; poets' reasons, like their rhymes, are sometimes cabalistic. Another poet, Paulo Gil, compared her to a percussion orchestra—two more poets for the *Anthology of Bahian Poetry,* both of the first rank—referring certainly to the moans and groans that Sylvia Esmeralda would break into when the hallelujah sounded.

The Adolescents

It had been Sylvia Esmeralda d'Ávila, the lawful wife of the juvenile judge, who introduced Olímpia to the particular indulgence of adolescents: Her friend immediately had surpassed her, becoming a connoisseur.

Possessed of a particular and unique charm, these strapping boys nevertheless demonstrated amusing limitations and sometimes suffered serious inconveniences. Their limitations were of time and money, of course, dependent as they were on their class schedules at school and the monthly allowances their parents gave them. But having to throw their lives into disarray in order to attend to the women unexpectedly was the least of the boys' worries; feeling a five-hundred note being discreetly placed into their pockets was more than pleasurable. Still, the inconveniences did finally end up being annoying. Terribly possessive of the women, these boys would often become unreasonable, impertinent. Inse-

cure because of their age, they sometimes behaved aggressively and inso-
lently. When one of them, judging himself irreplaceable, became
unbearable, Sylvia would fall back on Olímpia and vice versa, asking for
help; then they would exchange favors and boys.

One succulent morsel, a ravenous seminarian to whose juvenile
appetite Olímpia offered herself in her free time, was Elói, yet another in
a long string of young lovers proving to be inconsiderate. She had told
him that on that Thursday she couldn't meet him—that afternoon was
reserved for the senator, who was coming all the way from Brasília especially to discuss budgetary outlays, duty before all else. But Elói had
nonetheless telephoned from the archepiscopal palace, speaking softly
and hurriedly in fear of being discovered, to advise her that he would be
at the designated spot at the exact time and that he loved her. What spot,
what time, what was he talking about? The place and time in the note, he
said, and repeated where and when, then hung up immediately, leaving
her intrigued and confused. They hadn't made any date, hadn't set any
time; the little jerk must have invented the rendezvous to make her show
up. Having given the coordinates, he'd cut off communication before she
could argue.

In a sudden rage, Olímpia decided to let him rot in the sun of
Itapuã, their meeting place, in order to teach him not to lie. When her
anger passed, however, she felt sorry for him. If the poor devil had
plotted that trick, he'd done it because the life of a boarding student at
the seminary wasn't easy, and he had to take advantage of his day off.
She had no reason to punish him, and she even had the solution at hand:
She telephoned Sylvia and asked her to go in her place, to feed the
famished Elói out in Itapuã. A few months earlier the opposite had
happened: At the request of Sylvia, weary of so many demands, Olímpia
had taken ruddy Jonga in her arms and legs; he was a little sailor off the
yacht of that pleasant millionaire Tourinho Dantas.

Showing off her international ambience, Sylvia Esmeralda at first
played a little hard to get with Olímpia: "I'm with the Frenchmen from
Antènne 2 today," she said. She finally agreed to meet Elói, however—
she wasn't going to pass up a chance to please a seminarian—she still
hadn't laid one. "What wouldn't I do for you, girl?" When she said
good-bye, Olímpia's voice revealed a touch of annoyance: "Tell him that
since I couldn't come, I sent my best friend, and that he should forgive
me and have a good afternoon. You're the one who's lucky, girl. While
you're having fun, I'll be sucking the senator's limp dick—it makes me
sick."

"What about the kid—is he worth the trouble?"

"Worth it? An incredible lay!" Olímpia de Castro moaned, like an
airplane with engine trouble.

—§··—§

All in Good Time

In order to avoid any misunderstanding, let it be clearly stated that these two distinguished women didn't find pleasure only in filth during their morning chats. Besides being sexpots and gossips, they were cultured and involved; they would talk endlessly about art and literature as well. "I went to Jenner Augusto's exhibit, girl: Jenner's a hunk!" one would say. Or: "I read some poetry by Fernando da Rocha Perez, Nandinho, kid, he's a treat for the eyes." They had a similarly avid interest in politics, both in Brazil and abroad, and they would argue over it in perpetual disagreement.

Actually, in ideological matters, both were firm, intransigent, and sectarian, and they thought along opposite lines. Olímpia, who was the right arm of her entrepreneur husband, supported the dictatorship and found the military delightful—she believed they were saving Brazil from the abyss of atheistic Russian communism. In the vast and disturbed world, her idols were Franco, Chiang Kai-shek, Somoza, and Pinochet, and she kept her gold watch set to Washington time, the compass of the Americas. Sylvia Esmeralda, a bohemian by nature, however, and a student at the drama school, sympathized with the left, but she couldn't declare herself a militant because of her marriage and respectability as Dona Diana Teles Mendes Prado d'Ávila. But she swore by Mao, got all excited over the student movement in France in 1968: "Daniel is a sweet dish, kid." "Which Daniel's that, girl?" "Daniel Cohn-Bendit, the hero of the Sorbonne! He was on a TV program, he's a hunk of meat." Down in the depths of her Louis Vuitton purse, hidden in her wallet, she carried a small picture of Che Guevara that João Jorge—that rascal—had given her at the end of one incandescent afternoon when, after doing her pussy, he had done her mouth.

—§··—§

The Trick

The *samba de roda* was holding everyone's attention when Sylvia Esmeralda finally stood up from the table and took her leave: If she delayed fifteen minutes more, she'd be late getting to Itapuã. Sitting in between two literary eminences, essayist Ordep Serra and short-story writer Hélio Pólvora, she'd taken part in the brilliant debate over university criticism and fictional creation with nods of her head and loud interjections. It was an elevated conversation, or rather an intellectual debate; but it was also rather wearying, and certainly not worth missing the seminarian for. She'd made her appearance at the lunch for the French film crew, had been filmed from a distance, at medium range, and close up—maybe she'd be seen in Paris; she'd certainly appear in the society columns. During the taping with Caetano and Gil, Betânia and Gal, that night in the Teatro Castro Alves, she'd rejoin the crew. But she'd already paid tribute to culture, and she would now dedicate the rest of the afternoon to good works: She would let herself be screwed to help out a dear friend, she would wash the soul and bless the body of a seminarian in bed—a charity feast. Speaking of that, Patrícia's priest— what a southern hunk!

To begin filming the glory of Bahia for the episode of *Le Grand Échiquier* to be exhibited on the TV screens of eternal France, Nilda Spencer had decided, and Chancel agreed, to assemble in the Maria de São Pedro restaurant at the Model Market the most celebrated figures of the city's intellectual life, along with songwriters from the market and *berimbau* and *atabaque* players, culminating with the *samba de roda* directed by Zilá Azevedo, with spectacular dark girls, the dancers out of this world.

The atmosphere of the market, the rhythm of the musicians, Camafeu de Oxóssi's solos on the *berimbau*, the *atabaque* orchestra, all fascinated the Frenchman, while the *samba de roda* sent him into delirium: "Avec ça, ils vont craquer, les gars!" As for the intellectuals, they served as a frame for the picture; he would listen to a few and approve or reject their comments about Bahia. On Bahia, the originality of its people, the complexity of its mixed culture, Pierre Verger's speech was the last word.

Patrícia had translated the conversation with the notables as the camera taped the declarations by Professor Germano Tabacof, the poet Hélio Simões, the chronicler Raimundo Reis, the writer Sônia Coutinho —the camera lingered on her pretty face—the academician Itazil Benício dos Santos, Professor João Batista (who expressed himself in absolutely perfect French with a singing Sergipean accent), and several other conceited eminences. On the *samba de roda* Fernando Assis Pacheco, the Portuguese poet, poured out heady, lyrical phrases, keeping his glassy eye on the mulatto girls of the group.

At the end of the taping, the microphone still in hand, Patrícia dragged over a chair and sat down beside Father Abelardo, threatening to have it out with him about the charms of the women present, all of them drooling over him. Bold-faced Sylvia hadn't taken the trouble to be discreet about anything. Patrícia showed her fists: "If anyone of them lays a hand on you, I'll split her skull." Father Abelardo laughed, nervous, bashful, embarrassed.

Speaking of that, Patrícia told the priest that a little before lunch, someone had tried to play a trick on her over the phone. Pretending that he was Father Abelardo, the caller had proposed a date with her for that very afternoon. But she only had to hear the voice and realize that it had been a bad joke. She knew all the inflections of Abelardo's inimitable voice, the voice of a southerner from near the border, and he didn't call her "sweetie" or "my love," he called her "miss." She couldn't remember the proposed meeting place, however: only that it was somewhere in the vicinity of Itapuã.

At the sound of applause from everyone present, the Baianas of Zilá Azevedo, wearing their white smocks and colored flounced skirts, broke into the samba. They danced over to the luncheon table and one by one pulled the illustrious gentlemen from the academy and the university into the round to swing them about, swaying their bellies. Dr. Thales de Azevedo was applauded: neither his age nor his degrees seemed to diminish his drive. The labor court judge Carlos Coqueijo Costa had undoubtedly been born to it; he played the guitar and had the samba in his feet. Fernando Assis Pacheco attempted with Lusitanian drive to wiggle his waist, but without success. Jacques Chancel showed that he had skill, but it was Miro the Well-Loved, prince of honky-tonks, who dominated the group.

The camera rolled, and a month later the pictures of the party would run on French television. The festival of Bahia so warmed the heart of Nilda Spencer that, with a lump in her throat, she felt an urge to cry.

The Absent One

Nilda Spencer lamented the absence of Dom Maximiliano von Gruden at the lunch in the Model Market. Besides being a first-rate man of letters, the director of the Museum of Sacred Art was always an outstanding presence on television, with his white cassock, his elegant gestures, his actor's poise. She'd looked for him everywhere but nobody knew his whereabouts today.

Nobody knew his whereabouts at all, and at that very moment eager journalists and police were busy tracking him down. When they succeeded in figuring out the route that Lev Smarchevski's car had taken, they realized that Dom Maximiliano had gone to the Palace of the Archdiocese. Like the image of the saint, he'd disappeared without leaving a trace.

When he arrived at the Palace, the auxiliary bishop had brought Dom Maximiliano up to date on the information that the Federal Police agent had given him. Colonel Raul Antônio was convinced that the vicar of Piaçava was involved in the theft of the statue, for the purpose of financing subversion. Precious items were stolen from churches and sold abroad for hard currency to feed the land reform and urban guerrilla movements. Dom Maximiliano said he wasn't surprised—the colonel had telephoned him too that morning, aggressive, arrogant:

"All that was missing was his accusing me of complicity. The chief of the State Police, Dr. Calixto Passos, also thinks Father Galvão is the guilty party—in cahoots, just imagine, with Father Teófilo Santana of Santo Amaro. Then who—"

Dom Rudolph lifted his eyes from the German edition of Dom Maximiliano's book on the statue of Saint Barbara of the Thunder, which he had been thumbing through while he discoursed on the theft, pausing at one paragraph here, another there:

"I can guarantee you that the accusation is baseless. Father Galvão is innocent of that crime. His faults are others, albeit just as serious. He's got nothing to do with the disappearance of the statue—he just happened to be traveling on the same boat that brought it."

"Your Excellency seems quite convinced. How do you know?"

"I heard him in confession."

"Oh!"

"And what have you, Mr. Director, managed to find out? In the end, the matter is your responsibility, after all. What news do you bring me? I'm all ears."

The only answer Dom Maximiliano could give was to let his arms drop in a gesture that made obvious the extent of his helplessness. But that awful morning the distress of the museum director, his admission of defeat, and his near plea for clemency were a balm for the auxiliary bishop. Enjoying his triumph, Dom Rudolph moderated his tone of voice and changed the subject. Returning to the book, he commented:

"I'm going to read your book with the attention it deserves, but glancing at the pages, I already see that you attribute this statue of Saint Barbara to Aleijadinho. It seems to be rather a bold assertion, Dom Maximiliano. What basis do you have for forming such a controversial hypothesis?"

"A bold assertion—I won't deny that. When you finish reading the book, Your Excellency will find that this book is the result of hard investigative research that took me five years to complete. I scrutinized hundreds of documents, discovered inferences, found clues—everything leads to Colonial Ouro Preto and Antônio Francisco Lisboa, the marvelous Aleijadinho." Dealing with a subject that was dear to him, on his own territory, Dom Maximiliano warmed up, forgetting about his misfortunes, the accusations, the threats: "But what makes me most certain that Saint Barbara of the Thunder was his creation is actually something else."

"What something else?"

"The fact that Aleijadinho was a mulatto. Only a person of mixed blood could have sculpted it, a mulatto with both black and white blood."

The auxiliary bishop furrowed his Aryan brow in a frown and shook his head. "Dom Maximiliano von Gruden and the Passion of Race Mixing" had been the title of a paper that someone named Antônio Olinto had delivered at a recent colloquium on syncretism. When he received the program of the colloquium, Dom Rudolph had asked himself whether the description contained a double meaning, a malicious insinuation. It did not, he found out on reading the press coverage of the colloquium: It was only empty talk, a degenerate thesis, a conclusion that was suspect. Dom Rudolph put the book aside when he spoke again, abandoning the question of the authorship of the statue to return to the theme of its disappearance:

"I spoke to Dr. Odorico on the phone. I was puzzled by the virulence of the article in today's *Diário de Notícias*. All I learned from him was that he would place the pages of the newspaper at our disposal. He asked if you might not want to be interviewed."

Dom Rudolph cast his eyes out through the open window onto the square and the figure of the black woman came to him again, now malevolent. This was a cursed land, a land of reprobates.

"Either that sacred carving shows up, or I don't know what's going to become of our blessed Primacy of Bahia," he said in German. Used as shibboleths, certain words—*sacred, blessed*—sounded dirty. "We'll all end up in jail, accused of being thieves and Communists. Can you tell me anything new, director?"

"I can, yes, Your Excellency."

He told him of his decision. If the statue was not found by the time for the opening of the exhibit tomorrow, he, Dom Maximiliano von Gruden, would submit his irrevocable resignation and leave Bahia. He counted on his abbot to obtain a transfer. In the abbey in Rio de Janeiro he hoped to continue his museum work in silent obscurity.

Dom Rudolph was quick to approve and applaud the decision, which seemed to him the only proper one, and one that took into consideration the interests of the university, the Church, and Dom Maximiliano himself. Dom Rudolph's approbation and applause, however, pierced the wounded heart of the director of the Museum of Sacred Art.

—⚬—⚬

The Pond and
the Alligator

Father Soares was dozing in his after-dinner siesta when the reporters stormed the palace clutching microphones and cameras. Elói the seminarian, whose shift was coming to an end, found himself smothered with questions, and Father Soares was photographed with a look of openmouthed astonishment.

Both the seminarian and the secretary to the auxiliary bishop swore up and down that His Excellency, after his extended morning office hours, had left the palace and would not be back until the end of the afternoon. As for Dom Maximiliano, he had left for a destination unknown to Father Soares—lying was a part of the obligations of a competent secretary. But it was a pity that his position restrained him from saying more, since he would have liked to tell the journalists how Dom Maximiliano had been downcast, crestfallen, and humiliated, hadn't resembled at all his usual self, the wellspring of vainglory. On the rare occasions that he had appeared at the palace before, he had been so smiling, courtly, superior, that it had caused Father Soares to murmur, "Come off it, alligator—someday the pond's going to dry up, and I'll see the alligator dance." Today, a broken Dom Maximiliano von Gruden had stolen down the inner stairway to the garage, where he got into the auxiliary bishop's car. He'd left in the company of His Excellency, hidden in his shadow.

—⚬—⚬

Pretext and Value

With the intense activity of the police forces, both state and federal, on a war footing, it's a pleasure to take note that at the end of the afternoon Master Manuel and Maria Clara were released. They were ordered, however, not to leave the city, pending new depositions or allegations. The arrest of the perpetrators was considered imminent.

In the office of Colonel Raul Antônio, the press agent Epaminondas Costalima awaited Master Manuel and Maria Clara—another poet, yes, in Bahia you can find one or two poets on every streetcorner. Costalima had learned of their arrest, had come to confirm it and offer them assurances. He'd known the couple a long time—Master Manuel and Maria Clara were poor people, but they were utterly incapable of stealing anything. Colonel Raul Antônio said that he'd decided to let them go because nothing had turned up against them. Funny, how although Master Manuel was only a simple sloop captain, he seemed to be very well-connected. In addition to Epaminondas Costalima, who had come in person, a big shot had telephoned from Brasília, from the office of the minister of education: no less than the writer Herberto Salles, a member of the Brazilian Academy of Letters and director of the National Book Institute. He wanted to know the reason for the arrest of Master Manuel and Maria Clara, who were friends of his. *Friends of his,* that was how he put it, in an emphatic voice. He, too, Herberto Salles, was assuming complete responsibility for the sloop couple, he told the colonel, he was making a strong appeal, and so on and so forth. The colonel promised to take care of the matter and, without lying, said he was one of Salles's readers. In truth, as a young cadet with leftist tendencies, he'd read a novel by Salles about prospectors. Since then he'd evolved and had therefore abandoned his liberal leanings as well as the reading of novels.

What the colonel didn't mention to Salles was the real reason he was releasing the sloop skipper and his wife from jail: He was doing it to follow their footsteps in hopes of getting to Father Galvão's other accomplices. Offering Salles his assurances and pledges, the colonel demonstrated his sensitivity: "I'll keep your statement in mind. I'll do everything possible to take care of your request." With such pretexts he assured for himself the reputation of someone liberal and attentive. In fact, as far as the colonel was concerned, such pledges and assurances weren't of the slightest value. Intellectuals—a rotten bunch, he spat, rubbing his foot over it.

Roundelay of the Secret Police

On the streets the city cops, State Police, and the luminaries of the Federal Police were bumping into one another, hot on the trail of clues and suspects, tracking down intermediaries and witnesses, hiding places, dens of thieves, clandestine subversive operations.

The secret agents appeared on streetcorners in disguise, trailed priests, interrogated antique dealers and collectors. When Mirabeau Sampaio, an artist with a short fuse, quick to anger, saw Detective Expedito Bullyboy enter his studio and gallery and lift up a statue he was displaying off its pedestal—a statue carved in wood and signed by Frei Agostinho da Piedade—the crown jewel of his collection—he threw him out of his place. "Get out of here before I lose my head and give you one in the face, you son of a bitch!" The tale about the theft of the statue of Saint Barbara of the Thunder, a lie told by the director of the Museum of

Sacred Art, was becoming abominable, and Mirabeau couldn't take it any longer. Already interrupted three times in his work, Mirabeau hadn't been able to finish the Madonna that had been ordered by the banker Jorge Lins Freire on time. It was to be a birthday present for Dona Elcy, and the deadline for finishing it—and getting paid—was in jeopardy, all because of Dom Maximiliano!

Inspector Parreirinha had lost the trail of the vicar of Piaçava and was now comparing statues that were for sale in antique stores with the photograph of a Baroque statue of Saint Barbara venerated in a church in the Portuguese city of Guimarães. The photo was published in a book on the Minho region and had ended up in the files of the State Police along with a thousand other pieces of junk. Another inspector, Ripoleto, a bulldog famous for his sense of smell—wherever there was a free lunch he would show up, fork in hand—had headed for Santo Amaro with orders to interrogate the vicar there. He was also to listen to whatever the Velosos, Dona Canô and Mr. José, had to say, along with any other individual capable of furnishing information. And he wasn't to forget the vicar's girlfriend. As he instructed the inspector, Dr. Calixto Passos reaffirmed his conclusion: Father Teófilo had planned the robbery, and Father Galvão had carried it out. Hiding inside their cassocks, those wily devils were involved in the sale of antique statues under orders of priests, vicars, and bishops.

As for the agents of the National Information Service (with the lugubrious monogram SNI), they had arrived from Brasília with the object of setting up and carrying out Operation Crab Cunt, but they had been neither seen nor heard. They worked in the background, shadowed by disguises, incognito. They had set up a darkroom somewhere with the help of Madame Lia, the proprietress of a motel who had offered no objections—quite the contrary. Specialists of renowned competence, with apprenticeships in the CIA, and the PIDE, the supermen of the SNI boasted résumés that James Bond would envy. Heading up the team was one of the stars of the service (in their secret code, double-seven-O), known among his colleagues as Mule-Kick. One need only mention his name, and that was the end of somebody.

Matinée

From the window of the still-moving taxi Sylvia Esmeralda saw him in the sun, wearing a cassock, dragging on a cigarette. She found him beautiful and moving. Anticipating the pleasures of her afternoon, she put a fat tip into the driver's hand, and the gentleman effused, "Have a good time, missy ma'am, life is short." She waited for the taxi to drive away before she walked over to meet Elói and give him the message:

"Elói? Good afternoon, Elói. Olímpia couldn't come, and since there was no way to tell you—" She smiled at him with streetwalker eyes. She didn't have time to finish her sentence.

Two men jumped out of a big black car, their faces covered—they seemed to be in a hurry. They pointed their revolvers. One of them, Tarzan, pulled Sylvia and pushed her in the direction of the limousine: "Let's go, pretty—quick and quiet if you don't want to get hit." While King Kong, the other, grabbed Elói's arm and twisted it violently while smiling an almost cordial smile. Elói cried out. "Shut up," King Kong spat, punctuating the order with a slap.

Sylvia Esmeralda and the seminarian Elói were put into the car, where a third man, gripping a machine gun, was sitting next to the driver. He seemed to be the one in charge. The car took off, but it didn't go far. The motel they pulled up to was in the area, protected by high walls, and the gate was open, waiting.

Quico Promessa, the Promiser, had the bony, oblong face of an icon. When he took the list of the afternoon's callers from Elói's hands, he asked his colleague, without hiding his envy:

"You're going to take in a little movie, aren't you? At the Popular they're showing a great picture: *007 Versus Dr. No.*"

Elói smiled enigmatically, dreamy and proud:

"My double-0-seven is someone else . . ."

If he only knew.

To the Windward

Master Manuel and his wife Maria Clara were walking toward the naval arsenal where the *Sailor Without a Port* had been taken, chatting with their old friend Epaminondas Costalima along the way:

"That sloop of mine," the skipper bragged, abandoning his usual reserve, "sails so nicely that if I were to see it sailing through the sky one day, like a zeppelin or a falling star, I wouldn't be the least bit surprised."

That was precisely what happened at sunset on that very Thursday. Its sails filled with wind, the *Sailor Without a Port* was seen flying over the Sea Fort, cutting through the clouds as if it were cutting through the calm waters of the gulf. It sailed from the very beginnings of Brazil, from colonial times, crossing seas never before sailed, Portuguese and African seas; it weighed anchor at the port of Viana do Castelo, moored at São Vicente, Cape Verde, Dakar, Senegal, its holds crammed with hate, love, and poetry, a cargo of life and death.

Coasting along the sea lanes of the Bay of All Saints, the *Sailor Without a Port* circulated among the islands, flew over Maragogipe and Cachoeira, and dropped the heroes of Independence off on the island of Itaparica. At the sloop's helm was a black woman, stark naked, sometimes dressed in the gold of the sun, sometimes in the silver of the moon, hair of close-curled velvet, breasts of ebony, with a behind bigger than the sloop's stern. She was thirty feet tall at least, and her feet were at the mouth of the Paraguaçu River, while her head was on the dunes of Itapuã in the dark waters of Abaeté.

The *Sailor Without a Port* sails along the route of convents and temples and at all of them, blackwhite, whiteblack, Barbara Oyá got off the sloop and lingered on land. At the Desterro convent she danced with Vilhena in a licentious dance of nuns and noblemen—oh, what a delightful frolic! At the Convent of the Penitents, she wailed with the deflowered women at vespers and matins, the canonical hours. She opened the gates of the Benedictine abbey to persecuted students, to priests denounced as partisans of subversion.

She received the blessing of Mãe Menininha do Gantois, Oxum of Bahia, mother of goodness; she greeted Mãe Stela de Oxóssi on her throne of Opô Afonjá; and at the Temple of Portão she held in her arms Mãe Mirinha, who had incorporated the Caboclo Pedra Preta, the mixed-blood group of the Black Rock. She sailed underground beneath the city along the rivers of memory, in the light of midday and in the darkness of midnight; she was the imagination and the conscience, the dream of poets and novelists.

Thunderclaps announcing war without quarter were released from the mast of the sloop. Once more the enchanted one disembarked at the market ramp, the port of mystery. She drew night out of her saddlebag and spread it over the city: She went off for combat and revelry, fighting and fun. Meanwhile, at the Cloister of the Penitents, it was a different kind of night for Manela, a night of slavery, worse than death.

Master Manuel didn't care much for boasting and he wasn't in the habit of blurting out great tidings, but he reaffirmed that it was the truth of truths, proven and proven again: There was no sloop like his, not Guma's, not Rufino's, not even God's Love's, none on the waters of Aioká:

"She's capable of sailing through the air."

Giroflá

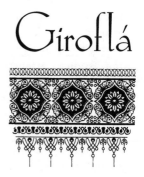

Oyá, night breeze, moonbeam, scent of jasmine, the refrain of a popular song, rose petals, iridescent bird, white cockatoo, wildcat, royal parakeet, blue lizard, green calango newt, glass snake, twelve multicolored beads, and a mother-of-pearl conch. Oyá would transform herself into a thousand disguises on her visitation to the artists, a nation very much to her preference because, like those beautiful madmen, she also spat fire, spewed flames out of her mouth. She wandered from studio to studio, seeing and appreciating, and wherever she passed she left a trace, an inspiration, a spark. The artist would sense the presence of somebody from another place and remember and recreate her: paint her on a canvas, sketch her on a piece of paper, carve her in wood, weld her in metal. She was vain; she knew she was beautiful, and she loved to contemplate her allegory in mirrors.

At the beginning of the nineteen eighties, a decade after the facts narrated in these memoirs, the museum curator Sílvia Athayde's attention was drawn to what seemed a surprising coincidence, an unusual circumstance worthy of investigation, clarification, and commentary. She plunged into solving the enigma and only came up asking more questions; lingering, she investigated, moved mountains, spent months gathering up the loose ends of the tangle. At the end of an arduous job she wrote and published a small essay, "Art in Iaô Time," and with some borrowed works she put together a curious and provocative exhibit that was talked about all over the country, from north to south, intriguing all the art critics. The veteran critic Antônio Celestino wrote: "Syncretism has been reaffirmed as a creator of art, and Brazilian originality is there in all its splendor."

Sílvia Athayde discovered and proved that during the short space of a few days in the seventies, the most important artists in the country had conceived and executed sculptures, oil paintings, carvings, designs, engravings, monotypes with a similar if not identical theme: the myth of Yansan, the cult of Saint Barbara. As director of the Art Section of the Development Bank of the State of Bahia, Sílvia Athayde succeeded in gathering together six such sculptures, three in metal, three in wood; two of the carvings, a tapestry, a set of tiles, and thirty-one pictures: oils, watercolors, engravings, sketches, and a pastel. At the time of the exhibit's opening, at the end of one clear and cloudless afternoon, lightning flashed over the bank building, and the growl of thunder resounded in a jubilant greeting. The absence of some of the pieces cited in her essay from the exhibit was lamented: It hadn't been possible to bring the big sculpture by Carybé from Rio de Janeiro, and the collector Edwaldo Pacote had loaned, and that with great reluctance, only one of the several Yansans by Tati Moreno: He'd once had a bitter experience when he'd allowed a Siron Franco to be exhibited in Switzerland and never saw it again.

Ten years had passed since the morning Altamir Galimberti picked up a mother-of-pearl conch and twelve multicolored shells from his work table and used those precious items for a frame made of bivalves that he had gleaned from the beach at Pedra do Sal—the night before, there'd been a full moon. These must be delicacies from Dona Zélia, Galimberti thought as he picked up the conch from the table, his good neighbor who was interested in his work and on her travels would bring him African periwinkles, shells from Polynesia, and other rarities. The frame would prove to be exactly the right size for a painting that Master Carlos Bastos hadn't painted yet. But when he painted it that afternoon, Saint Barbara of the Thunder appeared on the canvas. Cacá Bastos had admired her on the occasion of a festival at the church in Santo Amaro da Purificação. On the saint's naked foot he painted a blue lizard.

The Saint Barbaras and Yansans followed one after the other in the sculptures and paintings exhibited in the bank's gallery. In the panel by

Juarez Paraíso, bright with orchids and tiny diamonds, the saint and the enchanted one mingle in gold and copper, one born out of the other, interwoven: The two halves form a whole of contrasts and harmonies. Agnaldo's Saint Barbara of the Thunder, in brazilwood, is ambiguous: Crowned with nails, she rises up over buffalo horns, and cut into the wood is the slash of Yansan's cutlass. Seen from the right side the saint can be discerned, from the left the enchanted one, frontwise both of them, united. The Saint Barbara by Antônio Rebouças, an unusual artist, is a small masterpiece in stainless steel, depicting the mulatto woman in the swirl of a dance.

Thirteen prints by Hansen-Bahia were also displayed, twelve of which had been commissioned to illustrate Dom Maximiliano von Gruden's book. There was also one huge one, gigantic: Saint Barbara in the war of the thunderclaps, produced by the master engraver during those same tumultuous days. During those days of inspiration, Ilse, Hansen's young wife, had painted the merry ship of saints and *orixás*, a Coptic icon. The splendid carving by Zu Campos, the artist from the Ladeira de Santa Tereza, is entitled "Saint Barbara, She of the *Eiru*."

Jenner Augusto's oil, worked out with the demanding perfectionism of one who knows his craft, shows Saint Barbara of the Thunder, in the Alagados, the swamp, crossing an improvised rickety bridge over the mud. A train of altar boys accompanies her. Emaciated and famished, in their hands they hold copper swords and *eirus* aloft. The Yansan by Sante Scaldaferri advances along with the pilgrims in a landscape of ex-votos, a herd of goats among the bushes. Here the *eiru* is a sheaf of poisonous snakes, and instead of a sword there is a backlands musket. Corpses rot in the sun, slaves of the land are murdered. In the midst of merry banners, bordered in red, is depicted Jamison Pedra's Yansan. And on Lev Smarchevski's sea, Yansan sails among golden fish, amulets.

Mário Cravo forged a Yansan of Igbalé out of automobile scraps, a fearsome warrior woman, her arms extended, at her feet, in defeat, death. Yansan doesn't fear death; she guards the doors of the beyond for the *eguns*. Tati Moreno cut a whole sequence of Yansans out of metal, of different sizes and postures, all of them voluptuous. Calasans Neto, called Master Calá, king of Itapuã and environs, used a press and Chinese brushes. In the monotype, Saint Barbara of the Thunder; in the carving, Oyá; in the oil painting, both of them: Saint Barbara of the Thunder, riding a whale, Yansan mounted on a bird of prey, on the sea, and in the sky of Abaeté. The saint's face was that of the renowned lady Auta Rosa, Master Calá's wife, from the island; the hips of the enchanted one were those of Aíla, the marvelous cook. José de Dome, in his studio on the Largo de Sant'Ana, wrote the title of his painting on the back of the canvas that contained infinite variations of yellow: *Saint Barbara of the*

Thunderclaps and Yansan's Goat. The goat he painted a wine color. His friend and neighbor Rômulo Serrano conceived a lyrical still life of palm trees and *eirus* on sailcloth. Ruddy angels encircle Yansan, and fly over a colonial mansion, in the oil by Hélio Basto.

Genaro de Carvalho put together a tapestry in which the tools of the enchanted one and the symbols of the saint are mingled. Set in different types, he spelled out the greeting for the *orixá: Eparrei* Oyá!, depicting in the background the Largo do Pelourinho and the Taboão Elevator. It was Genaro's last work; he died soon after its completion. Nair placed Saint Barbara of the Thunder in a field of flowers, happy and carefree, playing with children. The Saint Barbara by Jorge Costa Pinto is now on the altar of the main church in Santo Amaro, amid lighted candles and silver sconces.

Willys imagined Saint Barbara conversing in Alfredo Santeiro's shop in Cabeça, with saints and *orixás* in profusion on the shelves. Lígia Milton saw Yansan and Saint Barbara in the oratory of the Cruz do Pascoal, holding hands. Licídio Lopes painted Oyá on the River Niger, which originates in Africa and flows into the Rio Vermelho. From the trunk of a breadfruit tree, Manuel do Bonfim sculpted a Yansan with heavy breasts and full hips, giving off lightning bolts. Cardoso e Silva, a painter of the churches of Bahia, reproduced the Church of Santo Amaro on canvas. He'd never seen it, but for Cardosinho, painter, poet, philosopher, mathematician, astronomer, and astrologer, a medium, a lack of firsthand knowledge was no handicap. He closed his eyes and saw the complete church, inside and out, the facade and the nave, the churchyard and the sacristy, the main altar and the altar of Saint Barbara of the Thunder. No one has ever painted or ever will paint the church of Santo Amaro with such exactness.

In all the nuances of *grená,* from cherry to dark wine, the lascivious flowers of Fernando Coelho unfold around the *eiru,* a ponytail, a woman's hair. Besides *grená* Fernando used white and red, the colors of Xangô, Yansan's husband. Floriano Teixeira, an Indian from Maranhão, a citizen of Ceará, a Japanese artist of Bahia, sketched with pastels a litter for Saint Barbara of the Thunder, carried on the shoulders of his closest friends: Milton Dias, James Amado, Wilson Lins, and the furnituremaker Armando Almendra. At the top of the canvas eight little windows open, with scenes showing Yansan's lovemaking in bed, in the river, and in the woods, with her husband and with her lovers. For the portrayal of lewdness no artist can top Floriano—sex is all he ever thinks about.

Luís Jasmim sketched the portrait of Mãe Menininha bowing to Yansan in a design of large proportions and great delicacy: it hangs in the Candomblé do Gantois. Rubem Valentim took the tools and weapons of Yansan and broke them down and put them back together again, in his

double role of master painter and *ogan* of the Axé do Opô Afonjá, initiated by Mãe Senhora. Out of splinters of wood Emanuel Araújo created
an abstract, but anyone who takes a good look at the object discerns
Yansan going off to war. Speaking of Emanuel, one should mention the
necklace made by Valdeloir Rego and worthy of the throat of the most
beautiful daughter of Yansan. Oyá, in the tiles of Udo Knoff, is called
Dana.

In the Saint Barbara of the Thunder, by Mirabeau Sampaio, the
splendid gold-plated statue of the saint of thunderclaps has an extravagant wine-colored halo. He hadn't painted it on commission, and for
many years he stubbornly refused to sell it. But how could he turn down
the millions offered by Antônio Carlos Magalhães? When the political
bigwig saw the painting, he decided to take it home with him no matter
what the cost. For that and other reasons his nickname was Toninho
Malvadeza, Tony Malice: he put an Uncounted amount of hard cash into
Mirabeau's hand. Even though the artist was rich and obstinate, how
could he refuse that kind of money? Mirabeau gave in to Malvadeza's
impertinence and let go of the painting; but the money evaporated, and
to this day Mirabeau regrets his choice.

We still haven't spoken of the Yansan in reinforced concrete acquired from the artist by the mayor's office in Rio de Janeiro during the
administration of Marcos Tamayo, placed in Cantagalo Park alongside
other notable sculptures. A monumental piece, it had become a sacred
object, an altar for worship: *Ebós* are left on its pedestal, trays of *acarajés*
are offered to it, and goats and kids are tethered to nearby trees.

Several other artists worked on the theme, but the list is already
getting too long—it's time for us to close off the entries. The curator was
criticized for not having limited herself to the pieces of greatest value.
But for Sílvia, the quantity of these works was just as important as their
quality, so extreme rigor was not exercised in the choice of material for
the bank gallery exhibit. It opened on the tenth anniversary of the mem-
orable exhibit of religious art at the Museum of Sacred Art of the Federal
University. It was not a coincidence, but rather a decision made by Sílvia
Athayde, who was thorough and attentive as well as capable and diligent.
Her research led her to conclude that events that had occurred in connection with that previous exhibit were directly responsible for all those
simultaneously created Yansans and Saint Barbaras, a magical coincidence.

When she returned from the show to her summer house on the
beach of Mar Grande, one of the visitors, Myriam Fraga, summed up for
Orlando and Beatriz, her parents, for Albérico, her father-in-law, for her
four children, the girl and the three boys, and for Carlos, her beloved
husband, the intense and acid debate that had swept up artists, critics,

and charlatans. *Giroflá,* she said, meaning that such absurdities happen with great frequency in Bahia, they're no cause for alarm, they're our daily way of life.

Mariner's compass, the spring equinox, the arcanum of poetry—Myriam gave the password and repeated it, and then they all understood the relativity, the participle, the price, the reason for things, *giroflá!*

The Events of Thursday Night

Dissension

Danilo was puzzled by Manela's absence from the dinner table. Had she fulfilled her punishment? he wondered. The door to her room was open—had Dadá allowed her out? Adalgisa had been acting fierce lately, keeping her niece on a short tether; there was no going out at night on the pretext of doing homework at the homes of her classmates; she went from the dinner table to schoolwork, prayers, and bed. Manela slept with the door locked from the outside, the key in the hand of her aunt, who was convinced that Manela was getting ready to elope. When Dadá got an idea into her head, she followed it to the letter: Lock the girl up, leave no room for wickedness. Danilo was bothered, but he avoided saying anything since the commentary was usually worse than the sonnet itself.

"Where's Manela?" he asked now, like someone who didn't really want to know, as he served himself a piece of steaming yam.

Adalgisa put her knife and fork down, stared at her husband, then told him about the events of the day. She told him how she had found the note, what it said, that the elopement was set for that night, Father José Antonio's intervention, and the visit to the juvenile judge. Manela's internment in the Lapa convent, finally, after all the mad running about, was the happy ending. God had protected and sustained her.

"You interned Manela at the Cloister of the Penitents? Is that what you're telling me?" His voice was hoarse, and his surprise was so great that it took him unawares. His face dumbfounded, Danilo shook his head, not believing what he was hearing.

"That's it exactly. I prevailed with God's help."

"Dadá, do you have any idea what you've done? Were you out of your mind?"

"I did what I had to do to stop her from leaving the house and prostituting herself with that devil. God helped me discover the plot just in time, but only I know all the doing it took. Now it's all settled—she's under the care of Our Lord Jesus Christ."

"Dadá, what have you done? Did you go crazy all of a sudden, or don't you have any heart? How could you be so wicked?" He pushed away his plate: "Quick! Get up, we're going to get Manela right now. I'm not going to let the poor girl spend even one night there."

"She'll come out of there when I say so. She'll stay there until she forgets about that chimpanzee, no matter how long it takes. and lower your voice—I don't want the neighbors to hear. If they ask about her, tell them she went off to spend a few days away, that she went to Itassucê's house in Olivença." Itassucê was a rich cousin of Danilo's and was married to a cacao planter; she was always inviting her relatives to spend some time on the plantation or at the baths in Olivença.

Danilo listened openmouthed to Adalgisa. Her manner was hard as always, but she was calm now that she knew Manela was safe from Miro's seduction, her virginity secure. Nothing awful could happen to her at the convent—quite the contrary. Secluded in a holy atmosphere, her daylight hours devoted to prayer, given over to divine fervor— masses in the morning, benedictions in the afternoon, prayers all along the way, examinations of conscience, spiritual retreats—her stay among the nuns would be like a bath in holiness for her filthy and hardened soul, threatened as it was with subversion by vice. Free of evil thoughts, triumphant over temptation, relieved of the weight of sins, grateful, disposed to obedience and respect, her niece could then return to the home that she had once tried to repudiate and defame. Adalgisa radiated satisfaction with her duty fulfilled: "God is my witness." She lifted up the pot to pour the milk.

Danilo stood up. "Let's go get Manela, Dadá."

"I've already told you to forget about it. She's in the convent by order of the judge—no one can take her out of there but me, her guardian. Sit down and drink your coffee. I didn't have time to make any soup. And keep your mouth shut. I don't want to give the neighbors anything to gossip about."

"I'm just as much her guardian as you. If you don't want to come with me, I'll go alone."

"You're not going anywhere. Stop all that. I told you already. Don't butt in where you're not wanted: I'm the one who makes the decisions about Manela, you hear? Now settle down and stop bothering me."

She put down the milk pitcher and picked up the coffee pot. Adalgisa didn't serve a full dinner as an evening meal; at most it was a bowl of soup, thin chicken broth. They were usually content with café au lait, bread, butter, and two or three side dishes: sweet cassava, yams, breadfruit, cassava or corn cakes, tapioca couscous, sponge cake, or fried cottage cheese. Danilo was crazy about sweet potatoes, but Adalgisa prepared them only rarely; they were gassy and Danilo, with age, was getting farty. Any event that took him off his daily routine affected his intestines. That was what happened on that Thursday night. The dissension had upset him, and he couldn't hold back his vigorous and loud discharge of farts.

"What's this, Danilo? At the dinner table? Have you no shame?"

The Head of the Family

Who wore the pants in the house on the Avenida da Ave-Maria? Adalgisa, obviously, most evidently—ask her neighbors, and you'll get no other reply. The termagant imposed and disposed, they would say; the poor man had the patience of Job, all he wanted was to live in peace.

Adalgisa had grabbed hold of the tiller from the very start of their married life, taking advantage of the inferior status Danilo was faced with in the early years. A clerk in a notary's office, almost a messenger boy, he'd earned a miserable salary. He'd gone up the job ladder step by step until he got to where he was, a head clerk with the hope and promise of one day being named substitute notary. The one holding that position, Eustáquio Lago, still hadn't retired, rickety as he was—he could barely stand on his legs.

When they got back from their honeymoon, because of a lack of money for rent, the couple went to live with Paco and occupied Adalgisa's old room. They slept in a single bed that was barely big enough for two people. Having succeeded in keeping her godmother's clientele and enlarging it—Doña Esperanza, punctilious, was choosy about her customers, she wouldn't do work for just anyone—Adalgisa contributed in a substantial way toward her and her husband's expenses. Paco Pérez wouldn't let his daughter and son-in-law contribute a penny toward the food budget, and the poorer he got, the more of a braggart and boaster he became.

Adalgisa enlarged her circle of customers in spite of the fact that she'd raised her godmother's already high prices. Her hats were in demand because her competitors in millinery couldn't hold a candle to the quality and elegance of her "parakeets," a nickname Danilo gave to her masterpieces. "Who's that pink parakeet for?" he would ask irreverently and playfully as he watched her carefully scrutinizing the perfection of a hat. She even received orders from Rio de Janeiro, and in their description of what the upper crust were wearing at high functions, society columnists would cite as a proof of good taste and refinement the hats displayed by the fine ladies "with the *griffe* of Adalgisa Correia, *la modiste distinguée.*" In *Sete Dias* Tereza de Mayo explained to those on the margins of society that a *modiste* is someone who makes hats, while someone who makes dresses is a *couturier.*

Danilo's low salary, their free lodging, his sterility as decreed by the medical specialist, and above all the aristocratic airs that Adalgisa continued to exhibit despite the vicissitudes of Paco Negreiro, made it possible for the hard-working and hard-driving wife to assume command of the home. Of a gentle nature, an affable creature, Danilo accepted the situation imposed by his better half without any apparent resistance, or at least without any overt protest.

Everything was fine as long as he could keep a few prerogatives, infrequent little enjoyments, the last barricades of *machismo:* his nights out two or three times a week with friends in downtown cafés, his passion for soccer (he never missed an Ipiranga game), backgammon and checkers on Saturday afternoons at Professor João Batista's wetted down with beer, and his dip in the ocean on Sunday mornings. His assiduous frequenting of houses of assignation wasn't part of the agreed-upon list. Here he employed the necessary caution, arriving home on time for his coffee and snack and some chicken broth at seven o'clock sharp.

Adalgisa also took charge in bed—and all the nasty little touches, the restrictions, the platonism—and the aberrations!—that governed Adalgisa's sad bed have already been mentioned here and certainly condemned by all. Let it only be stressed that the patient Danilo, a consummate optimist in spite of a history of almost twenty years of battle, still harbored lascivious intentions and appalling illusions. Even now, dreaming of miracles, whenever he saw her in her nightgown at bedtime he would run his hand over her behind: Your day will come, you tricky ass! He'd read that phrase in a magazine of erotic stories and had fallen in love with it. But it never went beyond a quick movement like the one described, since Adalgisa didn't even bother to scold him—she just curled up in the sheets and went to sleep. A wolf may lose his hair but not his vices. What had once been a burning flame, giving rise to quarrels, arguments, and exchanges of insults resulting in bad feelings, had become a weak flame, a flickering candlelight. Adalgisa had tamed the wolf.

The death of Paco Negreiro made the couple's economic situation all the more precarious. He had died suddenly, shortly after their first wedding anniversary. They had celebrated the occasion with the family: Wine was served at dinner, and they went to the movies with Dolores and Eufrásio to see an enjoyable Mexican film with Cantinflas. A massive heart attack hit Paco when he discovered his partner Javier García's swinishness. A few friends had given him good advice, and told him to clean up the situation at the scrap metal business. But Paco had listened with deaf ears; his fellow Spaniard had his complete trust since he owed Paco everything, starting with the money he'd put into the business. Paco had put up the capital and remained a silent partner at a time when the active partner, Javier, hadn't a penny to spare, only a great capacity for work and greed.

One afternoon, having gone to Água dos Meninos, where the scrap metal business was, looking for a few coins to gamble, Javier García told Paco that he no longer had any right to make withdrawals or to receive monthly payments of dividends. Javier no longer had to pay him anything. On the contrary, Paco had gone from creditor to debtor: He owed the firm a pile of money. Javier had the books and the signed vouchers to prove it. Francisco Romero Pérez y Pérez lost his color and his voice; he grew pale, gagged, and his eyes went glassy; he staggered among the chairs, and dropped dead right there in the scrap metal office. It was a place he had rarely visited, since the dirty, dusty environment was not to the taste of the former owner of a gourmet grocery, with its fine spices, imported wines, sherry and Málaga, Manchegan cheese, sardines from Vigo, and mussels.

Javier García contributed a modest amount to the funeral expenses collected by friends and family. The first-class funeral was held at the private chapel at the cemetery, with a funeral mass, a sermon, and a deluxe casket. Lots of people attended the wake, relating sentimental memories and spicy stories, the adventures of the deceased. In a corner of the chapel, in the small hours of the morning, a young black woman, Paco's last conquest, prayed for the soul of the Spaniard, distressed, her eyes moist. With a cortège of many people, the Spanish consul gave a speech as the coffin was lowered. The rich merchant's funeral was a consolation for Adalgisa.

The money obtained from the sale of the few objects of value that had belonged to Francisco Romero Pérez y Pérez barely covered the back rent owed for the apartment. Dr. Carlos Fraga, the family lawyer and an able curmudgeon, managed to negotiate a reasonable agreement for the liquidation of the scrap metal business; Javier García complained and argued, but he ended up turning over a few coins. Dr. Carlos dispensed with any fee for his services—he earned quite a lot looking after the affairs of the moneybags during the times when the cows were fat. Adalgisa didn't waste any time before depositing the pittance Javier paid into a savings account, already dreaming of her own house.

Adalgisa and Danilo lived in a boardinghouse for several months after that, in one room, then renting the house on Avenida da Ave-Maria. It had a kitchenette with a stove, a bedroom and living room, and a bathroom with a shower and a wash basin. They'd lived more than twelve years in the small but agreeable house. Adalgisa couldn't complain, except for the neighbors—a low lot, apart from Professor João Batista. By dint of the savings and the economies they made over so many years, their bank accounts grew fat, and Dadá began to study the classified ads.

One thing she refused to sell, even when most in need, was their charter membership in the Spanish Club, which had been transferred from Paco's to Danilo's, and they also continued to pay the monthly dues at the Galician Center. Nor would Adalgisa relinquish her status of a lady, following Doña Esperanza's example: Her godmother hadn't given in to the ways of poverty, and even in rough times she maintained her dignity.

Later, to these various troubles and tribulations, and Adalgisa's chronic migraines, was added the rearing of her niece, that Manela, who has so very little of the Spanish girl about her, who rejected her destiny as a lady, who went against moral principles, who sighed like a crazy woman over a taxi driver. It was a grave responsibility, a thorny task, but Adalgisa, by the grace of God, would see it through, even if she had to crack the girl's skull to save her soul.

The Insurgent

To save the wicked girl's soul, to carry out the order that God and the juvenile judge had assigned her and Danilo upon the death of her sister and brother-in-law, Adalgisa had to act on her own. The former prince of the playing field was of no help—he didn't get involved but kept quietly in his corner during Manela's constant mouthing off; and he didn't say a word when aunt and niece fought. On those occasions when the argument got more heated, degenerating into strife, obliging Adalgisa to apply her punishment, Danilo would pick up his hat in silence, almost sneakily, and take off. If a fight took place on the day of a soccer broadcast, he'd go over to the Quincas Wateryell, a sports bar that had a television set, to follow the game.

Not that Danilo was indifferent to the confrontations between Adalgisa and Manela, the aunt accusing, the niece asking forgiveness. He just didn't approve of the methods his wife employed to correct and educate the girl—and she knew it. When he first witnessed the reprimands, the punishments with the leather strap, he'd reacted by condemning the violence of the speech and the rigor of the corrective measures. He'd argued with his wife, indignant about the strap. In the course of their dispute he'd used the word "stepmother" to define her: "You're the worst stepmother in the world."

He never used that term again, ever. He hadn't imagined that Adalgisa would take it so badly, react so desperately, with the greatest depression, stung and hurt. Danilo was moved and stammered excuses, but Adalgisa refused to listen. Weeping, offended to the depths of her soul, she suffered an attack of heart palpitations that lasted all night long. When she recovered from the palpitations, she went into grief: misjudged by the one who should have supported and applauded her most, since Danilo was responsible for their niece's fate just as much as she, Adalgisa. In her view, she was carrying the burden of the guardianship all by herself, and when she tried to stop the madcap girl from getting caught up in evil ways, in return she received the worst of all insults: stepmother! She chewed on her pillow, wanting to die.

Fearing the deterioration of the peaceful and tender relationship, the pleasant and comfortable harmony that in spite of all the sorrows had characterized the couple's life up till then, Danilo decided to let things drift along in neglect, and he washed his hands of the mess. Danilo was like Pilate in the Credo, Father José Antonio Hernández stressed. Husband and confessor did not look on each other with kindly eyes. Danilo didn't know why, but whenever he met the Father Inquisitor, he felt an urge to punch him out, to smack him in the teeth, to kick him in the balls.

The relationship between uncle and niece, while neither intimate nor close, existed in a climate of kindness and affection, fortified by a marked mutual esteem. Danilo had tried to interest Manela in the soccer craze, but with poor results; instead, he taught her checkers and backgammon, of which she was a brilliant student. She was also outstanding at playing Patience, and laying the cards out on the dining-room table brought her easy victories over her uncle. "Uncle Danilo," Manela explained to Miro, "is a dear. I like him a lot. It's just that he doesn't stand up to Aunt Adalgisa. I think he's afraid of her."

Whether Danilo's discreet behavior was the result of fear or a prudence born of love, Adalgisa had grown so accustomed to it that she saw even his farting as a more serious matter than his amazing act of defiance at the dinner table. "If you don't come with me I'll go alone, right now" —the threat had caught her off guard at first. She followed Danilo's movements through the room with her eyes, not saying a word. She watched him put on his tie, his jacket, and his hat on his head.

"There's a limit to everything, Dadá," he said. "I'm not coming back without Manela."

He stopped at the door, his face contorted into a grimace of grief— obviously both physical and moral. He lifted his leg, releasing a flight of sonorous poops into the room, which perfumed Adalgisa's command:

"Get back to your seat!"

The Family That Dines Together Is Fine Together

Whether at the plantation or in the city, Joãozinho Costa imposed norms on his family life, with which he governed implacably. The family dinner on Thursdays was one such norm: Normally the family gathered around the large peroba table in the townhouse on the Corredor da Vitória: There was Scotch whiskey, and gin and tonic, and for Olímpia, Portuguese wine; there were delicacies prepared by black Pretinha, the cook brought from the Brazilian interior. Every so often, the family group would be enlarged by some close relative who was passing through the state capital, but as a general rule the Thursday dinners were held in the complete intimacy of the owners of the house, the son-in-law, and the two daughters, heiresses to the fortune, which was one of the largest in Bahia. There was an eleven-year difference between Olímpia and Marlene; in the years between them Dona Eliodora had given birth to a boy who hadn't lived long —dysentery took him before his first birthday. It had been an enormous blow to Joãozinho Costa. The landowner persisted in his desire for a male offspring, but when Dona Eliodora was with child again, she gave birth to Marlene after a difficult seven-month pregnancy.

"My flock"—the landowner would say, a follower of traditional values—"the family is the backbone of society." He required Olímpia and Astério to turn down any invitation that would conflict with the sacred dinner hour on Thursdays, and he would get quite furious when unavoidable circumstances caused the couple's absence: "The family comes ahead of the governor," he would reproach them. "It wasn't the governor, Daddy—it was the general," Olímpia would answer.

On this same busy Thursday, in the comfort of the living room that opened onto the garden and the swimming pool, the family was awaiting the arrival of Astério, who was very late. Dressed in a miniskirt, the agitated Marlene, a restless adolescent, couldn't tolerate her brother-in-law's tardiness, his lack of consideration. She checked her wristwatch—she had a date for eight-thirty that night at the Castro Alves Theater, where the French film crew were going to tape Caetano Veloso, Gilberto Gil, Maria Betânia, and a newcomer who was out of this world, Gal Costa. Marlene had been invited to the filming by Georges Moustaki, who she'd met the night before and had spent the whole day with. Short, dark, and flirtatious, Marlene had just turned fifteen. The society columnists had given wide coverage of her activities: her birthday festivities, her confirmation ceremony at the cathedral, the big lunch, the ball at the yacht club, the waltz she danced with her father—"a rural aristocrat, an endangered species," Terezinha de Mayo had written in *Sete Dias*. Fifteen was the preferred age, according to Moustaki; women began to age after fifteen, he said. Jacques Chancel had brought the composer of *Joseph* and *Le Métèque* along so he could sing on the program the songs that Bahia had inspired him to write: *"Bahia de São Salvador"* and *"Bye Bye Bahia,"* —composed in Paris on his return from previous trips.

Marlene watched the hands on her watch creep by and didn't try to hide her bad mood. Did Astério think they had nothing better to do than wait for him? What did he take them for? To leave Moustaki waiting by the theater door at the mercy of a bunch of crazy women was out of the question—she couldn't do it.

Even more nervous was the head of the family. Joãozinho Costa couldn't keep his seat warm, pacing back and forth, keeping his eye on the doorway, sharpening his ear to catch the arrival of the Beetle. Astério drove a little Volkswagen, while a Mercedes with a liveried chauffeur served Olímpia. This evening, however, Olímpia had arrived in a taxi—she'd come directly from the *garçonnière* that one of the secretaries of state, who was the senator's political protegé, had loaned him. The senator himself had been a pest.

Bedecked with jewels—the necklace alone had cost the price of a herd of cattle—Dona Eliodora Costa had the bosom of a diva, although her Belle Époque curves were imprisoned in a rubber girdle. Sipping a cocktail of fruit juices, she listened to Olímpia recount the latest news from Brasília. Her daughter was certainly something, Dona Eliodora thought. How could she have gotten to know so much, and so quickly? The recent misfortunes of Lieutenant Elmo—that pretty boy who was here with General Abdias, she asked—remember Lenoca? What happened to him? "I'll tell you," Olímpia said. "He was doing his thing in bed with Madame General, when the general showed up without any warning, and the little lieutenant wound up on the Colombian border.

Now he's going to have to make it with Indian women, the kind with saucers in their lips, poor thing." Out in the kitchen, downing a bottle of beer while he awaited the boss's orders, Zé do Lírio was telling Pretinha how much he missed Momi, his Indian woman: She was unequaled when it came to praying away groin bubos and curing the whooping cough.

Finally, a gray and anonymous envelope clutched in his hand, Astério crossed the threshold. "I was kept at the office," he said, making his excuses and distributing kisses to his mother-in-law, his sister-in-law, and his wife. "Our senator made a point of bringing to me in person the news that the minister has approved my proposal—the road contract is in the bag. Let's celebrate!"

Olímpia smiled timidly and discreetly, lowering her eyes to the floor: The tribute she had paid was well worth the trouble, no matter how insipid and wearying the senatorial afternoon in bed had been. The senator had announced that when he left her, he would pay a visit to his good friend Astério. "Visit Astério—for what?" she'd asked, surprised. To see his cuckold's horns, my pretty. While she was performing, Olímpia's thoughts had been of Sylvia and little Elói, the lucky ones: They were spending the bright afternoon in the merrymaking of fornication and its et ceteras, while she was struggling with her mouth to get the senator's tool up. Now when she found out that her effort of the afternoon had been rewarded, the payment due having been collected by Astério, Olímpia blessed the hours of her vexation and smiled at her husband. With his frog eyes, he contemplated her and found her beautiful and devoted, a blameless, unequaled wife. Olímpia had inherited her father's sense of family.

—❦—❦

The Photo Taken at the
Motel, or the SNI's Version
of the Artistic Nude

Astério waved the envelope at his impatient father-in-law:
"I haven't even had time to open it."
Joãozinho Costa, clapping his hands, ordered his wife and daughters, "Go ahead, go to the table—we'll be right there."
After the women had gone into the dining room, the father-in-law and the son-in-law went over to the lamp to get a better look at the photograph of Father Abelardo Galvão frolicking with Patrícia das Flores. Astério unsealed the envelope that bore the name of neither receiver nor sender and withdrew a negative and the eight-by-ten-inch color

photograph that they hoped to use to destroy the priest's reputation. Before Astério could look at it, Joãozinho Costa snatched it and savored the look that would appear on the face of the cardinal primate, that holy chameleon, when he saw it. In his presence the cardinal was so obliging and polite, so thankful—"How's the plantation going, Colonel?" he would ask. "Thanks for the barrel of dendê oil, liquid gold"—yet behind Joãozinho Costa's back, the cardinal was a protector of watermelon priests, green on the outside, red on the inside.

Now there they were, stark naked—except that it wasn't they: "What the hell is this? That isn't the priest!"

Astério de Castro took the picture back and exploded: "Imbeciles! Incompetents! Sons of bitches!"

The figures were not Father Galvão and not the girl from the theater. In the well-focused photograph Astério recognized not only Sylvia Esmeralda, the wife of the juvenile judge, but the seminarian that Olímpia was having an affair with. The kid was cheating on Olímpia! Astério fumed with indignation—but not over the boy's infidelity—that was of little concern to him. He kept up to date on his amorous wife's pastimes and only got involved when they threatened to disturb his business projects and lucrative deals. Then he would make her understand that she couldn't go too far with her fun.

No, he was indignant—furious rather—because on the telephone they'd promised to send SNI men of the greatest competence from Brasília. The presence of Agent 770 in charge was offered as assurance that Operation Crab Cunt would come off perfectly. Agent 770 was the ace of aces.

"And those shitheads want to win out over the Communists! All they know how to do is beat people up—they're only good for a clubbing! They're lower than shitheads!"

Her husband's roar made Olímpia return to the living room, curious. When he saw her, Astério stopped and tried to hide the photograph, but she'd already come forward and with a quick movement grabbed the envelope: She wanted to see what had so upset someone who always bragged of being unflappable.

She couldn't believe her eyes, and she covered her mouth with her hand, swallowing her exclamation of surprise: "Oh, my God, what's this?" She closed her eyes under their mascaraed lashes, then opened them to look again. In the color print, still damp from the darkroom, were Sylvia Esmeralda and little Elói, nakeder than Adam and Eve, while the cassock, the shorts, the dress, the slip, and the panties were at the foot of the round bed, a typical motel bed. The pair of them were side by side, photographed from the front; her eyes were bulging, dying with fright, while his face was fearful and his dick limp. Not even Sylvia's celebrated beauty mark, provocatively located above her pubis—it once inspired a sonnet from the budding Joca—salvaged the artistic nude shot from its mediocrity.

It was a most disturbing, most intriguing matter—Olímpia didn't know what to think. She closed her eyes again, and then she had to control herself to keep her calm. She suddenly realized the danger she'd been in and from which her rendezvous with the senator had saved her. Everything became as clear as a bell to her: If it hadn't been for her date, it would have been she instead of Sylvia who posed for the SNI. She recognized their handiwork—during the elections they'd done the same thing to the wife of a legislator, and now it was Olímpia's turn. They'd hatched a plot and sent a note in her name to Elói, setting forth the time and place for the meeting. He'd fallen for it like an idiot, and she would have fallen, too, if it hadn't been for her assignation with the senator. Sylvia had gone merrily into the mess—she must have been desperate! The reason grew clear: They must be trying to entrap her to demoralize Astério, she thought. But why had the SNI suddenly turned against him? Something serious must have gone wrong without her knowledge. Customarily Astério kept her informed of events and problems—why hadn't he told her anything about this?

"Astério, what does this photo mean? I want to know."

It was her father who answered, sputtering: "Nothing at all, sugar. A little trick we tried to pull. Fooling around." He tried to laugh, unsuccessfully.

Olímpia didn't take her eyes off Astério. He sensed that she was frightened and signaled to her behind his father-in-law's back to calm down. Joãozinho Costa, recovering from his tantrum, concluded, half-irritated and half-mocking:

"Who would have predicted that Dr. Prado d'Ávila, as stuck-up as he is, would turn out to have a cuckold's horns! You can't trust anybody anymore! Go to the table, I'll be right in."

He went into the kitchen, and Olímpia and Astério found themselves alone. She slipped the envelope with the photograph and the negative into her large white Christian Dior purse. Without the negative, they wouldn't be able to make any more copies. But how many of these could they have distributed in political and business circles already? Sylvia and her beauty spot were now exposed to the world. Olímpia drew close to her husband. "Do you know anything about this?"

"Everything. I'll tell you at home. It's not important."

"Don't lie to me, Astério! They're trying to get you, aren't they? Why?" She was whispering in spite of the fact that they were alone in the room.

"No, nothing like that—rest assured. Just a *quid pro quo*. At home." He held out his hand to her, and holding hands, they went into the dining room, the bullfrog and the airplane.

At the table, very agitated, Marlene swallowed the stuffed crab in two forkfuls, but passed up the fish with shrimp sauce, the steak with french fries, and the various desserts, even the milk, sugar, and egg sweets: "I'm not hungry, Mommy." She was only waiting for her father to come in so she could ask his permission to leave and run off into the arms of the *métèque: "avec ma guele de métèque, de juif errant, de pâtre grec . . ."* Marlene knew the words and music to the song by heart. Oh, Georges Moustaki—passion—his halo of white hair, fame—glory — waiting at the theater door! Daddy, why are you taking so long?

Joãozinho Costa ambled into the kitchen with measured steps. It was a good thing he hadn't let Zé do Lírio go, hadn't sent him back to Pernambuco, as his son-in-law had advised. He shook his big head: Astério and his crazy ideas. Astério exuded competence and bragged about his almost unlimited power, but he'd paid to see proof, and all he saw was a fool, a conman, a—a cuckold, the juvenile judge. Who would have thought it?

Argus in Action

Inspector Ripoleto of the State Police got off the bus in Santo Amaro at nightfall, and hardly had he stepped off than the locals recognized both his profession and his merits:

"Look, there's a cop hanging around here passing himself off as a tourist."

"And he's supposedly one of their best. Right away he wanted to know about the vicar's mistress. Calling Missy Marina a mistress, just imagine!"

Wrapped in his proverbial cape, hidden behind his dark glasses and the turned-down brim of his hat, conspicuously incognito, the inspector had been carrying out the mission entrusted to him by the chief of the State Police, a delicate and dangerous task: to interrogate the vicar, as well as the Velosos. The target of mockery, trickery, and violence, the inspector had nevertheless reached a precise and objective conclusion: The people of Santo Amaro had taken up arms and were ready to go to war.

All the more meritorious then, had been Inspector Ripoleto's actions in confronting the obvious ill will. He had encountered a great many difficulties, complications by the score: Anyone else would have given up, but he stood firm and persisted. He listened to the comical replies to pertinent questions that he had asked Mr. José Veloso, Dona Canô, and other suspicious personages of this agitated town. He heard mocking laughter behind his back—is it as Sherlock Holmes that he's disguised, or is it Tenório Cavalcanti's gunslingers? He swallowed insults from the vicar's housekeeper, Missy Marina, a great big woman with a ruddy face and hair on her chin. Enjoying the esteem and respect of her fellow townsmen, extremely offended by the indiscretion of the plain-clothesman, the vicar's *comadre* came close to slugging him: "I've got no cause to tell you about my life! Leave me alone, you nosy cop! Go ask your mother who the fathers of all her children are!" Some townsmen even murmured threats to him: People here have been known to send spies floating back to Bahia.

A revolt had indeed spread through the town, and the population was clearly on a war footing. Groups gathered on streetcorners, marched toward the square by the church, and cheered the vicar, Mr. José, and Dona Canô, parents of the boys. Emissaries departed for other towns around the Bay of All Saints by land and water transport—cars, trucks, oxcarts, motorcycles, bicycles, horses, donkeys, mules, launches, sloops, boats, canoes, and the yawl of the champion Dori Zarolho. Once they reached the other towns, they rallied support for their libertory yet puni-tive campaign, a sacrosanct crusade, drafting vessels and admirals, soldiers and sailors, enlisting them under the standard of Saint Barbara of the Thunder: All along the course of the Paraguaçu River the trumpets of Judgment Day resounded, and people ran about amid tumult and dust: The saint belongs to us!

Every day, copies of *Diário de Notícias* and *A Tarde* arrived on the Bahiana Line ship's morning run. Normally the newspapers were des-tined for the subscribers. On that Thursday, however, they'd become collective property, seized and socialized, passed from hand to hand. Everybody who knew how to read had read the stories by Guido Guerra and José Augusto Berbert, one saying that the statue had disappeared during the trip, the other describing the statue arrival's at the docks of Bahia in the presence of the reporter.

Between such contradictory items as those, what were they sup-posed to believe? Come now, what a question! There was no difference of opinion: *A Tarde* didn't exaggerate, it didn't publish false rumors—you could swear on the cross that what you read in its columns was true. As for the sensationalism of the pamphleteer Guerra in *Diário de Notícias,* it was nothing but a big lie, invented from beginning to end, most certainly at the request of somebody with influence who was interested in fo-menting confusion about the fate of Saint Barbara of the Thunder. Wasn't it much discussed that the director of the Museum of Sacred Art and Dr. Odorico Tavares, head of the Associated Newspapers of Bahia, were thick as thieves? There was no mystery: The statue had been stolen by a city slicker from the state capital, and when the uproar died down it would be discreetly incorporated into the museum's collection. It wouldn't be the first time, and it wouldn't be the last. Who was the thief, the conman in the state capital? Giving out names means running risks, but here's an interesting clue: Father Téo referred to him as Dom Mimoso, Mr. Darling.

Another rumor, this one bearing the obvious stamp of the opposition—insinuated that it was the governor who'd ordered the theft, with the intention of offering the thunder saint statue, the only one of her in existence, to the military candidate for President of the Republic. It was a rumor, yet it was based on some indications, various and proven. Along the way the name of a fiery colonel who was a devotee of antique statues surfaced. He'd stripped the state of Alagoas of its statues with the complicity of local politicians during the seven months he commanded the army garrison in Maceió. Sometime later, promoted to general and placed on reserve status, wearing the pajamas of retired officers, his stewardships and vainglory lost, he became a liberal. He applied the booty from his sack of Alagoas to the purchase of a penthouse in São Conrado, in Rio de Janeiro. Remembering his days of authority, the raids on the convents and churches of Penedo and São Miguel dos Campos, he explained that he'd acquired the luxury apartment with the help of God and the saints of the Church. The ingrate neglected to mention the aid of fawners and bootlickers.

Inspector Ripoleto smelled gunpowder in the air. He perceived signs of disorder, suspicious activity, and criminal incitement, but all afternoon, no matter how many townspeople he tried to interrogate, he had difficulty determining the extent and character of the riot in progress. Then, at dinnertime, he ate a sparse and terrible meal in a greasy spoon. The waiter was not only an idiot but clumsy—he didn't know how to answer any of the inspector's questions, and he spilled the tasteless contents of the platter all over the inspector's disguise, staining his jacket and his nearly clean shirt with fat and sauce. It almost seemed as if he'd done it on purpose.

The People in Arms

All the inhabitants of the town, as well as small farmers who came in great numbers from the surrounding areas, some carrying sickles for cutting cane, gathered that night to the light of torches and filled the square before the church to overflowing. "We want the saint!" they shouted.

Inspector Ripoleto mingled with the crowd and, so as not to be noticed, acted as one of the most enthusiastic demonstrators. He ended up leading a chorus of enraptured church biddies, broadening their hysterical shrieks with his thundering voice: "The saint belongs to us!" With his lively intelligence and the eye of a bulldog—gifts for which his envious colleagues wouldn't forgive him—the inspector realized that he was actively participating in a gathering preparatory to a demonstration—if not something worse—and was committing an illegal and punishable act.

It would be more than sufficient reason for his arrest and trial if he were caught by a police detective. The consequence would be all the more serious if a military policeman arrested him: The drubbing he would receive would scare a dog, a refined session of torture that would last until they obtained a full confession of his crimes against the state and the names of his accomplices and their leaders. That would be followed by a permanent stay in the dungeons of the security organization, the DOI-CODIs, for life; or rather, death.

Inspector Ripoleto shuddered just thinking of the unmentionable abbreviation, but he calmed down when he remembered that he was on duty. Disguising himself as a street rioter had been a stroke of genius worthy of his privileged intellect. He felt euphoric, thinking of the stupendous report he would deliver to the Dr. Calixto Passos, making him a candidate for a good promotion: "Mission accomplished, chief." He hadn't only been astute, he had also been careful, persistent, determined, hard-nosed; he'd honored the name of the State Police.

From inside the church, surrounded by wrinkled old women fanatics and excited reporters, the vicar of Santo Amaro appeared at the top of the steps. He was Father Teófilo Lopes de Santana, the popular Father Téo, who was called Teteo in the loving arms of Missy Marina when, after performing the devotions and tasks of the day, he would take off his cassock and put on his nightshirt with pink rosettes around the neck.

From the front of the church, which was both his stage and his tribune, the rude priest addressed the multitude. Indignantly he recounted every detail of the ignoble tale, using strong words, sometimes gross ones. He told of the request for the loan of the statue, his refusal, the insistence and pressure exerted on him, finally the order from above; then the embarkation—and the disappearance. The person responsible, the author of this Machiavellian plan, the one in charge of the theft had also disappeared. All that day, not to mention the night before, Father Téo had desperately tried to talk to the director of the museum on the telephone, but he had not gotten to hear his honeyed voice; Dom Mimoso had taken to his heels.

"Where has Dom Maximiliano, a citizen considered the flower of gentility, betaken himself?" the vicar asked the crowd. "The citizen has disappeared, taking along with him our Saint Barbara of the Thunder, our protectress." At the end of his speech—delivered with the ferocious tongue of a Father Antônio Vieira, who from his pulpit in the cathedral of Bahia used to excoriate the Portuguese nobility for their "art of theft" —the masses gave their vicar a rousing ovation: "Hurray for Father Téo, our defender!" "Hurray for the thunder saint!" "Down with the church robbers! Down with Dom Mimoso!" Inspector Ripoleto wondered who this Dom Mimoso could be, and since he couldn't find out, he shouted along with the indignant chorus: "Down with Dom Mimoso!" Rockets exploded in the air, lighting up the sky, filling the air with the smell of gunpowder.

An even greater ovation greeted Dona Canô, small, withered, and fragile, a jade saint. A daughter of Yansan, she galvanized herself into an insolent agitator, the head of a revolt, a leader of warriors. "Let's rescue our Saint Barbara of the Thunder, she belongs to the people of Santo Amaro, she belongs to us!" She said it with a soft and implacable voice, and the people lifted her on their shoulders. Once more there were fireworks.

A subversive act was definitely in the making, Inspector Ripoleto sensed, his nose sharper than ever. He ran his eyes over this crowd of Communists to calculate the exact number of subversives gathered on the square. It was a lengthy inspection because it required mathematics, and multiplication was not his forte, particularly when he had to do it in his head. In the interim the steps of the church had emptied, the vicar and the principals disappeared, as well as Mr. José Veloso, Araújo the goldsmith, Osvaldo Sá, the memoirist from Maragogipe, Miltinho the sexton, and all the reporters and photographers sent by the newspapers, not only from Bahia but even Gervásio Batista from the magazine *Manchete* of Rio de Janeiro, just back from the war in Vietnam.

They'd all disappeared into hiding to conspire or to a restaurant to savor a full dinner—wherever there's a journalist there's a freeloader, it's inevitable. Inspector Ripoleto decided to discover the scene of the crime —the eating place—and do it quickly, before both the conspiracy and the *maniçoba* were finished. *Maniçoba,* made of manioc shoots and meat, a specialty of the bay region, was the preferred dish of our luminary.

The inspector walked along asking questions of the people who were leaving the square after the rally, and though he refrained from the least bit of scolding, pushing, and bluster, he still somehow provoked a disagreeable reaction every time. Some bold young men surrounded him, took his revolver, insulted his mother, and led him out to the dock by force. Without taking his clothes off, they gave him a bath in the river —a kindly act because the heat was murderous. Then they put him aboard a small canoe with no rudder or paddles and turned him loose into the flow of the current—playful lads!

The fledgling sailor didn't navigate any great distance. A short way ahead, just before the river widens near a bend, the canoe came to a halt on a vast clump of water hyacinths—the realm of mosquitoes—between the rather proximate shores. Did the inspector leap into the Paraguaçu River and reach dry land with a few quick strokes? Didn't he? Well, just between you and me, quietly, let's share the most confidential secret: The Argus of the State Police didn't know how to swim. Now, let that detail remain buried forever—don't let the scoundrels in the State Police ever find out—our hero would become a laughingstock!

His muddy clothes drying on his body, the inspector listened to the atrocious buzzing of the mosquitoes. He'd never seen so many. The hat that could have protected him had floated downstream, a considerable loss; the wind was blowing and furtive sounds came from the indistinct shadows. In impotence and fear—that is, in the solitude of intellectuals—Inspector Ripoleto, who had been sent on a special mission to Santo Amaro da Purificação, thanks to his eagle eye and his ingenuity, spent the night sneezing and shivering from cold in spite of the ongoing heat wave. He'd done it to earn praise and promotion, but he barely escaped pneumonia.

The Perplexed

Leaving the Avenida da Ave-Maria amid a spray of farts and recriminations and finding himself on the street surrounded by the nighttime activity, Danilo realized that he didn't know what to do next. He wasn't coming back without Manela, he'd fumed—a very macho statement. Now how to fulfill his threat?

It occurred to him to look up the juvenile judge, but considering the hour, he rejected the idea. Besides, what could he do at the judge's by himself, without Dadá? Discuss their disagreement about his niece's internment? And Manela was his niece by marriage, while she was related by blood to Adalgisa—which of the guardians would His Honor favor? The aunt, certainly—moralistic and watchful, bristling with opinions about behaving like a lady. At best, he'd only be able to get the judge to countermand his order the next day, while Danilo was intent upon freeing Manela that very night. Hadn't he stated so categorically in the heat of the argument?

Rebellious, he'd gotten all excited, hadn't weighed his words, had overextended himself. Danilo now found himself standing on the sidewalk under a streetlight with the face of a fool. In the midst of his embarrassment he remembered Gildete, Manela's other aunt, related just as much by blood as Adalgisa, the guardian of Marieta, Manela's younger sister. He decided to go see Gildete, tell her what had happened, decide with her what measures to take. Gildete always had good advice, and she was resolute. Dadá would come out fighting and cursing when she found out that her husband was conspiring with her pest of a sister—she called her that and worse—but Danilo was ready for whatever might come. Dadá could go to hell. He took the bus to Tororó, where Gildete lived.

At Gildete's he found Miro, the crux of the problem. Danilo was already sick of hearing Damiana Sweet-Rice, his next-door neighbor, extol the virtues of the taxi driver, including the permanent and contagious joy that was his trademark: "That's a fine boy there, Mr. Danilo," she would say. "If I had a daughter, I couldn't think of a better husband for her."

But the helpless look on Miro's nervous face had taken the place of joy. By the time he'd parked his car at their meeting place a little before seven, he was already a bit suspicious: While he was at his sister's place, where he lived, at the end of the day he had received a summons from the juvenile judge, ordering him to appear before him the next day at three in the afternoon—with no explanation. Miro had stuffed the summons into his pocket, mystified.

Miro and Manela had a prearranged agreement due to the difficulty of their love affair: If after a half-hour wait she didn't appear at a rendezvous, he was to leave, since it meant that Aunt Adalgisa had discovered the plan or had grown suspicious of her and had locked Manela in her room. It happened with relative frequency. But on that Thursday, Miro wasn't willing to give up so easily. This was their only chance to elope, and they couldn't lose it. He hung around the entrance to the Avenida da Ave-Maria for a while, hoping Manela might somehow get away.

Professor João Batista told him he'd seen Manela when she'd come home from school at noon. All enthusiastic, she'd confided her plans with Miro, in secret, of course, of course, and her determination to meet him without fail. From Damiana, Miro found out that Manela wasn't locked up in her room—the sweets woman could vouch for it personally: A short while before dinner she'd stopped by Adalgisa's house to drop off some tapioca in sauce, a tidbit that Manela loved. She'd seen Manela's door open and her room empty. Manela had gone to study at Rízia's, Adalgisa had said. Damiana had been impressed by two things, she explained to Miro: One, she'd seen aunt and niece depart that afternoon— it couldn't have been four o'clock yet. Manela had waved to her as she went by, told her she'd see her later. Just by chance, Damiana had happened to be in her doorway an hour later, more or less, when Adalgisa returned home all alone. Since then nobody had laid eyes on Manela. The other thing that had made an impression on Damiana was Adalgisa's unrestrained joy. She couldn't contain herself, had been happy but nervous, acting strangely.

The other neighbors whom Miro asked knew nothing about

Manela. Uneasy, Miro went to Rízia's and found her watching television with her boyfriend. Manela? She'd seen her at school, but they hadn't made any plans to study together—that was one of Manela's lies to fool her aunt so she could go out with Miro. Didn't she have a date with him that night? Manela had told her so in confidence, all excited. More and more worried, Miro took off for Gildete's.

What to Do?

Danilo stood next to Álvaro, Gildete's son who was the medical student, who'd opened the door to let him in, and caught the tail end of Miro's harangue. He was talking in a loud voice, with lots of gesticulating, so apprehensive that he was on the point of giving up on his date with Manela:

"Missy Damiana saw the two of them go out in the middle of the afternoon, and she was at her doorway an hour later, when Dona Adalgisa came back—alone. Nobody's been able to tell me where Manela is. Besides what I've already told you, I don't know anything."

"Good evening," Danilo greeted them, appearing in the living room.

The two girls, Violeta and Marieta, came to welcome him and get his blessing. Miro nodded—he knew his sweetheart's uncle only by sight. Gildete got up from her chaise longue:

"What's going on, Danilo? Miro here is going crazy—he had a date with Manela, but she didn't show up, she's not locked in her room. She went out with Adalgisa, but she didn't come back with her. You coming here at this hour is a bad sign. What do you know?"

"I know everything." He looked around and said in a sorrowful, embarrassed voice, "Dadá's put Manela in the Cloister of the Penitents at the Convent of the Immaculate Conception."

"What convent is that? I never heard of it." Gildete entreated, but she didn't wait for an answer, she caught on. "Don't tell me that she put the girl—"

"In the convent in Lapa, the very same."

"The Penitents? Oh, this is too much! I won't stand for this!"

"What?" Miro went over to Danilo. "She's at the Penitents?"

"And you're to blame," Danilo retorted. "I think Dadá did a bad thing, and that's why I'm here. But the one to blame is this boy." He pointed to Miro. "Dadá got hold of a note he sent to Manela, setting a time for them to run off tonight. Adalgisa moved fast—she went to the judge, who issued the order."

"Me? A note setting a time to run away? What kind of a story is that? Who invented that lie? Tell me, come on! Show me the proof!"

"I saw a piece of the note setting up the meeting, don't deny it to me. It couldn't have been clearer: 'You're going to enjoy—' how did it go?, what did it say?—'the best of the very best'—everybody knows what that means."

"Oh! That note." Miro didn't calm down completely, but he moderated his tone. "I sent her a note, that's true. Setting a date for seven o'clock, that's also true. I wanted to take Manela to see the taping of the Frenchman's program at the Castro Alves. The best of the very best they are—Caetano and Gil, you've heard of them, haven't you? They're the best there is, aren't they? The taping must just be starting," he explained, a little less wrought up. "I've rented my car out to the French crew— they're good people, not stuck-up like some I know. I asked Dona Nilda, and she said it was all right to bring Manela. No one said anything about running away or eloping."

His eyes flashing again, he faced Danilo:

"I'm going to marry Manela with or without your consent or Dona Adalgisa's, but we never thought of eloping. Not yet." Indignant again, he pointed his finger. "Do you mean to tell me that they put her in the Lapa convent as if she were a whore? How low can you get? What are you going to do to get her out of there?"

Danilo didn't answer. He kept his calm, didn't become annoyed with Miro. He understood the boy's agitation, his drive, his revolt. He turned to Gildete:

"That's why I'm here, Gildete. So we can see what can be done to free the poor girl. I had an ugly scene with Dadá, and all I want is to bring Manela back home. But I really don't know what to do. I can't talk to the judge until tomorrow, and I'm afraid he'll side with Dadá over me. It might seem absurd, but she's done this thinking it's for the good of her niece."

"The witch!" Gildete couldn't control herself.

"It's just her point of view—let's stop worrying about Adalgisa. What I want to know is whether you've got any suggestions for helping Manela. That's why I came. You, Álvaro, maybe the boy—there's no time to argue. Manela must be going through the tortures of hell. I don't even want to think about it."

"You're right. You were always good to her." Gildete nodded, dismayed, feeling helpless. "Right off, I can't think of anything—but there must be some way. Let's sit down and wrack our brains. We've got to find a way out, no matter what."

Violeta and Marieta were weeping in each other's arms, a muffled, desolate crying. Álvaro suggested they find a lawyer:

"We can talk to Dr. Orlando Gomes—he's the best one in family

court. In fact, wasn't he the one who wrote the code? That's what the
newspapers said. He was a friend of the old man's, and he treats Mama
with a lot of respect. Do you want me to call him up, Mother?"

Miro interrupted as he put on his cap: "Pardon my bad manners,
Mr. Danilo. I didn't even thank you. You too, Aunt Gildete. It's just that
I can't stay here like this, pounding my head while she's suffering. I've
got to get Manela out of the convent, and it's got to be tonight. Tonight!"
he repeated.

He went out the door, and Álvaro got up, hot on Miro's heels. "I'm
going with him so he won't do anything foolish."

The Fortress of God

Police and reporters, one group as numerous as the other, were
crossing paths on the streets, going up and down slopes, sniffing in alleys
in search of two Catholic clergymen: a monk and a secular priest.

The secular one was a rioter, a trespasser, a robber of statues, a
womanizer: That was what was repeated over the telephone lines in
insistent calls to all the newspaper offices. The security organizations had
more than enough proof of the involvement of Father Abelardo Galvão,
the vicar of Piaçava, the one making the telephone calls said, in the
attacks on plantations in that municipality, at the head of peasants
he had personally armed and turned into outlaws. Indications were
being gathered that pointed to him as the main suspect in the recent and
spectacular theft of the statue of Saint Barbara of the Thunder. The caller
identified him as one of the leaders of a gang that specialized in the
pillage of churches, in the theft of statues and religious objects, active
throughout the whole Northeast.

Anonymous but precise, informed about the clergyman's public
and private life, the caller brought to light another fact of Father Galvão's
life: He was a seducer of virgins, a frequenter of motels—the scoundrel
was even shacking up with a young woman. Scandalizing his parishioners, he was sharing his bed and board with a shameless stage actress; the
anonymous caller promised to have new and sensational revelations in
this regard soon.

At the editorial offices of *A Tarde,* Renato Simões and Jorge Calmon
asked each other about the origin of the telephone calls. "It's easy," said
the editor-in-chief. "All you have to do is figure out who's the big landowner in Piaçava: I only know of one." Renato Simões agreed: "If it isn't
his doing, it must be his son-in-law's."

On the eight o'clock local news, a television shot showed scenes of the luncheon at the Model Market: the Baianas in the *samba de roda,* the Frenchman Jacques Chancel applauding the dancers, some of the celebrities present. The sharp-eyed Colonel Raul Antônio, who was also watching, spotted Father Galvão there, sitting between the ex-deputy Fernando Santana, whose rights had been suspended, and the loudmouth Dias Gomes, a confirmed Communist. The federals had thought he'd disappeared, but there he was, as large as life having lunch in the company of subversives, like a leading man on television. Gnashing his teeth, spouting threats, beside himself over such incompetence, the colonel gathered his bunglers together and demanded, amid threats: "I want some news about the priest immediately—tonight!" He ordered their vigilance redoubled; they must locate the perpetrator, even if it meant following his footsteps, right into bed. The police had lost track of him before the luncheon; the priest had mysteriously eluded both the State Police and the Federal Police. Inspector Parreirinha, as an excuse, said a solar eclipse had clouded his vision.

At eleven o'clock the newspapermen had been alerted about Father Abelardo Galvão, yet they still hadn't located him either—they'd been busy running around searching for the other man who'd disappeared, Dom Maximiliano von Gruden. The reporters and photographers who arrived at the archdiocese palace after the director of the Museum of Sacred Art departed had been unable to find out anything more about him. They were sure of only one thing: Dom Maximiliano hadn't returned to the Convent of Saint Theresa, the seat of the museum. Contradictory rumors were circulating about the monk's fate: He'd boarded a plane for Rio de Janeiro at the airport; he'd been arrested and was being held incommunicado at army headquarters.

At the museum, the journalists hanging around waiting for the director to return were yawning as they watched the workers set up the exhibit of religious art. Gilberbert Chaves and Lev Smarchevski had been joined by a third architect, Sílvio Robato, who was good for tips and anecdotes and helped the professionals of the press in their task of killing time. At the Castro Alves Theater, on whose stage the equipment of Antènne Deux was being set up, the police were sneaking around, keeping watch on the taping and filming the comings and goings, their eyes on Patrícia, who they hoped would lead them to Father Abelardo Galvão.

The two clergymen, the vicar of Piaçava and the museum director, were both actually quite near the theater—at the Benedictine abbey above the slope by Castro Alves Plaza. Father Abelardo stayed there whenever he came to the state capital. He'd been recommended to the abbot by his mentor, Dom Hélder Câmara, the celebrated archbishop of Recife, supreme head of liberation theologians, and the chief watermelon of the clergy, according to the militarists in power, who hated him.

Dom Maximiliano von Gruden, the tormented director of the Museum of Sacred Art, was a leading figure in intellectual life and his presence obligatory in the pomp of high society, but as everybody knew but nobody remembered, he was also an illustrious member of the Benedictine community. He kept his monk's cell at the abbey, a modest and austere one like all the others, different only in that on the wall hung a German print worthy of the original, of the Four Apostles by Jordaens.

One could imagine Dom Maximiliano hiding anywhere in the city; his circle of friends was wide, and the places where his intellectual curiosity and verve for life had taken him were many. It would cause no surprise for him to have gone to a painter's studio, a banker's mansion, the cellar of a bookstore, a student fraternity or a *candomblé* hideout. But no one ever would have thought to look for him in his cell at the Abbey of Saint Benedict.

Rising up on the top of the hill, looking out to the sea, the Abbey of Saint Benedict was a fortress of God; a memory of the homeland, a bastion of freedom, a refuge for the persecuted.

The Poets' Theater

The Castro Alves Theater was boiling over with police. "This place is crawling with cops," Nilda Spencer told Nelson Araújo. Cops, inspectors, detectives, secret agents dressed in character: cape, wide-brimmed hat, revolver bulge, soldier boys in civilian clothes, there was no lack of SNI agents. Assigned by their various respective civil and military bodies to be present for the taping for *Le Grand Échiquier* that Thursday night on the stage of the theater, it was impossible to deny them admission. Those whose explicit mission was to ascertain the whereabouts of Father Abelardo Galvão took note of every gesture Patrícia made. She would lead them to the watermelon priest, they thought.

Buried in the pockets of their capes, in the folds of their jackets, they were hiding sophisticated recording devices imported from the United States, Japan, and Germany, minimum in size, maximum in recording capabilities, the ne plus ultra in electronic equipment. Yet those masterful devices broke down with extreme ease, as we have already seen, on the streets of the city. Colonel Raul Antônio was most certainly right when he put the blame for such failures on the government agents who were using them. In Nipponese or Yankee hands, after all, they functioned flawlessly. The ideal thing, the colonel concluded, would be to import the human equipment as well. He would make an exception, in this regard, for torturers, since the local specialists owed nothing to the more savage and refined experts from countries of the First World, the civilized ones.

The massive police presence was all the more obvious because the Castro Alves was closed to the public that night with admittance only for some few invited guests. This was the result of the decision by the Antènne Deux team to tape there with four Brazilian musical stars, two composers and two singers. The ones whom Miro had described as "the best of the very best" in his ill-fated note to Manela: Caetano Veloso, Gilberto Gil, Maria Betânia, Gal Costa. They were the top names in *tropicalismo,* a musical movement to which seditious motivations had been attributed by the dictatorship, stamped as degenerate, criminal, subversive art.

Tropicalismo had already cost Gil and Caetano, the two leaders of the pack, dearly: They'd paid with imprisonment and exile for the songs that awakened hope, lifted spirits, and were banners for youth. They had recently returned from forced exile in London, following a period of jail, violence, and humiliation when their heads had been shaved, their guitars mute, their voices silenced. They returned as heroes, surrounded by the love of the people and the permanent vigilance of the police.

On their tiny recorders, the agents planned to take down for the knowledge and consideration of the competent authorities the statements that the two composers would make into the microphones of the French station. There was thus a considerable delay in taping due to a curious, even extraordinary combination of factors: While they were recording songs or talking about music, everything worked fine, but as soon as Caetano and Gil began to answer the political questions Chancel asked them, the receiving apparatuses manipulated by the secret police suddenly emitted deafening, unearthly feedback that filled the Castro Alves Theater. It was impossible to hear or understand a single word that was spoken. In the back of the hall, in the last row, a black woman of uncommon grace dressed in clothes like Patrícia's seemed greatly amused by the interference and the crackling. In the next seat her comrade, Exu Malé, was laughing. He'd come at her call to pluck the petals off the roses of the night with her.

By common agreement, Jacques Chancel and the tropicalists decided to postpone the interviews—they would cause a stir when broadcast in Paris—to another day and another place, one less susceptible to atmospheric disturbances. But while we are recounting the taping that was done that night, it's worthwhile to note some of the songs performed there, because Brazilians who happened to be in France were the only Brazilians who had the privilege of seeing the segment of *Le Grand Échiquier* dedicated to Bahia.

The first to perform was Gilberto Gil. He sang the *samba* with which he'd said good-bye to Brazil when he went into exile, "*Aquele Abraço*," ("That Embrace") whose lyrics said, "*A Bahia já me deu régua e compasso*" ("Bahia has already given me ruler and compass place"). It got the audience out of their seats, pulled by the irresistible sound. He was followed by Maria Betânia, whose voice of anger and revolt sang "*Carcará*," a song of war; "*Carcará pega mata e come, carcará não vai morrer de fome*" ("The falcon catches, kills, and eats, the falcon won't die of hunger"). Her hair flowing, her curved nose a bird of prey, she was at the same time the sweetness of the world, Dona Janaína, Inaê, Yemanjá, Betânia. Joy! Joy! Caetano exploded: He came walking against the wind, wearing no scarf, carrying no papers, but even the police, hearts of slime, blood of a cockroach, relented, having felt the breath of life and beauty. Then Gal Costa took over the microphone—she was still a timid little girl then—and with that voice that God gave her to seduce and dominate, she taped a song Caetano had composed for her, "Baby": "*Você precisa saber de mim, me ver de perto, baby, baby*" ("You've got to know me, see me close up, baby, baby").

Onstage, assisting Chancel, was a figure from a *candomblé*, the prodigious, captivating Patrícia. She was smiling into the cameras, but her anxious eyes were trying to spot her priest, her pretty boy, among those in the darkness of the theater. He'd said he was coming—why wasn't he here? Had he been caught up in the chains, the nets, the oaths of celibacy? Alas! Patrícia had never imagined that feudalism like that could survive in present times.

Also onstage, in silence, Georges Moustaki was following the taping, spellbound by those Brazilian rhythms, those tropical bits of rebellion. Marlene was kneeling by his feet, her head resting on his knees, in adoration. The mischievous Lenoca, naughty falcon, voracious baby, dazzled —"You've got to know about me, catch me, kill me and eat me, baby, baby."

News from Pernambuco

No, it wasn't the chains of celibacy, the oaths he took at his ordination ceremony in Porto Alegre that prevented Father Abelardo from meeting Patrícia at the Castro Alves Theater—from attending the taping, listening to the libertarian songs of Gil and Caetano.

When he went to the Benedictine abbey after the lunch at the Model Market, he'd thought and then thought again about the virtues of his obligatory chastity: A weighty promise, the subjection was more than fateful, it was fatal. Tonight, however, God had laid upon him another reason to stay within the confines of the Benedictine abbey: The news had come from Pernambuco, and it was frightening. Along with the other monks and friends at the abbey the vicar of Piaçava dedicated himself to prayer and reflections on the memory of a priest whom the police had murdered in Recife a few days earlier. They'd cut off his hands before they killed him, according to Dom Hélder Câmara's messenger, a Mr. Paulo Loureiro, who himself was just out of jail.

The victim's name was Father Henrique Pereira, a trusted aide to the archbishop of Recife and Olinda. He had been one of the originators of the idea of land communes, but above all, Father Pereira had been an influential presence among young people, who overcame their ideological differences and organized their energies around him in their struggle against the militarist, authoritarian state. Inexhaustible in his democratic preaching, Father Henrique had become a symbol of resistance to the dictatorship. On his way back from a meeting with some students, he'd disappeared, and his body had been found days later at the bottom of a gutter, his hands cut off, his face a bloody mass. Paulo Loureiro brought the photographs of the corpse to the abbey: The marks of torture could be seen on the priest's naked torso.

Perfidy and savagery characterized the political repression in Pernambuco. Small and thin, fragile in his white cassock, birdlike, Dom Hélder Câmara resisted all threats and denounced the horrors of the military dictatorship. His example bolstered the courage of the combatants and recruited new partisans. His fearless denunciatory voice crossed the borders of Brazil and resounded on all five continents, made itself heard by peoples and governments. The troublesome archbishop's envoy had come to the abbey in the company of a woman. She spoke alone with the abbot for more than three-quarters of an hour, then left to meet with Gil and Caetano just after the taping at the Castro Alves. They all knew each other from their exile in Europe.

Mr. Paulo Loureiro, a blond, middle-aged man from the backlands, lingered in the company of the monks of Saint Benedict and told them about the struggle in Pernambuco. He spoke of Gregório Bezerra, an octogenarian, in handcuffs, a rope around his neck, dragged through the streets of Recife like an animal. Everybody had seen that infamy—it happened in broad daylight, on the Rua Nova, the Princesas Docks, the Praça de São Pedro dos Clérigos, the Rua da Imperatriz, and the Rua da Aurora, all through the center of the city. He also brought news of Ariano Suassuna, Rui Antunes, Paulo Cavalcanti, Pelópides Silveira, all of them standing firm. Even puppet shows had been prohibited, as well as certain carnival dances.

Both as a guest and in solidarity, Mr. Paulo Loureiro accompanied the Benedictines to church to pray for the soul of Father Henrique Pereira, a sacrifice in the holocaust of the dictatorship. He didn't pray because he was an atheist, but he felt comforted nonetheless.

The Masters of
Angola *Capoeira*

On the Largo do Pelourinho, at the Angola *Capoeira* school of Master Pastinha, the First Grand Meeting of Angola *Capoeira* Masters had been set for that same Thursday night. It was a result of long preparations and enormous effort—Master Pastinha didn't want to die before putting down on paper and proclaiming in the press the code of honor of those who practiced the so-called sport.

Starting the next morning, the *capoeira* masters would be divided into committees, and the master would have them discuss the various problems affecting the study and practice of Angola *capoeira* in Bahia in a time of industrialization and tourism. They would talk about the possible dangers, especially the danger that *capoeira* would lose its character, or that the national martial art would be transformed into a folkloric exhibition, sumptuous or vulgar, rich or poor in agility and wit, a spectacle for the English to see, the Argentinians to applaud, the Americans to photograph. They planned to set up an organization with its headquarters in Bahia to bring together all the masters in the country for a Code of *Capoeira* Fighters that would establish norms of behavior, obligations, precepts. A draft of this code of honor had already been sketched out by Master Pastinha and written up by the short-story writer Vasconcelos Maia, a *capoeira* fighter himself, as were two of his children, a lawyer and an engineer.

A means of defense born in slave quarters, the creation of Bantu slaves, *capoeira* had been subject to the most ferocious persecution: Its practice had been prohibited, its practitioners punished. It was considered, along with *candomblé*, to be an expression of barbarism. In those days, the whole African component of Brazilian culture was being repudiated, knowledge of it erased, its manifestation forbidden. But *capoeira*, disguised as a collective dance, survived to the sounds of the belly *berimbau*, and its efficiency and beauty caught on; a ballet of magical steps, a fight with mortal blows, it attained the status of a martial art. Every day new schools were being opened, excellent teachers were proclaimed. It had been a lot of work to bring them all together, but Master Pastinha was used to overcoming difficulties, and no one could deny his unequaled mastery and his extreme honesty: "A human being formed out of generosity and civilization, one of the greatest, most illustrious people in Bahia," Glauber Rocha had written of him in the magazine *Mapa,* and the people venerated him.

Between that Thursday, the opening night of the First Grand Meeting, and closing night on Sunday, the masters would put on a show in the grand hall of the school, to the delight of those present. On Saturday morning they would be behind the Model Market, at the traditional stage for challenges, where they would be filmed by the crew from *Le Grand Échiquier.*

At the age of ninety celebrated years, blind and stooped, barely recovered from hemiplegia, but still steady on his feet, his head lucid, and his voice commanding, Master Pastinha greeted and welcomed the numerous masters from the seven gates of Bahia, from the island of Itaparica, from the towns around the bay. His wife Romélia, a vendor of *acarajés* and *abarás,* jerk-off cakes, caramel and white coconut cakes, would announce the name of each participant, and Master Pastinha would repeat it, giving the welcome.

Let us pause here to record the names of the masters and in that way illustrate and enrich this Bahian chronicle of religious and profane customs: not because doctors, intellectuals, millionaires, and politicians are among them, but because the masters who teach and preserve Angola *capoeira* are among the authors of Brazilian culture.

Let us begin where we ought to begin, by recalling the great ones from the past, citing their immortal names: Beetle, Chico the Great, Zé Dou, Tibiri Plenty Dough, Breeches, Ironbreaker, Sixty, Biluaca, Gasoline, Mumps, and Cobra, who died facing five thugs armed with fishscaling knives in front of Santa Maria Fort. They lived during the days of persecution and were familiar with the whip and the inside of a jail; they knew no fear.

Attending Pastinha's gathering and taking part in the First Grand Meeting were the masters whose real names or *noms de guerre* appear here, in the order in which they came through the door of the school where Romélia and the supreme master welcomed them. God's Love was the first, Waldemar da Liberdade came in the company of Traíra and Good Hair. Master Bimba, the creator of a regional *capoeira,* arrived surrounded by disciples who supported him in his dissidence. Camafeu de Oxóssi, dressed to kill, with a necktie and broad-brimmed hat, Coral Snake, Cat, Tapeworm, Paulo dos Anjos, masters emeriti. Jaime from Mar Grande, Vagabond, Jorge Satellite, René, Giant, Falcon, King Senac, Jairo Petroleum, Tamoinha, Senavox, Angola, Zé Poet, Deuce of Hearts, Boob, Miguel Moon, Mala, Diogo, Seven Ball, White Ball, Black Ball, and Caramel Cake, Hose, Red Mill, Pigeonhole, Medicine, Swollen Donkey, Luiz Gutemberg, Virgílio Costa, Milton Macumba, Cacao, Indian Poty, Gajé, American, Dimola, Sweet Mouth, Clay João, Little João, Big João, Maricota João, Luanda João, and Joãozinho, Lua de Bobó, Nô, Aristides, Good Fellow, Itapuã, Geni Loló, Alabama, Tame Snake, Little Green Snake, Ironwood, Daladé, Tininho Murici, Macau, Piauí, Rice Finch, Bluebird, Dinelson, Exequiel, Ferreirinha from Santo Amaro, Mário Good Goat, Benivaldo, Handkerchief Zé, Guts Zé, Monkey Zé, and Zezito Varig, Batista Basement, Decent, Jawbone, Bozó, Emanuel Son of God, Sausage, Buzzard, Redbird, Augusto Halfbreed, Stone Hammer, Roadrunner, Raimundo, Almir Loló, Lazinho, Sinval, Salis, China, Daltro, Lúcio Dendê, Lazaro, Edinho Square Crab, Tonho Matéria, and Doctor Manu. If anyone has been overlooked, may he pardon the clumsiness on the part of this ignoramus.

Some special guests, a few graduates appeared bearing the right to the title *master* even if they didn't yet follow the profession. Most of them were former students of Master Pastinha, and a few of Master Bimba. Among the latter were the rich landowner from Itabuna, Moysés Alves, while among the former was the writer Wilson Lins. Vasconcelos Maia has already been mentioned, but the writers present at the meeting were not limited to him and the author of *The Colonel's Thugs*. Several others, just as well known, lent their prestige to the Grand Meeting: Waldir Freitas de Oliveira, Vilvaldo Costa Lima, Ildásio Tavares, Antônio Loureiro de Souza, Antônio Risério, Luís Ademir, Jeovah de Carvalho, and Cid Teixeira, who documented the meeting in an erudite report for the Catholic University, with the collaboration of Rui Simões. Still other intellectuals from different fields could be seen: the theatrical *meteur-en-scène* Alvinho Guimarães, Guido Araújo from the movies, the press agent Fernando Hupsel, the sculptor Mário Cravo, the painter Carybé—that guy shows up everywhere, he doesn't have to be called!—the American professor John Dwyer, and Bruno Amado, a young lady-killer. All of them can be seen in the documentary that Siri filmed, produced by the businessman Renato Martins, a Maecenas by trade and vocation.

Songwriters and poets from the market proclaimed:

Bahia, minha Bahia,
Bahia do Salvador,
Quem não conhece capoeira
Não lhe pode dar valor.
Todos podem aprender:
General e até doutor . . .
(Bahia, my Bahia,
Bahia, my Salvador,
If you don't know *capoeira*,
You don't know what it's for.

Anybody can learn it:
Generals, doctors, and more . . .)

Doctors, movie-makers, playwrights, ethnologists, professors, moneybags, writers large and small, artists of chisel and brush—every type of person could be seen in the festive hall of the school. But where were the generals? The cat ate the generals on the way—but the prophecy must be fulfilled, and someday a four-star general will be seen winning *capoeira* matches, holding the *berimbau,* loosening his hands, thrusting his legs to the rhythm of the *martelo* and the *galope.* Anybody can learn it.

Of all the personalities who had been invited to the inaugural solemnities of the First Grand Meeting of Angola *Capoeira* Masters, only Danilo Correia was missing. The former soccer star for Ipiranga was Pastinha's former pupil and one most praised by the master, better even at doing the half-moon, the cartwheel, the blessing, the butt, and the kite tail than he was in kicking a goal, dribbling, and making a curved kick.

The Code of Honor

The level of excitement was high, and the room was packed; television cameras had already filmed the event for the eleven o'clock news. Siri and his crew—Siri's crew was his wife—were filming the champions in their boldest strokes from different angles.

Waldemar and Camafeu, two of the best soloists, were putting on a casual demonstration of the *berimbau* to the cadence of cane liquor and an old coin. Camafeu de Oxóssi's grave voice resounded throughout the hall, went out onto the pavements of Pelourinho and Maciel, and disappeared in the direction of Carmo and the Terreiro de Jesus:

Aruandê
ê aruandê, camarado.
Galo cantou, camarado
cocotocô.
(*Aruandê*
ê aruandê, comrade.
The cock crowed, comrade
cock-a-doodle-do.)

Waldemar, whose artistry on the *berimbau* on the Estrada da Liberdade brooked no competition from the others, turned his voice loose in the *capoeira* refrain:

Camarada ê!
camaradinho,
camarado . . .

In the center of the room Traíra and Good Hair performed, each
more agile than the other, more in control of himself, more tricky and
unexpected, more dazzling. No one who saw them leap their leaps will
ever forget the roguishness of the wily thrusts, the blows that were the
most difficult of ballet steps: *capoeira* kills! Bringing out classic songs, old
ones from the time of slavery, the Paraguay War, Camafeu and Waldemar put their hot male voices together:

Eu estava lá em casa
sem pensá, sem maginá
e viero me buscá
pra ajudá a vancê
a guerra do Paraguá
Camarada ê
camaradinho
camarado . . .
(I was at home there
not thinking, not imagining
and they came to get me
to give you some help
in the war in Paraguay
Camarada ê
camaradinho
camarado . . .)

Hands were clapping in applause for a movement by Good Hair
when Miro appeared in the doorway. It almost looked as if they were
clapping to greet his arrival—which wouldn't have been surprising, for
he was welcome at the school and at the home of Romélia and Pastinha;
they loved him like a son. Pastinha was a second father to his pupils.
When the old man had to move out of the city, Miro would go get him
in his taxi and take him back and forth and wouldn't charge him anything—not even the cost of the gasoline. "What could I charge him?"
Miro said. "I'm the one who owes him."

Accompanied by Álvaro, Miro was all worked up in a fury. They
applause for Good Hair died down, and then the new arrival clapped to
get attention for what he wanted to tell them:

"Excuse me, Master Pastinha, you people will excuse me for the
interruption—but it's something serious, a matter of life and death. I'm
asking for help."

"Who is it?" Pastinha asked Romélia. "I recognize the voice."

"It's Miro—Mirinho the Well-Loved."

"What brings you here, my son? From the sound of your voice I can see that you're in torment. Speak up, open your heart."

Miro had been one of Master Pastinha's pupils, he had done his cartwheels gracefully, but he had never finished the course. Where could he find the time? Time was short for him, with so many duties and beauties. Now Traíra and Good Hair stopped their match, and Waldemar and Camafeu laid down their *berimbaus.*

In a stumbling speech Miro told them that Manela, his girlfriend, had been dragged off to the Lapa convent, a cloister worse than the worst prison. She hadn't committed any crime, she hadn't offended anybody, hadn't threatened anybody, hadn't insulted anybody: If it was a sin to like somebody and want to marry that somebody someday, that was her sin. Her evil aunt—with the grim, intolerant soul of a Castilian; no, not a Castilian, the fanatical soul of a Francoite, a racist, a fascist—the step-mother aunt opposed the marriage because he was not only poor and a taxi driver but a dark mulatto. Manela was a light mulatto, a high school student; she attended the dances at the Spanish Club and the fairs at the new Church of Sant'Ana. She was an orphan under the iron heel of her guardian.

Romélia knew Manela, had given her her blessing, and they'd joked about the real name of the so-called "student cake." "What is it really called, Aunt Romélia?" she'd asked. "You mean you don't know, girl? Look here, you know very well, the name is *jerk-off. Student cake* is what church biddies call it. Jerk-off, just as tasty as the other kind." "Other kind? What other kind, Aunt Romélia? Tell me, please." "I'll bet you know perfectly well—don't play the fool." The two of them laughed, and Manela ate an *abará,* with lots of pepper, Auntie!

"Oh, what have they done to my girl, those rotten people!" cried Romélia.

"It can't be," Master Pastinha said, and repeated, "It can't be, I won't allow it. I won't permit it!"

In the code of honor of *capoeira* fighters, which Master Pastinha was submitting to this very meeting, the very first of its seventeen articles states that those who practice Angola *capoeira* have an obligation to go to the aid of those who call for help, those who suffer, the persecuted. Freedom is the lamp of the masters who study, practice, and teach that Brazilian art, because *capoeira* was born out of the struggle of slaves against slavery—that was what it said in the introduction to the noble document.

"Let's go get her out of there!" exclaimed God's Love, who was accustomed to sailing the broad breadth of the sea—he was a sloop master as well as a *capoeira* fighter.

"Right now," put in Coral Snake, who had no other profession besides making small talk, beating his gums at the market, eating ray-fish *moqueca* there, and playing dominoes with Merched the Arab. Apart from that, his only occupation was making love on the sand.

"Let's storm that convent—it shouldn't be hard!" was the advice of the halfbreed Traíra, who was ready for a riot. Known to the police as a troublemaker, he was always ready for action.

Mário Cravo, the sculptor, laughed under his thick mustache. He, too, was fond of a good prank and for that reason an idol of Traíra's. In the good old days he used to attack churches and convents to rescue statues—so why not rescue a maiden for her boyfriend?

"I'll go by my studio and pick up a lever to open the gate with no fuss. And a mallet."

The notorious Carybé rubbed his hands in sheer delight. The last time he'd freed a virgin cloistered by her family had been in Salta, Argentina, many years ago. Miss Nancy says that in order to carry it off, the gallant had to wear a red cape and mount a bay horse. It might even be true.

Álvaro shrugged off his last doubts. Gildete, his mother, would approve of the plan: "Let's go, then."

"There's no time to lose!" Miro the Well-Loved pleaded.

Master Pastinha extended his hand, and Romélia gave him her arm: "Hurry, my people, she's suffered long enough. Anyone who's a real *capoeira* fighter will follow me."

Master Pastinha, as old as he was, assumed command, headed for the stairs. If anyone was afraid of what lay ahead, the annals of the school didn't report this cowardice: All that appeared in that stew was the unanimity of decision. So even before being approved by the Grand Meeting, the code of honor was put into practice.

Out on the Largo do Pelourinho, on the illustrious square, Camafeu lifted his *berimbau* and opened his chest in the ancient song:

Negra, o que vende aí?
Vendo arroz de camarão
Sinhá mandou vender
Na cova de Salomão.
(Black girl, what are you selling there?
I'm selling shrimp and rice
Missy sent me to sell
In Solomon's grave.)

Manela too was in Solomon's grave; she'd suffered long enough, and even longer was the time of waiting, night without end. The *capoeira*

fighters made the black pavement of smooth stones tremble before the
Church of Our Lady of the Rosary of the Blacks:

> *Camarada ê*
> *Camaradinho*
> *Camarado . . .*

Arm in arm with Romélia, Master Pastinha led the vanguard of the
people. In his nineties, partially paralyzed, he was still intact, his code of
honor, the banner of Bahia.

The Question

What about Manela? This patient question was being vehemently
asked over and over that evening. Gildete telephoned lawyers, and Danilo
visited a magistrate. Damiana and Professor João Batista made inquiries
while the *capoeira* fighters boldly attempted their rescue. But what about
Manela?

Why have we allowed so much neglect, such total silence, to sur-
round the unfortunate girl? Isn't she, after all, the linchpin of the whole
plot? She may not be the only one, but she certainly figures preemi-
nently; the drama originates with her, and it is for her sake that relatives,
supporters, neighbors, acquaintances, and strangers, top figures in the
law and in high society, take action, but there's been little mention of
Manela herself—as if it weren't enough to bury her in the cloister, conceal her in the grave with base indifference. It's an absurd gaffe, an
unacceptable lacuna: We want to know about Manela, how the condemned girl is bearing up in this crisis.

After all, Manela had been taken to the Convent of the Immaculate
Conception under false pretenses in the midafternoon, and midnight was
already approaching. In a short time it would be Friday—the day for the
opening of the religious art exhibit, remember?—and up till now nothing's been said as to how she reacted, about the Bahia rerun of the
tragedy of the Capulets, the Juliet from the Avenida da Ave-Maria. The
tragedy of the Capulets—there's a literary note for you, even if it's hard
to conceive of Miro as Romeo, since he lacks a Latin profile and a
morbid tendency toward suicide. On the other hand, he's got more than
enough mettle to face and overcome the prejudices of his beloved's
lordly aunt: marriage, yes—suicide, never! But again, Manela or Juliet,
how is the persecuted maiden faring?

The one who is telling the tale should tell it in its entirety, skipping no details, without limiting the action to suit his convenience or the number of pages in the book. If it's told poorly, sloppily, with gaps, well, there are more than enough authors who publish those things they call the modern novel to the adulation of critics. No matter how pedantic and inept these kinds of authors may be, there's still hope: If they keep at it, they'll end up learning, the same way the doctors who study Angola *capoeira* eventually learn.

The question hangs in the air, demanding an immediate answer: What about Manela?

-⚜-⚜

The Mother Superior

Let's go straight to the source and get that answer, be precise and clear, give the most minute details. Details are the secret of novels, as one learns reading *Don Quixote* by Cervantes.

It is often said that a person who suffers develops great forbearance; Master Pastinha, the voice of popular wisdom, for his part, is accustomed to saying that the time of suffering is long and the one who suffers cannot see the end of it. That's why he quickens his pace at the head of the *capoeira* fighters heading for Lapa, where the Convent of the Immaculate Conception is located. In order to give a further touch of erudition to these poorly sketched lines, thereby ennobling the narrative, let us note that opposite the walls of the convent stands the house of Júlia Feital, who was murdered with a golden bullet by her fiancé, who was insane with jealousy. Even in killing her he wanted the best for her— a single bullet of solid gold, minted by him with all the refinements of love.

Manela's time of waiting and suffering was long and slow, made up of rosary beads recited in the convent chapel among the reduced community, a few old and weary nuns. Those young girls secluded for easing the way for a fiancé or lover were long departed. Manela was the only maiden taken in to preserve a virginity under threat from a filthy passion. The mother superior and Adalgisa left Manela in the Cloister of the Penitents—"I'm going inside," the aunt said, "I'll be right back." Once they were in the office, Adalgisa showed her the order from the juvenile judge. Father José Antonio joined them there, having come to bring the news in advance.

The mother superior was startled by the request. "It's been years since we took in the last one—a girl from the Baixo São Francisco," she said. "Her father brought a letter of recommendation from the bishop of

Barra. She died here, poor thing, from tuberculosis. Or from melancholy —only God knows."

To which Father José Antonio replied disapprovingly, "This house of God was founded by those who came before us to protect virtue and punish sin—don't forget that, Mother. You should celebrate the chance, Mother, to fulfill the order of the Lord when the occasion arises."

The mother superior lowered her head; she didn't argue against the judge's order, but she didn't show any enthusiasm for carrying it out, either. "I hope you won't be leaving her here for any great length of time, ma'am," she said. "It's no charity."

Then Mother Leonor de Lima—that was the mother superior's name—sent Sister Maria Eunice back to the cloister to fetch Manela. Sitting on a bench decorated with tiles, Manela had been killing time anticipating the pleasure of going to the Castro Alves that evening to listen to her idols, with Miro, as part of a most select audience. It would be a wild affair—her fellow students would die of envy! Adalgisa and Father José Antonio had avoided passing the cloister as they left the convent, silently, unseen. Manela stood up and followed Sister Eunice, expecting that she would meet her aunt at the exit.

When Manela reached the office, Mother Leonor offered her a chair, studied her, then said, "I've got some bad news for you, child. Be brave." It took Manela a while to understand what the mother superior told her. When she finally understood that her aunt was shutting her up in the Cloister of the Penitents, having obtained an order from the juvenile judge—the mother superior showed her the order, and there was the magistrate's signature—Manela leaped to her feet in a fury:

"I'm not staying here! I'm leaving right now!"

She shouted, pounded on the top of the desk, rejected the kindly hand that Sister Eunice held out, burst into screams such as hadn't been heard in the Lapa convent for decades; the girl from the town of Barra, the last penitent, her eyes swollen, had wept with quiet, desolate sobbing. Manela's great despair lasted several minutes, measured by the lugubrious ticking of the tall, ancient clock that stood in its mahogany case.

The mother superior's white hair showed beneath the hood that covered it; her face was thin, her hands bony. She remained calm, didn't tell Manela to be quiet. She let the girl carry on, accuse and insult her aunt, say what she thought of Father José Antonio—the shadow of a smile even crossed the mother superior's lips—and swear eternal love for her beloved Miro. At the moment of her declaration of love, when her rage and revolt were wrapped in the dew of tenderness, Mother Leonor de Lima finally spoke, her voice unexpectedly friendly:

"Listen for a moment to what I'm about to tell you, my child. Don't think I want to keep you here. I want you to stay the shortest time possible. I hope to God that your guardian will reverse the decision she's made. In my eyes it is an unfortunate decision, but I can do nothing about it. You're here by order of the juvenile judge."

She begged Manela to tell her her story, and Manela recounted it all. Between sobs, she told Mother Leonor of her parents, the automobile accident, her two aunts, Gildete and Adalgisa; Gildete had become Marieta's guardian, while she had gotten the second one who was . . . Manela fell silent—it wasn't easy to describe or classify Adalgisa, who was sometimes good, sometimes awful, loving and aggressive, a contradiction. "I think she's sick," she finally said.

Then she spoke of Uncle Danilo, a nice person who was intimidated by his wife's bad temper. Aunt Gildete, however, would stand up to Adalgisa. As for Miro, he was the light of her life—a joy, Mother—so nice, she was going to marry him. Aunt Adalgisa was against it because he was poor and dark, a handsome black man, Mother. As if Manela and Adalgisa weren't mulattos, too, a fact her aunt ignored completely. Did she really think she was pure white? At most she was a Bahian white in the sense people mean when they want to tease.

The mother superior spoke again, and her thin face opened up into softness; her weary eyes that had seen so many sad things grew large and lively, her voice was convincing, maternal. Manela had every right to feel herself a victim and to protest, she said, but when you really thought about it, there was no reason to despair, no reason to fall into bad thoughts. Certainly when her kindly uncle, her fighting aunt, and the boy in love found out what had happened, they would do something to get her out of the cloister, overturn the juvenile judge's order. They would have to overturn the order—without that, nothing else could be done.

Maybe it was too late to get her freedom that day, but tomorrow, certainly, they'd come and get her. Who knew, maybe Aunt Adalgisa herself would reconsider. If that didn't happen, she, Mother Leonor, would go to the cardinal, lay out Manela's case, and ask for his intervention. One night would be easy to get through if Manela had patience and faith in God. Enduring that test would be to her credit on the books of heaven: Someday later on, Manela would laugh when she thought of what had happened. The best thing for now was to calm down and wait patiently without punishing herself anymore. Sister Eunice would take her to the cell that would be hers during her brief stay in the convent— and it would be brief, my child—"I'll go to the cardinal, if necessary." Whereupon Manela accepted Sister Eunice's hand.

Even sheltered by so many arguments that seemed just, it wasn't easy to get through a night in the service of God, in Solomon's grave. A person who suffers has great forbearance, and the length of time suffered can't be measured on the clock, it's counted in the guts and in the heart.

Inquiries

Following Álvaro's advice, Gildete began by telephoning the residence of Professor Orlando Gomes. The person who answered the phone told her that the lawyer was in Portugal on a glorious trip—he was going to receive the degree of doctor *honoris causa* from the University of Coimbra. At that point Dionísio, Gildete's other son, returned from his job at the market, and his mother filled him in on what had happened. Normally a good-natured, phlegmatic individual, the lad went crazy: "I'm going to get her out of there if I have to tear the place down!"

Gildete asked him to calm down, they didn't need any more wild ones, and getting all heated up wouldn't get them anywhere. Dionísio's entrance reminded Danilo of a friend they had in common, Dr. Tibúrcio Barreiros: Besides being a reputable defense lawyer, he was also a good comrade. Dionísio approved of the idea of calling him—Tiburcinho knew everybody, he had a long arm and a good head, he'd tell them what to do even if he couldn't do it himself. Danilo got his number from the telephone book and dialed; he found the lawyer at home, no, he wasn't going out, if the Prince wanted to come over, he would expect him. "Prince?" Danilo asked. Something out of the past . . . Anyone who was once a king is always referred to as his majesty, the lawyer reminded him.

Dionísio didn't want to have any dinner: "I'm going with you," he told Danilo. "Me, too," Gildete decided. "I can't stand staying here doing nothing." The hard part was convincing Violeta and Marieta to stay home and wait for them to come back. Gildete promised to return and let them know what was happening, but even then she couldn't get them to stop crying.

Dr. Tibúrcio Barreiros, a jovial man in his forties, greeted them effusively: He had been expecting one friend, and he got three—to what did he owe such an honor? He pulled up an armchair for Gildete—"Sit down here, my saint." The lady of Tiburcinho's house, Dona Dagmar, a charming dark woman who was chic even at home at that hour, excused herself to go make some coffee. Gildete explained the story, interrupted here and there by Danilo, who was looking for ways to exculpate Adalgisa; and she was interrupted here and there by Dionísio, mouthing curses and threats.

Coming back from the kitchen with a tray of cups and the coffeepot, Dona Dagmar listened openmouthed: "In the Cloister of the Penitents?" she exclaimed, amazed. "Is that still in existence?" The director of an English program, well traveled, an executive, she couldn't understand the reason for the internment, the outworn, musty old prejudices. "Such ignorance!"

The lawyer said he didn't know how he could get Manela out that night. The juvenile judge, Dr. d'Ávila, was no sweet-smelling flower; he was not looked kindly upon in legal circles but was frowned upon and feared because he was in the confidence of the military gorillas; he was the worst kind of reactionary, a superfascist—Dr. Barreiros's left-wing sympathies and outspoken language were legendary. That evil bastard, a hypocrite besides, His Honor strutted about as a champion of morality, but he lived in brothels and kept mistresses, Dr. Barreiros said. Falser than Judas, he'd broken relations with Tibúrcio over a year before over some trifle, he didn't explain what. Danilo gathered that it had to do with a quarrel over a woman, he'd get the story on another occasion.

That night, the most they could do was try to get permission—not from the judge but from the nuns at the convent—for Manela's uncle and aunt to visit her. The presence of her relatives would be a consolation and a relief for the girl; knowing that they were doing something for her, she wouldn't feel abandoned. Danilo's position was of especial importance. Being her guardian and in disagreement with the measures his wife had taken, he could act against her, try to block her, seek annulment of the juvenile judge's order. It wouldn't be easy—that horned cuckold d'Ávila, that holy and arrogant cow, wasn't in the habit of changing his mind. But they shouldn't forget that in his view the husband was the head of the family.

"Tomorrow we'll see how to proceed. I'll need the prince's power of attorney. In the meantime let's make the visit. I don't know the mother superior of the convent, or who she is. Let me check with someone who can help us."

He'd taken the case with no interest but to be of service—that was how Tibúrcio Barreiros lived his life. He went to the telephone and made a few calls. Dona Dagmar, after serving the hot demitasse, joined the circle of lamentations: "I didn't think rubbish like that still existed. Rubbish from the dark ages," she said, still disbelieving.

Five minutes hadn't passed before the lawyer came back into the living room. "We're going to the home of Dr. Monteiro, the family court judge. An excellent person, and he knows the mother superior."

Dr. Agnaldo Bahia Monteiro met them at the door, asked them to excuse him for being in his pajamas, he hadn't known that his friend Tibúrcio would be coming with a lady. He led them into his study where he worked on his cases and wrote decisions; in the dining room the family was playing bingo, and laughter and exclamations could be heard.

Although Dr. d'Ávila was a colleague on the bench, Dr. Monteiro didn't disagree when Tibúrcio categorized the juvenile judge as a swine. The two His Honors hadn't gotten along ever since the time when it had fallen to the family court judge to fill in for the juvenile judge when he was unable to sit. It had been a brief period but long enough for Dr.

Monteiro to undo a number of rotten things that the title holder had decreed. "You couldn't imagine, my friends," he told them. "The wildest kinds of stupidities and arbitrary decisions!"

Could they visit Manela that same night? they asked him. It could be done, he said, who knew; there was some doubt because of the late hour, since it was a convent, and nuns live by their norms and precepts. But if they wanted to try, he'd give them a card introducing Danilo and Gildete, the girl's uncle and aunt, to the mother superior. He'd known her ever since he had worked on the settlement of her sister's estate: Mother Leonor is a straight shooter, he said, a woman of character. She had donated her part of her sister's inheritance to Sister Dulce's charity. The magistrate's eyes lit up, remembering, reflecting his thoughts:

"Sister Dulce is extraordinary, don't you think? A saint, a saint three times over!"

He scribbled the message on a calling card, stuck it in an envelope, addressed it "Mother Leonor de Lima" by hand and handed it to Danilo. "I think she'll give you permission," he said, "but you'd better go as soon as possible."

The "soon as possible" was delayed because Gildete wanted to stop by her house since she'd promised the girls she would, and they wouldn't hear of not going along with them on their visit. In the meantime Damiana and Professor João Batista had appeared, looking for information: The candy-maker was all swollen with tears, the professor was scandalized—he was cursing in French: *"Mais non! Merde alors!"*

Before all these relatives and neighbors go to the convent in Lapa, all in a group, let us reveal how the news of Manela's internment had reached the inhabitants of the Avenida da Ave-Maria in the first place. Damiana had found out from Professor João Batista, and he, astoundingly, from the juvenile judge himself. What link, you ask, can there be between the bulwark of authoritarian order and bourgeois morality, on the one hand, and the Francophile, liberal *bon vivant* (his own expression) professor on the other—they were antipodes, the crabbed face and the open smile?

Well, there was one link between them, and it was a place of leisure and recreation. It was none other than Anunciata's house, an ancient but well-preserved chalet in the Brotas district, surrounded by trees, sheltered from indiscreet eyes. There the paths of Dr. d'Ávila and João Batista, the distinguished magistrate and the honored professor, had crossed during the early hours of the evening. Both were good customers of the pleasant and comfortable seraglio. As the professor was emerging from the shapely arms of Mocinha da Briosa, the muse of the Military Police, His Honor was taking his leave of the thighs of Prudência Buceta Doce, Prudence Sweet-Twat, a most appreciated girl. In the hallway they met and exchanged good evenings. With the air of someone giving the latest news, the juvenile judge, Dr. Liberato Mendes Prado d'Ávila, let his colleague-in-recreation know that on the afternoon of that same day, he had sent a young underage girl to be interned in the Cloister of the Penitents; perhaps she was known to his dear friend because they lived on the same street: quite a neighborhood, wasn't it? The girl's aunt, a responsible person, had come to him before the minor went astray. *"Went-as-tray,"* he said, stretching out the syllables.

—§—§

The Processions Emerge
onto the Avenida
Joana Angélica

One group came from the Largo do Pelourinho, and the other from Tororó—the two groups reached the Avenida Joana Angélica at the same time, a mere stone's throw from the Lapa convent. The large procession and the small delegation joined, making a noisy demonstration—like a Carnival parade.

After crossing the Terreiro de Jesus, the Praça da Sé, and Misericórdia, the *capoeira* fighters had gone down the Ladeira da Praça, come out opposite the fire station, crossed the Praça dos Veteranos, gone up the Ladeira da Independência, and occupied the Campo da Pólvora, where Frei Caneca, the revolutionary, had been shot.

The caravan had swelled on every corner, picking up adherents along its path. Crowds of onlookers and drifters enlarged the ranks: students, prostitutes, bohemians, gamblers, scientists coming out of a meeting on technological development, subliterates, and tourists, and Councilwoman Amabília Almeida. They went along without knowing where or why, drawn by the *berimbaus* and the singing. Bringing up the rear were the urchins known as the captains-of-the-sands, doing *capoeira* leaps, cartwheels, and half-moons, they had the mastery of it in their blood, it was as hereditary with them as their roguishness. There certainly was going to be a huge commotion somewhere, and nobody wanted to miss the spectacle.

The group formed by the relatives had been increased by neighbors —Damiana had run to recruit them—and had then left Gildete's house in Tororó de Cima. Aunt and uncle, cousins and friends, all hastened their steps in order to get to the convent in time for a visit. As an offering for a happy ending, the superstitious neighbor Alina had promised a month of sexual abstinence to the Slave Anastácia, a recent saint in the popular anthology. Her husband, Sergeant Deolindo, had put on his Briosa team shirt to impose respect.

On the Avenida Joana Angélica the two hosts mingled, intertwined, without any previous plan but still not by chance—everything that happened that night had direction.

It was in that instance of fraternization when, at the players' touch, the *berimbaus* of war resounded louder, and the song of the Angola *capoeira* brought the residents to their windows. Saint Barbara of the Thunder had rung the bell at the ancient entrance to the Convent of the Immaculate Conception where, by order of the juvenile judge, the Cloister of the Penitents had been reopened.

‑ξ‑‑&

The Order Signed by
the Juvenile Judge,
Dr. Prado d'Ávila

When she heard the bell, Sister Eunice, the sister on duty as the doorkeeper, opened the peephole, looked out, and recognized the saint —after all, they'd traveled together on the sloop from Santo Amaro to Bahia two nights before. On their arrival, the enchanted one had gathered up her cloak and taken off.

It is an unpardonable slip, an inexplicable omission—*mea culpa! mea culpa! mea maxima culpa!*—that we have omitted from our account of the events of Thursday morning any news or mention of the following fact: Sister Eunice had received an early visit from Inspector Parreirinha at the Convent of the Immaculate Conception. The policeman announced that he had come to learn something from her in strictest confidence: Who had stolen the statue? Stolen? she replied. Who said anything about its being stolen? The saint had simply walked off on her own two feet, Sister Eunice told the inspector—she'd even waved goodbye to the sister. The inspector threw up his hands: Ye gods! he thought. Not a word made the slightest sense. These convents are filled with senile old women! This investigation was going nowhere.

Tonight, when Sister Eunice saw Saint Barbara of the Thunder through the peephole, just outside the convent, standing in the entrance, Sister Eunice smiled, withdrew her eye from the peephole, pulled the bolt, and opened the small door. The saint returned her smile. "Good evening, Eunice. May the peace of the Lord be with you," she said.

"Your blessing, Saint Barbara. Your Grace here—did you come to spend the night? Please, come in, this is your home."

Saint Barbara of the Thunder gave her her blessing. Immediately she handed the nun an official document with a stamp, date, and signature, all the bureaucratic requirements.

"I am putting into your hands an order of release signed by the juvenile judge for the girl Manela Pérez Belini, who by a previous order from same was interned here this afternoon. Is Mother Leonor de Lima still up?" she asked. She was happy to learn that the mother superior was deep in her first sleep, the heaviest one.

"She's already retired—she must be sleeping. But I'll call her if Your Grace wants."

"It's not necessary. Put the order on Mother's desk—she'll see it tomorrow. Hurry, bring the girl right now. I'll wait here. There's no need for me to come in."

Sister Eunice picked up the order, looked mechanically at the date and the signature—a scrawl—and went off swiftly with small little steps, almost tripping along, she was so happy. How nice! The guardian had repented, the judge had issued a new order revoking the awful one! Saint Barbara of the Thunder had come in person, she must be the girl's godmother. Hurry, hurry—she musn't keep her waiting, neither the saint nor the girl; the poor thing, having put on the habit of a novice, she hadn't eaten even a mouthful of food. She was in the chapel, praying with the nuns, she'd run out of tears. She'd lain down on her cot dressed as she was, unrecognizable in her novice's habit; Manela was no more, she'd ceased to exist. During vespers Sister Eunice had accompanied her on her bitter path, and her heart bled with pity for the girl. Now she quickened her pace, murmuring a prayer of thanksgiving.

Manela didn't even bother to change her clothes, so as not to lose any time. She ran out, excited—she, too, imagined that Adalgisa was repentant—her aunt was unpredictable, she acted on impulse, without thinking—Adalgisa must have realized the inhuman thing she'd done. When Sister Eunice opened the door for her, Manela kissed her hand, then crossed the threshold; the door closed with a dull creak all by itself —the bolt was drawn and locked at the same time, locking the nun in the room. Unable to say good-bye to Saint Barbara of the Thunder, Sister Eunice prayed for her with a song that her grandmother, Iá Kaçu, had taught her:

Saint Barbara, brave woman,
thunderclaps and lightning's flashes,
lend me just three pennies
to free me from slavery's lashes
Saint Barbara, Thunder Woman.

When Manela reached the entryway, a black woman dressed in wine-colored clothes, pretty as a picture, smiled at Manela, handed her an *eiru* made of horsehair, and vanished.

—§—§

The Novice

A gift from the sea to the city of Bahia, immersed in heat, the night breeze lifted up the borrowed costume of a novice, loose and baggy, billowing out—only a winding sheet could be larger. It was a strong breeze, almost a gust of wind.

Exalted, Manela took a deep breath—she was free! She felt the same fullness that had possessed her in January on Bomfim Thursday, when on the steps of the church she'd sprinkled Miro's head with the waters of Oxalá. Too bad Miro couldn't see her in a novice's habit—he would have doubled up with laughter, he always enjoyed things. He must be angry, she thought, waiting for her to show up for their meeting. "I couldn't come, Mirinho," she would tell him. "They locked me up in the Cloister of the Penitents." She looked around, trying to find the black woman who'd given her the *eiru,* but the black woman had disappeared. The person she saw before her was none other than Miro himself, arm in arm with Romélia. Behind them, a crowd was streaming into the small square where the Lapa convent stands at an angle to the College of Bahia.

Mute and slow, the *capoeira* fighters were no longer singing, no longer plucking their merry *berimbaus.* They were advancing, worried, because the time for action was drawing near, and no one could foresee the course of their deeds, not Miro—not even Master Pastinha. From the mingled gathering suddenly, all at once, the figures of Aunt Gildete and Uncle Danilo stood out. Aunt Gildete was waving an envelope in her uplifted hand: the note sent by Dr. Agnaldo to the mother superior. Miro's shout when he spotted Manela in front of the main door shook the earth and moved the sky:

"Manela! Oh, Manela!"

"Manela? Where?" Master Pastinha asked.

"Right there—dressed as a nun!" Romélia pointed.

Manela scarcely had time to smile at her lover, wave to Uncle Danilo, and catch a glimpse of Aunt Gildete. When she tried to call them, to go over and embrace them, her mouth and feet no longer belonged to her. Yansan took possession of her and rode her.

So as it was she came out dancing along the sidewalk by the convent, went down to the square—there she went. Master Pastinha couldn't see, but he could guess what was happening. He raised his hands and lowered his head as is obligatory and greeted the *orixá:*

"*Eparrei,* Oyá!"

The people repeated as a chorus, the palms of their hands at face level turned toward the enchanted one: "*Eparrei,* Yansan, mother of thunder! *Eparrei,* Oyá!" Manela's face glowed, her body loose in the novice's habit, in the swirl of the dance, more beautiful than Miro had ever seen her: He bowed reverently.

Yansan ran the length of the square from end to end, showing the people her warrior's dance, by the one who had no fear because she'd faced death and conquered it. She stopped in front of Master Pastinha and clasped him to her breast, prolonged the ritual embrace, shoulder to shoulder, face against face. She went off to greet her favorites, the deserving.

She began with Gildete, opening her arms to gather her aunt and protector in them. Gildete wobbled on her feet, spat to one side, pulled off her shoes, and became Oxalá returning Yansan's embrace: She'd come to assist the *iaô* in a trance. Oyá held Uncle Danilo close to her heart and gave him the *eiru* to signify that he was her little father and in the auction of the slave woman he would buy the freedom of the *iaô* for ten *réis* of strained molasses. Finally she reached Miro, who, respectful, reverent, was waiting. Oyá danced her steps of war and victory only for him: The body of the enchanted one trembled, her mouth filled with saliva, her voice hoarse with love, goddess and loved one. She grasped Miro by the legs and held him, an *ogan* of Yansan, there in front of the convent, dressed as a novice.

Dancing without cease, escorted by Oxalá, Oyá set out for the Candomblé do Gantois, where Mãe Menininha was waiting for her, for only then could she grip the knife and weigh the anchor of the boat. The multitude accompanied her toward the Federação, to the Largo de Pulquéria. The breeze gusted into a wind, and lightning and thunderclaps tore the clear sky, the calm night, in the proclamation of freedom. Oyá Yansan was dancing through the streets of Bahia.

The *Barco* of the *Iaôs*

Dancing, dancing, Yansan went up the steps by the door to the Candomblé of Gantois. Inside the darkened temple—only a lamp with a few candles gave off a thin yellowish light—with Cleusa and Carmem, *iyakekerê* and *iyalaxê*, as acolytes, Mãe Menininha received her, sitting on her throne. The entourage that had gathered in the Largo de Pulquéria gradually broke up.

"I was waiting for Your Grace, my Mother."

Mãe Menininha touched the head of the *iaô* stretched out at her feet. In the set of conch shells, in the rosary of Ifá, the *iyalorixá* had seen her and watched her: Oyá ordered her to reserve a place for a daughter of hers in the crew of the *barco* that was leaving that night for the mystery of the cabin, the ports of initiation.

The rest were already gathered. There was an Oxum, just like the *mãe de santo,* an Ogum, an Euá, two Xangôs, an Oxumaré, two Oxalás, one old and one young, and—something that rarely happened—an Ossãe from out of the jungle. No Oxóssi appeared—he was too busy with the big hunt in the woods. Nor did Omolu or Obaluayê, who was curing an outbreak of smallpox in the backlands of Xique-Xique. Obá, it was said, didn't come on purpose, to avoid meeting Yansan, with whom she had had a quarrel caused by jealousy. Manela embarked on the crowded ship to become a saint.

Mãe Menininha do Gantois took the razor—she would use her tremendous powers to shave the heads of the chosen ones, open the way for the manifestation of the *orixás.* The sound of the *adjá* silenced the roar of the thunder, and the candle lighted in the *peji* extinguished the lightning flashes.

That Long Day of Friday's Passions

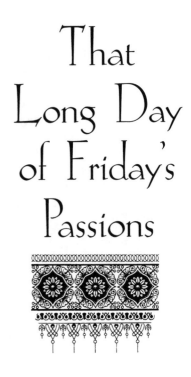

Preparations for War

As Friday morning began, Inspector Ripoleto, sleepless, feverish, dirty, his clothes damp, his face swollen from mosquito bites, his stomach empty, his mouth dry, was watching from his shipwrecked canoe the unusual activity of boats and people on the docks by the River Paraguaçu.

In response to the summons of the vicar of Santo Amaro, sloops and schooners were arriving from all along the river, and from towns and villages around the bay, there to be transformed into warships. The Invincible Armada was making ready to sail, right under the inspector's nose.

Armed groups were receiving orders from the now-bellicose Father Téo. The women were armed with rosaries and prayer books, with flowers picked from private gardens to decorate the litter of Saint Barbara of the Thunder on the return voyage; the men were armed with dendê palm leaves and sugar cane stalks. Dona Canô was passing out little holy pictures to the volunteers; on the front, in color, was the image of the saint, while on the back were some facts of dubious historical merit. The cards were leftovers from a past festival and advertisements for a distillery that specialized in jurubeba brandy. Young men from Santo Amaro, in blue jeans and various tunics—T-shirts, leather jackets, in loud designs—sang songs by the unrivaled Caetano, who'd been born in their town.

Balanced unstably in the canoe, under such trying conditions, still suffering from last night's ill treatment and insults, Inspector Ripoleto nonetheless hadn't yet lost his talents as a first-class investigator. He'd kept to his post, worn down but vigilant. That so many vessels were gathered at the anchorage, not to speak of the continuous coming and going of people—all that early-morning bustle looked extremely suspicious to him; hunger and the mosquitoes had further sharpened his perception. Obsessively he tried to make mental notes of details and movements, guessed at the depth of the water, the force of the current, the speed and efficiency of the mosquitoes, in order to form a firm opinion and transmit it, when he had a chance, to the state secretary of public safety.

To extricate himself from his predicament, to obtain transportation to the state capital, to appear before his superior, and to render an account of his mission, assigned and fulfilled: these were the inspector's immediate objectives. Because of his handicap, however, the secret of which we share, it wasn't easy for him to leave the canoe and reach the shore. He was at the brink of despair when suddenly everything resolved itself, albeit with a few complications.

Those tiresome village lads who had attacked him and shipped him off the night before, now rescued him and led him to the sloops, which were being made ready for the punitive expedition, and put him on board. Indeed, not only had they taken Inspector Ripoleto out of the canoe and out of the clump of pickerelweed, but, without his having even asked, they were actually giving him transportation to the city. It would have been a perfect solution, had it not been for the facts that his arms were tied behind his back and his feet bound, and that he was less an inspector than a hostage.

—◈—◈

Reading the Papers:
1—The Advertisement

On that Friday morning the newspapers in the Bahian capital—all of them—ran a spectacular full-page advertisement with a photograph of the statue of Saint Barbara of the Thunder, in the center, enlarged and reprinted (without authorization) from Dom Maximiliano von Gruden's book. Although the book wasn't yet on sale in bookstores, the author had given out a few copies to critics and friends.

The headline, in large block letters—THIS SAINT HAS DISAP-PEARED!—effectively caught the readers' attention and aroused their curiosity. Designed with the skill of first-class professionals—the layout was by Vera Rocha—the advertisement, in boldface, gave a succinct and exact report on the statue, pointing out its inestimable value. Its authorship had been attributed to Aleijadinho by one who understood such treasures, Dom Maximiliano von Gruden, a prominent authority, a notable sage. To give some idea of the importance of the missing statue, suffice it to say that the director of the museum had written a whole book about it in German.

Under the photograph, in large letters, was printed the offer of reward: "If you have any clues or information leading to the recovery of the statue in the photograph, you will be eligible to receive"—the amount was given in cruzeiros—"the reward offered by"—the name of a most powerful and prestigious firm—"a company that, working hard for the progress of the nation, defends with equal enthusiasm the preservation of our patrimony: the statue of Saint Barbara of the Thunder." The copywriter for the ad agency, a prizewinning adman, had outdone himself; his boss, Mr. Sérgio, congratulated him on the conciseness and elegance of his copy.

We have omitted from our account of this exemplary text the amount of cruzeiros because, with inflation galloping along and gobbling up everything, the value of the reward, extremely high at the time, would now seem ridiculously small. Nor have you been informed of the name of the company that underwrote the prestigious advertisement costing all that dough—albeit a tiny fraction of its colossal profits, an expense, furthermore, that was tax deductible. Is it necessary to explain the reason for this omission? Even though the reason is obvious, it's worth repeating it: Never will the dazzling but decorous pages of this chronicle of religious and cultural history serve as a publicity vehicle, even if subliminal, for a multinational corporation. Subliminal and, let it be added, gratuitous—no proposition ever reached our hands.

Those who wish further information regarding the advertisement—

the amount of the reward, the social motives of the firm placing it, whether anyone responded, whether the reward was paid, whether all that ballyhoo was worth anything—those interested parties should contact Mr. Sérgio Amado. Director of the agency responsible for the creation of the advertisement and its distribution, he's the one who can clear things up—not this poor scribe who struggles, pounding his typewriter with two fingers—one of those ancient manual ones that nobody uses anymore in the twilight of this century of electronics and computers —to defend the slim royalties that income tax, alas, will cut in half at the source.

Reading the Papers:
2—The Interview with
the Vicar of Santo Amaro

Besides the page devoted to material paid for by the multinational corporation, the Friday newspapers dedicated substantial space to the disappearance of the statue of Saint Barbara of the Thunder, including headlines on the front page, editorials, commentaries, columns, and special feature articles.

Worthy of mention is the lead editorial in *Diário de Notícias,* which appeared in all italics at the top of the third page. In it, the editorial board of the Associated Newspapers of Bahia congratulated itself for the newspaper's spectacular scoop of the day before. *Diário* had been the only paper in town to lift the veil of mystery surrounding the arrival of the statue on the docks of Salvador. While *Diário's* competitors had gone along with the official version—that the statue was unloaded peacefully and the director of the museum received it in the presence of reporters (sic!)—"your paper," the lead editorial apprised its readers, witnessed and reported, accompanied by exclusive photographs, the illustrious museum director's despair when he learned of the disappearance of the saint.

Had it not been for the reporting by *Diário de Notícias,* the people of Bahia would still be unaware of the theft of the statue—and it had been a theft, what else could it have been?—a daring deed undertaken in broad daylight. The museum director had tried to hide it, evading the truth, telling the press that everything was shipshape, or more appropriately, *sloop*shape, in this case. Was it an international gang, as Colonel Raul Antônio, chief of the Federal Police, maintained, or had it been another removal of antique statues from the altars of poor churches and chapels for the homes of millionaire collectors, as the secretary of public safety asserted? The staff of *Diário de Notícias* had made every effort to dispel such confusion and clear everything up, the lead editorial said, to serve our readers: "The newspaper that informs—accurately," the editorial triumphantly stated.

The hero of the day had been congratulated by the publisher, Dr. Odorico Tavares, in person—he had patted him on the shoulder: "Congratulations, Guido, another exclusive"—and became immediately a candidate for a raise in salary. But Guido Guerra didn't rest on his laurels. A copy of the newspaper under his arm, he took off very early Friday morning for Santo Amaro, intending to get an exclusive interview from the vicar. He got there before any other reporter, accompanied by the photographer Gervásio Batista Filho—son of the famous photographer for *Manchete,* like father, like son—who drove Guido to Santo Amaro in the newspaper's Volkswagen Beetle.

Father Téo welcomed Guido with a readiness to stone him to death —some weeks before, that same scoundrel had written a story that had thrashed him from start to finish, showing a thoroughgoing lack of respect. Guido's earlier article had criticized the vicar for initially refusing to lend the statue to the exhibit, then had ridiculed him, called him regressive, behind the times, tight-fisted, with "a medieval, elitist mentality incapable of understanding the cultural needs of the masses," saying that he didn't deserve to be vicar of Santo Amaro, land of the Velosos, or to have custody over such a valuable image. He'd finished him off with one final epithet: Buzzard in a Cassock.

Father Téo was not a man to let a challenge go unanswered. So when Guido introduced himself so confidently on Friday morning, the vicar, before even greeting him, said: "Guido Guerra?" then looked the writer's fragile bone structure up and down. "I've really been looking forward to meeting you—to tell you that the Buzzard in a Cassock is the fine lady who's your mother!" He flung quotations from the acerbic article, with its pathetic humor, back into the journalist's face. He'd been particularly hurt by the taunt about his mentality: he, Father Téo, medieval and elitist! That was the real laugh! Then he refused Guerra the interview.

Guido Guerra wasn't a reporter to be cowed by a no, not even one roundly accompanied by words of spleen and contempt: blockhead, smartass, cretin! Guido apologized, confessed that he'd been off the mark in his interpretation, though never in his facts. He appealed to the vicar's ignorance, saying his job was at stake—a classic lie—either he got that interview of he would be fired, and if he were fired, how could he feed his wife and two innocent children? He invented the family on the spot—he'd only just begun to court Celi—but the weeping little children succeeded in hoodwinking the ferocious Father Téo. *Diário de Notícias* ran the interview the next day on the front page with a double headline:

PEOPLE OF SANTO AMARO WILL COME TO RECLAIM STATUE—
SAINT'S PLACE HERE, NOT IN MUSEUM'S HOARD

Professional probity led Guido to mention his disagreement with certain declarations the subject of his interview made. He stayed clean, didn't compromise himself: Tomorrow they wouldn't be able to accuse him of allowing lies, falsehoods, and calumnies to pass unchallenged. An eyewitness to Dom Maximiliano von Gruden's despair on the waterfront, he couldn't second the vicar's opinion that the director had planned all the confusion so that he could appropriate the statue of Saint Barbara of the Thunder for the museum's own collection. This assertion, which the newspaper printed, was made with the sole responsibility and risk falling on Father Teófilo Lopes de Santana, who had said, "Write it down, young man, publish it, and I'll assume all responsibility."

Why did Father Téo believe this? In the stubborn and difficult struggle between the monk and the vicar over the loan of the statue—lend it, don't lend it—Dom Maximiliano, normally obsequious and honey-tongued, had lost control. He'd gone overboard and become scornful. This was a statue worthy of display in the Valladolid Sculpture Museum, or in any other museum in Europe or the United States; relegating it to a backwater out in the boondocks was an absurdity. The parishioners of Santo Amaro couldn't facilitate the visits of tourists and those interested in studying it, couldn't even guarantee its safekeeping. Someday when the vicar least expected it, thieves specializing in church and convent artifacts would get their clutches on it, and then, bye-bye saint. The place where the statue of Saint Barbara of the Thunder would not only be safe but could be seen and admired by thousands and thousands of visitors, he had argued, was the Museum of Sacred Art of the University of Bahia.

The vicar needed no further evidence to lay the blame at Dom Maximiliano's feet, to call him a THIEF in capital letters, and to finger him for the police. No doubt he was in cahoots with certain church dignitaries and glib journalists. The vicar refused to authorize Guido to cite the cardinal as one dignitary involved in such machinations. As for glib journalists, the vicar said, "Don't get me into trouble, but if you want to, my dear young man, you can give your own name as the best example of a rattlebrained journalist involved in Dom Mimoso's scheme"—the vicar was also handy when it came to ridicule and epithets.

When Guido turned off his tape recorder and shook the priest's hand as way of saying thanks and good-bye, Guido said roguishly, " 'Dom Mimoso'—I like that. It wasn't right for me to call you a Buzzard in a Cassock—please forgive me. But to make up for it completely, in the interview I'm going to give you the title Dove of the Divine."

"Dove of the Divine, my dear young man, is the mother of you know who . . . If you call me the Dove of the Divine in your newspaper, I'll come by and split your head open, and later I'll ask God's forgiveness." He took measure again of the journalist's thin bone structure, his long-nosed, ugly, dirty face—a long-legged bird, father of two small children. "I'll do something worse: I'll come by, and in the presence of your own colleagues, I'll tweak your ears. And I won't have to ask God's forgiveness for that."

Laughing, Guido took his leave of the vicar, then went into a bar and sat down with Gervásio Filho. They ordered a full pot of coffee with two cups. Guido turned on the tape recorder, and as the cassette spewed back the priest's indignation, he began to write up the interview. The parishioners in the bar who had been angrily discussing the case of the statue fell silent when they heard Father Téo's voice, watching Guido out of the corner of their eyes. The reporter quickly filled sheets of paper with his schoolboy scrawl. He didn't look over the pages again, leaving all corrections for the copyeditor. The task of transcription finished, he handed the sheets of paper and the cassette to the photographer, who doubled as driver, and sent him off to Bahia, urging haste:

"Give this stuff to Kléber—tell him to fix it up. As soon as you develop the film and pick out the pictures you're going to use, set one aside for the priest. Get back into the Beetle and come on back here. This is going to light a fire, friend Gervásio!"

Reading the Papers:
3—Special Articles,
the Society Column,
and a Poem

The editorial in *A Tarde*, a masterpiece written by Mr. Cruz Rios, raised some questions, gave no answers, but made a single noteworthy affirmation. It was incontrovertible, the editorial said, that the statue of Saint Barbara of the Thunder had reached the capital on Wednesday evening at dusk, as "our readers learned from yesterday's edition, which carried an exhaustive feature story on this momentous event." Reporters from *A Tarde* had been present at the statue's arrival, it continued, "as is customary on such occasions. Our newspaper spares no effort to furnish the general public, which honors us with its preference, with accurate information." *A Tarde* is not in the habit—like certain tabloids in their thirst for notoriety—of resorting to cheap sensationalism; nor is it here to toot its own horn, the editorial said. The editorial writer passed over its reporter José Augusto Berbert's claim to have personally witnessed the museum director's euphoria as he laid eyes on the statue and touched its wood when he received it Wednesday evening. That was merely a minor detail, apparently, not worthy of explanation or mention. Only the reporter himself was in a position to account for his statement, but Zé Berbert hadn't set foot in the newspaper office all that Thursday. Perhaps he was trying to avoid running into Dr. Jorge Calmon, *A Tarde*'s editor and publisher, or who knows, perhaps he was lying in wait for his friend Dom Maximiliano to get out of the museum director the explosive interview that he could hardly deny him. One hand washes the other, and the two together can wash the slate clean.

On the editorial page of *A Tarde*, two articles, equally delightful, discussed the statue from different angles. An undisputed authority—the author of a small but learned pamphlet that had been the first serious study of the statue of Saint Barbara of the Thunder, published more than five years before—Ary Guimarães synthesized what was known about the statue, including Dom Maximiliano's recent attribution of it to Aleijadinho. Ary Guimarães found it more likely that the sculpture was the work of a Bahian disciple rather than the master from Minas Gerais himself.

The other article was signed by Paulo Tavares, a scholar of literature and art and the author of a *Dictionary of Characters in Bahian Fiction*, which had won a prize from the Brazilian Academy of Letters. Tavares had dug up out of his files everything that had ever been written about the famous statue: articles, accounts, essays, pamphlets, studies, references in newspapers and magazines, Dom Maximiliano von Gruden's book, still to be released in Portuguese, and the story by Guido Guerra that was published the day before in *Diário de Notícias*. Tavares's survey of this literature complemented Ary Guimarães's article, leaving readers of the editorial page well-informed indeed.

As for the progress of the investigation, *A Tarde* opened its columns to a succinct statement from the chief of the Federal Police: "We are on the trail of the perpetrators; an arrest may be announced before the day is out. But the matter is complicated—it goes beyond a simple robbery from a church." And the newspaper also carried the prolix expatiation of Dr. Calixto Passos, chief of the State Police: "It is a simple matter, more or less, just another of countless thefts perpetrated of statues; our people are piecing together evidence, but we have almost located the guilty parties." In addition to these statements the newspaper referred to the anonymous phone calls that had been received in the editorial offices, trying to link a certain priest to the disappearance of the statue. *A Tarde* devoted two lines to the accusation—but protected itself from the possibility of a prank by withholding the name of the accused.

The society column revealed from unquotable but unimpeachable sources, the names of the important people who were expected on morning flights, from north and south, for today's opening of the exhibit of religious art, a cultural and social occasion that would extend into a weekend of lunches and dinners, cocktail parties and soirees, and boat trips around the Bay of All Saints. Expected from Rio were "the physician to Hollywood stars and Arabian princesses" Ivo Pitanguy; the director of the Museum of Modern Art, Niomar Moniz Sodré; the academician Eduardo Portella and his wife Célia; the owners of two art galleries, Giovanna Bonino and Ana Maria Niemeyer; the collector Gravatá Galvão; and Messrs. Carlos Leonam and João Condé, inevitable presences at events such as this. From Fortaleza came Mr. and Mrs. Paulo Elpídio Menezes; he was rector and she, Zuleide, was director of the Museum of the Federal University of Ceará. From Belém do Pará came Ruth and Rodolfo Steiner, aristocrats from the Island of Marajó. From São Paulo came a numerous and varied delegation: the director of the Museum of Art, Pietro Bardi; Lina Bo Bardi, architect and founder of the Museum of Modern Art of Bahia; the Siciliano brothers, booksellers interested in getting a contract for national distribution of the Brazilian edition of Dom Maximiliano's book; Drs. Fanny and Joelson Amado, all arriving in the private plane of the rich *marchand de tableaux* Waldemor Szaniecki. The tycoon was flying in with Belinha and would take advantage of the occasion to extort some oil paintings, watercolors, and sketches from Carybé and scrounge around the city after canvases by Di Cavalcanti and Pancetti. While the others were wearing themselves out eating and drinking, he, Lindinho, would be hard at work.

On the front page of *A Tarde*'s second section was a sketch by Floriano Teixeira, meticulous, strong, and beautiful, showing the statue from the front and in profile. Below it was a poem by Godofredo Filho, written in 1958 on the occasion of a visit to Santo Amaro by the distinguished bard; it had been forgotten in a drawer, from which the ruckus about the statue had finally drawn it out. Another poet of good reputation, Carvalho Filho, considered Godofredo's poem premonitory, as he later said in a speech to the Bahian Academy of Letters, concerning the publication in *A Tarde* of the "Ballad of the Mulattery and Negritude of Barbara the Thunder Woman, A Saint Both Dual and Singularly Brazilian." The poem had been premonitory, he showed with critical acumen. A pilgrim on a night of pilgrimage, vigil, and revelations, in the frenzy of the confusion regarding the saint, in the delirium over the black woman, the poet had created the poem at daybreak, ambiguous, divinatory, eternal.

Making Up

At peace with her conscience, Adalgisa slept alone. It had been a tense and weary day, one of bitterness and exaltation, and as soon as Danilo had stormed out and she finished washing the dishes, she retired to her room. She wasn't interested in television; her husband's rage hadn't affected her to the point of bringing on insomnia.

Only a few times, not many, during their almost twenty years of married life had he gone out slamming the door behind him, all worked up, shouting, saying he was going to do something he wanted to do. Hours later, he would return, a lamb, his rage over, the disagreement forgotten. Usually he'd bring her something nice as a peace offering: a European fruit, an apple or a pear, a bar of milk chocolate, a red rose.

On Thursday night, kneeling by her bed, she said her prayers, which that night were lengthened by a few Our Fathers and Hail Marys to please the Lord, who had protected and favored her in her struggle, leading her to victory. She lay down without a worry, unconscious of the hubbub that stirred on the Avenida da Ave-Maria later on. She knew that when she awoke, she would find Danilo in bed beside her, pleasant and cordial, as if nothing had happened: He wouldn't bring up the quarrel again, wouldn't disagree about Manela's internment anymore. Free of doubts, she fell asleep and passed the night with an agreeable dream in which she was present at Miro's arrest, watching the chimpanzee being carried off by two policemen into the presence of the juvenile judge.

On awakening, as she had expected, the first thing Adalgisa saw was Danilo. But he was no longer in bed, he was coming out of the bathroom, having taken his bath, with his shorts and shirt on, getting ready for his day at the notary's office. He said good morning to her without a trace of anger; she answered, smiling, and shut herself up in the bathroom, taking the radio with her. Danilo finished dressing, went to the door for his copy of *A Tarde* delivered each morning, and sat down in the easy chair to read the news while he waited for coffee to be served. He was reading the various articles when Dadá emerged from the kitchen carrying a tray with the slices of breadfruit, Minas cheese, and cinnamon crackers.

Danilo commented, "Everybody's talking about that business of the statue."

"What business?" Adalgisa limited her reading of newspapers to the crime news and the society pages.

Danilo waited for her to come back with the pots of milk and coffee, then told her about the matter that had gotten the whole town worked up: the statue of Saint Barbara of the Thunder, which had been sent from Santo Amaro for an exhibit, had vanished into thin air upon its arrival. That was all the paper talked about.

"It's worth a fortune," he said. "It looks like it was the vicar of Santo Amaro who sold it, and there's another priest involved—it's a big mess. It's going to end up in the house of Dr. Clemente Mariani or some other rich guy, they spend their lives buying up old artifacts, supporting a mafia of hoodlums." He was laughing, having a good time, his face merry, affable. "They say a vicar is quicker—"

Adalgisa peered closely into Danilo's face. Open in a smile, his face seemed all lighted up, euphoric over his rhyme; an indubitable proof of his talent, he would repeat it to his colleagues at the office. Adalgisa wondered at her husband's strange behavior. "The theft of a statue of a saint is no laughing matter—it's a sin, and a very serious one. I don't know how a priest can make a business out of dealing in statues and how you can laugh at it that way."

"The saint of a quicker vicar . . ." Danilo was beaming, happy with the variations on his wordplay. *Wordplay,* what an ugly term! Let's say it in French, as would Professor João Batista: *calembour*—the word melts in the mouth like a gumdrop!

Danilo got up from the table, stretched, put on his jacket, took his hat, and headed for the door, whistling. Adalgisa found his behavior stranger by the minute. He'd even forgotten to ask as he customarily did, "Do you want anything from outside, Dadá?" A pro forma question, but attentive all the same. Dadá, accustomed to hearing it and answering, "Nothing, thank you," noticed it was missing. There was, indeed, something else surprising about Danilo's behavior. On previous occasions when they'd made up after altercations and quarrels, he would smother her with attention; but this time he hadn't brought her the usual nonsense, flowers, fruit, chocolate, or some other olive branch. The bigger the fight, the greater the consideration and niceties of the reconciliation. Well, the fracas of the night before had been among their fiercest, comparable only to those of the earliest days.

Surprised and puzzled, wounded in her self-esteem, she watched him open the door so confidently, calmly, on top of the world. He didn't even say good-bye to her. Adalgisa couldn't stand it, so she provoked him. "Didn't you say last night that you wouldn't come home without Manela?"

The door half-open, his hand on the knob, Danilo turned to Dadá, his face calm, his voice neutral, and he said, "Manela didn't want to come home. She went to take her initiation ceremony at the Candomblé do Gantois."

By the time Adalgisa got her voice back, her husband was long gone. It was no use running out after him, dressed as she was and in her slippers. He was just getting onto the bus at the far end of the street.

Humiliation

It was a monstrous, abominable humiliation for Adalgisa to learn about it in all its sordid details from the mouth of Damiana Sweet-Rice —a common nobody! The neighbor woman had seen her run by, had stood waiting in her doorway, stepping out to meet her as she came back with her head bowed. Damiana didn't even say good morning to her in her haste to let the cat out of the bag, to fling the news in the face of her stuck-up snob of a neighbor. Aware of Adalgisa's horror at anything having to do with *candomblé,* the candy-maker couldn't hide her soul's satisfaction at the prospect of filling the ear of that awful stepmother, that pretentious woman, detestable bigot. Giving her a comeuppance she wouldn't soon forget.

"You've heard, haven't you, Dona Adalgisa? The news about Manela?"

Adalgisa's first impulse was to turn on her heel and go into her house, as if she hadn't noticed Damiana. But her desire to know won out over the prospect of the mockery that her neighbor was sure to subject her to.

"Heard what?"

"Manela was prettier than ever last night when the saint possessed her in front of the Convent of the Immaculate Conception. I saw it all."

Damiana didn't say what had induced her to go to the Lapa convent in the middle of the night; nor did she say anything about how Manela had gotten out of the Cloister of the Penitents. But with an abundance of detail and manifest enthusiasm she described the celebration on the square, the dance of Yansan accompanied by Gildete's Oxalá—"It was a thing of beauty, Dona Dadá. Manela's Yansan was right up there with the ones they talk about most in the city, including Oyá Oiaci, the Yansan of Margarida do Bogum, celebrated everywhere."

She mentioned people who were present, witnesses who would confirm her story: In addition to Gildete, present were Professor João Batista, Alina, Sergeant Deolindo, and Master Pastinha—"Master Pastinha in person, yes ma'am. Mr. Danilo must have told you the basics, even if he didn't go into detail, because he was there, all excited, and Yansan honored him by giving him the *eiru.*" Damiana, too, had been embraced by the enchanted one in a show of friendship, but the most sensational moment—didn't Mr. Danilo tell you?—happened when Manela lifted up Miro as an *ogan.* Where could Manela have gotten the strength needed to lift her boyfriend by the legs and dance the dance of presentation with him hanging there? It must have been the superhuman strength of an *orixá,* or the strength of love, who knows? "One way or another, my dear, you should have seen the two of them together in the thin arms of the *iaô*. I'm sorry you weren't there—you would have liked it, my dear Dona Dadá!"

The lump in her throat was choking her, the pain in her head was eating at her eyes, and her brains were frying; in spite of all that, Adalgisa managed a thread of voice to ask:

"How did she get out of the convent?"

Showing her white teeth in her fat, fleshy mulatto's mouth, her laughter unleashed, uncontained, Damiana excused herself. "Oh, you'll have to pardon me, but I don't know how that happened, my dear Dona Dadá." Abandoning niceties and hypocrisy, Sweet-Rice Damiana released her anger at her neighbor for all her past insults, nastiness, and evil deeds. "All I know is that she got out—God helped her. And I know something else that I can tell you: Whoever locked that poor thing up in the Cloister of the Penitents hasn't got a heart or a soul, she's an evil woman, a miserable person. And that's the truth, my dear Dona Dadá!"

—❦—❦

News, Even Though Vague, of Sylvia Esmeralda

Adalgisa abruptly turned her back on Damiana and slammed the door in her obnoxious face. She stopped in her living room to catch her breath, afraid that something would happen to her. She went into the bathroom, wet her face with cold water, and she could hear her heart throbbing.

She picked up her purse and headed for the Sant'Ana Church in Rio Vermelho. On the bus she said her rosary, nearly suffocated by the smoke that the man next to her was sucking out of his cheap cigar with great pleasure. As she moved her lips in prayer, the lout with the cigar watched her out of the corner of his eye. The bus was stopping at every corner—would it never get there?

Father José Antonio was performing a baptism when she arrived, and Spaniards were clustered around the font. Adalgisa gave them a wide berth in order to avoid running into anyone she knew and went to wait in the sacristy. The priest took a long time in coming, since he was baptizing the offspring of a wealthy family who had a right to a sermon. Finally he arrived in the company of the parents, grandparents, and godparents, and Adalgisa couldn't avoid the greetings. Father José Antonio signed the baptismal certificate for them, received his gratuity, and confirmed that he would attend the commemorative feast. When they bustled out, he took off his surplice and stole. In the empty sacristy, he went over to his favorite parishioner, sensing her nervous state:

"What brings you here so early, child?" When he was alone with Adalgisa, he spoke to her in Spanish, ignoring her Brazilian nationality. "Why are you standing? What's wrong that makes you tremble so?"

"Manela's run away from the convent."

"Run away? From the Lapa convent? Impossible, child! I don't believe you."

Adalgisa told him what she knew, a jumbled narrative in which her husband Danilo, a neighbor woman, Master Pastinha, and *orixás* were all mixed together. It made no sense, and the priest began to think that his good sheep from the Lord's flock was not quite right in her head. As they got older, church biddies often lost their marbles and went about babbling nonsense, imagining things. Usually when it happened, it was senile old women.

"I don't understand," he said. "The best thing is to go have a talk with the mother superior and find out what happened. Come, child."

On the bus he revealed to Adalgisa that he hadn't liked the mother superior's reaction yesterday when she received the order for Manela's internment. The nun hadn't made any effort to hide her disagreement with the order. Now he went into a rage: She was a liberal—disgusting! Ill-mannered, such insolence! The mother superior was one of those modern nuns who are more like—but enough. He didn't think it likely, but he couldn't rule out the possibility that Mother Leonor herself had facilitated the girl's escape—what other explanation was there? If such an outrageous thing could be proven, the mother superior would pay dearly for it. He, Father José Antonio, would go to the auxiliary bishop about it.

When Mother Leonor de Lima saw the priest enter her office, she limited herself to wishing him a good morning. But she greeted Adalgisa's arrival warmly: "I can only praise your decision to let the child go free after all. A sinner who repents her error is doubly worthy of God's grace. You have given me delight."

The nun's boldness, her lack of consideration, left Father José Antonio almost apoplectic. He interrupted the mother superior's euphoria and demanded a full explanation of Manela's flight. She must tell everything, blow by blow, he said, or he would report her to Dom Rudolph. The mother superior didn't bother to reply—she took the order from the juvenile judge out of the drawer and showed it to him. The priest read it and reread it, examined the paper, the stamp, and the signature: There was no possibility of doubt—it was the judge's order, signed and sealed.

Adalgisa also stopped to read the release order. "Danilo managed it —just as he said!"

"Your husband?" Father José Antonio wanted confirmation. "But the judge stated in my presence that only at my request and no one else's would he change the order—do you agree with this?" he asked in Spanish.

Father José Antonio took pride in speaking Portuguese almost as beautifully as Spanish, with absolute grammatical perfection; only his tight-lipped accent gave him away as an immigrant. But at times like this when he lost his composure and got flustered, he mixed up the two languages, confused pronouns, and fell back upon his mother tongue.

He wanted to take the order with him, but the mother superior categorically opposed this. She did, however, permit a photocopy to be made at the College of Bahia, next door. As he put the photocopy into the pocket of his cassock, Father José Antonio sputtered angrily in a mixture of Spanish and Portuguese:

"Keep the cell ready, Mother." He raised his finger fervently. "The sinner will return—immediately!" Then: "She'll come back, possessed by the devil, *puede que sea* necessary to exorcise her," he fumed in the purest Spanuguese.

"She'll return, with faith in God." Adalgisa picked up the cue.

But nothing happened as *pronto* as the embattled Falangist predicted, because the juvenile judge hadn't appeared in court that morning. The clerk who received the priest and Adalgisa advised them against going to the judge's residence. "The judge isn't at home. His wife, Dona Diana, fell ill, something serious—she had to go to the hospital right away. Dr. Prado is with her, and you won't find him here until afternoon —if Dona Diana is feeling better. Come back at three o'clock—no use showing up any earlier."

Dona Diana, the juvenile judge's wife, the esteemed Mrs. Diana Teles Mendes Prado d'Ávila, was the garland of aristocracy. Of course, in theatrical circles, in the corruption of Cuckoldland, she is known to us as none other than Sylvia Esmeralda.

Exile

A wounded lion, raging out of his mind, Dom Maximiliano von Gruden paced in his modest cell, his narrow cage, his roars echoing down the dim corridors of the Benedictine abbey.

No, scratch out that whole sentence. The image is not only a cliché but false. Delicate and elegant, balding, there is no way in which Dom Maximiliano resembled a lion with sharp claws, or his hair a majestic mane. The sentence is also bombastic and cheap: The long corridors of the Abbey of Saint Benedict are bright, not dim, and no roars, no clamor, no shouts were heard, only sobs. The mourning for Father Henrique Pereira, murdered in Pernambuco by constables of the military government, was no louder than the funeral prayers in church accompanied by the organ. In that hushed assembly of priests and laymen, the protest did not explode into demagogic speeches, collective hysteria; rather, it took the form of a reaffirmation of conscience and an aim to continue and enlarge the opposition, even if the fight for justice and freedom meant more hands would be chopped off, more bodies dismembered, more corpses thrown into sewers. Dom Maximiliano von Gruden didn't take part in these religious services or civic conversations; he had meditated in his cell.

His vigil last night had lasted an eternity of humiliation and dishonor. Then although fatigue finally dulled his eyes, it did not free his heart of the dagger plunged into it, or put his affliction to rest, or mitigate the loss or his feeling of defeat. Dom Maximiliano, sleepless in the earthly void, had written a brief letter of resignation, addressed to the rector of the University of Bahia. He was leaving in his hands the office of director of the Museum of Sacred Art that he had performed for more than ten years with both efficiency and enthusiasm. It was said and had been written, rightly, that the museum owed to Dom Maximiliano its perfect organization, the value and high quality of its collection, and its national and international reputation.

This renown was confirmed in the silence of the cell. Outside he knew they were waiting to slaughter him, drag him through the mud, blame him, crucify him. In his telephone conversation with the rector on Thursday morning, he'd thought of mentioning his request for resignation in case the statue wasn't found, but he had kept his mouth shut; there was still time and hope. In his conversation with the auxiliary bishop he'd said that he was prepared for resignation and exile. His Excellency had agreed: Dom Maximiliano couldn't really remain in his post or in the city after such a grotesque occurrence. Resignation and exile—are they really much different from death?

Exile? Yes, *exile* was the exact word. Born in the mists of Germany, after having trudged along the pathways of the world, Europe and Asia, North America, marooned in many ports, exhausting himself in work, in study, searching for a convivial home, he'd discovered the blazing light of Bahia—the promised land that welcomed him. In the breezes of the Bahian sea, in the excitement, the inventiveness, the cordiality, the art of kindness, the rites of friendship, the mingling of races as a condition of life, a fountain of humanism, he'd found himself and he'd stayed. He'd crossed through desert and storm to know himself.

On that satanic night on the deserted dock when the statue had disappeared, when Edimilson had been in the dementia of his visions, Dom Maximiliano, stunned and lost, had cursed the hour God had brought him to Bahia to live and work. He had cursed this country where everything was mixed up and confused, where no one could distinguish between reality and dream, where the people believed in miracles and witchcraft. A voice of malediction, ungrateful, backbiting, the perfect ass had had no idea what he was saying and hadn't been long in repenting his words. Now, when he realized that he might be obliged to go away, to leave the city and the sweet, dark people who inhabited it, the people of Bahia, he knew that living on any other ground would seem like exile.

Who knows, the alert and daring scholar, the brilliant intellectual, the competent curator, might be able to survive and work in another abbey, another museum or research center for religious art. But to live life as Dom Maximiliano had hitherto enjoyed it, there was no territory outside of Bahia. No, there wasn't!

He'd used a lot of paper saying why he was going away. He'd written page after page, a small essay, a vivid memoir, an explanation and a plea for forgiveness. But he finished none of his three attempts to make his statement and say farewell. Each time the statement was smaller, until finally he stared at the concise half-page that remained. All that it said was that he was leaving his position and going away, never to return.

When dawn broke, Dom Maximiliano went to the church, kneeled, and made the sign of the cross. In the kitchen the monks gave him some coffee and a slice of bread, and he sent out for the newspapers. He asked them to tell the abbot that he was there and would like to see him as soon as possible.

The Abbot

While Dom Maximiliano waits to be received by the abbot, who is still busy revising his homily on the murder of the Pernambucan priest, to be read on Sunday during mass, let us take advantage of this pause to leave the twisting path of the narrative once more.

Respect and friendship behoove us to introduce into the plot the abbot of the Abbey of Saint Benedict, Dom Timóteo Amoroso, with the honors due him, which he avoids out of modesty. Let us salute his inspirational presence in a tale where numerous priests and poets rub elbows, some excellent, some terrible, in both doctrine and verse.

Before donning his white cassock, the fragile Timóteo lived in the world, a citizen like anyone else. Married, with children, he knew life through more than hearsay. He took holy orders only after his wife died, when he felt her absence sorely; he sought consolation and joy in God. He was a poet, wrote verse, but he didn't publish anything—poetry is simply an inherent part of every instant, of every step he takes in life as a functioning human being.

Dom Timóteo Amoroso had revived in Bahia the tradition of the outstanding missionaries who were not content to advise Indians and blacks to be submissive as they baptized them. Father Manuel da Nóbrega, who had arrived with the first Jesuit settlement, opened a college in the wilderness and helped make Bahia part of the world, the most beautiful of all. Later, the voice of Father Antônio Vieira, miraculous and implacable, a tribune of natives and slaves, thundered in the cathedral church of Bahia. The Holy Inquisition, not content with persecuting him in life, tried to silence that voice of fire for centuries after. They tore down his cathedral church in an attempt to extinguish the echoes of his denunciations of thieves, cowards, torturers.

Two friars, who were also sculptors, Agostinho da Piedade and Agostinho de Jesus, gave these saints of heaven faces, expressions, and attributes, gave them eternal life as they recreated them in wood, stone, and plaster sculpture. Frei Caneca, the spiritual forebear of Father Henrique Pereira, had fled from Pernambuco and was shot on the Campo da Pólvora, in the very heart of the city of Bahia, to serve as an example. Several others, whose names have been omitted because of the historical and religious ignorance of the author of this chronicle of customs and manners, devoted themselves to the city and to the people with self-abnegation and love. But none did so with more self-abnegation or greater love than Dom Timóteo Amoroso in his Abbey of Saint Benedict.

A few days before that Friday, when students were attacked by police constables, civilian and military, for demonstrating on Castro Alves Plaza, Dom Timóteo had flung open the doors of the abbey to shelter and protect them. Banners and posters of the demonstration that had been broken up by clubs still were visible behind the grillwork of the abbey. If the constables wanted to tear them down and destroy them and seize the students who had carried them, they would have to invade the abbey and trample the thin monk who denied them entry with outstretched arms. None dared do it, so the curs remained growling on the square at the top of the slope.

On the occasion of the festivities commemorating Menininha do Gantois's fifty years as *mãe de santo,* guardian of Afro-Brazilian rites, of the culture of African slaves, persecuted and denied, the major *iyalorixá* in the city and in the nation, Dom Timóteo held a congratulatory mass in the church of the Abbey of Saint Benedict and exalted her priestesshood. Mãe Menininha watches with zealous love over the *orixás* and the people of Bahia.

These moments, two gestures, two actions among dozens of similar, equally exemplary ones, are sufficient to measure the stature and excellence of this character who is going to enter our tale only to hear Dom Maximiliano's confession.

—

The Sermon of the Miracle

No reference will be made here to what was said or heard in confession—the secrecy will be maintained intact, as is ordered and ordained by Holy Mother Church.

Let it just be said that Dom Timóteo received Dom Maximiliano with the admiration, esteem, and patience that the illustrious monk, garland of the Benedictine order, had always deserved. After absolving him of his sins and giving him the penance due him, Dom Timóteo promised to help smooth the way for his transfer to the abbey in Rio de Janeiro: Dom Maximiliano planned to leave as soon as he handed over the directorship of the museum.

Seeing that he was resolute if not enthusiastic about his decision, the abbot stretched the interview into a friendly conversation. He asked Dom Maximiliano why he had doubts about divine mercy, the power of God, and the existence of miracles.

"Miracles happen—they take place before our eyes at every instant," the abbot said. "It's only pride that prevents us from seeing and recognizing them."

What was it that Edimilson had seen on the dock, if not a miracle? he asked. Why did Dom Maximiliano question his assistant's account and doubt that still another miracle could happen? Miracles were the daily bread of God Almighty, he said. Here in this city of Bahia, there were so many gods and such prodigious happenings that one lost count of miracles and no longer paid any attention to them, so simple and commonplace were they.

"Isn't simply living under the conditions that people do a miracle—and one of the greatest?" he concluded.

The abbot didn't delve further into the theme of the poverty of the people because of the urgency of attending to the monk's agony. Dom Maximiliano's affliction threatened to grow in desolation, become disaffection. The abbot fastened his blue eyes of light and water on the hunched shoulders, the tormented face of the wise curator and suffered with him. He had no balm for the open wound but the parable of the master and the disciple in the solitude of the docks.

He said that our knowledge frequently limits us, making us intolerant, proud, single-minded, and incredulous. Edimilson, that cross-eyed angel of the Lord, didn't let knowledge limit him or make a sectarian out of him. He would never become so infatuated, presumptuous, or heavy with self-esteem that he lost his belief in miracles. "Don't let knowledge limit you, dry up your imagination, or reduce your fantasy, my son, my brother, my teacher, Dom Maximiliano. Greater than our knowledge is the grace of God and poetry."

The Rewards of Martyrdom

As the vicar of Piaçava, Father Abelardo Galvão had learned some things from his own experience, while he knew many other things from what he heard. He had heard and heard again, ever since his mystical adolescence at the seminary to which his undefiled vocation had brought him, concepts, affirmations, limits, duties, and prohibitions. The limits were narrow, the prohibitions many.

His father, a doctor at a prestigious hospital, had envisioned Abelardo with a stethoscope on his chest, assisting him at the hospital and in his practice. His mother, an avid reader of novels, wanted him to become a man of letters, a university professor. But it was his maternal grandmother who supported him in the melee. Rich and domineering, she imposed her decision from the domains of her ranch: "I want to see my grandson enthroned as a bishop, to kiss his episcopal ring, and give him a blessing—me to him, not him to me." Her name was Edelwais dos Reis Rizério, and she had been widowed while still quite young, before the age of thirty. Every inch a woman, she was grand, eye-catching, and imposing.

His grandmother used binoculars to scan the horizon of her ranch from the porch of the big house, but not even with binoculars could the vicar of Piaçava see a bishopric as his choice and preference. In her rare letters to him, Grandmother Edelwais complained, "What kind of an idea is this one you've got of fighting for a diocese in Bahia?"

"Your glasses deceive you, Grandmother," he replied. "A dignitary's ring, a bishop's miter—these are inaccessible honors." In fact, even his vicarage in the dirt-poor backlands parish was now in doubt, since the auxiliary bishop had delivered the ultimatum: Either he ceased his communal action—subversive, Dom Rudolph had called it—or he would be removed. "I'm neither bishop nor half a bishop, Grandmother, only a threatened priest," Father Abelardo wrote. "Behind His Excellency stands the shadow of the landowner Costa, who holds the power of life and death over his tenants. These are bad omens, Grandmother."

What was close at hand, and this was certain, was martyrdom. There before Father Abelardo, within his grasp and well in sight in the news that Mr. Paulo Loureiro had brought from Recife, was his own destiny. Once, when Father Henrique Pereira had been giving his analysis of the national political situation, he had said, "We're returning to the days of the martyrs." He'd also used the word *comrades* in referring to those who were present.

Father Abelardo agreed. They were returning to the heroic times of spreading the Gospel, when Christian martyrs paid for their sacred mission with their lives. They were dangerous yet elevating times, the days of the Church of the Poor in the world today. Split down the middle, the Church of Rome vacillated between the rich and the dispossessed; it was just as divided as society. Only a handful of progressive priests stood up to the legion of reactionary cassocks. At this threatening but passionate juncture, Father Abelardo looked over the small circle of clerics and laymen gathered, and the word *comrades* had a fraternal ring to it, it broke down barriers, dissolved differences, did away with distance. He remembered the words of his grandmother at his ordination ceremony: "I demand that you be a *whole* priest, not one of those loafers who parades down the Rua da Frente here in Porto Alegre, those fops, perfumed dandies, clever gigolos of God." Grandmother Edelwais had no moss on her tongue; she rode and attacked with spurs.

Whole, his grandmother had demanded; he could be that at least, since he would never be able to offer her a bishop's ring to kiss. He'd enlisted in the army of the poor under God's orders, had served in the ranks of the poorest of all—the landless, the serfs. By doing so, he was fulfilling the oath that he'd made when he had lain on the church floor to receive the blessed sacrament. A southern ranch owner, his grandmother knew the poverty of her ranch hands, but she couldn't begin to imagine the misery of peasants in northeastern fields.

In spite of threats, insinuations in newspapers, pressure from his superiors, and sinister messages, Father Abelardo was fulfilling his oath. Of those who were disposed to act bravely, how many had already given their lives in sacrifice, been murdered by thugs: police, gunmen, or private bodyguards under the orders of the landowners? It was a long list, and it kept growing inexorably—a week didn't pass in which a priest wasn't killed in the backlands barrens, on a rural plantation, or on the banks of the River São Francisco, wherever serfs dared demand possession of the land they were tilling.

The vicar of Piaçava, whole, was fulfilling his oath, too, when he preached resistance instead of submission to parishioners reduced to extreme poverty, living like animals. But was bravery sufficient for a

Catholic priest to be whole? Or was the strict observance of the oath obligatory? As he prepared for martyrdom, Father Abelardo Galvão decided to tear from his burning breast any vestige, the smallest glimmer of an inclination toward disobedience to the vow of chastity that he'd assumed. No, he couldn't allow the hot coals in his breast to take fire; he had to extinguish them once and for all, so that the fire fed by the flames of sin would never again burn his heart. Just the day before in the automobile, at lunch, when they had taken leave of each other—"So long, I'll see you at the theater"—Patrícia had brushed her lips against his, hers wet and hot, his dry and avid. If he fell into mortal sin, could he be a whole priest? Oh, Grandmother, it's harder than you think.

In truth, he didn't really know what his grandmother thought. As a matter of fact, didn't people whisper about the rich widow and the local priest? Canon Jesuíno Santo Domingo had commanded *gaúchos* during the southern insurrection, rode horseback in his cassock, a carbine hanging from his saddle, like a character out of one of Érico Veríssimo's novels. He was sleeping with Grandmother Edelwais, the ranch hands and their women whispered with a tinge of laughter. They didn't censure the affair—they found it amusing, natural. A whole priest—what did his grandmother mean?

The Chosen One

"For important reasons, I'll tell you about them," Father Abelardo explained to Patrícia over the telephone when she wanted to know why he'd stood her up, having made a firm date to meet her at the Castro Alves Theater. "I was praying for a martyr and searching out the consequences of his martyrdom." "Martyrdom?" Patrícia was puzzled, and he explained: "We're living in the days of the apostles and sacrifices once again. Fulfilling the mission of Christ can mean terrible persecution, vile calumny, iniquity—it can cost you your life," he said, his voice excited, almost happy. He had an urge to call her comrade, but he held his tongue.

Patrícia listened to his solemn declaration with some impatience. Friday was the busiest day on the filming schedule for *Le Grand Échiquier,* because today they were going to shoot an improvised Bahian Carnival in Pelourinho, with the participation of Afro groups and *afoxés,* the Internationals, the Children of Gandhi, and the Bloco do Jacu, the latter under the baton of the composer Waltinho Queiroz and his most loving mother and most lively reveler, Dona Luz da Serra. Starting the day before, people were summoned by radio and television stations to come en masse today at three in the afternoon to the Largo do Pelourinho, where the Trio Elétrico of Dodô and Osmar would be the centerpiece of the improvised festivities. Nilda Spencer guaranteed Jacques Chancel that thousands of people would appear, two or three thousand as a conservative estimate, and the Frenchman was quivering with excitement.

"You can explain it to me later," Patrícia cut him short. "No, I don't mean it that way. The thing about martyrdom interests me a lot. But right now I've got to hang up—I'm up to my neck in things . . . I'll expect you at two o'clock at the school—two in the afternoon, of course. . . . No, I won't have any time for lunch, so bring a sandwich if you can . . . Yes, ham is okay, but I'd rather have mortadella, I like it better. . . . I like you too much, did you know that? Well, now you know it, my favorite martyr, my Saint Sebastian—and put on a nice starched shirt so you can be on television," the bold girl told him over the telephone.

Crazy as a bedbug, she was, Father Abelardo thought. She didn't say two words that made any sense to him, moonstruck and captivated as she was. What was that business about a starched shirt, and television? Again? Hadn't she been satisfied with the luncheon at the Model Market? What would the auxiliary bishop say if he found him in front of the cameras amid actors and half-naked *samba* dancers? And when they parted, there would be the brushing of the juicy lips again. She had teased him about martyrdom: *My Saint Sebastian, I like you too much, now you know it.* Oh, Grandmother, to be a whole priest was a most adverse and risky task!

He had wanted to explain to her about a whole list of ideas that bothered him, including the idea that Christ's mission was a task for the chosen. He didn't feel worthy, deserving of it. If God chose him for martyrdom, however, if he placed him among the chosen, he would take his position—he wouldn't run from it. But Patrícia had hung up before the vicar of Piaçava could assure her that danger didn't frighten him, wouldn't make him abandon the poor or give up the demand for a land commune or silence the word of God. He was fiery, burning, impassioned, ready and waiting for sacrifice!

The Gunman

What Father Abelardo Galvão didn't know was that on the Largo de São Bento, standing across from the abbey in a rain cape, dark glasses, and wide-brimmed hat, chewing on a matchstick, was Zé do

Lírio, waiting for him so that their paths would cross at the right place, at the best moment for the bullet of sacrifice. He had six in the chamber of his revolver, but he'd never had to use more than one for such assignments.

A religious man was Zé do Lírio. He feared God and Father Cícero, the patron saint of bandits and highwaymen and, by extension, of gunmen, although not, however, of policemen, torturers, elite guards, and other criminal elements. Zé do Lírio had heard mass in the abbey church, his thoughts turned toward heaven, that pretty and bountiful place where music is heard all day long and people eat manna, a tasty foreign food. His eyes had been fixed on Father Abelardo.

He needed to get a fix on the vicar's features so he didn't make another mistake like the one in Caruaru. That time, he'd kept watch on the wrong fellow, drunk a glass of cane liquor, chewed a piece of jerked beef, seen his face close up. The boy had had some of the features of the guilty party, but the resemblance wasn't really even that close—it didn't go beyond Carlitos's little mustache, which had been responsible for the confusion. Now, in the Church of Saint Benedict, Zé do Lírio begged God's forgiveness once more. By his count, he must have sent a good two dozen scoundrels into the other world. He felt no remorse: If someone was willing to pay him to dispatch a living soul, he reasoned, there had to be a good reason for it—nobody threw money away. But the weight he carried on his shoulders for that one killed by mistake outweighed his successes. He even had a mass said for the repose of his soul.

He had engraved the face of this stiff-collar in his mind—he must be a no-good, a scoundrel, Zé do Lírio thought, one of those evil priests who doesn't recognize the law of God and who wants to take land away from its owners without respect for property deeds, fences, or boundaries. Or maybe the priest had had a taste of one of the colonel's daughters; both of them were pretty, especially the married one, and these priests today don't stick to their duties but go around prowling, screwing —except for those that would rather have it in the ass. Zé do Lírio didn't criticize priests for screwing—anyone who found a juicy twat and didn't take advantage of it didn't deserve the kingdom of heaven, he thought. But the ones who offered their assholes—those he detested—they were a devilish breed.

Colonel Joãozinho Costa had paid him in advance because that Friday he was taking an early plane—he'd been called away suddenly on urgent business. Zé do Lírio saw through the ruse: The boss preferred to be far away at the hour of justice. It was God's justice, Colonel Costa had told Zé do Lírio, since lawyers' justice is all fouled up, and these bastardly priests are raising hell, invading other people's property at the head of bands of thugs.

On the Largo de São Bento, in the coolness of the morning, Zé do

Lírio, his heart cleansed of guilt, his conscience pure, the fulfiller of duties, awaited the condemned priest, for whom there would be no escape. The sentence had been handed down by the one who had the right to do so; the work had been well paid for, and Zé do Lírio had photographed the priest's face on his retina. The Reverend Father was as good as dead. You could already pray for his soul.

The Potentates

The first plane out of Brasília that Friday afternoon was full of legislators leaving for the weekend to visit their families and their properties and make contact with their electoral constituencies. But His Eminence the Cardinal Primate and the Magnificent Rector of the Federal University were flying in the other direction, from Brasília into Bahia.

"Our aircraft is full of potentates," commented Deputy Hamilton Trevísio, a radical, in a loud voice. Perhaps it was because he found himself the traveling companion of these two important figures that he felt free to endorse and promote among students the concessions that the cardinal and the rector had wrung from the minister—of war, not education. In reprisal for the student strike and the recent demonstrations, the students of the university were threatened with losing the academic year and their stipends.

Iron-willed, the minister of war had kept the cardinal primate and the rector waiting in his outer office for fifteen minutes. In spite of the appointment made the day before, he was counting on the passage of time to crack the shell of these two civilians who acted like big shots. Finally, he'd begun the audience by scolding the rector: "Keep those delinquents under control," he'd said. "What's become of your authority?" He went on to blame the cardinal for the unruly activity of priests: "How far will they go? They're worse than Communists—but we've got our eyes on them, and their cassocks won't give them immunity. Immunity is finished, for the good of the nation and the security of its institutions." Having put the rector and the cardinal in their place, he was ready to listen to them. He argued over the reasons they gave him, but he ended up agreeing to their request: He would give orders to the minister of education, he said, and they should go see him. When he said goodbye to them, he was almost pleasant.

Civil and courteous, the minister of education and culture had received the cardinal and the rector immediately, even though their visit wasn't on his calendar; he made no complaints about the telephone call from the war minister's office, he was magnanimous. The father of several university students himself, he said, he was living the problem with his own flesh and blood. Inexperienced youths, idealists, these students were the favorite prey of the Communists, and those Brazilians in the service of Russia were leading them into subversion. The problem wasn't just young students, either; there were certain priests, weren't there, Your Eminence? In land occupation and even in the guerrilla warfare in Pará, priests were playing an important role as dangerous and insolent agitators. He, the education minister, knew better than to confuse those Marxist priests with priests of the Church of Christ, that bastion of society and of the worthy Revolution of 1964, for which it was the inspiration. Their rhetorical efforts were pathetic, the minister said; if it hadn't been for the Revolution, where would we be today? With soviets, gangs, atheism. Atheism—declared by law, imposed by bayonets, Cardinal! Then he softened his voice, withdrew his red bayonets, became friendliness personified. He reaffirmed his acceptance of the invitation to attend the opening of the exhibit of religious art: He would be there Friday evening to cut the inaugural ribbon before returning immediately to Brasília on the ministry's private jet. Besides being comfortable, small jets were most useful, they let you move around quickly, keep the government responsive. He embraced the rector and reverently kissed the cardinal's ring.

During the ninety-minute flight, weary, humiliated, satisfied, victorious, restored to their customary dignity, the cardinal and the rector exchanged mutual praise and congratulations. The irresponsible students' school year had been saved, and the threat of expulsion from the university avoided—the rest was of little import. It wasn't easy being either a rector or a cardinal under a military government, when ministers wore boots and spurs, rode their horses, and exercised their arbitrary wills, the grumpy, ill-mannered little despots. The two men didn't speak of such disturbing things, but had words of sympathy for the minister of education. The rector knew him well, they had a working relationship and met frequently: "He's a cultivated man. A fine orator, a brilliant intellectual. The soldier boys don't trust him—they criticize his liberalism."

The cardinal recognized his qualities, but added, "Poor fellow, I don't envy him his job."

But he said no more, preferring to lead the conversation into another thorny matter that was upsetting them: the disappearance of the statue of Saint Barbara of the Thunder. They'd barely mentioned the matter during their errand in Brasília, bearing the weight as they were of the student situation and the repressive measures; they didn't have time to comment on the lamentable event. On the plane, however, the saint had imposed herself between the two potentates.

"It's a typical mess from our dear Dom Maximiliano. Another one," the rector said, putting his finger on the sore spot.

Merciful, the cardinal came to the defense of the monk: "Dom Maximiliano is a scholar, and scholars as a rule are given to confusion."

"Some of them too much so," the rector said pitilessly.

The cardinal primate didn't respond. He was thinking of the vicar of Santo Amaro and the uproar he must have been raising at that moment. Father Téo wasn't a doctor, there was nothing of the scholar about him, and he'd certainly forgotten all his Latin from the seminary by now, but he was a hard nut to crack. In a certain way, he—the cardinal—had forced him to loan out the statue against his will, and he felt responsible.

The Invincible Armada

At that moment the vicar of Santo Amaro, the unbearable Father Téo, at the head of the town notables, was making final provisions for the departure of the Invincible Armada for the state capital. Their objective was to rescue the saint and bring her back to her altar in the Purificação church—no matter where she might be, they would find and retrieve her.

For Father Téo there was no doubt as to the statue's whereabouts. He knew that it had been hidden in some cranny by the director of the Museum of Sacred Art, that so-and-so Dom Mimoso, with the complicity of the cardinal primate. Once the people of Santo Amaro put the thieving friar up against the wall, he would have to confess to the robbery and restore the saint to her altar. No cardinal on earth could save him from that.

That morning, Santo Amaro was running the risk of becoming a ghost town. Its inhabitants were turning out en masse, voluntarily; the vessels, even as numerous as they were, were insufficient to carry the thousands who wanted to take part in the expedition to Bahia. The difficult part wasn't recruiting people, it was stopping them from fighting over a position in a vessel, or a poster, a palm branch to carry. Finally Dona Canô Veloso, who was experienced in dealing with problems and disorders and in finding and imposing equitable solutions, managed to convince the ungovernable crowd of people that each family should send one representative. Even so, the armada's galleons would weigh anchor loaded to the gunwales. Santo Amaro was no sleepy hamlet.

Starting at noon, the first sloops set sail. Some of them had already arrived at Santo Amaro completely full, in a merry uproar. The combatants carried varied and copious provisions: sandwiches, fruit, hard-boiled eggs, roast chickens, codfish cakes, fried fish, sliced jerky with onions, roast beef with mushroom sauce, pork chops, shrimp pies and pastries, sugar cane slices—an endless list that stirred up the appetite, made the mouth water. And this was not counting the cases of guaraná soda and beer, or the bottles of cane liquor, prohibited as they are. Aboard the rich men's launches, of which there were only four, whiskey was flowing freely.

The little old women from the Sisterhood of Our Lady of the Good Death, from Cachoeira the Heroic, occupied one of the liveliest boats. Dressed to kill, they wore their white skirts adorned with lace and embroidery over starched petticoats, their blouses displaying the scapular of the order: chains of eighteen-carat gold with two plates of the finest goldsmithery. Black, laughing, ancient, almost all of them were in their eighties, and some were over ninety: Badu, at seventy-six, was the baby. The dean, Maria Pia, had been born in the time of slavery. She had no teeth, but she was sucking pieces of sugar cane, softening them with her gums.

Hemmed in by the young sportsmen who'd been taking care of him since the night before, Inspector Ripoleto's arms had been untied so he could eat a chicken drumstick and some day-old bread, two bananas, and a guava. At least he wouldn't starve to death. They tied his arms behind his back again when he finished because when he'd gone into the woods to pee, he'd tried to escape. In spite of his discomfort and fear— might they not drown him halfway across?—he was still conscious of his duties. Inspector Ripoleto tried to set down in his unfortunately weak memory the instructions that the leaders were giving and the demands being written on banners and posters: "We Want Our Saint Barbara of the Thunder!" "The Saint Belongs to Us!" "Down With the Museum's Imperialism!" "Long Live the Saint!" "Down With Dom Mimoso!" "Long Live Father Téo!"

Because the Invincible Armada would have to dock at the state capital with enough time left to disembark and march to the Convent of Saint Theresa and lay siege to the museum before the exhibit opening that evening, at three in the afternoon, anchors aweigh, it was only waiting the order to sail. Sails to the wind, crews ready and equipped, troops prepared for the good fight, sailor girls and quartermaster women clutching palm branches, posters, and flags, the Invincible Armada of launches, schooners, and sloops was about to leave the port of Santo Amaro and sail down the channel of the Paraguaçu River heading for the market ramp in Bahia. Such a squadron hadn't been seen since the time of the Dutch wars.

The vicar of Santo Amaro, Father Teófilo Lopes de Santana, said his farewell to Missy Marina. Then, outfitted with a whistle, surrounded by his children and parishioners, with the reporter Guido Guerra and the photographer Batista serving as orderlies, he assumed the command post in the bow of the *Flying Packet:* a Batavian admiral, a hero of the Second of July, a knight of hope, Saint George of Cappadocia.

The Decision

After his meeting with the abbot, Dom Maximiliano von Gruden was pondering the best way to get from the Benedictine abbey to the museum and take refuge there without being spotted or besieged by newsmen on the street. Keeping watch in the courtyard of the Convent of Saint Theresa, some of them were killing time playing cards, while others listened to music on their transistor radios. The well-connected José Berbert de Castro had taken shelter in Roque's studio across from the convent and museum, dozing in the easy chair of the "sought-after con artist"—that was how he had described him in one of his columns inspired by the disappearance of the statue.

After much reflection, reviewing the ordeal that had been inflicted on him during the last two days of hell on earth, and thinking about the days awaiting him from that day forward, Dom Maximiliano made a final resolve. Now that he was ruined—only the miracle predicted by Dom Timóteo could save him, although in spite of the abbot's preaching, the director still refused to believe in miracles—it was better to confront the situation with his head held high than to run away. He'd decided what he would do when the hour of his crucifixion arrived, so why go on like a coward incapable of acceptance and resolve? Ready for anything, he felt relieved. A Japanese samurai, defeated and dishonored, heroic and suicidal, he slipped into the pocket of his cassock the weapon with which he would commit hara-kiri before his implacable judges: his request for resignation. Since he'd resolved to resign and leave, what more did he have to fear?

In a last gesture of gallantry, he straightened his rumpled cassock. All he lacked was a mirror with which he could adjust his downcast, dejected face to present it as proud with a trace of melancholy. His paleness would suit the role well. Feigning disillusionment and helplessness, then, he left the abbey on the Largo de São Bento, mingled with the hurrying pedestrians, and walked up São Pedro, ignoring the couple who whispered as they passed him. On Piedade he turned the corner, then continued along the Rua de Baixo; in the distance saw Dr. Odorico Tavares, who was no doubt on his way to his newspaper office, arm in arm with Professor Edwaldo Boaventura, with whom he was conversing and laughing a lot. He must be laughing at Dom Maximiliano, the monk concluded gloomily—it couldn't be otherwise.

Why in heaven's name had Dr. Odorico—who had always been his friend, had backed him up consistently in his controversial management of the museum, lent him items from his own collection for exhibits, written congratulatory pieces about him in *The Compass*—why had he suddenly changed so completely into a sworn mortal enemy? He'd given the bellicose Guido Guerra carte blanche in *Diário;* why was he dragging his old friend through the mud?

Dom Maximiliano was sure he knew the reason. It must be because his intemperant, loose tongue was incapable of resisting gossip. Although he was as obsequious as anyone else, behind people's backs he whispered and gossiped. Dom Maximiliano bites the hand that feeds him, he imagined Dr. Odorico telling Professor Edwaldo. There's always someone who'll betray a confidence. And in order to intrigue, people exaggerate an irreverent remark until it becomes biting, perhaps vulgar or insidious. But it had been a joke, a jibe, nothing more, transformed into an insult in the repeating.

Dom Maximiliano passed by the *Diário* office, but nobody noticed his provocative gesture. He felt an urge to go in—but to do what? From the top of the stairway that connects the Rua de Baixo with the Rua do Sodré, Dom Maximiliano contemplated the Santa Tereza convent, the courtyard in front, the garden alongside; it was one of the most beautiful buildings in the city, set into the incomparable landscape of sea and mountain: his museum, his house, his life.

He saw a thick-set fellow, wearing a leather jacket, facing the Ladeira de Preguiça, pulling on the bridle of a small, slow-footed donkey. On the animal's back was a large lump, and the packsaddle frame, enormous, worn, and irregular, reached down past its belly. Dom Maximiliano cast his eyes on man and ass, noticed the frame, then closed them to preserve that instant in his memory. Then he began down the stairs, step by step, greeting neighbors with nods along the way.

He stopped in front of the atelier of the woodcarver Zu Campos and watched him hard at work chiseling into wood. The artist gave a friendly smile when he spotted the monk.

"Good afternoon, Dom Maximiliano."

"What are you making, Zu? What saint is that?"

"Well, isn't it obvious that it's Saint Barbara? Can't you see the *eiru?* If the one from Santo Amaro doesn't show up, you can put this one in its place, Dom Director."

In a small carving hanging from the wall beside the door, an angel was flying over a sky of blue flowers and pink birds.

"How much do you want for the angel, Zu?"

"The Mulatto Angel? Do you like it?"

"Very much."

"Is it for you, or a present?"

"For me."

"For you it doesn't cost anything. Everything here is yours, Dom Maximiliano."

Dom Maximiliano knew that if he insisted on paying, the artist would be offended. "Well, if that's how you want it, thank you very much. I'll send someone over for it in a little while. I'm going to give you a remembrance, too: the book I wrote about Saint Barbara. The statue from Santo Amaro, the Thunder Woman. Yours is turning out almost as pretty as she."

He wanted to tell Zu Campos that he had planned for the next year to hold another exhibit of religious art of Bahia, this time for contemporary art, beginning with Presciliano and going up to Zu, Wanda do Nada, and Osmundo. It would have been a followup to the exhibit that would open just before nine o'clock tonight without any Saint Barbara of the Thunder or any *eiru.* But now those plans would remain in the ex-director's head, would never be realized—what was the use of talking about it now, announcing it? He would be the ex-director a few hours hence.

He took the last steps, and as soon as he set foot on the street, he found himself surrounded by reporters, their tape recorders running, barraged by questions. From the door of Roque's studio, Zé Berbert, agile despite his corpulence, crossed to the director. Sought after for so long, Dom Maximiliano was suddenly available right there, after they'd imagined he was in Rio de Janeiro on his way to Germany.

Impassive, a touch of melancholy on his proud face, as pale as marble—or better, as ivory—maintaining his measured pace, Dom Maximiliano didn't stop. He continued toward the convent without answering the reporters but also without chasing them away. Zé Berbert grabbed him by the sleeve of his cassock.

When he got to the door that led into the museum, the master of himself, his voice calm, he turned to those around him.

"A moment of attention, my friends, please," he said. "Listen to what I am going to say, and don't interrupt me. Ever since yesterday, my dear friends of the press have been wanting to hear from me. Let me speak to you." He looked at his wristwatch. "It's two forty-five, a quarter to three in the afternoon. At exactly eight-thirty tonight, half-past eight on the nose, or five hours from now more or less"—he looked at his watch again, corrected himself—"five hours and forty-one minutes from now, the exhibit of religious art of Bahia is going to open, to which you are all invited. At that moment and only then will I have anything to say. Only five hours, a little more, it won't hurt you gentlemen to wait."

He smiled at Zé Berbert, crossed the threshold, and locked the door from the inside.

The Marked Saint

Dom Maximiliano had to grasp the railing for support. It was absurd—his eyes were dim and his stomach empty because he hadn't had lunch—yet he wasn't hungry. His mouth was bitter. He pulled his handkerchief out of his cassock pocket and wiped the drops of sweat and faintness from his face. He put on a mask of boldness—no one was going to laugh in his face. Then he went up the small set of stairs.

In the rooms set up for the exhibit, a few people were moving about in silence. Jamison Pedra, artist and architect, came over to greet the museum director.

"I came to add the final touches," he said.

"That's very kind of you."

Then he was surrounded by the others. Gilberbert Chaves informed him, "We're finishing up. Among the important pieces, the only ones still absent are Mirabeau's. I proposed sending for them, but he refused, he said he'd bring them here himself. We've already picked out the places where they'll be displayed."

Dom Maximiliano couldn't help but smile at the news of Mirabeau's precautions. A prize-winning sculptor, a designer, and a painter with a great many customers, as well as a collector, Mirabeau Sampaio owned the best collection of antique statues in Bahia.

"I'm surprised that he's even consented to lend the pieces. Afraid I wouldn't ever give them back."

No sooner had he spoken than the aforementioned Mirabeau Sampaio came into the room. In his arms, held with the care one uses in carrying a newborn baby, was the coveted statue of Saint Catherine of Alexandria. Antiquarians and collectors sighed over her, and museum directors dreamed of her because her cape bears the signature of Frei Agostinho de Piedade. She was one of the only four pieces our famous master signed, the greatest master after Aleijadinho, Mirabeau bragged, the proud owner. Dom Maximiliano went over to greet him:

"Would you allow a poor mortal to take that precious thing in his arms?"

"Be careful—it's heavy."

Heavy and large. With his thin hands and long fingers, Dom Maximiliano got a good grip on it, and once again admiration lit up his face and greed darkened his eyes as he examined the rare and authentic signature. Watchful and nervous, Mirabeau followed the director's inspection of Saint Catherine. He smiled, comforted, when he saw Dom Maximiliano hand her over to the robust Sylvio Robato. She was out of danger—and the mark hadn't been discovered, the director hadn't noticed it. Nor could he have. Only he, Mirabeau Sampaio, knew where, locked in his studio, without any witnesses, he'd carved the sign that would identify the statue upon its return. Not that he believed everything they said about Dom Maximiliano, but as the saying goes, a safe man dies of old age.

Nor did Dom Maximiliano mean it when he joked, "Let's find a special place for it—the prominent place it deserves. Who knows, maybe our dear Mirabeau will be convinced that this Saint Catherine of Alexandria shouldn't continue on in a private collection. Its place is here, in the Museum of Sacred Art. Who knows, generous person that he is, maybe he'll make us a donation."

Generous or not—there were doubts—Mirabeau failed to see the humor in the jokes. No, Dom Maximiliano was not to be trusted; even now his story about Saint Barbara of the Thunder was confused. Joke for joke, threat for threat, he answered in kind:

"Watch out—I'll take it back. No donation, no sale, no swap— positively no swap." Angry now, Mirabeau had changed the tone of his voice.

Dom Maximiliano took it as a misunderstanding. In order to calm down the grumpy fellow, for a second time that afternoon, he thought of mentioning his plan for an exhibit of contemporary religious art. The saints painted by Mirabeau, his sculptures, the Pietà, the Christ would have figured prominently in it. But again he remained silent; tomorrow he wouldn't be the museum director anymore. He felt an emptiness in his chest as he took Mirabeau by the arm. "Let's go pick out a spot for your Saint Catherine," he said.

Accompanied by assistants, the two collaborators, co-defendants in so many machinations and sharp deals, went through the rooms. The exhibit was practically all in place; imposing, it spanned colonial times through the end of the nineteenth century, bringing together treasures of immeasurable value and beauty. In the center of the main room an empty platform awaited the statue of Saint Barbara of the Thunder. Dom Maximiliano had an assistant go get a certain small table from the storeroom—a rare piece from the time of Dutch rule—and on it he placed the statue of Saint Catherine of Alexandria, recreated in Bahia by Frei

Agostinho da Piedade. The sculptor had liked the statue so much that he'd signed it, and the signature was in plain view.

Dom Maximiliano sent Almério the doorman to get the other pieces Mirabeau was loaning—he'd left them in the car under the eye of Edgard, his helper. Mirabeau had still been a young dandy, a playboy, beloved of the Argentine girls of Bataclan, when he'd hired Edgard as chauffeur and bodyguard. Now they were growing old and cantankerous together.

In spite of his curiosity, Mirabeau Sampaio refrained from alluding to the disappearance of the statue reported in the press; nor did he mention the police's visit to his studio. He was both tight-lipped and sharp-eared. But at the end of their inspection of the exhibit, when he found himself standing at the entrance to the main hall saying good-bye to Dom Maximiliano, Mirabeau couldn't resist.

"What about Saint Barbara of the Thunder? Have you decided where you're going to place her yet?" he asked, as if he weren't interested and didn't know anything.

Taken aback, having no prepared answer, Dom Maximiliano, without hesitating, said the first thing that came into his head. "Right here where I'm standing, right at the entrance. What do you think, my dear Mirabeau?"

Without waiting for an answer he shook the collector's hand and let the others escort him to the stairs, because all aflutter, the "angel" on duty had come to tell him:

"The cardinal is on the phone, sir."

The cardinal greeted Dom Maximiliano affectionately, then asked about the problem of the statue. He'd just been given a long account by the auxiliary bishop, but he wanted to hear the museum director's version. Dom Maximiliano told him everything he knew, holding nothing back. Nothing outside of what was in the papers had reached his ears today, and he hadn't reason for a shred of hope. From the abbey he'd called the chief of the State Police, he said, and Dr. Calixto Passos had insisted on naming Father Téo as a suspect—no, not as a suspect, as the indisputably guilty party. The director offered the cardinal no opinion of this accusation—His Eminence might not approve of his indiscretion.

On the other end of the line the cardinal exclaimed, "Who? Father Téo?" "Yes, he, the vicar of Santo Amaro, precisely." Once more Dom Maximiliano kept his opinion to himself and went on telling what he knew. He'd tried to contact the chief of the Federal Police, Colonel Raul Antônio, but was unable—the colonel had sent a message by an underling saying that he had nothing to report. Dom Maximiliano ended up declaring that he was happy he was still free, but how long he would be, only God knew.

The cardinal promised to convey any new information to him as soon as he spoke with Colonel Raul Antônio. Before hanging up, he asked the director if Dom Rudolph's information was correct: that Dom Maximiliano was intending to resign the directorship of the museum and leave Bahia if the statue weren't found in time for the exhibit. It was true, yes.

"Do you think that's absolutely necessary?"

"I can't see any other way out, Your Eminence."

Perhaps he hoped, who knows, to hear a word of disagreement from the cardinal, an objection, a refusal to accept his resignation, an order to remain at his post. He didn't hear it. His Eminence only said regretfully:

"A pity, a great pity, but really, there's nothing else you can do."

The cardinal could at least have mentioned his role in obtaining the statue, Dom Maximiliano thought; he bore part of the responsibility, he'd put pressure on the vicar of Santo Amaro. But most likely the cardinal had forgotten that detail. On this *via crucis,* Dom Maximiliano was carrying his cross alone. There would be no Simon of Cyrene to help him in his climb up Calvary.

The Motorcyclist

The next thing Father Abelardo Galvão knew, he was on the rear seat of a motorcycle, his hands on Patrícia's naked belly. Clinging to her, his arms encircling her body, he felt its contact and warmth as they rode through the center of the city, from the drama school in Canela to the Largo do Pelourinho, where the crowd was gathering.

"Come with me," she'd ordered. "We're late as usual. Jacques has already left with Nilda, and Guy's been over in Pelourinho for a long time now. Two cars just left, all filled up. But we'll get there ahead of them," Patrícia announced. Father Abelardo didn't know how, but he soon found out—when he found himself on the motorcycle. Going sixty miles an hour.

Hanging loose over his Lee jeans was his colored shirt, the only one he'd brought along on the quick trip, apart from his clerical garb and the two simple T-shirts with Mário Quintana poems printed in white on the black fabric. As for Patrícia, the best one could say is that when she put on her showy and brief outfit, she got undressed. Under the print wrap-around it was easy to see that she wore only her white panties. Tied around her waist by a knot, opening and closing, the skirt displayed her thighs and derriere openly. Over her breasts, the band that held in her opulences was showing more than it was hiding. She'd rolled her Indian hair around the top of her head and studded it with flowers, the crown of a queen. A Carnival queen, for a Frenchman to see and film.

Before she covered herself with a motorcycle helmet to protect her crown and makeup from the wild wind, Patrícia had been parading about the drama school barefoot and almost naked, provocative. Exposed to the wind and to people's stares, she was a monument, a statue in the sunlight, vigorous, radiant. But statues don't move—they are fastened to pedestals, static in museums, like the Venus de Milo, Rodin's Eve—but Patrícia was going back and forth, and as she walked she swayed and her skirt opened.

She was sensual but not lascivious, voluptuous but not lewd. Father Abelardo could not discern a trace of indecency, he decided as he contemplated Patrícia. He didn't turn his eyes away, and yet he didn't feel he was sinning. It was as if he were watching the flight of a seagull, an acacia in bloom, a bird of paradise. Could it be?

Those restless candidates for stardom in the firmament of the performing arts, the students from the acting division, dressed in identical nudity, were running out to two parked cars, one of which was Miro's. The priest was puzzled by Sylvia Esmeralda's absence, since yesterday she had been the most excited one about Carnival. Father Abelardo asked about her. "Poor Sylvia, she got sick last night," said Patrícia. "But Dona Olímpia de Castro, a rich woman, her friend, phoned from the hospital with news: Sylvia is still in bed, but she's out of danger. Poor thing!" Patrícia felt sorry for her; falling ill right at the height of a Carnival commotion, the likes of which wouldn't be seen again in a hundred years.

Their crazy conversation was interrupted constantly as Patrícia made decisions, hurried people up, gave orders to colleagues, to drivers, and to him, Father Abelardo Galvão. After they filmed the Carnival scenes—he would be up on the music truck with their small group of privileged people—she'd take him along to join in a *caruru* dinner, with more than a thousand pieces of okra. In Piaçava the vicar had gone to *carurus* for Saints Cosmos and Damian—it was a traditional custom in the interior too. This one was for Yansan, and it was to be in the Santa Bárbara market, in the Baixa dos Sapateiros. They would leave directly from Pelourinho for the merrymaking—it was only a step away. Jacira do Odô Oyá had asked that Patrícia bring the whole film crew, not forgetting Mr. Jacques, that hunk, or that chic little Frenchman, the one with the earrings who looks like a queer but isn't.

That was how now, when he least expected it, Father Abelardo Galvão found himself involved and associated with people whose lifestyle he'd only known previously from hearsay. Everything about his surroundings was new to him, from the students' shameless, amusing language to their brief, casual clothing. Foul-mouthed, indecorous, they used and abused freedom—sexual freedom included, as rumor had it. The rumors seemed to be true from what he could observe, although they didn't seem to merit the customary labels *evil, degenerate, dangerous.* In fact, he was finding them to be pleasant, cordial people, good companions; no one held his status as a priest against him, and the ones who knew about his village activities congratulated him for them in solidarity. Hanging out with this dubious theater and television gang, with the stars of shows by Eros Martins Gonçalves and of films by Glauber Rocha—bohemians, liberals, and libertarians—he, the bashful hick priest, didn't feel at all strange or out of it. On the contrary, he felt relaxed and comfortable.

Patrícia was guiding him through that labyrinth, giving him cues, filling him in. The *caruru* of the enchanted ones, she told him, was a festival linked to the traditions of *candomblé.* It wasn't an obligation that it become a ritual feast of the *axé,* when the *orixás* come to sing and dance with the priestesses and the *iaôs.* But that could happen.

"Haven't you ever been to a *candomblé*?"

"Not yet, but I'd like to. I've heard it's very beautiful."

"I'll take you someday. Did you know that I'm a daughter of Yansan? I shaved my head and received the saint—didn't I ever tell you?"

"No, I never knew."

"It's best that you know because you don't fool around with Yansan's people—they're serious, fierce. And your saint, which one could it be? From your ways I think it would be Oxalá, but I'd rather it was Xangô."

"Why Xangô?"

"Because Xangô is Yansan's husband." She laughed impudently.

Priests can't marry, Patrícia, he thought. Their vows won't let them. Priests are sworn to celibacy, to chastity. But he didn't say anything to her, he swallowed dryly. Maybe those wild remarks were just joking around, a city girl having some fun at the expense of a little country priest. On the motorcycle, as he touched her body, as he felt the firmness of her flesh on the palm of his hand, the curve of her stomach, when he suddenly and unexpectedly recognized the shell of her navel, the vicar of Piaçava, the preacher of the Land Pastoral, the candidate for martyrdom, wondered where in the devil the decisions he had made at daybreak had gone, when he had been getting ready to give his life in sacrifice. He had been austere, firm, incorruptible, steadfast. Steadfast, fuck—as any of the students at the drama school would have reacted, if you'll excuse the curse word. He was fragile, reckless, the wind was carrying them away, unsustainable. He was suffering martyrdom right there at that moment, straddling the rear seat of the motorcycle, between heaven and hell, between hallelujah and malediction.

He was trying to keep his distance but found himself clinging to Patrícia's body. If he were not to be thrown off the vehicle onto a curve, over the speed limit, he had to clutch her, and not even his fright stopped him from feeling the softness of the world beneath his hands. A warning chill crossed through his body from head to foot, stabbing his balls. Does a priest have balls, Abelardo?

The trip from Canela to Pelourinho that seemed endless and mad to Father Abelardo Galvão, the vicar of the indigent parish of Piaçava, the pastor of that reviled community of the landless, actually lasted only a few minutes. Ignoring traffic signals, Patrícia's comet sped past buses and cars, Miro's taxi, Jenner Augusto's Mercedes—it was a spaceship in a flight of screaming skids. All the while the priest's votive hands touched Patrícia's concave stomach, a realm of dreams and sin. The right hand, or maybe the left, now one, now the other, creeps along, finds the navel, moves off, goes away, comes back, stretches out; the navel is an abyss, the crater of a volcano, the depths of hell; the right hand or maybe the left slips along, there's no strength of will capable of holding it back. Bent over the handlebars, rising up from her seat, Patrícia rides with her back pressed against the priest's chest, a priest in danger of death and condemnation for eternity. What does a whole priest mean, Grandmother? Tell me. A priest has balls like any other man—did you know that, Grandmother?

In the clutches of temptation, in danger of a fall, on the road to excommunication, Father Abelardo Galvão traveled to the Frenchman's Carnival. Then he would go to a *caruru* for Yansan, the wife of Xangô. Alas, Patrícia, even if he belonged to Xangô, a priest still couldn't marry, Patrícia—alas, no.

The Impossible Concessions

Having made an appointment to meet Father José Antonio at the courthouse at three in the afternoon, Adalgisa went home. To say that she was indignant, furious, wouldn't begin to describe her state of frenzy. Yet although she was a bundle of nerves, she was at the same time resolute, alert.

She was at the point of exploding when doors and windows opened as she passed—the neighbor women were eager for news and ready to savor her misfortune. She'd decided not to talk to the neighborhood riffraff, not to give them the satisfaction of any news, not even the smallest piece of information, the pleasure of a complaint, the slightest recrimination—the supreme joy of gossip. They were wasting their time, those nobodies, those repulsive women, she thought. She passed them by, holding her head high, and walked up to the door of her house, her face so tight that not even Damiana, the lead intriguer, who was enjoying this moment immensely, dared ask her anything. The gargoyle contented herself with laughing when she saw the ugly face Adalgisa wore. He who laughs last laughs best was an insignificant consolation, but on this occasion Adalgisa had no other.

Danilo was going to get a piece of her mind when he arrived home for lunch. Based on what she'd heard and on what she imagined, Adalgisa had determined the role her husband had played in the disastrous events of the night before. She knew Danilo was not a man who could draw up and execute such a precise and complex plan—he'd used up all his capacity for initiative on the soccer field and had turned the rudder of the ship over to his wife.

No, it was Gildete—that pesky busybody, that tramp, that trash, who had taken charge, who had thought out the scheme and directed it from beginning to end—with the help of the chimpanzee, that stinking nigger. Adalgisa could just hear her arguing to Danilo: Since he was Manela's guardian just as much as Dadá, why didn't he go to the juvenile judge right away? she would have said. Then he would have laid out his reasons, told the judge about the girl's upbringing under Adalgisa's rod. Or, rather, he would have invented a pack of lies, describing Adalgisa as a monster, an unnatural, heartless woman. That must have been what happened, and things like that must have been said about her, to convince the judge and obtain his countermanding order.

As she surmised what had happened, furious and offended, Adalgisa considered herself above all unjustly maligned. To rear her adopted daughter according to God's law, to protect her from vice and sin, to make a lady out of her, she'd been killing herself, her health had suffered, she hadn't known a moment of rest, she had sacrificed herself. But instead of thanking her for her self-abnegation, her relatives—including her own husband—had dragged her through the mud, stabbed her in the back. It must have been her—from that *macumba* woman—who had had the idea of stirring up the filth of the neighborhood, of dragging along Professor João Batista, the damnable Damiana, and the rest of the riffraff so they could all witness Manela's infamy and Adalgisa's defeat. But she still wasn't defeated; he laughs best, et cetera and so forth.

She was counting on a decisive weapon—Danilo himself. When he arrived home during his lunch hour, he would hear some things he'd never heard in his life. He'd hear what Adalgisa had to say, what she hadn't told the witches in the neighborhood. She had never been so furious at him, not even during the honeymoon at the beach or during the first months of their marriage, when Danilo had tried to force her into his degrading practices. She had had to be tough, to say ugly things then; that was nothing, however, compared to the tongue-lashing that awaited him now.

After she read the riot act to him, Adalgisa would make him accompany her on her visit to the juvenile judge so he could retract his miserable slander against her. He would have to state that he was in complete agreement with the internment of Manela in the Cloister of the Penitents. Did His Honor the judge know that Manela was taken in last night by the Candomblé do Gantois? she would ask.

Two would have to act as one: either Danilo would give in, lower his head, and act the way she wanted, or their marriage—publicly considered to be the perfect union of two loving hearts with a single will—would go down the drain. He'd go with her to the juvenile judge, or he would leave, there was no third alternative. And he had to do it immediately, or the door to the street was open.

She could consent to everything her husband did, willingly or unwillingly, except for two things. She would not permit him to side with Manela on an occasion like this, to encourage her to run away, to allow her to succumb to shamelessness and idolatry. That was the first of the two inadmissible actions. We already know what the second is—it's been commented on more than enough during this narrative. Never, ever, would she accede to the requests he had whispered to her in bed during the passage of almost twenty years, with indecent language, depraved to the lower depths, such baseness, moral defect, filth. No: not Manela, and not in the ass. ¡Olé!

It happened, however, that in the confusion of that ill-fated morning, Adalgisa had forgotten that it was Friday. So distracted was she that she hadn't remembered the notaries' lunch or the brains with manioc mush. Every Friday for more than twenty years, Danilo's boss, the notary Wilson Guimarães Vieira (besides being his boss, he was a friend), would take a group of co-workers and guests to a restaurant in the lower city, the Colón, where they would eat an omelet whose flavor ranged from the sublime to the divine. Adalgisa would take advantage of her husband's absence to prepare and enjoy brain stew, her favorite dish. Danilo was allergic to brains and, strange as it may seem to us, the tail of the animal as well.

What Adalgisa didn't know, or was never interested in knowing, was the notary's reason for those weekly lunches. Fridays are dedicated to Oxalá, and on Fridays his children, men and women alike, dress in white and celebrate him. The notary Vieira celebrated him by holding a lunch for friends, washed down with Portuguese green wine. A permanent yet special guest, Professor João Batista enjoyed a plate of snails as an appe-

tizer, though Danilo rejected them. Besides being a refined delicacy—
escargot in French, *lesma, caracol* in Portuguese, *igbin* in Yoruba, sun-
watcher in any language—the snail is the food of Oxalá.

—✥—✥

Corridor and Anteroom

Adalgisa arrived at the juvenile judge's chambers before her three
o'clock appointment. She couldn't stand to wait at home any longer.

She'd tried in vain to get in touch with Danilo. When she'd gone
out to call him from Mr. Martínez's bakery, the neighborhood riffraff
had once more taken up posts at their windows to watch her pass; she
had responded with disdain. The notary's luncheon guests had already
left the Cólon restaurant, said the waiter who had served them when he
found out who it was; he was attentive but sorry—Danilo had just left in
the company of Dr. Wilson. To ease her conscience, Adalgisa called
Danilo's office, knowing ahead of time that she wouldn't reach him
there. The notary and clerk conniving after the Friday blowout wouldn't
return to work until after three. They would prolong their lunch hour
with a drink or two, with this or that person, with other idlers, a censurable male habit allowed only reluctantly.

At the judge's chambers, she waited in the hallway so she could go
in along with Father José Antonio when he arrived. She was pacing back
and forth, went over to the elevators, unsure of herself because of the
absence of Danilo, the trump card she had been counting on to win the
game with the judge. All the more dependent on divine help now, she
made a promise: If God would help her get Manela back into the cloister,
starting with next Friday she would give up her brain stew for a year. On
one previous occasion—the illness and recovery of her godmother—
she'd gone three months without tasting her favorite dish.

Her migraine headache wasn't leaving her a moment of peace—it
burned at her temples and dimmed her eyes. Her legs were aching
from pacing along the hallway by the time Father José Antonio finally
appeared, excusing himself for his delay; there had been terrible traffic, he said; the bus was falling apart, barely dragging along. In truth,
he'd lingered at the baptismal lunch, filled his belly, and thoroughly
enjoyed himself. At the door to the judge's chambers, the clerk finally
came from inside, slowly, smoking a cheap cigar, and received them.
He recognized them—there was still no news of the judge, he said; if
they wanted, they could sit and wait in the anteroom. Was it an urgent matter? he asked. Very urgent, they replied. "Maybe he'll come,"
the clerk said. "If he doesn't come, he'll call." He turned and went

off, coughing long and hard—he suffered from a long-standing tobacco-based bronchitis.

For Adalgisa, waiting in the anteroom was less wearying, less agonizing: At least she was sitting down, and Father José Antonio had managed to boost her sagging morale.

"Don't lose faith, *hija*," he said. "There's nothing to it. I'll take charge: Dr. d'Ávila knows me from way back. We were colleagues at the Anticommunist Crusade seminar that Major Saturnino gave after the Revolution. We share the same ideals."

Still, something nagged at him, leaving him puzzled: "I can't imagine what brought Dr. d'Ávila to change his mind, to heed your husband's request. It's as if in only a matter of hours, water changed into wine. Something very serious must have happened. But no matter what it is, we'll clear this business up. Don't be upset—our cause is holy. God is with us, *Dios es grande, hija mía.*"

As they moldered in the anteroom, a well-stuffed Father José Antonio began to doze off, the sweat pouring off him in the deadly heat. The air conditioning had broken down more than a year ago. It was after four in the afternoon when the judge finally put in an appearance. Although he had gone home and taken a shower and changed clothes, His Honor's face still showed the signs of his sleepless night and the restless morning at the hospital.

Father José Antonio, fawning, asked the judge about Dona Diana, his virtuous wife. Dr. d'Ávila said he was worried, and Father José Antonio promised to pray for her rapid recovery. Adalgisa added her good wishes. She didn't know Dona Diana personally, but she'd heard the greatest praise for the beauty and elegance of the judge's wife from her friend Dona Olímpia de Castro. "I'm a milliner, and Dona Olímpia is a customer of mine," she added.

—§——§

A Simple Rondeau:
The Dedicated Woman

The juvenile judge had been able to return to his chambers because Adalgisa's distinguished customer, Dona Olímpia de Castro, had abandoned her many social activities—including a cocktail party organized by the promoters of a Caribbean cruise—to stay by her friend's bedside. Being with her during the bitter crisis, this most strange and sudden illness had left poor Dona Diana talking to herself, saying nothing that made sense; she seemed stark, raving mad. In her delirium she'd called for Olímpia; it was the only name that came to her lips.

The day before, upon returning home relaxed after giving nourishment to his body at Anunciata's house, Dr. d'Ávila had found his wife sprawled on the bed thrashing, kicking, and howling, her eyes wide. Called in at once, Dr. Rubim de Pinho had diagnosed a serious nervous crisis and given her a shot of sedative. It seemed advisable to put her in the hospital, to get her away from her usual surroundings. That was what they did. It had been a hard night for the juvenile judge.

In the morning, at a reasonable hour—these high-society ladies go to bed in the wee hours, then sleep late—Dr. d'Ávila had phoned Mrs. Castro and asked her to forgive the intrusion, but it was an urgent and delicate matter. Diana had been hospitalized with a nervous condition. He went further: It wasn't a simple case of the jitters. Dr. Rubim de Pinho had diagnosed it as a violent hysterical crisis. She kept asking for Dona Olímpia.

Dona Olímpia, showing good manners and sensitivity, listened almost in silence, inserting a few exclamations here and there. She showed great interest and concern, but she didn't seem surprised. The night before, she said, she'd tried to talk to Sylvia—"excuse me, I mean Diana" —she'd called several times without managing to reach her. "I'll hurry right over there," she now promised, "as soon as I get up and dress." She'd answered the anguished call in bed, at eleven o'clock in the morning.

Around one-thirty that afternoon, Dona Olímpia appeared at the hospital, dressed as if she were attending a fashion show. When Dona Diana—that is, Sylvia Esmeralda—who until then had been wrapped in a sheet from head to toe, heard Olímpia's name pronounced deferentially by the judge, she sat up in bed. She grasped her friend's arm and her eyes went wide, staring at her as if her life depended on it.

"Go take care of your duties, Your Honor," Dona Olímpia suggested to the astonished judge and husband. "Leave this poor creature in my care—I'll have her cured in the blink of an eye. It's nothing more than a case of frazzled nerves. Your wife, Dr. d'Ávila, is a sensitive person —the slightest thing triggers her nerves. Go attend your children. I'll take care of this child."

No, the judge's morning hadn't been easy either.

A Double Rondeau: The Nuts

The juvenile judge stopped to greet Adalgisa and Father José Antonio, then led them into his chambers, where they'd been the day before.

He asked them to have a seat and sat down behind his paper-strewn desk. In spite of his worry over his wife's mental state, he made an effort to be pleasant—he had a high regard for Father José Antonio. "How can I be of service to you?" he asked, weary and bitter, his mind far away, in the hospital. "Did the cloister take the bad girl in?"

Because Adalgisa had been expecting to hear an explanation, his question disturbed her. It didn't make any sense, and she stammered in bewilderment, "Yes, sir—in the afternoon. . . . But last night, you ordered her let out."

It was the judge's turn to be perplexed. "Whom did I order let out? I don't understand. What do you mean, my dear lady?"

"You—" Helplessly, Adalgisa looked to Father José Antonio pleadingly.

The priest lifted his hand, raised his voice, and chose his words carefully. "You can let me explain, *hija mía*," he said. "Listen, my dear Dr. d'Ávila, to what has happened. Yesterday afternoon we took the girl to the convent and left her there in the peace of *Dios*"—he said *Dios* in Spanish, then corrected himself—"of God. This morning Dona Adalgisa here came to tell me that her ward had left the cloister in the middle of the night. We went there, and the mother superior confirmed the fact: She really had allowed her to leave, and she'd done so in accordance to an order from you, my dear friend."

"An order from me? What kind of craziness is this? Who issued it? Who spoke in my name? I want to know who committed this abuse so I can put him in jail, bring charges against him."

The imbroglio was becoming more and more difficult for Adalgisa to comprehend: Her migraine had settled in, along with nausea, and she felt palpitations in her chest. Father José Antonio was also losing his grasp on things; "*Quid pro quo de lo copón divino,*" he said, mixing Portuguese and Spanish. "*Nadie* spoke in your name. *Fue* a written order."

The judge hesitated as he heard this absurdity: a dialogue of misunderstandings, a conversation of fools:

"A written order of mine? That's absurd! There's no such order!"

Father José Antonio held out his hand. "Where is the order, child?" he said in Spanish. "Give it to me."

Adalgisa took the photocopy out of her purse; the priest grabbed it, ran his eyes over it, and handed it to the judge. "A signed order. See for yourself."

Dr. Liberato Mendes Prado d'Ávila, His Honor the Chief Juvenile Judge for the District of Salvador, Capital of the State of Bahia, took the piece of paper, certain that he was dealing with a bunch of nuts—just as he had been since the night before. First Diana had been sprawled on the bed, her body wracked by spasms, howling as she begged forgiveness.

Now and then, confronted with flagrant evidence, she'd given bungled explanations, lame excuses, badly put together. She'd never asked for forgiveness before, since her husband was the only one to blame. Why was she begging him for forgiveness all of a sudden?

As the judge ran his eyes over the photocopy of the document, he frowned. The more he studied it, the more astonished he became. Its authenticity was absolute, undeniable. Dumbfounded, Dr. d'Ávila asked, "What is this? What does this mean?"

He stared at the photocopy again, studying every detail. Everything was correct—the paper, the stamp, the signature—and it was his signature, no doubt about it.

"Someone forged my signature." He raised his voice so he could be heard in the next room. "Mr. Macedo, come here, quickly."

Mr. Macedo, the clerk, ambled in slowly, dragging his feet, chewing on the stub of his cigar, stubbornly clearing his throat. He'd grown old in the courthouse, had served many judges, some better than others, some worse. But Dr. d'Ávila outdid the worst of them—he was a prick, in Mr. Macedo's expert opinion.

"Take a look at this, and tell me what's going on."

Mr. Macedo glanced at the document and found it in order; the only exception that could be taken to it was that it hadn't been drawn up during business hours. "Did you fill it out at home, or were you here last night?"

"Not at home and not here, nowhere. Somebody forged my signature." He stopped to look yet again at the photocopy. "A perfect forgery. I want to see the original. This piece of work was done by someone familiar with my signature, somebody with access to stamps, to official paper. Mr. Macedo, what have you got to say for yourself?"

"I've got nothing to say, judge, I know just as much about this as you do, no more, no less. I spent last night at home. I watched an eight o'clock program on television, then I went to bed. It seems that Tarcísio and Glória are going to get married . . ."

Knowing only too well that the judge was a master at creating confusion, was accustomed to making a fuss, Mr. Macedo wasn't upset that suspicion had been cast on him. Dr. d'Ávila was obviously up to one of his tricks—he had invented this chicanery of a forgery and was conducting an inquiry to fool these two suckers, the priest and the gorgeous babe. He practically licked Adalgisa with his eyes—that devil of a priest had it good, he thought. Those Jesuits dined well, on the best fare. Mr. Macedo turned, cleared his throat, and was about to go back into his office when the telephone rang. He answered, handed the receiver to His Honor:

"It's from the hospital."

⟿⟾

A Telephonic Interruption
for a Piece of
Auspicious News

The caller was Dona Olímpia de Castro, that most charming lady, with some good news. Our dear patient, our delicate girl, she said, is much better now—practically recovered. She'll be able to go home to-morrow.

Dona Olímpia's voice was habitually lax and sensual—a voice from the cunt, the poet Cid Seixas had versified in the throes of passion. Now it was melting into sugar, mellifluous, enwrapping. After an upset like that, her terrible crisis, the poor dear Diana needed a period of rest to help her forget, to let her recover her tranquillity and the joy of life. "Don't you think so, judge?" "Yes, of course," he replied.

Well, by happy coincidence, Dona Olímpia de Castro explained, she herself was just then making preparations to take a Caribbean cruise aboard a very modern Italian ship—twenty-five days of sea and tropical islands, with total relaxation. "What do you think, my dear judge?" "Why, it sounds fine to me."

Since he had agreed, Dona Olímpia said she would give the good news to the poor convalescent. It was superb that Dona Diana could join Dona Olímpia since her husband couldn't accompany her, she said, because of business—poor Astério, he had so much to do, he hadn't any time to relax!—and now she would have the company of her best friend. "Thank you so very much, judge!" and hung up. Dr. d'Ávila held the receiver to his ear, stunned. It took him a while to realize that he'd just give his wife, our poor girl, a cruise through the waters of the Caribbean, so she could recover from her upset, from her terrible crisis—but the cause of the crisis hadn't been revealed to him. Dona Olímpia had given him no explanation; nor did he expect to hear one from Diana. Diana had asked his forgiveness, but for what he didn't know. Was it worth knowing? Most certainly not!

Thoughtfully, the juvenile judge put down the phone and returned to the absurd nonsense, the brain-teaser: the photocopy of the release order signed by him sitting on his desk. Could he have been out of his mind, maybe?

Pathetically, Adalgisa stood up and interrupted his thoughts: "What about Manela, Your Honor? What's it going to be? Do you know where they took her? To the Candomblé do Gantois!"

The Carnival of the
French: A Brief Report

Nilda Spencer had promised Jacques Chancel that two to three thousand people would be gathered on Pelourinho for the improvised Carnival so that Antènne Deux could show the French people an authentic Bahian Carnival. But she'd been modest in her prediction. At least five thousand revelers were already dancing to Dodô and Osmar's music truck when Patrícia and Father Abelardo, after leaving the motorcycle in front of the old medical school, strolled down the Rua Alfredo de Brito on foot, making their way through the crowd. People were arriving from all over. The music truck had been set up at the top of the square, between the Municipal Museum and the Rosário dos Negros Church.

Before the facades of the big townhouses, a wooden platform had been erected, from which a camera was filming wide panoramic shots. Three cameras were circulating among the crowd, picking up details. Each detail would leave the French viewers open-mouthed, drooling.

On the Rua Gregório de Matos were concentrated the *afoxés* and the Afro groups, a good half dozen of them, each with its own powerful music and its radical negritude, the product of Brazilian miscegenation, unmistakable. In front of the headquarters of the Children of Gandhi *afoxé*, the glory of Bahian Carnival, its members were warming up: From within the building came the throbbing of drums. Participants from the Bloco do Jacu, wearing turquoise shrouds, were waiting, seated on the steps of the church. An enthusiastic group of girls from the drama school had joined them and were beginning to dance on the church steps. The people came down from Carmo and the Terreiro de Jesus, they came up from Taboão, they poured in from the Baixa dos Sapateiros. They came along already leaping and singing the songs of Gilberto Gil:

> Yansan, Yemanjá, call Xangô,
> Oxóssi, too, tell to come see
> Children of Gandhi,
> Oh, Father in Heaven,
> It's carnival on earth. . . .

Accompanied by Nilda Spencer, Jacques Chancel surveyed the various groups and decided on the sequence of the parade, unable to contain his excitement. The only sad note was the absence of Sylvia Esmeralda; he'd counted on seeing her in a wrap-around, showing off her body today. He asked Patrícia about her after she'd settled the priest in by the music truck among the high-ranking figures, including the French consul, Jacques Falah, the Portuguese poet and journalist Fernando Assis

Pacheco, the American Frances Switt, and several other foreigners then came over to join the team.

"*Où est Sylvie? Je ne la vois pas.*"

"*Elle est malade.*"

"*Comment, malade? Quel dommage! Moi qui avais pensé faire la fête avec elle—la fête du carnaval, bien sûr.*"

"*Seulement du carnaval?*" Patrícia hinted maliciously.

Nilda Spencer exploded in laughter, and the Frenchman couldn't help swinging his hips.

"*Elle est si belle. . . .*"

The two belles laughed in merriment—but shouldn't they be weeping over their friend's misfortune? Poor Sylvia. When she finds out that Jacques Chancel, the head of the production, a celebrity, charming and sought-after, for whom she'd sighed, languid and romantic, and offered herself—that none other than he had missed her at the moment they started shooting and had said, loud and clear, that he intended to *faire la fête avec elle, faire la bombe* . . . She might die of sadness when she hears, the unfortunate Sylvia. Why did she have to get sick on Carnival day?

Improvised, staged, directed, the Carnival broadcast on the *Le Grand Échiquier* segment dedicated to Bahia was worth all the money spent, all the effort expended. It was a splendor of music and dance—the costumes, the beautiful women, the *samba*, the *frevo*, the groups, the *afoxés*, the embassies from African kingdoms, the magical movement of people in both individual and collective festivity. The foreigners were being treated to a spectacle that had no equal anywhere.

They watched the parade of the Children of Gandhi, grand in their austere white, with Gandhi in front leading the goat. They saw the Bloco do Jacu pass, *há-ja-cu-no-pau;* they were singing, the shrouded girls and the ones with open skirts, derrieres on display. At the head of the girls came the composer Waltinho Queiroz, marking the rhythm, and at his side was Luz de Serra, his mother, letting everything out; she looked more like his sister. They saw Georges Moustaki, a Greek from Alexandria, a Parisian from the Île Saint Louis, a Carnival Bahian with a thin cotton wrap around his body, hugging and kissing Marlene de Costa, who was more naked even than the girls from the drama school. They saw coming down the Largo do Pelourinho, led by President Rubinho, the Internationals, parading to music by Vinícius de Moraes that had been composed especially for the group *hors concours*. They saw this, that, and the other, and the cameras recorded the explosion of joy and freedom. Some of the more observant television viewers would catch a brief glimpse of Father Abelardo Galvão, casually perched up on the music truck platform, holding a tambourine, his eyes fastened on Patrícia down below.

Around the music truck Patrícia was passing from arm to arm, the camera accompanying her steps, documenting the dance that extended out from her and was multiplied into thousands of dancing and acrobatic feet. The French would see her, Indian, black, and white: The Dutch girl Patrícia da Silva Vaalserberg, the Baiana Patrícia das Flores, an exuberant mulatto girl.

At a certain moment they would catch her in a panoramic shot and then in a close-up, as a space opened up and she was engulfed in the admiration of the people. There, to their clapping, she could dance all by herself. Camafeu de Oxóssi, one of the Children of Gandhi, in the supreme elegance of his *afoxé* costume, was beating on a matchbox and imitating a master of ceremonies, while Patrícia, the standard-bearer, queen of the Bahian Carnival, was twirling in the most difficult of dance steps, exaggerating the cadence, swaying her hips in the dance, the *samba* in her feet, knocking herself out so that the French would understand what Carnival, the greatest festival of the Brazilian people, was like. And so that, up by Dodô and Osmar's music truck, her handsome and virgin priest would see her and desire her.

Euclidian Epic

Relating Zé do Lírio's marathon in Pelourinho is a narrative task worth of a Homer, a Shakespeare, or an Euclides da Cunha, in partnership with a Dostoyevsky or Gogol: a Greek tragedy and a Russian novel. Too heavy a task it is for the slovenly, sloppy scribbling of an obscure troubador of roundels, with rhymes in -*ão* and -*ado*, this Bahian author of popular literature. Lacking the grandeur of *aedos*, not to speak of the psychological refinement of the intimists, their brilliance of style, their artistic quality, all the anonymous pamphleteer has is the fearless courage of an ignoramus—he goes limping along with only that.

For an eternity, for two hours amid the Carnival hubbub, the turmoil, all those naked women offering themselves, gross and shamefully whoring themselves, Zé do Lírio, sometimes hurriedly, sometimes slowly and introspectively, was accompanied by fear, danger, slavery, and death. He drew up plans, analyzed their details, committed abuses, broke laws, reflected, imagined, was jailed, was subjected to a verdict and sentenced, went down to the depths of hell, was killed and saw himself dead.

His struggle to overcome his difficulties had already begun in front of the drama school, when the son-of-a-bitch stiff-collar had climbed up behind the crazy girl on the motorcycle, gotten a grip on her, and taken off like a shot. Zé do Lírio had caught a taxicab on Campo Grande to follow them, but the bike was already long gone, impossible to catch. The driver calmed him down: "Take it easy—they're on their way to the Carnival on Pelourinho." God certainly does help his own, because the taxi dropped Zé do Lírio off in time for him to see the two lunatics climb up onto the music truck. The wild girl came right back down again, leaving the stiff-collar among the big-shots. A more womanizing priest he'd never seen—not content even with Colonel Costa's married daughter, even if she was a little chubby.

Seeing him settled in, Zé do Lírio went about studying the terrain and the conditions, so he could carry out his job at just the right moment. A mark can't be sent off to the land of stiffs just like that; in complicated cases like this one, he had to plan carefully, using mathematical precision.

First he thought he'd shoot the priest while he was up on the music truck—it would be easy to take aim at him from any second-story window in the surrounding buildings. Zé do Lírio had even found the ideal spot: the room on the upper floor of the Municipal Museum where a sensational collection of Baiana torsos was on display, more than three hundred of them. He'd gone into the museum through the side door while the museum officials, male and female, were gathered on the walk in front of the main entrance, joining in the revelry. From a slit he opened in the window, the assassin admired the disheveled locks of the priest close by, making a perfect target. Perfect hell—it was damned risky! In spite of the complete certainty of his aim, all Zé do Lírio needed was for the poor bastard to shift a few inches, and someone innocent would drop in his place. Besides, the other idlers wouldn't stop moving around—they kept changing position, swapping places. As easy as it seemed, Zé do Lírio knew it was also impossible. He left the Municipal Museum the way he'd gone in, sneakily, taciturn.

He studied other routes, but he couldn't find one that was workable; all were risky, offering no guarantee of success. Zé do Lírio might find himself with another mistaken corpse on his hands: One was a heavy enough burden to bear, and he hadn't the strength for two. After a lot of reflection, he came to the conclusion that he had no other choice but to accept the worst, the danger of getting caught red-handed. The worst had happened once, but Colonel Ulisses Cardoso, who'd given him his order and who in fact gave all the orders in the state of Alagoas, an honest man, had come to get him out of jail as soon as he found out about the blunder that the police had committed. Today the experienced and crafty Zé do Lírio easily recognized several policemen concealed in doorways who were every bit as interested in the priest as he was. As soon as he arrived he'd recognized Inspector Parreirinha: He didn't know his name, but he'd never forgotten that imbecilic face. But even though he was surrounded by cops, running a great risk of getting busted, facing a trial, and getting sent up for thirty years, he had to fulfill his contract. He couldn't let his name and honor as a reliable man be the object of public scorn.

He was a reliable man, an upstanding, competent, and let it be added, patient professional. If he weren't upstanding, competent, and patient, that holy Joe of a priest would escape with his life, as jaunty and pleased with himself as ever. The gunman stationed himself behind the music truck, his eyes on his prey, prepared to wait as long as it was necessary. A fellow Pernambucan, a halfbreed, had climbed up onto a donkey to get a better look at the scene. Yes, the priest was sitting high and mighty up there on the truck with their lordships, but when he came down, Zé do Lírio would open fire and then get the hell out: If he could make it to the Ladeira do Ferrão, he'd be home free. He girded himself with patience and restraint, took the liberty of a few quick glances at naked bellies and thighs, round breasts, and red-ant asses. But as a person of responsibility, he spent most of his time watching the condemned man.

The festivities stretched all the way from the cathedral to the Carmelite convent. Two more music trucks had appeared on the street of their own accord, without any invitation or contract; one parked on the corner of the Rua Alfredo de Brito, the other by the entrance to the Ladeira do Taboão. *Ranchos, afoxés,* and Afro-groups that had not been in the planning for in the production now showed up, coming spontaneously to take part in the revelry. Worth mentioning among them were the Baron's Block, the Apaches of Tororó, the Owl Block, the Olodum, the Merchants of Baghdad, the Youth of Garcia. With their habitual albeit not excessive tendency to exaggeration, the reporters later calculated that ten thousand merrymakers had kept on *samba*-ing until early morning; they hadn't come because of the television cameras, they'd come from the seven gates of the city to join in the Carnival.

In order to convey some idea of the success of the Frenchmen's Carnival—an expression we have stolen from a column written by the poet (encore!) Rui Espinheira Filho—it's sufficient to repeat the official figure given to the press, a precise number. Of the more than two thousand members of the Children of Gandhi *afoxé* who usually paraded at Carnival, five hundred ninety-seven answered their leaders' call today. To complete our information, let us quote Tereza de Mayo, indeed plagiarize what she wrote that Sunday in her column in *Sete Dias:* "Pelourinho was transformed into a stormy sea of dance, a tempestuous ocean of breasts and bare hips, a hallucinated, surrealist utopia, while eternal France, the France of Voltaire and Sartre, was bowing low to Brazil once more." It was a succulent description, adorned with all the pomp of fantasy and erudition and a touch of justified chauvinism. Well put, Terezinha.

The crowd reached the height of its delirium when the cameras, taking their last shots, documented the unequaled splendor of the parade of the Children of Gandhi; Jacques Chancel, in the first row, embracing the *afoxé*'s president. It was then that Patrícia went to get Father Abelardo so they could celebrate together amid all the people; until that moment she'd been working and he'd only been watching. Waving to catch his eye, shouting so he could hear her, she told him to come down. Zé do Lírio stirred, moving away from the stocky man who'd dismounted from his donkey and, sitting on the curb, dozed off. Only a migrant from the backlands could fall asleep in the midst of a masquerade! The donkey was chewing on a colored poster that had been pulled off the wall. The people, all roused up by the parade of the Children of Gandhi, were cheering.

Zé do Lírio gripped the .38-caliber Taurus revolver in the pocket of his raincoat. He had six shots, and all he needed was a firm hand, unerring aim, and unswerving faith in God. Good-bye, you stinking little priest, your final hour has come! Take your leave of your life and your hot box—you won't be doing any *samba* with her, you won't be screwing her in your excommunicated bed—it's all over for you. No more dividing up other people's land, or feeling up a woman's breasts—priests weren't made for that. So long, you stinking little stiff-collar—who told you to screw around, anyway?

Father Abelardo had come down from the music truck holding a tambourine and Patrícia put her arm around his waist. Zé do Lírio came forward, aimed his revolver at the back of the doomed man's neck from a yard away, and pulled the trigger. But someone bumped his arm—it leaped like a broken spring—and the bullet sped off toward the horizon. Zé do Lírio turned around, ready to liquidate the brazen person who had dared to push his elbow. But he saw no one except the dozing man and the donkey, who was busy chewing the printed paper, tasty and nutritious as it was.

The couple was still dancing a Carnival step, and Zé do Lírio had no time to figure out what had happened. He forced his way through the crowds and took aim at the head of the lewd priest,—but once more his arm shook, and the bullet disappeared into the air. The same thing happened on his third, fourth, and fifth tries, until there was only one bullet left in the revolver. Zé do Lírio was going slightly crazy.

A man from the backlands like Zé do Lírio may die, he may kill himself if necessary, but he doesn't become discouraged. Because a man from the backlands, as Euclides wrote, has first of all his courage. Zé do Lírio saved the last bullet for himself. Realizing that the priest had a pact with the devil, he sat down on the curb to make himself more comfortable. He missed his wife, Índia Momi, a good woman who could cast a spell and at the same time a ball of fire in the hammock of sleep and desire. He aimed the Taurus revolver at his chest, at the exact spot where his disconcerted stout heart was beating hard, bade farewell to life, to Pernambuco, that land of brave men. He pulled the trigger, felt the blood flow, staining his raincoat, considered himself dead, laid his body down, and pounded the sidewalk. What he didn't realize was that the dampness was coming not from blood pouring out of his wounded heart but from dirty water coming out of the barrel of the revolver. The Taurus had been turned into a child's plaything.

The Migrant and His Donkey

The halfbreed migrant who'd been dozing next to his donkey up till then got up quickly—he was in a hurry. Short and stocky, he had long arms like a monkey. He easily picked up the gunman and placed him over the large, worn packsaddle in a huge lump. He patted the donkey with its clumsy bundle and led it down the steep slippery Ladeira do Ferrão at a trot. At a bus station where the Recife connection takes on passengers, he deposited Zé do Lírio, who at this moment was coming back from the other world, on the bus.

Dom Maximiliano von Gruden had seen the halfbreed, leading his slow, peaceful donkey going down the Ladeira da Preguiça, on his way back to the museum. In fact, on that afternoon a lot of people saw him without giving it any thought, and if anyone did pay any attention to him, it was to chuckle at the comic figure, the familiar figure of a northeastern backlands farmer exiled to the state capital by the drought that had killed his livestock and children. If he'd had a long beard, he could have been taken for a holy man from the backlands of Canudos, a comrade of Antônio Conselheiro. If a weapon had been hanging from the packsaddle atop his sluggish donkey, he could have been a bandit, perhaps a survivor of Virgulino Ferreira Lampião's band. He could have been a pilgrim from the backlands of Cariri, a devotee of Father Cícero Romão, the holy godfather and patron. Or he could have been a canecutter, a riverbank dweller from the São Francisco, a gatherer of dendê, piassava, and carnauba palm; and if he'd worn a leather hat, he could have been a drover from the brush country, an accordion player, or a dancer at peasant feasts, of mixed blood; he had the face of a Sergipean votive offering.

He was, in fact, a fearless northeasterner, audacious and brave, with his curmudgeon of a donkey little larger than a goat. Those rare people who know about the *padê*, who can read the *taramesso*, the ones from Ifá's mat, the sorcerers, those who know all waters, the confirmed, the

babalaôs and the *eluôs*, the *akirijebôs*, the comrades of the Comrade—
they and only they knew that the thick-set man dressed in a faded and
tattered jacket that reached down to his knees, wearing rope-soled sandals, smoking a homemade cigarette, with cane liquor on his breath, was
Exu Malé, the adjunct, the partisan, the milk-brother of Yansan who
came in answer to her call.

As the mulatto and the donkey walked up the Ladeira do Papagaio
in Rio Vermelho, a worn and ancient leather strap could be seen on top
of the packsaddle.

Becalmed

The Invincible Armada proceeded down the River Paraguaçu with
the rhythm of a celebration. The serene waters carried the sloops, the
launches, the schooners amidst religious and profane chanties, Carnival
sambas, church hymns, and protest songs, several of which were forbidden by the censorship and condemned by the regime:

> Going against the wind
> No scarf, no documents,
> The sun looks down on crime
> Spaceships and guerrilla war . . .

There were twenty-eight vessels all told, their sails puffed, multicolored banners on their masts, a few of them cloth, most of them
made of wrapping paper. The river breeze respected them. As it passed
by river ports, the expedition was greeted by people gathered on the
shore. In certain river villages processions were held, and litanies were
prayed for the success of the rescue.

When the Invincible Armada entered the waters of the Bay of All
Saints at the end of the afternoon, however, and became visible from the
islands where people were also gathering in solidarity with it, the unexpected happened. A complete, absolute calm fell over the waters, not a
breath of wind stirred them, and the sea became like a blue-green carpet,
so still and flat that it looked as if a person could walk on it. An ill-
omened silence descended over the boats.

How long were they going to be halted on the water? They had to
land at the market ramp before nightfall if they were to make it to the
rally at the Santa Tereza convent, near the entrance to the Museum of
Sacred Art, just at the moment when the director was receiving the
governor and the cardinal for the opening of the exhibit. "The Saint

Belongs to Us"—they were carrying twelve banners and fifty-two signs. Would they get there in time?

"We're licked, Father Téo. This calm could last for days." The fiery Guido Guerra was suddenly dejected.

"Be quiet, man of little faith. Saint Barbara of the Thunder won't permit that to happen. It's just a passing calm; the wind will be coming up soon, just enough." The vicar was trying to bolster people's spirits, but he too had lost his euphoria.

That was when they heard an ancient song, born in slave quarters, coming from the sloop *Night Flower,* carrying the little old ladies of the Sisterhood of Our Lady of the Good Death:

Saint Barbara of the Thunder
Lend me three little pennies
Of lightning and thunder
To buy my freedom with
Saint Barbara of the Thunder

Dona Canô, mother of music and poetry, improvised:

Saint Barbara of the Thunder
Give me three pennies of wind
With lightning and thunder
Put an end to this calm. . . .

The chorale took shape, covered the sea, the green-blue mantle, and rose up to the sky. Wherever she was, doing whatever she was doing, Saint Barbara of the Thunder finally heard and paid heed. If anyone has doubts this happened and wishes to wager, then put up your money—the challenge is accepted. The winner eats for free, and the loser pays for the fireworks.

—&—&

The Merry Troupe

Adalgisa received complete satisfaction. When she left the juvenile court, she was carrying a new order from His Honor Dr. d'Ávila giving her control over Manela, her niece and ward, and returning her to the Cloister of the Penitents in the Convent of the Immaculate Conception.

There Manela would remain until her guardian—and no one else—came to take her out. Along with Father José Antonio, two bailiffs in the service of the court accompanied her. Their mission was to see that the order was carried out, for better or for worse, using the strength of the law—and the police, if necessary. The bailiffs would be there to help, in case the slightest resistance—obstructions, arguments, protests—was offered on the part of the Gantois people, or the *candomblé* niggerdom, as the juvenile judge put it.

They got off the bus at the corner of the Avenida Cardeal da Silva, a symbolic name, and walked in the direction of the slope leading up to the Largo de Pulquéria where, modest and majestic, the Ilê Iyá Omim Axé Iyamansê rises, the house of the Candomblé do Gantois. Happier even than Adalgisa, Father José Antonio was glowing. Euphoric, his belly full of food and satisfaction, he kept kissing the crucifix that hung down on a long silver chain over his well-tailored black cassock. A dandy, was Father José Antonio Hernández. In his youth in Seville the young cleric of military bearing had participated in Falange parades, and he had aroused passions: Two devout women, one a wealthy widow in her forties, the other a young girl, had sighed over him—the adolescent suicidally; so had a bullfighter of celebrated bravery and notorious faggotry. While the girl had threatened to kill herself by swallowing her breviary, the Balzacian woman had lured him with presents; the glorious *maricón*—who'd vanquished dozens of defenseless bulls in the arena—visited him in the sacristy, swiveling his hips and making indecorous propositions, even trying to kiss him on the mouth.

Our devotion to truth—the guiding principle of this Bahian chronicle and perhaps its only virtue—demands that we reveal that this flourishing and pampered Falangist, obsessed with his Holy Mother Church and the Generalissimo, has rejected these three lovesick creatures, the two females in heat and the mad matador. If anything sexual happened with the cleric, if there were any stain, it was only in his dreams, a venial sin that a little soap and an Our Father would wash away without leaving a mark on the sheet or a blot on the soul.

José Antonio had been deaf to the girl's hints (for words that are crazy, ears that are hazy), was indignant at the widow's advances and rejected them, albeit without refusing, out of courtesy, her presents: silk pajamas, blue and yellow shorts, bottles of perfume, the silver cord with the vermeil crucifix—it was worth a fortune, perhaps, but not enough to corrupt him. It had been more difficult to spurn the fatal passion of the matador, because for a long time the young braggart José Antonio, a fanatical frequenter of bullfights, had idolized El Rijoso. He had tried without success to develop a comradely relationship with the matador, but the depraved El Rijoso was fierce and demanding—all or nothing, *camaradería un cuerno!* Disappointed, he went off to fight bulls in Mexico, where he fell in with a mustachioed mariachi musician, *pendenciero y malo, olvidando el amor sacrílego.* Father José Antonio's pure virtue had survived intact.

Tagging along behind the priest and the milliner were two cops. The mulatto Joselito Massaranduba was one, a gentleman on in years, the father of numerous progeny, and an *ogan* of Oxóssi in the Ilê Ogunjá; the other was pale Paulo Cotovia, still a bachelor although engaged, an amateur musician, a drummer, in his free time. Adalgisa and Father José Antonio were busy talking about the strange confusion of the release order with the judge's forged signature. According to the priest there was no mystery behind it; the inquiry would confirm His Honor's suspicions.

Dr. d'Ávila had made no secret of the fact that he suspected the clerk. Mr. Macedo had access to the judge's chambers at any time, and to sealed paper and stamps; he was familiar with the judge's signature, all the easier to forge it. All that remained to be cleared up was who had put him up to it, and how much he had been paid.

Gildete was unquestionably the culprit, Adalgisa panted. That *candomblé* woman, along with Danilo, had put up the money, the gratuity—they'd paid for the forgery. The most likely possibility was that that viper was a friend of that Macedo. These riffraff all knew each other, and they stuck together in all their escapades, Adalgisa explained.

Prattling like that, they approached the Candomblé do Gantois. On the Avenida Cardeal da Silva they spotted a stocky stranger approaching, leading his donkey by the bridle.

Adarrum

Toward the end of the afternoon of that Friday of unleashed passions, the antennae of Bahian television stations, whose towers rise up in the neighborhood of the Largo da Pulquéria, picked up the sound of the *adarrum*. Resonating, it summoned the *orixás* to the first stop at the ports of initiation, on the ship of *iaôs* anchored at the Candomblé do Gantois.

Of great magnitude and mystery, the call was all-powerful. Transmitted by satellite, it resounded from north to south, east to west, from the coast to the swamp, and across the seas. From continent to continent, from country to country, it was heard across all frontiers. What signal, never heard before, was suddenly vibrating on all channels? Where was it coming from, what message did it convey, what blessing or disaster did it presage, what tidings did it forebode?

Gathering in congresses, assemblies, seminars, and councils, the most notable scientists were split along their favorite ideological lines, placed as always in the service of power. Or more precisely, in the service of those who held power. The wise men of the West, patrons of retrograde and reactionary western civilization, declared that the signal had been sent from the planet Jupiter. The sages of the East, preachers of the civilization of bureaucratic and authoritarian socialism, disagreed in chapter and verse: The signal was coming from Neptune. Erudite communications and classic insults were exchanged.

The debate grew heated, and the crossfire between Washington and Moscow, between right and left, was intensified. A liberal coalition was formed, with two principal wings: that of center-right, that of center-left. A violent radical manifesto attracted various extremist tendencies ready for armed conflict with either Jupiter or Neptune, it didn't matter which. Dissidence grew, thousands of books were written—the presses groaned, publishing them in Roman, Slavic, Arabic, Hebrew characters, and in Chinese, Japanese, Korean ideograms—films were made, videotapes, cassettes, and computer programs. An unknown group of Sino-Japanese theoreticians announced, to worldwide acclaim, the subtle theory that the signal originated from Pluto, the symbiosis of Buddha and Marx.

In Africa, Cuba, and Haiti, the *orixás* heard the call of the *adarrum*, left their good life, the hunt, the bath in the river, the gathering of jungle leaves, the stroking of heads, the game of moaning without feeling pain, and crossed the sky, heading toward the land of Bahia.

The War Upstairs

At the sound of the *adarrum*, the migrant halfbreed patted the donkey and quickened his pace, approaching the respectable troupe bent on carrying out the moralizing mission ordered by the juvenile judge. Traffic was heavy on the Avenida Cardeal da Silva; cars were whizzing by at top speed. Paying no attention to traffic laws, the man and his donkey suddenly began to dance like two mad creatures.

As soon as Mr. Joselito Massaranduba and young Paulo Cotovia came face to face with the strange man-and-donkey pair, they lost their serious mood. They began to spin about, doing the same saraband—they were obviously familiar with it. Father José Antonio didn't recognize the pagan character of the swaying, which was in fact a hex dance, a proper greeting for Exu, the prankster: *Laroiê!* Even so, he grew indignant as he witnessed the degrading scene: two servants of the law lapsing into debauchery in the middle of a public thoroughfare, in the company of a vagrant. And what was there to say about the ass? Who'd ever heard of a waltzing donkey? Furthermore, the dancing was disrupting traffic, forcing vehicles to slow down, brake suddenly, turn, and skid.

"What's the meaning of this? *¿Qué hacen ustedes?*" He was getting his languages mixed up, a dead giveaway that sudden disorder and brash behavior had rattled him.

The migrant, the comrade, the northeasterner of the crossroads, Exu Malé, black urchin, opened his mouth wide and showed his glowing metal tongue, to provoke the respectable priest. "Be gone!" the worthy man exclaimed, offended. The donkey replied with a barrage of farts, while Exu turned to Adalgisa. Confronting her, eye to eye: Elegbará's eyes were two hot coals. Adalgisa gave the first shudder that announced the coming of the *orixá;* she raised her hand to her mouth and called for help: "Save me, Mother of God, help me, Father in heaven!"

The opponents were arrayed against each other in the immense struggle sung of by the poet Castro Alves, of fanaticism and tolerance, prejudice and knowledge, of racism and mingling, of tyranny and freedom in the fight between the *abicun* and the *orixá,* in the war of Upstairs. This battle is joined everywhere in the world, at every instant. To this day there's no end in sight.

The onslaught was swift. Drivers and passengers continued indifferently along their way in their speeding cars without realizing that there on the Avenida Cardeal da Silva, which bears the name of that indomitable sectarian and rigid guardian of dogma, at the bottom of the Largo de Pulquéria, which in turn commemorates the *iyalorixá* born a slave, caretaker of the enchanted ones in the persecuted religion, a poverty-stricken and sweet creature, meanness and grandness were confronting each other, yesterday and tomorrow, the vocation of death and the joy of living. Fighting on the side of obscurantism was Father José Antonio Hernández, the Falangist, the swastika guts, the anathema mouth, the atomic balls. Fighting the guerrilla warfare of humanism were the three *orixás* from Africa, Oxóssi, Xangô, and Exu Malé. In their mad whirl of running after money, the passersby passed blindly with the urgency of getting somewhere—anywhere—as quickly as possible. Only a girl, Rosane Novoa, a secretary, at the wheel of her thirdhand jalopy, slow and steady, asked her husband why in the devil that priest at the roadside was in such a fury, clutching a crucifix and running toward a lady on her knees. Her Humberto had no idea, and couldn't care less.

Mr. Joselito and young Cotovia, Oxóssi and Xangô, the lover and the husband, danced around Adalgisa in steps of greeting and reception. They offered her invitations for the *caruru* announced for the market in the lower city. Adalgisa twisted and bit her mouth, her eyes glittered: She'd stopped seeing the sunlit afternoon around her and sensed only the breaking of dawn, the morning of birth. Her lips mumbled inaudibly, as the *abicun* gave three leaps into the air, each one higher than the one before. Father José Antonio, astonished, lifted the crucifix over his head, shouted in Spanish, his voice loud with fright and condemnation,

"*¿Qué te pasa, hija? ¡Contrólate, desgraciada!*"

The anointed, illuminated Spanish woman did try to control herself; the Catholic woman of the Holy Inquisition did try to shake off her trance, to escape the saint. She ran her hands over her body, from top to bottom, as if to push away the force of the *orixá*, to deny him passage through her. Adalgisa, there at the side of the road, tried to slam shut the door that had been opened when her mother had embarked on her initiation without imagining that she was carrying Paco Negreiro's daughter in her belly.

"*¡Espera, hija! ¡Voy a librarte del demonio! ¡Ahora mismo!*"

Adalgisa fell to her knees, her hands outstretched, her arms lifted up to heaven. Above all, she didn't want to cease being a lady. Gripping the vermeil Christ, Father José Antonio hastened to exorcise her:

"Get thee behind me, Satan!"

Satan didn't get behind him—on the contrary—he didn't obey the command at all. Seven Leaps, the migrant man, swiftly fell onto the exorcist, accompanied by his dancing donkey. The stocky man brandished the leather strap that he'd taken off the harness, as the jackass danced to the rhythm of a *paso doble*, farting, shitting, and kicking. In his attempt to escape the whip, Father José Antonio received a poorly shod hoof on his rear end, and the donkey, satisfied no doubt, opened his lips, showed his teeth, and brayed, sacrilegious and brazen. The priest was stretched out in the shrubbery on the avenue's divider. Up ahead Adalgisa was prostrate, her exhausted body stretched out, her head bursting with the headache that was about to leave her forever. Her breathing was rapid, and her heart of stone was bleeding. It was hard to believe!

Later it came to be known that on that occasion Father José Antonio Hernández—a hero of the mouth, a coward in the guts—hadn't been born for martyrdom, refused to sacrifice himself. He raised his arms in surrender at the approach of the three demons, who no doubt were to put an end to him. He knew that Communists were accustomed to gelding priests before killing them; Father José Antonio wanted to save his life and, if possible, keep himself intact, even if he never used his balls properly and pleasurably, except perhaps in dreams. For him demons, Communists, *orixás*, and hippies were all one and the same.

Those fearsome assassins, playful and somewhat unruly *orixás*, encircled him, laughing. They contented themselves with just a small bit of mockery: In the blink of an eye they undressed him and took his shoes off, leaving him stark naked except for his dirty socks and the silver cord with the vermeil Christ. Then Exu Malé gave him a whack on his skinny behind and sent him packing.

Father José Antonio tumbled down the slope, scratching himself on the thorns of the hedge planted with various ginger lilies and touch-me-nots, of red and yellow blooms. Falling and getting up, he crossed the Avenida Garibaldi and came out on Ondina, where passersby shouted:

"Look at the naked priest!" He found refuge in the house of Dr. Carlos Mascarenhas, a millionaire—nicknamed Carlinhos Ukelele and Carlinhos Cat-Paw, owing to his skills with orchestras and with a deck of cards. Carlinhos recognized the collector of alms, and even though he didn't have a high opinion of him, he welcomed him in lordly fashion, inviting him to join him in his late afternoon Scotch and soda:

"Are you playing Adam, my good Father? Running away from a cuckolded husband? Was the generous lady worth the trouble?" He raised his glass in homage to the aforementioned generous lady.

So that Father José Antonio could get back to his church without being spotted by urchins, Carlinho loaned him the wrap he'd worn in the last Carnival—the black shroud of a poor dead man, a white skull in the middle of the chest. He also gave the priest a pair of dark glasses to hide his face.

The Ark of the Alliance,
or *Oxumarê*, the Rainbow

The three enchanted ones took the packsaddle off the back of the donkey and put it on Adalgisa, who was twisting in the pain of the *abicun*. A bit large on top of her hips, the saddle lent even greater beauty to Dadá's behind, the tail that Danilo has sighed after.

At the *peji* of Gantois, in the secret chamber of those to be initiated, Yansan had just mounted Manela, a beautiful *iaô*, a fiery colt. There would be uncontrollable madness in the circle of initiates when this one made her appearance.

Having established her rights on Manela's head, her steed confirmed, Oyá left her resting, lying on the mat, her head shaved, her face painted blue and white, on her ankles the *xaorôs* of subjection. Yansan smiled tenderly, and only then did she announce herself on the avenue with a flash of lightning, the war cry, and thunder. She leaped beyond the television towers, landing on Adalgisa. Then she ordered Exu Malé to place a saddle on the rebel and mounted her that way, fulfilling her promise of long ago. The only reason she didn't use spurs was the single tear the otherwise heartless guardian had shed when she left Manela at the Cloister of the Penitents.

Forty years after she had been made a saint soon after her conception in the womb of Andreza, her mother, Adalgisa abandoned her clandestine state of *abicun* to take on the glorious role of a daughter of Oyá Yansan. She became the Yansan of the Saddle, cited so often in the oral annals of *candomblé*. In her hand, instead of the *eiru*, she held a leather strap—the very same one.

Oxumarê—the rainbow, the two-headed snake, Saint Bartholomew with his trident, ark of the alliance—stretched out its solar spectrum in the skies of Bahia and opened the seven-colored fan, the road of mystery. The donkey was the first to set out along that way, kicking the air. According to certain mediocre chronicles of scant inspiration, this was the same ass mentioned in the New Testament that the Holy Family rode on their flight into Egypt. Perhaps it was the Maître Âne of Perrault, the legendary ass that shat not dung but shiny gold coins, because on the ground on Cardeal da Silva, in the midst of the donkey manure, three copper coins were found, one of twenty and two of ten *réis*.

Inseparable, Oxóssi and Xangô, Yansan's two loves, entered the rainbow through the blue-green and red and white doors. Together they left for the jungle, the desert, the river, the capitals of Africa, Lagos, Luanda, Praia, Porto Novo, the Gulf of Benin, and the lands of Aioká. They went off singing a *frevo* by Caetano:

> If you've split it in two,
> you've learned
> that it comes from the other side
> of the side
> that's beyond the side
> that's beyond
> the side that's beyond. . . .

Mr. Joselito Massaranduba and young Paulo Cotovia now found themselves all alone on the avenue. What had become of the prudish priest, they wondered, sweet music on the outside, stale bread on the inside, and the still-tempting woman clutching his cassock? It didn't bother them that the two zealots had taken off without saying good-bye —they were accustomed to dealing with inconsiderate, stingy people— not even a thank you or a few coins to wet their whistle. Mr. Joselito, having been invited to Jacira's *caruru*—she was a good friend of his— dragged his colleague along to have some fun:

"It's going to be a humdinger!"

Laroiê! There went Exu with a somersault, shutting the door to the rainbow behind him.

Oyá had already gone in and out of the city, packsaddle on her back. *Eparrei!*

The Caruru

From the Terreiro de Jesus to the Largo do Carmo, in the historical center of the city, the Carnival of the French burned until dawn. The last revelers stopped dancing only when the morning bar was taken off the rainbow door to brighten a hallelujah Saturday.

The French themselves, by the way, had left around five in the afternoon, right after the last takes. They'd gotten great shots—the immense panoramas of the crowds *samba*-ing, and the close-ups of Patrícia's bare body, challenging, panting, offering itself opposite Father Abelardo Galvão, who had been forced into the Carnival in the throes of agony.

Leaving their television equipment at the hotel, the foreigners all accepted the insistent invitation and rushed to the *caruru* of Jacira do Odô Oyá at the Santa Barbara market. Miro took on the job of transporting them. Everyone attended, from the boss, Chancel, down to the young man with curly hair and an earring who looked like a fairy but maybe wasn't.

Jacira's *caruru* wasn't being held for any special reason that came to mind. She wasn't making good on any promise, she wasn't proposing an *ebó*; it was simply to honor Yansan, the patroness of the market, the saint of the stalls. Euá was on his way after bathing in the fountains, cisterns, and pools of the city and at the springs on Itaparica.

The *eluô,* coming from the festival at Gantois two nights before, had whispered to Jacira that the enchanted one would be in the city on a visitation, busy with some important work. The one who whispered was in the know—she wasn't just anybody, one of the usual gossips of the *candomblé* houses. A *caruru* would be a fine pretext for Jacira to gather her friends, good friend that she was, and to greet Oyá, her mother, to whom she gave full credit for everything good that happened to her in business and in love. She invited everybody and his cousin to attend.

And it was a worthy *caruru,* complete with twelve grosses of okra. The stall owners chipped in to buy the ingredients, and the drink stands furnished cases of beer. Dr. Zezé Catarino, a well-to-do attorney, came with quarts of *batidas* ordered from Vilar and Deolino, suppliers to the market. These cocktails were made with lime, coconut, cherry, plum, and tangerine, and there was nothing sour about their abundance, diversity, and quality. The lawyer's wife, Dona Regi, a wealthy *grande dame,* was also a daughter of Yansan. A confirmed saint, she honored Yansan at her home every December 4 with superb food, caviar, and champagne at a dinner for select guests. Yansan didn't disdain the honor just because it came from a rich white woman—she cultivated no prejudices.

Jacira de Odô Oyá didn't have enough fingers to count her friends on. She had good friends not just among simple folk who earned their daily bread by the sweat of their brow, bosom friends, her equals—but also among the high circles of finance and politics, and among intellectuals. Before she took over the booth at the market in the lower city, Jacira had managed a discreet house in Amaralina. She'd inherited the shop from her only brother, a bachelor, a wastrel who had been shot to death in a brawl during a night of carousing.

The *caruru* was so well attended, it would be easier to list who *wasn't* at Jacira's revels. It just isn't possible to include the names of all the grand dukes and duchesses who licked their lips there—and the *caruru* couldn't have been more delicious if it had been put together by the blessed hands of Anália de Yemanjá. Everyone was sipping *batidas,* chatting, laughing, and having a good time. Let the list here be limited, then, to the few names of characters whom we have already mentioned in these memoirs of Yansan's visitation to her city of Bahia.

In an animated conversation with Jacques Chancel, our dear and always welcome Professor João Batista was making use of his purest French. In spite of his Sergipe pronunciation, he explained the *caruru,* *vatapá,* chicken *xinxim, quitandê,* and other delicacies of Afro-Bahian

cuisine with great expertise. The art critic Antônio Celestino was escorting and caressing two excellent female curators—women with great
minds and great bodies—as well as another who just had a good body.
Lacking a university degree to display, she was showing her tail, which
was worthy of any honor, including that of doctor *honoris causa.* In the
entourage of the nobleman from São João del Rei was found the Portuguese poet Fernando Assis Pacheco, a man fascinated with Bahian customs, indeed seduced by them. The bard from Coimbra bravely downed
several deep dishes of *caruru,* sipped with pleasure *batidas* of different
flavors, and as came to be known afterward, picked up at the festivities
the inspiration for a dazzling poem about late-night insomnia. Continuing their lunchtime and afternoon relaxation, the notary Wilson
Guimarães Vieira and his faithful clerk, Danilo Correia, were busy savoring the delights of the okra and the ice-cold beer. The popularity of the
former Ipiranga star, absent from the soccer field battleground for so
many years, was still alive—people came over to shake his hand and give
him a hug. "How're you doing, Prince Danilo? Didn't Dona Adalgisa
want to come?"

The fact was that Adalgisa didn't frequent places like that; she
would never have appeared at a *caruru.* Danilo had brought his boss and
friend to the lower-city market for the purpose of delaying his own
return home, where he would have to confront Dadá's fury. There would
be hell to pay. But even though he had no regrets about his bold disobedience of his wife's orders the night before, he was now torn between
pride and fear. He'd decided not to go home until late tonight after tying
one on: If he were roaring drunk, her anger would be tolerable. In any
case, he'd still have to endure at least a quarter-hour of complaints,
insults, and threats. Then Dadá would be seized by another headache,
reeling with a migraine. God's will be done.

Let us mention, finally, Father Abelardo Galvão, the vicar of Piaçava
on his troubled visit to the state capital. He was trying to affect a gay
mood, he honored the *caruru,* he sipped a plum *batida,* nectar of the
gods; but still he couldn't suppress the apprehension that was making
him silent and withdrawn. It wasn't the presence of the Federal Police
agents and Inspector Parreirinha, who were barely keeping up with the
poet Assis Pacheco in their consumption and praise of the *caruru,* that
was making the priest subdued. The preoccupations of the Land Pastoral
preacher were all with Patrícia, who'd lost all restraint and seemed bent
on bringing about his abject surrender. She held the priest by the arm,
put food into his mouth, ran her hand over his face and through his
wavy hair, and whispered into his ear. She called him my Saint Sebastian
all full of arrows, my Lamb of God, my Christ Child, my little lamb, my
Infant Jesus of Prague, my beauty. She called him love, in a low voice,
grabbed him, rubbed up against him, bit his ear, gave him a kiss on the

neck—and she wasn't even drunk, although she was rather high. She was a girl of Yansan, restless and ready: now or never. Father Abelardo was caught between two fires, between the cross and the cauldron. A priest can't marry, Patrícia, his vows won't let him, he thought. But Patrícia didn't seem to understand or even be aware of the fatal prohibition. Not only did she reject it, the priest's heart rejected it, burning with wicked love. And his balls—well!

Lots of *candomblé* people attended. Besides Mother Olga de Tempo, Olga de Yansan, Queen of Alaketu, there was Father Air de Oxaguian, the *babalaô* Nezinho, Manuel Cerqueira de Amorim, with a saint's house in Muritiba, Mário Obá Telá, a shoe repairman and a font of wisdom, the *babalorixá* Luís da Muriçoca, an adept of Exu of the Seven Leaps, Father Balbino de Xangô, Aurélio Sodré, *ogan* of Bogun, dressed in elegant white because it was Friday, Oxalá's day. In addition, the guests' attire was predominantly white—even those who didn't belong to the saint observed the rule.

It was getting past seven in the evening, the gorging was coming to an end, and the carousing was just beginning. The market was overflowing when, at the suggestion of the *babalaô* Nezinho, some musicians took the *atabaque* drums out of Arab Jamil's stall where they were kept for safekeeping. There were more than enough drummers at the *caruru*—an *alabé* was even at hand. They set up the orchestra in the main area after the plates and pots had been removed. The *atabaques* began to throb and a few initiates began to dance—the first to take the floor was Gildete, needless to say. Olga took up the song of greeting for the *orixás:*

> *Agô lelê*
> *Agô lô daké*
> *ô xaoorô*

Then she greeted Yansan, mistress of the feast, patroness of the market:

> *É ialoia*
> *ê ialoia ô ô*

She didn't finish her song: Having passed through the Carnival of the French, Oyá now appeared in the main door. She came in swaying her body, murmuring greetings, spitting fire, the packsaddle on her back, the leather strap in her hand. No one had ever seen Adalgisa, the Yansan of the Saddle, before, and they were startled. A shudder ran down the aisles of the market; Jacira do Odô Oyá lay face-down on the ground as if she were in a temple. The secret she'd been told was true: Yansan was indeed in the city, she'd accepted the *caruru* and come to celebrate. Oyá lifted the acolyte up and embraced her three times. The saint unleashed herself, Odô Oyá mounted Jacira, and the dance began.

All the Yansans were coming forward, one by one. The guests crowded in, they all wanted to see. The pounding of the *atabaques* grew, accompanied by the *agogô* and the calabash. Olga do Alaketu took off, a horse at the gallop, like a shot, a thing of beauty! Then Oiaci appeared, a *vodun* of the Jeje nation, he mounted Margarida do Bogun, Margarida de Yansan, the wife of the *ogan* Aurélio. After that it was the turn of Vera do Veludo, who'd just arrived from Rio de Janeiro that day.

Before Father Abelardo was aware of it, Patrícia, taken by the saint, tore off her shoes and joined the circle. The five Yansans danced around Oyá of the Saddle, who was presenting to the people her daughter Adalgisa, for forty years an unyielding *abicun,* now a docile and obedient *iaô.* Speaking Yoruba, the Latin of *candomblés,* Yansan ordered them to take the saddle off. The people had already seen Adalgisa in the streets of the city; most of them had laughed, thinking it was a masquerade party, but some had understood and smiled discreetly. Nezinho, Mário Obá Telá, and Gildete obeyed her, putting the saddle in Jamil's stall. When the festivities were over and they went to retrieve it, nobody could find the big heavy object. It had disappeared, just like Saint Barbara of the Thunder.

Six Yansans had appeared at the *caruru* in the market in the lower city, all of them fatally beautiful; Adalgisa's Yansan was the most incomparably beautiful of all. Only those who'd seen her dance, her full breasts quivering, her monumental hips going up and down, knew how many pieces it takes to make a packsaddle.

Danilo had remained at the rear of the market, polishing off a beer while passionately discussing a penalty that the Paraíban referee had called and that had recently given the game to Santa Cruz from Recife over Bahia. The referee had left the field a little the worse for wear, but he considered himself lucky. Suddenly Danilo heard his name shouted. It was the notary Wilson who was calling to him, all excited, flabbergasted. The former prince of the playing field went over to him, mug of beer in hand, and looked to where the finger of his boss and friend was pointing. He almost fell over backward at the sight.

"My God—it's Dadá!"

Mounted on Adalgisa, her roan, Oyá came toward the good Danilo, and gave him the leather strap. Then, taking him by the legs, she lifted him up the way Manela had done with Miro and presented him to the people: one more *ogan* in Yansan's court, her favorite.

With night coming on, the festival slowed down, and everybody began heading home. Oyá turned Adalgisa, Saddle Woman, over to the *babalorixá* Luís da Muriçoca with instructions to watch over her. For forty days Adalgisa would occupy the center of the *ilê* to learn the points, the steps of the dance, the chants of the saint. She would be freed forever of her headache, her fanaticism, and her meanness:

I've shut the door already,
Now I want it opened.

The Opening

The Sentence

The sentence was handed down at seven o'clock, when the blackness of night replaced the shadows of dusk over the sea of the gulf and the mountains of the city. The exhibit was all set up; even the last-minute details had been taken care of.

Dom Maximiliano had doublechecked everything—nothing had escaped him. He led his four assistants and friends—Gilberbert, Lev, Sylvio, Jamison—to the outside door and thanked each of them for his help with just the right words. He didn't mention the decision he'd made, but they suspected something was afoot. This reserve was not typical of the monk's behavior.

Then Dom Maximiliano gathered the workers together and gave them their orders, peremptorily as usual. No one, no one—no matter how high an authority—was to be allowed into the rooms where the exhibit was displayed before he, Dom Maximiliano, gave the order. The high authorities—the cardinal, the three military commanders, Dona Regina Simões, the mayor, the auxiliary bishop, Dr. Norberto Odebrecht, the bankers Angelo Calmon de Sá and Lafayette Pondé, Dom Timóteo, and Carybé—all would wait in the director's office, and the rest of the invited guests and the press in the regular galleries. Now Dom Maximiliano was going to retire to his quarters, they should call him only when they got news from the airport of the arrival of the minister of education. Before that, he didn't want to be disturbed. The workers, from guards to curators, realized that he was tense and melancholy and surrounded him with affectionate obedience, though they were disconsolate. They wished that their director, accustomed to laughing and joking, would make some wisecrack about the event to relax his nerves and cheer up his workers.

Before withdrawing, he spoke to the cardinal on the telephone, heard the sentence, and frowned. His hand trembling slightly, he lowered his head: There would be no last-minute pardon from his sentence.

—✎—✎

The Mystery of the Statue
Up in Smoke: The Federal Police
Investigation Down the Drain

On this late phone call, the cardinal passed on to Dom Maximiliano a report he'd just received on the Federal Police investigation of the mystery regarding the theft of the statue of Saint Barbara of the Thunder. Starting off with the correct assumptions, then pursuing clear leads, the astute police had swiftly arrived at categorical conclusions. Not only had the luminaries of the organization shed light on the puzzle that had originally seemed so intractable, they had completely solved it, bringing everything out into the open in less than forty-eight hours, an honorable record. Of the State Police investigation, the cardinal had heard not a murmur: If there were any results to be announced from that quarter, it would certainly be in never-never land.

Colonel Raul Antônio, chief of the Federal Police in Bahia, had come to see the cardinal in person rather than send an underling. The act was proof of his courtesy and consideration, something to bear in mind in times of a military dictatorship: Not only was Colonel Raul Antônio the regional chief, he was also the highest authority in the state. He'd spent almost an hour giving His Eminence a thorough report, including a great number of technical details. He'd expounded theories, made accusations, named names. He'd even expressed certain reservations regarding the generally pristine performance of the officers under his command. They'd gotten quick results, to be sure, but still, they'd lost time. Lost time—yes, sir, they'd gotten to the airport too late, they hadn't been able to recover the statue.

The cardinal didn't find it necessary to pass on to Dom Maximiliano the details of the conversation, the names and places mentioned by the colonel. One name was that of Father Abelardo Galvão, notorious for his involvement in the heated land question and accused in the press of instigating, if not commanding, the attack on the Santa Eliodora plantation. He was without question the key to the solution of the enigma. The fact that he had traveled from Piaçava to the state capital by way of Santo Amaro—taking the long way around, with the obvious intent of sailing on the same sloop as the statue—was what had first attracted the colonel's attention. Then the colonel had discovered the priest's sinister presence aboard Master Manuel's sloop—in spite of Dom Maximiliano's evident forgetfulness of it when he gave his deposition, a curious omission.

Hot on the trail of the priest, the Federal Police had identified the hiding place where the gang had kept the statue: the Abbey of Saint Benedict. All the pieces fell into place then: a subversive priest, an abbey permeated with Marxist ideas and agitators against the rightful military regime. Polite but firm, Colonel Raul Antônio paid scant attention to the questions His Eminence raised: "Excuse me, Your Eminence, but we've got proof." He'd raised his voice just enough to deflect any argument: "We know all about the Abbey of Saint Benedict and the abbot."

While doing surveillance on Father Galvão, watching his lodgings at the abbey, the federal cops had observed the arrival of a woman at the abbey. She'd remained there for more than half an hour—nearly an hour. They found her suspicious, given her furtive behavior and her foreign outfit: chamois boots, gray tailored suit, gloves, and hat; all of it elegant. They had noted her time of arrival by taxi and her departure in an abbey vehicle. Once informed of this, the colonel had set the well-oiled machinery of his federals into motion, and after exchanging messages with other state forces and with Brasília, it had been possible, in only a few hours' time, to identify the nocturnal visitor to the abbey. Did His Eminence know who it was?

"No one less than a sister of Miguel Arraes, the Communist leader who headed the government of Pernambuco in 1964—a most dangerous agitator. Violeta Arraes."

"Violeta Arraes?"

"Does Your Eminence know her?"

His Eminence made a vague gesture—a cardinal knows so many people, how can he remember them all? The colonel didn't press him, but went on with his story. Once her identity had been established, it had been easy to retrace the steps of the subversive woman in Bahia,

where she'd arrived the day before. After leaving the abbey, she had gone
to pick up her luggage at the house where she was staying. Guess whose
house? Caetano Veloso's—he hadn't learned from the lesson we gave
him, he was in need of another. From there she went to the airport.

"When we got there, her flight, nonstop to Paris, had already left,
carrying off La Pasionaria of the Capibaribe and our statue."

La Pasionaria of the Capibaribe—where had Colonel Raul Antônio
picked up the nickname? On the streets of Recife? In the files of the SNI?
By his account, Arraes's sister had conspired in Pernambuco with Dom
Hélder and other partisans of her exiled brother; she'd come to Bahia to
pick up the stolen statue, with the specific task of taking it out of the
country and carrying it off to Europe, where it would be sold to finance
subversion. She'd carried out her mission, a well-planned, perfectly executed one; the gang had taken care of everything, timed matters perfectly. "She was traveling with a French passport, under the alias of
Violeta Gervaiseau."

There had been a large, heavy box among her luggage, the colonel
told the cardinal. She'd asked the baggage man to put a "fragile" sticker
on it, since it contained items of popular Pernambucan crafts, ceramics
by Master Vitalino and Severino de Tracunhaém.

Thus had the Federal Police, in a display of extraordinary efficiency,
deciphered the mystery of the disappearance of the statue within less
than forty-eight hours; but the scrupulous Colonel Raul Antônio would
accept no congratulations for it—he'd arrived at the airport too late.

"We missed it by less than twelve hours. The plane took off at one-
thirty in the morning, and it was a little after noon by the time we got to
the Varig counter." The colonel struck his breast in penance. "Your
statue, cardinal, is in Paris, out of our reach. The mystery has gone up in
smoke, our efforts down the drain."

He went on to vow to continue their war on church thefts until they
broke up the gang and put the bosses and accomplices behind bars.
They'd lost one battle, but the final victory would be theirs.

"And the one who's going to lead us to the big bosses is Father
Galvão. He is an important figure in the gang. We're going to let him go
free, and without knowing it, he'll lead us to the others. When the eggs
are cracked, there'll be a lot of surprises, Your Eminence." As one intellectual to another, he ended by pulling his Shakespeare out of his vest
pocket. "There's something rotten in the state of Holland, my dear cardinal."

The cardinal didn't correct him: Holland or Denmark, the chief of
the Federal Police was alluding in his fashion to the ideological disarray
in the Church. Under a military dictatorship, with its threats and hu-
miliations, who has any respect for a cardinal, even if he is the primate?

The Chalice

The cardinal passed the disastrous news on to Dom Maximiliano over the telephone: The statue had gone up in smoke. All and any hope was lost, and things were in a sorry state indeed.

He went on to expound on the colonel's extraordinary theory, which was already all too familiar to the monk. These thefts of Church possessions were no doubt being perpetrated to finance land seizures and urban guerrilla warfare, he said. The story would have been unbelievable, except that the Bahian chief of the Federal Police had presented the solution all wrapped up in conclusive evidence gathered by his investigation. Saint Barbara of the Thunder had been taken out of Brazil by Violeta Arraes.

The cardinal knew her from way back: Violeta Arraes Gervaiseau. The name wasn't an alias as the colonel had said, but was from her marriage to the French economist Pierre Gervaiseau, a courageous and generous Nazarene. And knowing her as well as he did, the cardinal believed she had done everything of which she'd been accused: Violeta Arraes or Gervaiseau was capable of much worse.

Before he hung up, His Eminence asked Dom Maximiliano whether he didn't think it better to skip the opening, to send an aide to the rector with his letter of resignation from his post. The director, long-suffering and sour, retorted, "I will resign in public, Your Eminence, when I declare the exhibit open. I will drink this chalice down to the last drop."

How could the cardinal respond to such a melodramatic statement? Not knowing what to say, he answered, "In that case, I'll see you later on," and he hung up. He pictured the monk, tasting the bitterness of the chalice. Drop by drop, he could measure the extent of the director's misfortune. Dom Maximiliano was given to colorful language, but the cardinal detested rhetoric. He regretted the fate of the Benedictine—a wise, hard-working, creative man—and he didn't know of anyone capable of replacing him. Poor Dom Maximiliano, he would undergo a night of torture.

No matter how long it seems to last, a night has only so many hours, and then it's over. The next day Dom Maximiliano would board the plane for Rio de Janeiro, far from all this bedlam, while he, the cardinal primate, would have the vicar of Santo Amaro nipping at his heels. The vicar possessed no colorful language, no baroque rhetoric, only base, jeering vulgarity. These ruminations weren't merely idle self-pity, for just then a secretary hurried in to announce that Father Téo had landed at the market ramp at the head of an army of inhabitants of Santo Amaro. The cardinal felt a chill run up his spine.

Consummatum Est!

Dom Maximiliano's crucifixion began at eight o'clock, give or take a minute, when he was told that the statue, his Saint Barbara of the Thunder, had been smuggled to France. The police had demonstrated their usual stupidity, their balky, bureaucratic, foot-dragging incompetence. The monk had reached the end of his path of stones and thorns; he'd come to the strait gate, the final point; all that was left now was for him to go into exile. Stay in Rio, go back to Europe—where could he start over? He would decide later. At this moment of his consummation he wasn't thinking about tomorrow; he was carrying bygone days in his breast. The Bahia years—happy, exciting. *Consummatum est!*

Within an hour he would be greeting the minister of education and culture, the cardinal, the governor, the rector of the university—all powerful, intelligent people. He would proclaim the opening of the exhibit of religious art organized by the Museum of Sacred Art and by himself, its director. There the exhibit was—ready and waiting in all its splendor, almost complete. The opening should have been Dom Maximiliano's hour of triumph, of fame; the applause at home should have echoed overseas, become the high point of a life of scholarship and research. It had turned out to be the contrary. Standing before the television cameras, he would take out from the pocket of his cassock the piece of paper bearing the terse statement, his resignation from the directorship. He would inform those present of his irrevocable retirement. *Consummatum est!*

Now all alone in his soon-to-be former office, he began his climb up Calvary. During the afternoon he'd clean out his desk, and his suitcase full of personal items was already in the Beetle. Now he was all alone beside the telephone, he and his sadness. The sadness pained like the centurions' whips on Golgotha. Dom Maximiliano got up and headed toward the other end of the building, where a small stairway led to the storeroom and his quarters. In order to get there he went through the galleries of the exhibit. He walked slowly, lingering to look at the pieces with loving eyes, engraving the dazzling sight in his mind and his heart. At the end of each room he turned out the light. He left the exhibit in darkness, carrying it with him. *Consummatum est!*

He hadn't touched anything in his quarters, there hadn't been time and he hadn't had the strength or courage. He'd given the key to Emanual Araújo, a good friend, and asked him to take care of removing his belongings and shipping them to Rio. He only turned on the small light by the head of his bed and went to the window; if he had to weep, it would be then and there, not at the moment of his departure: He wanted to leave with his head high and his eyes dry. In this proletarian neighborhood, night was dissolving fatigue and frustration, falling amid yawns, complaints, and the sound of music. Roberto Carlos was singing on a jukebox, someone was drawing a song out of a guitar, a transistor radio was blaring a sports event, three men around it were arguing, the fat woman was waving her hand, and in the shade of a jasmine in bloom a girl cashier from the supermarket and a boy with a motorcycle were taking advantage of the darkness. He would even miss this less-than-grand spectacle. What wouldn't he miss? *Consummatum est!*

He let his sight wander over the old rooftops on the slopes, over the sleeping streets of the lower city, over the bay where stars were twinkling, the lanterns on boats, beacons on the breakwater, over the black hulk of São Marcelo fort—the shell of an enormous turtle. His eyes damp, his heart undone, Dom Maximiliano let himself go as anyone would, but nobody heard the strangled sound of his sob or saw the tears running down his pale face. Crucified, *consummatum est!*

The sound grew louder; in the beginning a distant murmur, it soon drew closer, louder, the stamping feet of people on the pavement. Dom Maximiliano focused his eyes and saw a demonstration coming up the Ladeira da Preguiça with the singing of church hymns; they were the pilgrims from Santo Amaro da Purificação, and they were coming to rescue their stolen statue. When they reached the front of the convent, Dom Maximiliano recognized the vicar of Santo Amaro, Father Teófilo Lopes de Santana; he was clutching a sign that read DOM MIMOSO IS A THIEF! Dom Mimoso? Who could that be if not he? Dom Mimoso— how base! Lord, why so heavy a cross? *Consummatum est!*

The demonstrators occupied the Rua do Sodré and took up positions across from the museum. In the streetlamps, Dom Maximiliano could decipher what some of the banners and signs said: THE SAINT BELONGS TO US! WE WANT OUR SAINT BACK! THEY'VE STOLEN SAINT BARBARA, THUNDER WOMAN! ARREST DOM MIMOSO! DOM MIMOSO IS A FAG! Dom Maximiliano lowered his head, and the nails of crucifixion were hammered into his hands and feet, barefoot, naked, exposed. The tears ran down his chin—*consummatum est!*

A rap of knuckles on the door; it was Nelito, the smiling little mulatto, the black "angel," a fugitive from a cornice. A phone call had come in from the airport saying that the minister of education, accompanied by the governor and the rector who had gone out to meet him, had just left for the museum. The office and the regular galleries were overflowing; the cardinal was growing impatient. It was the cardinal who'd sent for him now.

"Thank you, Nelito. Wait for me."

He wiped his eyes before turning on the light in the bathroom; he washed his face, groomed himself quickly, adjusted his cassock so that it hung properly. He examined himself in the mirror: a melancholy face, a romantic profile, fatally pale, a pretty figurine, an ivory friar. Hidden were the wounds of defeat, the marks of weakness under the makeup of virile misanthropy, consumed but dignified. *Consummatum est!*

"Let's go, Nelito. I'm going to tell you something that nobody knows yet. They'll know in a little while. I won't be here tomorrow. I'm going away."

"Going away, boss? But you can't! What about the museum? Without Mr. Director, what's going to happen? I don't believe it, boss—you're joking."

Glory to God in the Highest!

Turning on the lights, illuminating the galleries of the exhibit, Nelito went ahead of Dom Maximiliano von Gruden, who was walking with the step of a condemned man, pushed on by the executioner and his second who, invisible, framed him and imposed the stoic cadence of their walk upon him. With no other witness but lively Nelito, Dom Maximiliano crossed over to his banishment, losing not for a moment the solemn look on his face, the decorum of his white cassock, the necessary dignity. It was a funeral procession.

Irritated by the cherub's euphoria, Dom Maximiliano scolded him: "What's this, Nelito? Show a little more respect."

"Tonight there's a full moon, boss—a party night for the exhibit. Nelito's happy."

Dom Maximiliano wouldn't see the black angel anymore, leaping in front of him like an engraving by Debret. Today's festival, Nelito, didn't belong to us, he thought. It belonged to the auxiliary bishop, the rector —to all the ones who don't like me and who covet my position as director—they number in the dozens. I'll be far away, I won't have any say in their choice of my successor; if it's Liana, so much the better.

"Listen, Nelito, I'm going to wait by the door. You go down to the bottom of the stairs. Don't let anyone up here until the minister arrives. Nobody—not even the cardinal."

Nelito went ahead to carry out his order. The sound of voices was coming from the galleries—snatches of conversation, women's laughter, the swarming of guests moving around to get a place in line for the entrance, behind the privileged people gathered in the office. The large clock on the wall, itself a museum piece still in use, had just struck the hour. In a military dictatorship, a minister, even a civilian one, would have had the power to determine the exact time, to stop the hands of clocks, to slow down the swinging of pendulums to announce the precise nine o'clock opening of the exhibit of religious art of Bahia: the precise moment of consummation.

By the time Dom Maximiliano von Gruden reached the end of his Calvary walk—that is, the entrance to his exhibition—he was a mere shell of a person, a corpse en route to the grave. He forced himself to be strong and lifted his chest, but his heart wouldn't respond; undone in sorrow, his eyes pained him with their dryness.

It was at that moment that he looked and saw but didn't believe. No, it wasn't possible. He forced another look at the exact spot where he'd told Mirabeau Sampaio that he was going to place the statue of Saint Barbara of the Thunder, at the entrance to the exhibit. There she was, the magnificent statue, on the floor without a stand, without a litter —just like a living person, like you or me. It seemed impossible—he had to blink to believe what his eyes were seeing. Yet suddenly he wasn't startled anymore—it seemed normal to him for Saint Barbara of the Thunder to be smiling and winking at him, calling him back from exile to those unparalleled shores of Bahia.

Dom Maximiliano fell to his knees, praised the Lord and prostrated himself at the feet of the saint and kissed the fringe of her cloak of thunder. He looked like a son of Oyá in the *dobalé* of obedience and partiality.

Surrounded by television cameras, by radio microphones, His Excellency the Minister of Education and Culture appeared in the doorway to the exhibit. By that point Dom Maximiliano von Gruden, director of the Museum of Sacred Art, was waiting for him, composed, standing beside the statue that was thought to have been stolen and taken to Europe. Whole, proud, smiling, Dom Maximiliano had a touch of arrogance in his voice when he said:

"In the presence of His Excellency the Minister of Education and Culture, the Governor of the State, His Eminence the Cardinal Primate, in the name of the Magnificent Rector of the Federal University of Bahia"—a pause, and he raised his voice—"under the blessing of Saint Barbara of the Thunder, I declare the Exhibit of Religious Art of Bahia to be open."

The microphones recorded his words; and the television cameras relayed via satellite, from the Oiapoque to the Chuí, to millions of Brazilians, the monk in the impeccable white cassock, the wisest monk in directing museum affairs, the wisest and handsomest, standing next to his protégée and protectress, the famous statue. Then they showed him autographing copies of the book he'd written about her, about Saint Barbara of the Thunder for all the notables. The book defined her, giving her a birth certificate, the exact date and the name of her father—the sculptor whose fingers had been eaten away by leprosy, the divine mulatto, Aleijadinho.

Glory to God in the highest! The hallelujah Saturday began at nine-twelve in the evening of that Friday of passions.

Hail
and Farewell,
Saravá 3 Times,
We're
Out of Here

Mail from Readers

This is an innovation in the novel: Mail from Readers, pages where the author answers the questions of those who undertook the penance of following the plot, the tribulations of the characters—not to mention those of the author, as a matter of fact, suffering the atrocious pains of lumbago just now. Such a journalistic genre is unheard of when it comes to works of fiction, creative things. This is a Bahian novel, however, and as such, it is attuned to the dernier cri in literary innovations, open to the ideological winds unleashed by perestroika. The days of elitism and bureaucracy are over, *harasho!*

The author's own inability to renovate or innovate is notorious. He is known to be unable to renovate the weak writing, to revolutionize the structure of the narrative, to deepen the Freudian introspection of the beings condemned to life by the powers of destiny, to present love as an aberration, to be difficult to read, to be modern and boring. Such incapacity eats at the author's flesh, gnaws at his insides, embitters his days of senility, his nights of dotage. Can this Mail from Readers be just another form of dotage?

It would be well to pay heed to the curiosity and demands of readers who have borne witness in solidarity with the scribbler's persistent daily efforts to fulfill his duties by telling a tale to amuse, and by amusing himself, to change the terms of the theorem and better the world. It is the undeniable audacity of an author on in years, a veteran of lost battles, who has yet to bring literary critics to an orgasm of pleasure as they read his manuscripts, deficient in expression, devoid of ideas, plebeian.

No one who disagrees with this innovation is obliged to read the pages that follow. In truth, the tale ended a couple of pages ago; these pages of Mail from Readers serve only to follow up on some of the details and consequences of the plot.

The Repercussions

The nationwide repercussions, with Lusitanian echoes, of the exhibit of religious art of Bahia were extremely positive and congratulatory. As a byproduct the book by Dom Maximiliano von Gruden on the statue of Saint Barbara of the Thunder was already a classic at its birth.

Dom Maximiliano is overjoyed; he fritters away his time basking in his own glory, strutting about like a turkey—make that a peacock; he spreads his feathers in the neighborhood of the convent, having a word with Roque the frame-maker, another with Zu Campos the woodcarver, his white cassock parading up and down the museum garden. Leaping around him, Nelito, the mischievous cherub, carries the useless breviary. Dom Maximiliano has no need for reading; he passes between beds of daisies and angelicas, a shepherd of images and angels. We will leave him that way, enjoying life.

The press devoted entire columns, big headlines, with photographs here and there, heaping the most baroque adjectives of praise on the exhibit and the book. As for the statue's disappearance, an episode that held the city in excitement for forty-eight hours and ultimately furnished the populace with the basis of a suspenseful television series, current opinion holds that it was nothing but a stroke of genius to promote the exhibit and the book, conceived and executed with evident precision and astuteness by Dom Maximiliano; with the active collaboration of the journalist Guido Guerra, of course, intriguers worthy of each other.

Far from denying this opinion, Guido is content to laugh out of one side of his mouth, with his roguish eyes of a lewd parrot. If a parrot eats grain, a parakeet gets the fame. José Berbert de Castro doesn't look like a parakeet—more like a cockatoo, relaxed and victorious. He was able to return to the offices of *A Tarde* and face the now-affable Dr. Jorge Calmon, who patted his head. Once more, without resorting to sensationalism, Dr. Simões's newspaper had struck just the right note, had given the correct information after all. At the moment of the arrival of the statue, the reporter from *A Tarde* had been present to take note of the event and report that it had in fact arrived safely, as expected.

Leaving aside the competition among the organs of the press, let the articles signed by illustrious names be noted here. In his "Courtyard of the Arts," Antônio Celestino, whose integrity had been cast into doubt for no valid reason, sang the praises of the exhibit: "A panoramic, monumental overview of the immeasurable wealth of religious art gathered and preserved in Bahia." In the same article he extolled Dom Maximiliano's book with frilly Minhotan adjectives: "A major work on Brazilian creative arts, owing to the golden pen of the master *inter pares,* it clears up all the obscure aspects surrounding the statue of Saint Barbara of the Thunder, even answering definitively the question of its authorship. Bahia can rejoice: We possess one of the most beautiful pieces ever created by Aleijadinho's genius."

In his column "Compass Rose," our daily allotment of good prose, Dr. Odorico Tavares didn't mute his praise for the exhibit and the opening, even though he maintained certain qualms concerning Aleijadinho. Suggesting the hypothesis would have been fine, he said, but asserting, as Dom Maximiliano von Gruden was doing, that the statue of Saint Barbara of the Thunder was in fact the work of Aleijadinho was simply too bold. Obviously, Dr. Odorico still harbored some resentment.

Bombastic is the word that describes the article by Clarival do Prado Valladares of the International Association of Art Critics: extravagant and long, full of quotations in many languages, especially German, it praised Dom Maximiliano to the skies. On the other hand, he noted, the thesis with respect to authorship had already been hinted at by Clarival himself, in his essay on "The Cosmology of Saint Barbara of the Thunder." On the problem of authorship, he'd written, "the work of an anonymous sculptor, doubtless a disciple of Aleijadinho." Of the three masters of Bahian art criticism, one born in Portugal, another in Pernambuco, Clarival had recognized the light of day first and had done justice to the museum director, anointing him with the oil of praise, with the incense of encomium.

Nor was the praise limited to the local applause of Valladares, Celestino, and Tavares; it extended across the country and was echoed overseas. There was an article from Gilberto Freyre—we feel obliged to start with him. Published in *Diário de Pernambuco,* reprinted in Rio, São Paulo, and Fortaleza, and in *Diário de Notícias* of Bahia, translated into

Spanish and appearing in the columns of *ABC* in Madrid, the master from Recife, playing for applause, took over the thesis of "the eminent von Gruden" and made it his own, vouching for Aleijadinho. Revealing what nobody yet knew, discoveries he'd made to be published soon in a new edition of the *Historical and Sentimental Guide to Recife,* he postulated the existence of three statues by Aleijadinho in Recife alone; a Saint George, a Saint Benedict, and an Our Lady of Sorrow. The Saint George belonged to the collection of Abelardo Rodrigues, the Our Lady of Sorrow was the property of Tânia and André Carneiro Leão, and the Saint Benedict, a unique treasure, could be found on the Apipucos estate, the fief of the great Gilberto, master of us all.

Another statue attributed to Aleijadinho turned up in Rio Grande do Sul, according to a good-humored article by Moacyr Scliar in a Porto Alegre newspaper. The young writer had recourse to the testimony of his uncle, Henrique Scliar, an old anarchist and lover of art, who'd come to own a Christ sculpted by Aleijadinho but had had to sell it in order to support his painter son Carlos in his European apprenticeship. "How can you authenticate the authorship, how can you know it was the work of the genius, uncle?" Moacyr had asked the question as a gangling boy in short pants. "All you have to do is take a look at it, and you'll see," the good Henrique had answered peremptorily.

Another leading authority, Pietro Bardi, in *O Estado de São Paulo,* praised Dom Maximiliano's book but rejected the scholar's authorship assertion incisively. Neither Aleijadinho nor anyone like him had created the statue! The dates didn't jibe, much less the characteristics of the sculpture, which were more suited to Frei Agostinho da Piedade than to the mulatto Antônio Francisco Lisboa, the Aleijadinho, son of a Portuguese colonist and a black slave woman.

What caused real surprise was an extensive article that took up almost a whole page in *O Globo* of Rio de Janeiro, by Otto Lara Resende, a writer from Minas Gerais—where Aleijadinho had lived and worked—and a member of the Brazilian Academy, on "The Origins and Authorship of Saint Barbara of the Thunder." The monk's book was nothing but a heap of nonsense, according to Dr. Resende—with all due respect for the noble bellettrist, the possessor of a dazzling intelligence, his books were the finest of Brazilian fiction. Humor dominated the debates he enjoyed so much. We must state without fear of error or injustice, however, that Dr. Resende's article, intended to be biting, was certainly the product of either regional xenophobia or envy, and was the only truly negative one among all the many written about the exhibit—which he didn't see, a bad sign already—and about Dom Maximiliano von Gruden's book. Could the writer have read or at least thumbed through the book? Not likely.

ALEIJADINHO BELONGS TO US! was the title of the diatribe in

which the choleric Resende thrashed the director without pity or compassion, showing him no mercy, calling him an adventurer and a charlatan whose pen was in the pay of secret interests. Alluding to the slogan of the nationalist campaign "The Petroleum Belongs to Us," echoing the cry of the demonstration of the people of Santo Amaro, "The Saint Belongs to Us," Resende's article breathed narrow regional chauvinism. It denied the existence of any pieces by Aleijadinho outside his home state of Minas Gerais, except for those few registered in the archives of the Museum of Ouro Preto itself. Next to that Mineiran museum, Resende wrote, the Museum of Sacred Art in Bahia "is nothing but a common convent sacristy."

Not content with having stolen Minas's access to the sea, he said, the Bahians had now decided to take possession of the Mineirans's glorious artistic patrimony. Before long, whenever the name of Aleijadinho, the genius of Ouro Preto, came up, based on Vicar Gruden's book people would say that the artist had been born in Cachoeira, that the sculptor had been established in Santo Amaro da Purificação. That was what all those colonialist Bahians want. Hadn't Mr. James Amado just written that Guimarães Rosa was more a Bahian novelist than a Mineiro? It was just one piece of insolence after another!

Honesty obliges us to recognize that Mr. Resende's insults and invective were cloaked in an overwhelming amount of erudition, which made his Catilinaria a veritable encyclopedia of the statues and, most especially, of the creativity of Aleijadinho, replete with literary references, generally French, from Flaubert to Proust, from Hugo to Sartre, from François Villon to Jacques Prévert. It's impossible not to admire it, or the captivating prose style and the Mineirism, a peculiar and virulent kind of xenophobia.

The cloud that academician Resende's article caused was compensated for by the appearance of "The Revelry of Saint Barbara, Fled from Antônio Francisco Lisboa's Studio and Found in Bahia," a short poem by Carlos Drummond de Andrade, which the poet sent to Dom Maximiliano as thanks for his gift of a copy of "the superb edition of your splendid book." What now, Otto?

To close this limited review of quotes from news stories, chronicles, and articles dealing with the exhibit and the book, let us speak of the interview conducted by Fernando Assis Pacheco, that "special envoy of the Portuguese press"—that was how Dom Maximiliano had introduced him at the news conference that Wednesday, just before all the confusion began. Accompanying the interview, in which the museum director put forth his ideas, made his bold assertions, and exuded his personal charm, was an excellent profile of Dom Maximiliano drawn by Pacheco. "He admits to the age of fifty-five, fifteen of which have been lived in Bahia, but his eloquence and wit are cultivated and enduring; the master of other poetic skills beyond the world of statuary, I heard him expatiate on the poetry of the Galaico-Portuguese *Cancioneiro*," the journalist wrote in good Lusitanian style. He didn't stop there: "Drawn from the memories of his lifelong love affair with Saint Barbara of the Thunder, the book is mad, bright, and metaphorical, and most assuredly exhaustive." Dom Maximiliano reveled in it.

As for his reporting, Assis Pacheco narrated in merry Sunday prose, with a wealth of detail, the story of the disappearance of the statue and the two days of panic among the population. He painted a picturesque view of the city stirred up by the theft of the statue, a possession of the people. In addition, he described the luncheon at the Model Market, the *samba de roda*, the Carnival of the French, and Jacira do Odô Oyá's *caruru*.

He rudely demolished the police theories, both Federal and State, as empty assertions proven wrong by events. A presumptuous colonel, a swashbuckler posing as an intellectual, had said, "The statue was carried off to Europe!" A rattleheaded lawyer, a blockhead know-it-all, had announced: "The one who stole the statue was the vicar of Santo Amaro himself!" No doubt the two buffoons were long since discharged.

The Portuguese bard was mistaken, however, when he announced their discharge. The chief of the Federal Police continued his revelation of foul plot of the Communists, both those in coveralls and those in cassocks. If the statue was not carried off to Europe, it was because of the efficiency of the Federal Police. Violeta Arraes, perceiving herself followed and possibly to be arrested at the airport, had decided not to take the statue out of the Abbey of Saint Benedict after all. The chief of the State Police, once he was in possession of the reports of Inspector Parreirinha and the terribly flu-ridden Ripoleto, fingered the sacristy once more—in this case, that of the main church of Santo Amaro da Purificação. In sacristies, vicars and sextons were freely planning and putting into motion the ever-more-frequent thefts of church and parish possessions. When the vicar of Santo Amaro saw he had been found out, Dr. Calixto Passos maintained, he had retreated and organized that farce of a protest.

The Truth About the Poem

A poem that Fernando Assis Pacheco wrote caused an angry debate in which pen-pushers from here and from there took part; the publication of its first draft here will help this dull chronicle take on literary merits that have been lacking in it up till now.

Before we transcribe the poem, however, it is proper to make mention of the discrepancies that exist between the original text and the one that was published in Lisbon several years later. Inspired by Jacira do Odô Oyá's *caruru,* which took place on the Friday evening of the exhibit opening—a full day and night of gorging—it was published the following week by Edições Macunaíma. It was a limited, numbered edition, noncommercial, illustrated with a black and white woodcut by Calasans Neto for the enjoyment of a privileged few, according to the title page. A second version of the same poem was published in Portugal. It constitutes, along with other no less admirable verses, the volume *Variations in Souza,* published under the imprint of Hiena Editora.

In the Macunaíma edition, the poem and the woodcut are printed on a hand press by the artist on a sheet of wide, thick Chinese paper made especially for wood engravings. Alongside the handwritten poem appears the print, in which the flanks of a fog-shrouded mountain of an apocalyptic and sensual creature, half-mare, half-woman, rise up. Master Calá's illustration doesn't figure in the Portuguese edition; the text is one of the last poems in the collection, the third from the end.

Although these modifications conserved the structure of the poem itself, they had the obvious end of concealing its inspiring muse as well. Why they were made, we don't know: roguery on the part of the poet, Galician sobriety, who knows. Perhaps it was the jealousy of Dona Rosarinho, Pacheco's well-endowed wife, that was at fault. If two of Portugal's most renowned critics, Messrs. José Carlos de Vasconcelos and Antônio Alçada Batista, couldn't explain the modifications despite numerous monographs—and they might well have, being in possession of numbers six and seven, respectively, of the Bahian edition—it would be much too pretentious to attempt to resolve the controversy here. Let us content ourselves with noting the discrepancies between the two editions.

Down to cases, then. Where the original text reads *Adalgisa,* in the revised edition it is *Maruxa. Bahia* has become *Orense;* the *Bahians* are transformed into *Burgos,* and the *iaôs,* written with Yoruba spelling, are simple dolls; Adalgisa's magnificent rump was discovered in a market and not a restaurant. That was all—just enough to expel the defenseless

Adalgisa from literary history and to sabotage Bahia, the perpetual victim of the unscrupulousness of certain poetasters.

In order to complete our bibliographical information, it behooves us to reveal that four of the ten copies that were numbered and signed by the poet and the artist were taken to Portugal. Number one, the poet kept so well hidden that he never set eyes on it again. The second he gave to Dr. José Maria Assis Pacheco, his father; two others, with fawning inscriptions, were given to the critics Alçada and Vasconcelos. The remaining six copies stayed in Brazil. Number two remained with the beloved of the illustrator, Doña Auta de Calasans Neto, his queen, his rose; the others, in no enumerated order, were distributed among the following personalities: Antônio Celestino, in whose banker's apartment Pacheco had stayed for more than a month; Carlos and Myriam Fraga, who had put up and fed the Portuguese poet, so adept with fork and flagon, on his visit to Mar Grande; the novelist João Ubaldo Ribeiro and his stoical Berenice—living with a genius is hell!—for the same Itaparican and gustatory reasons; and to counselor James Amado, as proof of devotion for his sweetness of character; James Amado is a creature made of honey, without thorns, a flatterer. The remaining copy was appropriated by another Amado, James's eldest brother; present at the occasion, a *profiteur*, he made off with it.

All this verbosity having been expended, you genteel ladies and distinguished gentlemen are now invited to read the poem inspired in Fernando Assis Pacheco by Adalgisa, Yansan of the Saddle, while the enchanted one possessed her at Jacira do Odô Oyá's *caruru*. More precisely, by Dadá's triumphant ass.

—૪—૯

The Poem in Its
Original Form

ADALGISA'S RUMP

A rump revealed, one August in Bahia,
Round to the eyes, a magnificent orb,
A bottom like a bison, your buttocks, Adalgisa
Beguiled my walk through the market stalls

Of all the rhymed asses of ancient memory
Only yours has the compass of true poetry
A tail bound for glory, oh unrivaled *iyawô*

Rolling your hips, you take our breath away
Our lips, fair Adalgisa, long there to stray

So plump, so cleft, so high, it rivals
The white and leavened dough, cooked in the far off Bahias
Where oh how Adalgisa sings! tropical bird, Homeric siren
And I, a lost Ulysses, bow my head in this tavern
Longing for your broad pelvic perfection
Foundering in my sleep but not in affection.

FERNANDO ASSIS PACHECO
Bahia, stormy, on an August night

The Day of the *Ôrunkó*

Many are those who were curious for news of Manela—and there are a lot of questions to be asked. But is there anyone who doesn't care to know the fate of the ship of *iaôs* that weighed anchor from the port of Gantois?

On course to Aioká, it sailed through the depths of the sea, from dock to dock through the dark waters of an extinguished memory, as if it carried some vile stain on the body of the nation. Difficulties and distances, recovered sounds, gestures, feelings, the sands of the desert, the humus of the jungle, enchantment, spells. The ship returned from humdrum days, loaded down with vestiges, colors, rhythms, echoes, and hints, jewels and gravel, good and evil things that make up a nation; the *iaôs* were piling them up on the sacred ground of the *jurá oluá*, the sanctuary. They were waiting around to be reborn and already being reborn, securing the saint, learning the steps and the accents, the trot and the gallop, a herd of young horses, of mounts. Manela and her *erê* were busy in the labors of Yansan.

A head shaved by the razor of the *éfun* is a broad entrance door, an open exit door, and the hair of the armpits and the fuzz of the pussy are narrow, sloping doors, hatchways for unexpected visitations for possession. Manela learned the chants, at least seven for each saint, the different beats of the *atabaque* orchestra, *rum, rumpi,* and *lé,* from the *alujá* to the *adarrum,* in the seventeen days of circumnavigation, until Mãe Menininha determined the day of the *ôrunkó.*

That most festive and glorious day, the day for giving the name, when Yansan in the crowded shed of Gantois finally leaped, rose up into the air all covered with rubies and purple grapes, and announced for the first and last time the name of the newborn, the Oyá of Manela. The Oxalá of Gildete, majestic, and the Yansan of Adalgisa, powerful, accompanied her in the course of the revelation.

The name is heard and forgotten, is never repeated, and no one memorizes it. Only the mother and daughter, the *iyá* and the *iaô*, know how to pronounce it. The name of the Yansan of Manela was proclaimed, a hoarse shout, heard and forgotten at a fine big name festival, with a lot of fanfare and a certain pride. In the temple decorated with multicolored streamers, scores of guests, countless people, gathered. Along with *ogans* from many other saint houses, present were the *babalaô* Nezinho, the *babalorixá* Luís da Muriçoca, Miguel Santana Obá Aré, Camafeu de Oxóssi, Sinval Costa Lima, Master Didi, Carybé, and Pierre Fatumbi Verger, Ojuobá, escorting a son of Elegbará, whose Christian name was Severo Sarduy, a sweetheart with words who came from Cuba via Paris. The Avenida da Ave-Maria appeared *au grand complet*, to quote Professor João Batista, Francophile. In the dining room and kitchen of Cleusa's house next door waited the sumptuous viands of Afro-Brazilian cuisine: three goats, two dozen chickens, and a dozen guinea hens had been sacrificed for the *ebó* of the name. First-rate chow, plentiful and appetizing.

On the Sunday following the day of the *ôrunkó*, the ceremony of the *panã*, the auction of the *iaôs*, the slave market, took place: their *xaraôs* on their ankles, the *kelê* of their *orixá* around their necks. Manela was bought for a good price by Danilo, her little father. But even before he bought her and became responsible for her for the second time, he'd underwritten the name festival without worrying about expenses. Had he won the sports lottery? That was the only way a clerk in a notary's office could afford such luxury. Danilo never had any luck at gambling, but he had good friends, lots of them, and a person who has friends never wants for anything.

On the name festival day Miro, laughing with all his teeth, picked up Gildete and Adalgisa together in his taxi. The two aunts were all excited—they'd hated each other in the past to the same degree that they liked each other now. They had even begun to look like twin sisters, fertilized in the same egg. Adalgisa, tamed, jovial, free of migraines and of her father confessor, had turned completely around and without ceasing to be a lady had become a person just like anybody else. Without ceasing to be a Catholic, she was a fiery steed for the enchanted ones in the circle of saints, Adalgisa of the Saddle.

Anyone who wants to know still more about these matters of saints, voodoo, *candomblé, macumba,* possessions, mixed blood, and *orixás* should try to put a little money together and take a trip to Bahia, the capital city of dreams. Go to a saint's house, to a temple, to Engenho Velho, Axé Yá Nassô, to Gantois, Axé Yá Massê, to Centro Cruz Santa de

São Gerônimo, Ilê Moroialajê of Alaketu, to the Candomblé do Portão, *peji* of Oxóssi and the halfbreed Pedra Preta, the Pilão de Prata, Ilê de Oxumaré, Bogum, territory of the Jeje nation, to the Ilê Axé Ibá Ogun, Candomblé da Muriçoca, where comrade Exu Seven Leaps can be found, to the Village of Zumino-Reanzarro Gangajti, of Neive Branco, and to the Bate-Folha, Angolan soil in Beiru, the Kingdom of Time. Go to any of the thousand *candomblés* of the various nations of Africa and the indigenous nations, Nagô, Jeje, Ijexá, Congo, Angola, and mixed blood located in Bahia. You'll be well received in all of them, with liberality and generosity. If you come in peace, you may enter.

Anyone who stops by will be able to see at a glance, the beauty and the freedom of the *candomblé*. If your heart is in it, you'll see a lot more —you'll rub elbows with the *orixás*. Those poor temples, persecuted only yesterday, keep the saga of slavery alive, the prohibited songs and dances, the condemned memory can be recovered there. The keepers of the *orixás* are the noblewomen of Bahia, each one more majestic, more beautiful and wise than the one before, princesses and queens, *iyás,* the mothers of the people.

The traveler, be he rich or poor, be she black or white, young or old, educated or illiterate, no matter who, as long as they come in peace, they will be able to participate in the festival of the *candomblé*, where gods and mortals are equal, to sing and dance in their universal communion.

Manela put on the thunder cloak of Saint Barbara and lifted up the *eiru* of Yansan. Oyá had already named her, and anyone who heard it has already forgotten.

The Holy Man

We regret to inform the feudal colonels, the landowners of unmarked dominions without fences or gates, the masters of whole regions, of electoral districts, of legions of serfs; the wheedling politicians, the employers of assassins, the little fathers of the poor—we regret, gentlemen, to inform you that one of the most competent professionals of death, Zé do Lírio, a Pernambucan gunman famous in many states, the one with infallible aim, has abandoned his profession forever.

Six shots fired and failed: five at that swine of a priest, one at his own chest to die like a brave man. A message from God was sent through the mediation of Father Cícero Romão Batista, the saint of the backlands, of whom the migrant riding his donkey was one of the twelve apostles. Zé do Lírio invoked penance. He called upon rich people to renounce their worldly goods, called the poor out for the final pilgrimage to the

Cariri, and preached the abandonment of work and the practice of prayer.

He succeeded in gathering a fairly large band of fanatics together with imprecations and litany; they were already calling him Saint Joseph of the White Lily; they asked for his blessing, begged for miracles, and he performed them. When they asked for food to kill their hunger, he told them to go into pastures and slaughter a few head of cattle for a frugal repast. They drank at water holes.

The paramilitary police under command of the army, waging the war against subversion, took him prisoner, gave him a masterful beating with bayonet scabbards, accused him of being a dangerous Communist, and put him on trial for stirring up the peasant masses, even saying he was a Marxist-Leninist. They sent him off, shackled to a gang of criminals, to serve time on Fernando de Noronha. On the same devil's island he lives in peace today, praying to God Almighty and playing in the hammock with India Momi, his wife, who went along to keep him company while he awaits the roar of the trumpets heralding the Apocalypse. Zé do Lírio—a reliable professional, a good man.

A Plea for Living Together

Under the rich full moon fastened to the Itapuã lighthouse, Patrícia stole a kiss from Father Abelardo Galvão. A kiss on the mouth, it had the taste of crime and homemade ambrosia.

Father Abelardo Galvão had just told her that he had decided to prolong his stay in the city for a few days, to attend the lectures of Dom Pedro Casadáliga, the legendary Clareteano, the bishop and poet from the prelacy of Araguaia, on agrarian reform and the Land Pastoral. In the minicourse, limited to a restricted circle of priests and laymen, at the summer house in Pedra do Sal, Dom Casadáliga would narrate the saga of his missionary activities against poverty in an attempt to change the land statutes. Dom Timóteo had obtained enrollment for the vicar of Piaçava. Quivering with excitement at the news, Patrícia threw her arms around his neck and stole the kiss: a real kiss, on the mouth, not just a brushing of fearful lips.

Father Abelardo shuddered in his southern *gaúcho* shell; a macho man by birth, a fiery cowboy, he was chaste only by the obligation he had assumed at the foot of the altar. They'd gelded him, but they'd forgotten to remove his balls—a moral and physical contradiction, antidialectical. On unwillingly breaking away from the kiss, at the cost of

great will power, the priest proclaimed the drastic truth in a loud voice
so she could hear and act accordingly. In order not to fall into temptation, he'd kept repeating the litany to himself during the last forty-eight
hours:

"A priest can't get married, Patrícia!"

Fear clouded Patrícia's medallike profile, jubilant in the moonlight,
her Indian woman's straight hair, her white woman's blue eyes, her black
woman's hungry lips:

"Who's talking about marriage?"

Tell me, Father Abelardo Galvão, you and your oath of celibacy
sworn at your act of ordination, tell me: Who said anything about marriage? Life, my love, is easy and simple, a sweet intimacy when we open
our eyes to catch sight of it and free our hearts of shackles and impedi-
ments, of foolishness. Come, my love, brush the cobwebs from your
tonsured head, come to your senses, face reality. Don't pretend you don't
understand; don't play deaf, stupid, innocent—it's no use running away
from the matter, talking about something else. Be a man.

That business of priestly celibacy that you people talk about so
much, proposing radical solutions to it, changes in canon law, the condemnation of a wornout dogma in a papal encyclical—that soap opera
was resolved here a long time ago without any need for theology or
councils: They did it in their little Brazilian way. José de Alencar, the one
who wrote about Iracema, my cousin, was the son of a priest, didn't you
know? You know now.

I'm not asking you to marry me, she said. I'm not asking you to
deny the cassock that you wear so little, to stop being a priest. I know
that your vows prevent you from getting married, you'd lose the right to
priestly duties, the motivation of your life. Marriage, my sweet reverend,
is something that never entered my head. I'm asking you to live with me.

A pastor of the Church, a missionary in the lands of misery, your
apostolate serves the poorest of the poor, the disinherited, the landless,
the serfs. You don't want to deny your promise, Christ is your master,
your banner is Nazarene. Well, hold it high, and honor the lesson of the
Master—why would you have to abandon your preaching? I'd never ask
you to do that. I'm a sheep in your flock, a black sheep, a wild goat
leaping from rock to rock in the brushland. I support your struggle: land
for the people who work it, I'm on your side, in your trenches.

You keep on saying that the vow of chastity for priests is a holdover
from the Middle Ages, a political act by the reactionary Church that
served the rich, that things are different today. Any day now a forward-
looking council will do away with that nonsense, and love will no longer
be a sin, either mortal or venial, it'll be the grace of God. Brazilian priests
didn't wait for that revolutionary council, they resolved the matter an
easy way, with no theological theorems, without recourse to the light of

doctors or doctrine, with their faces and their hearts, the way God likes. God closes his eyes and smiles; he never raises his voice to condemn them, and he receives them in his bosom when they die, almost always with the smell of sainthood.

I only ask that you love me, nothing else. Here I am, dressed in the light of the moon and the stars, sprinkled with the salt of the waves, smelling of the sea, my face damp, my heart leaping, and the unholy weariness of waiting for you, my ochlocrat, I'm asking for your hand as a friend here, in concubinage.

Do you think that with the exception of a few rare fanatics and mental weaklings, priests really practice chastity? Or that those who practice it are going to die on the sly in the arms of whores like that good cardinal in Paris—I forget his name? Or even those who in broad daylight make families, have children with their mistresses, more devout and devoted than I—aren't they fathers of exemplary families? Without need for a marriage with a sealed piece of paper, they join together under the law of the forest, which is the true law of God. I want to be your mistress, a vicar's whore: a priest's mistress who becomes a headless mule on Fridays and runs about frightening people. A priest's donkey, you hick.

I want you to get me pregnant, I want to have a child of yours, born in the backlands of Piaçava on the blood spilled by the feudal lord's, the colonel's orders. Speaking of that, do you know they tried to kill you? Did you know that Joãozinho Costa hired a gunman from Pernambuco to dispatch you to an early grave? It was Oyá who saved you, at my request—she canceled the sentence and wrote down the word *love* instead. I bought your life, I paid for it with the price of a goat.

Love isn't a wrong, it doesn't offend God, it isn't a wicked, an ugly, dirty thing, it isn't a sin or a curse. Come, my beauty, let's put an end to this nonsense. You're going to be an even better priest, a great one, a priest nobody can find fault with after you learn the taste of my kiss, how to moan in my arms, hear my cries of love when the apples of my breasts ripen in your hands, after you've tasted the wild honey in the cool jug of my stomach, resting your head in my lap. Come, my Christ Child, my Jesus of Nazareth, I'm going to crucify you.

If you don't want to come, if you refuse me your hand in concubinage, if you're deaf and blind, don't want to hear or see, if you're that stupid and ignorant at this point, if you prefer masturbation, pornographic dreams, nocturnal pollution, the dirty and the ugly, if you're a southern or backlands copy of Father José Antonio Hernández, the Falangist, then I'll go away and never want to see you again. They've invited me to Paris for the festival of Bahia on Antènne Deux. It's going to be wild, that celebration, *la grande pagaille, la paillardise, la bringue,* just imagine what it's going to be like! Do you want me to go to the blowout with the French? There's one who's a sweetheart, he wears an earring but he's not gay. Or do you want me to stay in Bahia and take your virginity, my dear? Make up your mind, I'm asking you to live with me. Will you give me your hand?

In the garden of the lovers, Patrícia da Silva Vaalserberg, Patrícia of the Flowers, black sheep in the Lord's flock, Yansan's goat, having finished her discourse, having emptied out her sack, stole another kiss from Father Abelardo Galvão, vicar of Piaçava. It was another kiss on the mouth, with tongue and teeth, wet with the sea breeze; it never ended.

A whole priest, Grandmother, with God's grace. In the distance, most certainly in the dark lagoon of Abaeté, a chorus of angels and demons sings hallelujah to the sound of the flute and the ukelele. The music of Tom Jobim. A whole man, Grandmother.

Voyages and Voyagers

During the course of this tale of such vast reach, we have frequently had recourse—and we express our thanks here—to the society column edited by Julie, Julieta Isnesêe, a journalist of good credentials, well-informed and widely read. Everything that happens in the festive universe of the upper city and behind the scenes in culture, hot news, fresh news, first-hand gossip, finds mention and comment in the cordial space of Julie's chronicle.

The columnist noted with pleasure and a touch of envy the sailing of a dandified group of moneyed vacationers for a Caribbean cruise aboard a luxurious Italian liner. In the list of lucky ones, standing out among the livelier figures, were two distinguished, worthy acquaintances of ours. Olímpia de Castro, the airplane, was dressed as a sailor girl in a garb specially made for her figure and her boldness. Her inseparable chum Diana Teles Hooks-and-Hints, or Sylvia Esmeralda on the lists of combat, was dazzling in miniskirt and T-shirt bearing the image of Saint Barbara of the Thunder, printed in color. The T-shirt was from a promotion by Chaves the bookseller, who never misses an opportunity. Recovered from the nervous crisis that had put her in the hospital, Sylvia Esmeralda is a living joy.

They were traveling by themselves, which was the only thing to pity about them. The executive Astério de Castro couldn't leave his command post in the construction business, his public works projects, his many businesses, his contacts with ministers, generals, senators, colonels. He had bills to pay at the end of the month, handouts to distribute, and financing to receive, and the competition was fierce. The most worthy juvenile judge, Dr. d'Ávila, in addition to being hard at work in his patriotic battle against juvenile delinquency, found himself caught up in the inquiry to find out who had forged his signature. The two poor lonely wives, dying with longing for their husbands; they tried to kill their yearning in the arms of tourists, and ship's officers; the first mate was fought over, while boys on vacation topped the list.

Julie's column also reported the honor of an invitation that Nilda Spencer had received: Antènne Deux was requesting her presence in Paris to collaborate in the showing of the Bahian *Grand Échiquier*. Jacques Chancel wanted her sitting beside him in the auditorium on the night of the telecast. Nilda Spencer flew over carrying a reservoir of tears to shed while seeing and hearing the parade on French television sets. The music of Bahia, its customs, its *samba de roda,* its Angola *capoeira,* its *candomblé,* the rows of houses, the simple people, the masses at Carnival, a life so long-suffering and so ardent: It was all captured in *La Chanson de Bahia.*

Nilda didn't travel alone. Dona Eliodora Costa had asked her to look after her daughter Marlene. Lenoca was still a little girl, whose fifteen-birthday present was a study trip to Europe, a month of sopping up culture. Julie foresaw that Lenoca, in a restless expression of the power of youth, would take the greatest advantage in a marathon encyclopedia: museums, lectures, a quick course in French civilization at the Sorbonne, concerts, theater, l'Église de Notre-Dame, Le Lapin Agile, l'Opéra, le Grand Palais, and le Crazy Horse.

It was learned, not from Julie's column but from the mouths of eternal gossipers, that the child Lenoca, as soon as she arrived in Paris with the desire to celebrate her fifteen springs properly, had let go of the hand of Nilda, who thanked God for it. Nilda had no vocation for standing guard over anyone's pussy, and she found herself extremely busy with the final details of the *mise-en-scène* for Chancel's program. Lenoca took her leave, promising to phone.

She absconded to a sixth-floor walkup on the Île Saint-Louis, whose address she carried, along with dollars and traveler's checks, in a silk belt next to her skin, sewn by Dona Eliodora. A merry and multinational band greeted her there: beautiful *demoiselles,* none of them older than fifteen, likewise in their springtime. They took in Lenoca with extreme kindness, showed her the two floors of the apartment, room by room: the musical instruments, the recording equipment, the books, the little green garden, the sheets of the composer, who was traveling but might be back at any moment: The life of an artist is tiring; the life of a famous artist—don't mention it!

The fillies were busy and having fun weaving a garland to crown him bridegroom when he returned, *le pâtre grec.* There were sixteen *jeunes filles* all told, and their names were Benedicte, Nadja, Nadine, Vera, Veronique, Vasso the Greek, Anna, Rachilde, Bonza the black girl, Valentina, Alexandre, Renée, Remedios the Sevillian, Oula, and Maria Les Sept Merveilles, copper-colored.

The Miraculate

In order to praise it publicly, to applaud it, I reveal the name of the only charitable soul who remembered to ask after the poor unfortunate: It was Anny-Claude Basset, a Franco-Brazilian writer, a sensitive heart, who was the only one who demanded news of Elói the seminarian. Elói the seminarian, who had posed nude for the photograph by the SNI, do you remember?

The victim of an ambush of fate, he'd suddenly seen the barrel of a revolver pointed at his head, a machine gun aiming at his chest. Trembling like a green reed, naked and limp, he'd begun to cry, then pissed all over himself.

Considered to have disappeared by the seminary, he was discovered at Boca do Rio, shaking with fever, his memory gone, masturbating endlessly. Amnesiac and onanist, a harmless madman escaped from the asylum, pathetically nude.

Brenda Hallstatt, an aging and moneyed Swiss woman, had established her residence at Boca do Rio more than five years ago. She lived in the company of the ghost Artur, whom she'd bought at a sale in Saint Gaudens and who'd turned out to be a drag. She never learned Elói's name, where he'd come from, or the reason for his delirium. But Brenda adopted him: *l'Inconnu du Fleuve* was what she named him, and he answered to it. Through the intermediary of a spell cast by Mãe Mirinha do Portão, at the instance of the halfbreed Pedra Preta, she returned the ghost Artur to his mountainous origins in Haute Garonne.

Romantic and perverted, using the natural resources of hand, mouth, and twat, Brenda rapidly cured *l'Inconnu* of his mysticism, of the malignant fever, and his tendency toward masturbation. The former seminarian never got his memory back; nor did he have the slightest need for it. He dedicated himself with considerable success to the profession of sexual slave. He led a pampered life, only rarely dreaming about a revolver threatening him, a machine gun aimed at him, and an impassive photographer shuffling plates. When it happens, he pees in bed. In the opinion of Brenda, who is Swiss and Freudian, it's due to an Oedipus complex.

—&—&

The Cure

In the Ilê Axê Ybá Ogun, after forty days in the chamber, Adalgisa made full payment for seven years of negligence, for obligations that the *abicun* had stopped observing. She went in an *iaô;* she came out an *êbômin.*

She came out washed and consecrated, and when she went back to the Avenida da Ave-Maria, she was received in triumph, a merry uproar in the festive neighborhood. There was food and drink, music on the phonograph of the pretentious Alina and Sergeant Deolindo; Damiana outdid herself with sweets, and Professor João Batista obtained from the prestigious circle of acquaintances Spanish red and white wine, Portuguese green wine, sherry, manzanilla, Brazilian vodka, and Paraguayan whiskey of the most respected Russian and Scottish labels. The singing and dancing in front of the houses went on into the wee hours, but around midnight Dadá and Danilo withdrew, saying they were going to get some rest.

They didn't get any rest. Yansan had spat fire into Adalgisa's private parts, and for the forty days of the confirmation she'd carried buffalo horns hanging from her waist: an aphrodisiac more potent and powerful than holly or ivy. Adalgisa got fired up, and that night of socializing in the neighborhood became the night of her first orgasm. Danilo practically fainted with pleasure. As hungry and thirsty as he was, he didn't drink from the pitcher like one parched; nor did he try to allay his hunger with one big meal. They decided to go back to São Paulo Bluff to celebrate their twentieth wedding anniversary, a second honeymoon. The first one had lent itself to the play on words—honeymoon, hungry moon —when the former prince of the playing field broke the cherry of his virginal spouse with a sledgehammer, thereby closing up her twat with hasp and padlock and turned someone who was already puritanical frigid.

Adalgisa ceased being a puritan, but she didn't become profligate; she retained a certain shyness in lovemaking that increased her charm and seductiveness. She continued being every inch a lady, even if she let herself go in bed; she ceased being a fanatic, but she remained a good Catholic; she goes to mass every Sunday in the company of Gildete, but she doesn't go to confession anymore, and she has never laid eyes on Father José Antonio Hernández again. She adores Miro, and the solemn ceremony of asking for Manela's hand in marriage has already been set. Just one more detail before Dadá and the Prince take the ferry to São Paulo Bluff: Adalgisa has now been cured of her headaches and Danilo of his farting.

—❦—❦

Happy Ending

In the modest wooden house loaned them by the Queirozes, Laura
and Dário, acquaintances of twenty years' standing and lots of conversations about soccer, harmony ruled. In a great and animated letting go,
Dadá was carrying twenty years of delay in her luggage and two decades
of ignorance. She made up for it.

In her forty days in the chamber at the Candomblé da Muriçoca
she'd paid back seven years of obligations and learned the ritual of the
orixás. In fifteen days and fourteen nights on the beach of São Paulo
Bluff, covered with moonlight, in the caress of the breeze, Dadá paid
back everything her importuning husband was due, and she owed a lot
—alas for lost time! She'd learned, on the tip of her tongue, so to speak,
the lessons of her capable and persistent teacher—the prince of bawdy
houses, the wise hound dog, Danilo-good-in-bed, Danilo-wild-and-
horny—to use the vernacular expression of Elisa, the Queen Bee.

If after these succinct and shameful considerations, anyone hopes to
read fifty animated pages narrating the second honeymoon, commemorating the twenty years of married life, as was done for the first, that
person will be disappointed, mistaken. Mistaken? All those appreciative
people, Lord help us, mistaken about what kind of literature this is?
Regardless, these readers will be left watching boats, sloops crossing the
waters of the gulf. The bedroom door of the honeymooners is locked,
and we're not ones to peek through the keyholes.

The one left saying " Oh, come on, now" will be the one who hopes
to regale himself with erotic expressions, roguish, exciting details, sighs
and moans, sweet talk: "Come, my little pervert, my wild whore, golden
tongue, velvet twat, hard ass," tender things like that, delicate, romantic,
divine expressions of love. The cherry-popping will not be told.

Cherry-popping? But hasn't that happened already, twenty years
before, on the original honeymoon, on the linen sheets in Dr. Fernando
Almeida's house? On that occasion, clumsily and hastily, Danilo had
indeed broken Adalgisa's cherry, encrusted under the forest of curly hair
at the mouth of the world, virginal. But the second time, after twenty
years, it was the cherry of the asshole, called the back door by those in
the know, that he screwed, and enjoyed the delight, with the startled
acquiescence of the one backdoored.

It was on the seventh night, exactly halfway through their vacation,
that Danilo took the rear end; it was a night with a full moon. They'd
walked a long way beyond the houses, barefoot along the magic road of
moonlight, they'd taken off their bathing suits, gone naked into the sea,
he chased her amid laughter, they rolled in the waves, bounced on the
hard, wet sand, startling crabs. The foam of the waves tickled Dadá's

nipples, and Danilo's prick was pointing skyward. The salt kisses, the devouring mouths, the free hands—they went back to the house, quickening their step, they were in a hurry. And so it happened.

When we were describing the wedding, the difficult, unhappy honeymoon, we promised to tell about the melodrama and the happy ending. The melodrama has been narrated in all its difficult detail, winding up and winding down, appointment and disappointment, something out of the sad past. Now it's time for the happy ending.

Danilo, let us agree, deserved his happy ending because after twenty long years of puritanism on the part of fanatical Adalgisa, he never lost heart, he kept on asking. It took a long time, but he finally realized his most daring dreams. Dadá was more fiery and complete in bed than he had ever hoped. Now Danilo has to make use of all the competence and enthusiasm in his male character, forces that are happily still not lacking in him. But for some time now, he's been taking the guaraná powder sent him by Eduardo Lago, a friend in São Luís do Maranhão, a soccer fan.

And here we come to the end of the tale of Adalgisa and Manela, descendants of the Castilian Paco Pérez y Pérez and the black woman Andreza, aunt and niece, both daughters of Yansan. Yansan came to Bahia on a visitation to straighten out their twisted lives, put an end to evil, to teach goodness and pleasure, the joy of living. She put on the cloak of thundercaps of Saint Barbara, her alter ego, sailed on Master Manuel's sloop, sowed confusion, went beyond the limits of disorder and danger, saved the life of a watermelon priest, and all in all had a fine time. She spelled things out divinely with Dorival Caymmi, with Carybé, and with your servant here, thank you very much, three *obás* of Xangô, three doctors *honoris causa* of the school of life, three lads from Bahia, a musician, a painter, a novelist, *saravá!*

The Return

The exhibit of religious art was an absolute success—it couldn't have been greater. There were countless visitors, comments of resounding enthusiasm in the guest book, wide repercussions, as is well known. It lasted for a month, but the figure of Saint Barbara of the Thunder remained a week longer still in the Convent of Saint Theresa, in the museum workshop, the object of the special care of restorer Liana Gomes Silveira, of celebrated skills.

Always on the safe side, always mistrustful, Father Téo grew impatient at the delay and went to bring back the statue in person: His relations with Dom Maximiliano von Gruden were still unsociable, marked by antipathy and suspicion. He had to be patient for two more days, amidst cursing and grumbling, because the museum director had taken an unexpected trip and only he could sign the order returning the statue.

But every dog has its day, and so one sunny and breezy Sunday morning, Dom Maximiliano and his helper Edimilson Vaz, a Marxist and a visionary angel, back in his function as adviser, carried the statue in the museum van to the market ramp, where the *Sailor Without a Port* was once again moored. Master Manuel and Maria Clara took charge of taking it onboard, placing it on the litter in the stern of the sloop. Courteously, Dom Maximiliano said good-bye to the vicar of Santo Amaro, who was no less polite: "Excuse my rudeness, that's just the way I am." "Think nothing of it," Dom Maximiliano begged him; he didn't worry about misunderstandings, tricks, and evil insinuations—he could understand and even justify them. They shook hands, the vicar and Dom Maximiliano. In the museum safe, under lock and key, Dom Maximiliano had kept the document signed by Father Téo testifying to the fact that he had received the figure of Saint Barbara of the Thunder in a perfect state of preservation. He'd even had the vicar's signature notarized.

Two newspapermen accompanied the statue back to Santo Amaro —Guido Guerra for *Diário de Notícias,* José Berbert de Castro for *A Tarde,* with their respective photographers, Gervásio Filho and Vavá. The two brilliant reporters' stories, albeit each in his own style, resembled each other in their description of the trip, the stop at the mouth of the river, and the unloading at Santo Amaro. The trip went peacefully, there were fireworks and speeches at the docking, and the unloading was an apotheosis.

From the waterfront of Bahia, the *Sailor Without a Port* had been escorted by a convoy of several sloops to the mouth of the Paraguaçu. There, where the river meets the sea, the gateway to the bay, the sloops halted. Rockets shot up to announce the happy return, and using an old loudspeaker, Antônio Brasileiro, a troubador from Feira de Sant'Ana, the last bard to poetize in this manual of versification, declaimed a ballad in praise of the saint: "The Triumph of Saint Barbara, Thunder Woman, on the Delta Wings of the People." Fish rose to the surface to hear him, hyacinths burst into bloom, and rhymes flew off in the morning breeze.

Along the course of the river, the escort consisted of devoted sloops that came from ports around the bay, a whole swarm of them. Around the neck of the carving was the reliquary of the sisterhood of Our Lady of the Good Death, and the little old ladies from Cachoeira waited anxiously on the docks at Santo Amaro. Saint Barbara of the Thunder seemed satisfied to be going back to her altar; she smiled as she listened to Maria Clara's love songs, at the ritual points of *orin orixá*. The breeze came along to play on Master Manuel's callused hands: Hosanna!

In Santo Amaro the unloading was a consecration, celebrating the victory of the people and defeat of all the swine who'd tried to steal a possession of the town. It was now more valuable than ever because, as had been proven over and over again and as can be read in the book, the image of Saint Barbara of the Thunder was sculpted by Aleijadinho, at the request of the vicar, to be especially venerated in Santo Amaro da Purificação. The population accompanied the procession en masse, taking turns carrying the saint's litter; in front went Dona Canô and Mr. José Veloso, parents of the happy children. Epiphany!

Placed on its modest altar in the main church, the controversial statue remains there today. It had disappeared and caused a lot of talk. In the opinion of Father Téo it never should have left. It had cost him a lot of labors and curses to bring it back—the famous, the one and only, the true Saint Barbara of the Thunder.

The Entry

At the doors of bookstores, places for meeting and talking, comments were whispered among people of letters about an entry concerning the statue of Saint Barbara of the Thunder with a colored photograph in the *Universalenzyklopädie der Religiösen Kunst*, recently published in Germany (Piper Verlag, Munich).

"Die Heilige Barbara des Donners"—the entry, accurate and concise, sings the praises of the beauty of the statue, speaks of its great artistic worth and its fantastic commercial value on the specialized market, making reference to the book by Dom Maximiliano von Gruden, *Der Ursprung und der Schöpfer des Gnadenbildes Barbara, die des Donners*, and his thesis that the author of the sculpture was Aleijadinho. The entry concludes with the information that the original statue is part of the notable collection of the Museum of Sacred Art of the Federal University of Bahia, while the object of the popular cult and public devotion in the main church of Santo Amaro da Purificação is a copy.

With that frightening Germanic information, doubt is awakened, the debate is rekindled, veiled denunciations are fed, public accusations are stimulated—and we come to the end of the story—all that's left for us to say is so long, *au revoir*. Dismounting from the back of the sluggish donkey, that same one, the dancer, at the crossroads where paths blend and faces mingle, I furnish the *ebó* owed Exu: an *ebó* of blood with a bottle of cane liquor and half a dozen cheap cigars.

Laroiê! I say in greeting, and the chorus of comrades answers me, *Laus Deo! Axé,* good people, I'm on my way, until we meet again.

On the Quai des Célestins, in Paris,
from May to October 1987;
from February to July 1988.
In Bahia, August 1988.

Glossary

abicun: in *candomblé,* a child who dies shortly after birth to torment parents: said to be born over and over again

adarrum: in *candomblé,* a drumbeat to force descent of gods

adjá: small bell used in *candomblé* rituals

afoxé: ritual procession group of *candomblé* and at Carnival; an Africanized version of *bloco;* for example, the Children of Gandhi Afoxé

agogô: musical percussion instrument of bells and rod

akirijebó: frequenter of *candomblés*

alabé: lead drummer of a *terreiro* of *candomblé*

aluj á: a special drumbeat for Xangô

amalá: in *candomblé,* a food offering to Xangô

atabaque: large war drum

axé: the ethos of *candomblé;* also, the vital force that animates all things, particularly present in sacred objects or beings; also, a sacred object; also, the name of a *terreiro* of *candomblé,* such as the Axé of Alaketu; Axé Ya Nassô, the Axé Yá Massê, or the Axé do Opô Afonjá

axôgun: in *candomblé,* a male assistant priest who performs animal sacrifices

baba: father

babalaô: in *candomblé,* a priest of the cult of Ifá; diviner

babalorixá: in *candomblé,* a male cult leader

Baiana: a woman from Bahia; also, a Bahian woman who wears traditional white processional costume of turban, lace blouse, and long skirts

balangandã: Afro-Brazilian amulet worn by Baianas

Barbara of the Thunder, Saint: Christian saint merged with Yansan and Oyá in syncretistic Afro-Bahian religions; known as Barbara Yansan or Barbara Oyá

barco: a boat or ship; in *candomblé,* a group of *filhos* and *filhas de santo* who are initiated at the same time

barracão: a large shedlike room or hall where *candomblé* ceremonies take place

berimbau: two-stringed musical instrument, of African origin, for *capoeira*

bloco: in Carnival, a large organized dance group; examples are Bloco do Jacu, Youth of Garcia, Baron's Block, Apaches of Tororó, Owl Block, Olodum, and Merchants of Baghdad

Bomfim or **Our Lord of Bomfim;** deity closely identified with the city of Bahia; an invocation of Jesus as "Lord of the Good

Ending"; represented in a miracle-working crucifix in the church of his name. In *candomblé* Bomfim is identified with Oxalá; Oxalá is identified with Jesus in this form

Bomfim Thursday (second Thursday in January): *see* Washing of Bomfim

bori: in *candomblé*, an animal sacrifice; also, the "feeding the head" ceremony of making offerings to the head; also, the first stage of initiation into *candomblé*

caboclo: in Afro-Brazilian religions, a native Indian spirit

caipirinha: drink of cane liquor and lime juice

candomblé: Afro-Brazilian religious ceremony partly of Yoruban origin; it is most widely practiced in the city of Bahia; it is regarded as more African than other Afro-Brazilian religions like *umbanda*. Also, a particular *terreiro*, such as the Candomblé do Gantois and the Candomblé da Muriçoca

capoeira: a foot-fighting martial art devised by Brazilian slaves from Angola that subsequently evolved into a kind of athletic ballet dance, very stylized; accompanied by *berimbau*

Children of Gandhi Afoxé: one of the oldest *afoxés*, founded in 1940s; its clubhouse is on the Rua Gregório de Matos

Church of Bomfim, on Sacred Hill: center of popular worship and focal point of Bomfim Thursday religious festival; cleansed in washing ceremony with waters of Oxalá

dobalé: a salutation between those with female ôrixás

doburu: popcorn

ebó: in *candomblé*, a sacrificial offering to *orixás*, especially for magical purposes of divining

êbômin: in *candomblé*, a *filha de santo* who has completed initiation

éfun: in *candomblé*, chalk designs on initiates' bodies

egun: in *candomblé*, spirit of the dead

e i r u: a ceremonial scepter of oxtail or horsetail

e k e d e: in *candomblé,* a female initiate who is not in trance but who is in charge of *filhas de santo* who are in trance; also, a ritual assistant and dignitary of a *terreiro*

E l e g b a r á: counterpart of Exu; of Dahomean origin

e l u ô: a diviner

e n c h a n t e d   o n e: see *orixá*

E n g e n h o   V e l h o   C a n d o m b l é: famous *terreiro* of *candomblé* in Bahia; also known as Casa Branca, or White House

E p a r r e i!: a greeting to *orixás*

e r ê: in *candomblé,* the child form of an *orixá;* when a *filha de santo* undergoes initiation, she spends about a week "incorporated" by her *erê*

E u á: an *orixá*

E x ê - ê - b a b á!: ceremonial greeting for Oxalá

e x u (f. *exua*): one of a class of originally African deities or spirits transplanted to Brazil; in *candomblé,* a spirit who performs the role of "slave" of an *orixá;* popularly thought of as a devil

E x u: *orixá* of doors and paths, who guards thoroughfares of city of Bahia; priapic, associated with copulation. Also, an initiated person who "belongs to" Exu

f i g a: good luck gesture, charm

f i l h a   d e   s a n t o: in *candomblé,* daughter-of-saint; a female initiate who experiences trance (m.: *filho de santo*)

f r e v o: frenetic musical style and dance from Recife

g a ú c h o: person from Rio Grande do Sul; also a southern cowboy

g r i n g o, *gringa* (Sp.): foreigner; not derogatory

g u a r a n á: plant; the soft drink made from it

i a b a: in *candomblé,* a female *orixá*

i a ô: in *candomblé,* a *filha de santo* who experiences trance; also, an initiate in seclusion; same as *iyauô*

i a ô - d e - é f u n: in *candomblé;* same as above

I f á: orixá of fate

i l ê: house of *candomblé,* such as Ilê Axé Ybá Ogun, Ilê Iyá Omim Axé Iyamansê: (the house of Gantois Candomblé), Ilé Iyá Nassô, and Ilé Ogunjá

i y á: mother

i y a k e k e r ê: in *candomblé,* a substitute for an *iyalorixá;* also, "little mother"

i y a l a x é: woman in charge of altar *axé*

i y a l o r i x á: in *candomblé,* a high priestess; she sits on a throne in her *terreiro.* For example, Mãe Stela de Oxóssi is the *iyalorixá* of the Axé of Opô Afonjá. See *Mãe de santo*

J e j e   n a t i o n: one of the Afro-Brazilian nations

j u r á   o l u á: in *candomblé,* a sanctuary

k e l ê: initiate's necklace; sign of submission

l a m b r e t a: a drink

l a r g o (Port.): small square

L a r o i ê!: in *candomblé,* a salutation to Exu

l é: smallest of three ritual drums

m a c u m b a: an Afro-Brazilian religion that deals mainly with *exus*

m ã e: mother

mãe de santo: in *candomblé,* a female religious leader or priestess who heads a *terreiro;* watches over initiates in trance and invokes *orixás;* also called an *iyalorixá*

maionga: ritual bath

Model Market: a huge indoor bazaar in the lower city area of Bahia; notable for selling statues of *candomblé* deities and *capoeira* displays

obá: in *candomblé,* title of the ministers of Xangô

Obá: Yoruba goddess of the river Obá; third wife of Xangô

Obaluayê: same as Omolu

ogan or *ogan da sala:* in *candomblé,* a lay protector or guard, selected by *orixás* and subject to a minor initiation ritual; does not go into trance but acts as a ritual assistant and dignitary

Ogum: *orixá* associated with iron; also, an initiated person who "belongs to" Ogum

Omolu: male *orixá* of contagious diseases and their cures; associated with the earth

Opô Afonjá: see *axé*

orixá: generic word for a spirit, either male or female. Originally Yoruba or other West African deities, they were transplanted to Brazil by slaves and became part of Afro-Bahian religions. Each *orixá* has his or her own color, song, animal, insignia, holy day, etc. In *candomblé,* initiates "receive," or go into trance with, an *orixá.* An initiated person "belongs to" an *orixá,* who becomes the "owner" of that person's "head." *Orixás* can mount those who belong to them and "ride" them.

ôrunkó: name-giving day for initiates

Ossãe: *orixá* associated with leaves and herbs

ossé: offerings

"owner of head": the *orixá* to whom an initiate "belongs"; in initiation, ritual objects are set up in a *terreiro,* sacrifices are performed

to get the *orixá* to take up residence in the person's head: for example, Miro's "owner of head" is said to be Exu; Yansan is "mistress" of Patrícia's "head"

O x a g u i n h ã: youthful form of the *orixá* Oxalá himself

O x a l á: the male *orixá* of procreation; father of the gods, he is identified with Bomfim in *candomblé;* because of his prominence, he is identified with Jesus Christ; his day is Friday. Also, an initiated person who "belongs to" Oxalá, like the Oxalá of Carmem

O x o l u f ã: elderly form of the *orixá* Oxalá

O x ó s s i: male *orixá* associated with hunting; also, an initiated person who "belongs to" Oxóssi

O x u m: female *orixá,* associated with love, beauty, wealth, and luxury; associated with fresh water, fish, mermaids; closely identified with city of Bahia; one of Xangô's wives. Also, an initiated person who "belongs to" Oxum, like Mãe Menininha do Gantois

O x u m a r é: male and female *orixá,* associated with the rainbow

O y á: a name for Yansan; also, a person who "belongs to" Oyá

p a d ê: propitiatory offering before a feast to trickster god Exu, so he won't spoil the festivity

p a n ã: a ceremony in which foods made by initiates are sold at a "market" or *quitanda*

p a x o r ô: staff of Oxalá

p e j i: sanctuary on a *candomblé* altar; the Peji de Yemanjá is the altar of Yemanjá

r e c e i v e   a n   *o r i x á:* in *candomblé,* to go into trance

r u m: largest of three ritual drums

r u m p i: middle of three ritual drums

s a m,b a: a Brazilian dance, accompanied by songs in 2/4 rhythm, syncopated drumming *samba de roda:* circle formed for dancing *samba*

saravá!: hail! in *candomblé*, a greeting to *orixás*

Sisterhood of Our Lady of the Good Death: sisterhood in the town of Cachoeira (near Bahia), founded by freed women slaves in the mid-nineteenth century, partly as a religious group and partly to work to free slaves; acted as an early cooperative bank to buy people their liberty; today, its dignified matriarchs preside at *candomblé* celebrations in Cachoeira

taramesso: diviner's ceremonial table

Tempo: male *orixá* associated with sacred trees, the weather, and time; also, an initiated person associated with Tempo, like Mother Olga de Tempo

terreiro: a house or center of *candomblé*, both as place and as institution; where *candomblé* ceremonies take place, especially animal sacrifices, food and drink offerings, and drumming and dancing, to induce *orixás* to descend into bodies of initiates; headed by a *mãe de santo*

toada: sad song

Trio Elétrico: in Bahian Carnival, musical groups parading atop trucks wired for sound, with banks of speakers on all sides

tropicalismo: Brazilian musical-cultural style of independence against the 1960s dictatorship, founded by Caetano Veloso; notable for double entendre lyrics to avoid censorship

umbanda: an Afro-Brazilian religion widespread outside Bahia city; less "African" than *candomblé;* uses Portuguese language

vodun: priest

Washing of the Church of Bomfim, or the washing ceremony: an annual festival that takes place in the city of Bahia on the second Thursday in January, second only to Carnival in scale; it involves a procession to the Church of Bomfim and the cleansing of it with the waters of Oxalá; a raucous celebrating follows until early morning

waters of *Oxalá*: waters fetched from a spring for Bomfim Thursday washing ceremony; they are associated with female *orixás;* the Baianas literally wash the Church of Bomfim and the square before it with these waters, thereby bathing Oxalá, the father of all the *orixás*

***Xangô*:** male *orixá,* associated with storms, lightning, and thunder; Yansan's husband. Also, an initiated person who "belongs to" Xangô

***xaraô*:** ornamental ankle bracelet

***xinxim*:** chicken dish; in *candomblé,* the food of Oxum

***Yansan*:** female *orixá* associated with wind, thunder, and storm; in Africa, she was the goddess of the Niger; in Bahian *candomblé,* she is a wife of Xangô; aka Oyá Yansan; also, an initiated person who "belongs to" Yansan, like Andreza de Yansan, Olga de Yansan; the Yansan of Margarida do Bogum; the Yansan of Iybalé; and Adalgisa, Yansan of the Saddle

***Yemanjá*:** a female *orixá* associated with the sea; also known by the names Aioká, Dadalunda, Janaína, Kaiala, and Mukunã; queen of the sea; mother of waters and all other *orixás;* her day is February 2. Also, an initiated person who "belongs to" Yemanjá, like Maria Clara

SOURCE: Jim Wafer, *The Taste of Blood: Spirit Possession in Brazilian Candomblé.* University of Pennsylvania Press, 1991.